Ali Harris lives in Cambridge with her husband and three children.

Prior to having children, Ali was  of women's magazines including
ELLE.

She is the author of three previous
bestsellers *Miracle on Regent Street* and
written after a prolonged break following the loss of her baby girl, late in pregnancy.

https://aliharrisauthor.substack.com

instagram.com/Aliharriswriter
facebook.com/Aliharriswriter

Also by Ali Harris

Written in the Stars
A Vintage Christmas (novella)
The First Last Kiss
Miracle on Regent Street

THIS WASN'T MEANT TO HAPPEN

ALI HARRIS

One More Chapter
a division of HarperCollins*Publishers* Ltd
1 London Bridge Street
London SE1 9GF
www.harpercollins.co.uk
HarperCollins*Publishers*
Macken House, 39/40 Mayor Street Upper,
Dublin 1, D01 C9W8, Ireland

This paperback edition 2025
1
First published in Great Britain in ebook format
by HarperCollins*Publishers* 2025
Copyright © Ali Harris 2025
Ali Harris asserts the moral right to
be identified as the author of this work

A catalogue record of this book is available from the British Library

ISBN: 978-0-00-870846-7

This novel is entirely a work of fiction. The names, characters and incidents portrayed in it are the work of the author's imagination. Any resemblance to actual persons, living or dead, events or localities is entirely coincidental.

Printed and bound in the UK using 100% Renewable Electricity
by CPI Group (UK) Ltd

All rights reserved. No part of this publication may be reproduced, stored in a retrieval system, or transmitted, in any form or by any means, electronic, mechanical, photocopying, recording or otherwise, without the prior permission of the publishers.

Without limiting the exclusive rights of any author, contributor or the publisher of this publication, any unauthorised use of this publication to train generative artificial intelligence (AI) technologies is expressly prohibited. HarperCollins also exercise their rights under Article 4(3) of the Digital Single Market Directive 2019/790 and expressly reserve this publication from the text and data mining exception.

To my sweet baby girl Poppy, and to all the babies held forever in our hearts but not in our arms. This is for you.

Foreword

This Wasn't Meant to Happen was inspired by my daughter, Poppy, who died six months into my pregnancy ten years ago. Writing this story about a fictional couple, Sofie and Rory, who suffer the stillbirth of their son, Leo, has been the most challenging, cathartic and fulfilling accomplishment of my life.

Whilst baby loss was an unexpected personal plot twist for me, I have never wanted that to be the case for readers. It's my great hope that those who may have experienced the devastating loss of a baby (or babies) in pregnancy, birth, or beyond and who find themselves here will feel both seen and held throughout this story. And those who haven't might find a language and deeper insight with which to support friends, family or colleagues it may sadly affect in the future.

Whatever has compelled you to pick up this book, read the blurb and make it as far as this page, before you go any further I want to both thank you and reassure you that whilst this book is about loss, more than anything, I consider it to be a profoundly beautiful and life-affirming love story, just one that has been too rarely written about outside of the community it directly affects.

With love and deepest gratitude,
Ali x

Part I

If people do not believe that mathematics is simple, it is only because they do not realise how complicated life is.

John von Neumann

Chapter One

I've been pacing inside the toilet cubicle at my office like a caged lioness for the past minute with my eyes squeezed shut. When the alarm on my phone goes off, it sends shockwaves through my nervous system. I look down.

Two lines. Like an equals symbol.

Two lines equals *pregnant.*

This was not meant to happen. I lean against the wall, my forehead resting against the cool tiles. I feel sick: I'm not sure whether it's with adrenaline, elation, shock or fear. Marriage I'd got my head around, but having a baby? That's never been part of my plan. I made that clear to Rory when we first became serious:

'If you want to be with me,' I'd told him when we decided to move in together, 'you'll have to be happy with just me. That's the deal. No ring, no kids, okay?'

'Okay,' he'd said, kissing me lightly on my forehead. 'But I think you'll change your mind. In fact,' he'd smiled, 'I'll even make a bet on it.'

'Oh, really? How much?' I'd teased, used to this kind of verbal sparring with him.

'My whole heart,' he'd answered, unexpectedly seriously, which had made me lose my breath.

I'd pulled away. 'But,' I'd protested, 'there's no data to back that up. What makes you so sure?'

Infuriatingly, he'd shrugged. 'I'm not. You're a total enigma. Also, you're stubborn, impossibly hard to read at times, clever, controlling, and the most freakishly organised person I know ... and sexy, did I mention sexy?' he'd added, when he realised I was glowering at him. 'It's true! I thought so from the moment I first set eyes on you, nine months ago. You were stuck in the middle of a field, cows to your left, a pen of pigs to your right. That, I thought to myself, is the sexiest creature I've seen ... today,' he'd grinned cheekily and pulled my hips to his as he lowered his mouth to my ear and gently kissed behind it.

'*Thanks.*' I'd laughed, despite myself.

'... And *hot*,' he'd added, his lips working their way down my neck.

'Let me guess,' I'd said, pushing him away playfully. 'Due to the free coffee I was handing out...?'

'SO hot,' he'd murmured, and he'd pulled me closer to him again so his lips could settle lightly and finally upon mine. 'I burned my tongue because of you.' His eyes were glimmering with mirth as he flickered his tongue lightly into my mouth. 'In fact, I *think* it still needs some help to heal...'

'Well, let's see what I can do...' I'd kissed him deeply in response, feeling my legs weaken as he pressed his body against mine and I found myself falling back in time to our very first meeting, at the Dorset County Show in Dorchester the September before. I'd been there helping Mum who had a stand promoting Per's Place – my parents' café in Swanage (my dad's name being 'Per').

Alongside reporting on the usual livestock shows, show jumping and horticulture for *Meridien News*, Rory was also a judge of the annual bake-off. Mum had entered her infamous breakfast muffins.

He'd strolled over while we were setting up. He was overdressed for both the heat and the occasion in a white shirt stretched tantalisingly over his broad shoulders, loosely knotted tie and blazer. His reddish-blonde hair was neatly gelled back but at odds with his smiling, sun-kissed cheeks and childishly mischievous eyes. He looked like an overgrown teenager masquerading as a journalist. He wasn't my type, at *all*.

This Wasn't Meant to Happen

Over the past decade, I'd had a parade of relationships with a certain type of man. Like Rob – the one before Rory – who was a highly intelligent but emotionally distant and socially awkward geologist who put rocks above romance. He'd ticked a lot of boxes until, one evening, over a romantic meal for our first anniversary, he'd proposed, completely out of the blue. 'Sofie,' he'd said in his grave, reedy monotone as he knelt down over dinner and presented a Dorset amethyst ring, 'you're a rare gem and I want to spend the rest of my life with you. Marry me?'

I was horrified. Rob had shown no indication of wanting us to be that serious. We'd never even discussed moving in together. I quickly explained my non-negotiable stance: that I never wanted to get married and couldn't be with someone who wanted that from me. He said it was fine, he understood, but his defeated, hangdog expression said the opposite. As did the way he clung to me in the following days, which he'd never done before. We staggered on for a few more weeks, but the feeling of being in sync had gone.

'Not all marriages end up like your parents', you know,' Nisha had said when I'd told her what had happened, in a FaceTime debrief. My best friend since she joined my high school from London in the middle of Year 8, Nisha was now a consultant paediatric neurologist at Great Ormond Street Hospital, and just like she'd been at school, my go-to for everything. We talk at least two to three times a week – or as often as her job allows. 'Look at my mum and dad,' she'd added.

This was true. Her parents, Arj and Sita, were both local GPs who had been happily married for close to thirty years. Stable, steady and reassuringly similar, their home became a second one to me after Dad had died. It was Sita who encouraged my love of cooking during this time, when I found it hard to be either at home or at the café as there were too many memories of dad there. I'd always loved cooking with him after his fishing and foraging trips, and in those early weeks of my grief, Sita also patiently and painstakingly taught me how to make the best curries. I fell in love with the ritual of it; the complex equation of spices, the delicate chopping, dicing, frying and stirring. It was just what my grief-stricken brain needed.

'I don't want to build my entire life around loving someone, only to risk being completely devastated when they leave. I'd rather make that choice now, than take that chance.'

'Your dad *died*, Sofie,' Nisha had pointed out gently, knowing I wasn't talking about Rob anymore. 'In a terrible, tragic accident. It was bad luck.'

'Or you could say he made bad choices,' I'd countered. 'Either way, I'd rather not make myself unnecessarily vulnerable to that sort of pain by committing to one person for the rest of my life. Did you know forty-two per cent of marriages end in divorce in the UK?'

Nisha had tucked her dark, bobbed hair behind her ears and sighed as she stared at me with the kind of unwavering intensity that had ensured no bully ever bothered us much, despite our geek status at school.

'Statistics don't provide the full picture, Sofie. Life can be random and surprising in wonderful ways, *especially* when you take risks.'

My silence – and raised eyebrow – spoke volumes.

'Look,' she went on, 'it's totally fine if you don't want to fall in love and have a family, not everyone does. But I know I'd do anything to have it. *Anything*,' she adds fiercely. 'My worry is that you're making that choice out of fear. Instead of thinking the worst, why not believe that it *could* last forever; that you could be *happy*? Put aside the statistics for once and just focus on the positive outcome.'

'Easier said than done, Nish.'

As an actuary, it's my job to advise on financial risks for the life insurance company I work for. By using my knowledge of economics, probability theory, statistics and investment theory I can assess the likelihood of an event occurring and its possible financial costs. Statistics and probability analysis are the beating heart of what I do.

I'd remembered this conversation with Nisha about risks a year or so later, when I was standing in front of Rory, and he was asking me to move in with him. Rory – the opposite to what I thought I wanted: someone openly and quite unashamedly searching for love and commitment. Someone positive, sociable, spontaneous and brimming with both self-belief and hope. For the first time, I did what Nisha had asked of me: I considered the most optimistic outcome. After all, here was someone I *could* see myself being happy with. Imagining our life together made me feel like everything I'd ever run away from was suddenly something to run *to*.

'What makes you so sure this is going to last, Rory?'

'Let's just call it a feeling,' he'd shrugged. 'I know when something is just ... meant to be.'

'Rory!' I'd cried out, in frustration. 'Answer the question properly!'

He'd taken my hands in his then and stared deeply and unflinchingly into my eyes. 'Because I'm sure of *me*. Long ago I made the choice to always count myself lucky. I chose it even though my dad left before I was born. I chose it when my mum went, too, and left me with Gran. Then again when I failed my exams and Gran helped me sort myself out, supporting me until I got my first job in TV. I've got everything I ever wanted because I *choose* to focus on the possibility of good, not bad. Look, I know that there are risks to everything, and life can throw some unexpected shit at you, but' – he'd pulled me even closer to him, then – 'I've also learned to hold on tightly to things I know are good and be grateful for them. We're good together and we're going to go all the way. I believe in us, Sofie, more than I've ever believed in anything. And I can see us having it all: house, marriage, kids – the lot. Does that answer your question?'

I'd stared at his smiling, optimistic face, his dancing eyes and the deeply embedded dimples.

'I think,' I'd replied cautiously, 'it's hard *not* to believe every single thing you say, Rory King.'

And now, just like he predicted, we're not only married but pregnant. I look down at the pregnancy test, at the two distinct lines in the aperture.

Suddenly I'm filled with unexpected and cautious joy, and it occurs to me that, as usual, my Mr Positive – my Rory – was right.

Seven and a half months later

'You can do it!' Rory says, with the positivity he often uses to gear himself up to deliver a difficult news report. I half expect him to add an air punch like he did the day we met, and for a brief, terrible moment, mid-contraction, I want to punch him. But he looks down at me so lovingly that I feel terrible for having such an

ugly thought. Who can blame him for not knowing how to handle this? I don't, either. When the contraction eases, I slump back on the pillow and take a moment to glance at him.

His usually perpetually cheery face looks like it has been put in a vice, simultaneously tightened and stretched beyond recognition. His fair skin is so many shades paler than normal, I worry that if I squint he might disappear into the walls themselves. His crown of shaggy sunset-gold hair, usually perfectly coiffed for work, is limp and bleached of colour. The thought triggers yet another surge of doubt.

I can't do this.

3.141592…

It's too hard.

Rory hovers at my bedside, not quite knowing what to do.

I grab the bowl that the midwife placed next to me and throw up into it.

'Are you okay, Sofie?' he says, stroking my hair, fear plastered over his features.

'No.' I begin to cry as the contraction intensifies. I know that this is an impossible situation and Rory is doing his best.

'I wish I could take the pain away. I'm sorry…' he says desperately.

3.14159265358979…

'Rory, you don't need to apologi-ooooww!'

I've moved into full birthing-cow mode. I squeeze Rory's hand until it turns white. 'Just stay with me,' I gasp. 'That's all you have to do. Okay?'

He nods. His lips are trembling; his temples ripple as he clenches his jaw to stop them. I know he's doing everything he can to keep it together for me.

'This is too hard,' I whimper as I look up at him. His youthful, carefree, puppy-like face that I fell for, just over six years ago, has aged, reshaped, remoulded because of this experience. He's not just my husband anymore. He's already become an anxious, over-protective father, too.

'I wish I could help,' he says again despairingly.

'You can promise never to get me in this state again.' I force out a laugh but it turns into a cry of real anguish and he kneels next to the bed. I watch his Adam's apple rise and fall as he swallows, his olive-green, gold-flecked eyes soften with love and fear as he grasps my hands between his. His gold wedding ring glints and shimmers in the bright room, sending tails of light swimming around it. I think of our wedding day on the Isle of Purbeck, just three years ago. How we stood together looking across the cliffs to Old Harry Rocks as the sun set, painting a pink wash over the sky and the silvery, mercurial sea. Our guests gathered on the sloped lawn, so busy chatting, drinking, celebrating, that they were oblivious to our private moment. We were in our blissfully happy bubble, surrounded by love and good wishes and subsumed by a flood of hope, as bright as the sunset itself. A life together stretching ever onwards towards the horizon.

'And you're sure you don't mind that it will only ever be the two us?' I'd asked him then, for the hundredth time.

'You'll always be more than enough,' he'd promised then. I hold on to the tail of that promise now, even as I feel myself being torn apart.

'Sofie,' he says softly when the contraction finishes, his forehead against mine, 'I know this isn't how we imagined this experience would be, but I love and admire you even more because of it. I'm in awe, truly.'

I close my eyes and nod, stifling another sob as I feel another contraction begin.

'I'm so scared, Rory,' I whisper.

'I'm right here with you, okay?' he murmurs, his voice hoarse. 'Everything is going to be okay. You can do this Sofie. We can do it.'

Chapter Two

A sudden urge to throw up overcomes me as I think about the prospect of giving birth. I dry-heave into the sink, turn on the tap and watch the water swirl down the plughole. I feel like another version of my life, the one in which I'm *not* pregnant, disappears along with the water.

I rinse my mouth, wash my hands and look up in the mirror again. My pale face is punctuated with frown lines from years spent hunched over monitors, trying to both predict and control the future. I peer closer, looking for something in my reflection that I haven't seen before. Something beyond my short, neat, naturally blonde hair, moss-green eyes and the Scandinavian nose I inherited from my father. Someone innately maternal beneath my immaculately smart clothes and filed nails: the unfussy look of a professional woman completely in command of their life. Try as I might, I don't see a mother there. All I feel is poleaxing panic.

I look at my phone again, at the app that charts my periods. My last one was May 28th. I then open a fertility calculator to work out my due date. The answer comes back quickly. February 21st. Just over seven-and-a-half months. A few weeks ago, I had a sickness bug that stopped me from going to work. And, I realise now, stopped my contraception working. I'd been so busy at work, that I just presumed stress had delayed my period.

This Wasn't Meant to Happen

This is it. I'm pregnant. Not through choice, probability or persuasion, but by accident.

I stare at the screen and the two lines observe me back, defiantly, as if to judge me for not feeling instantly overjoyed or excited.

'I'm scared, okay?' I whisper and then roll my eyes at myself for talking to a wee-covered window. But saying those two words out loud helps clarify for me that my fear isn't about not *wanting* to do this, it's more … what if I *can't* do this? I've always worked hard to be successful in my career, acing all the professional exams I've taken. But this? You can't revise for this. You don't qualify to be a mother. Nor are you rewarded enormously for the effort - at least, not for a while from what I've heard. But even knowing all this, my anti-baby stance begun to waiver when I turned thirty-five, last September. I didn't tell Rory because I knew he'd immediately try to accelerate things. The change started when I was out for a birthday dinner in Bournemouth with my old uni friends, Emma, Inge and Sal. Inge and Sal both had small children; Emma was trying for her first. The three of them spent all night obsessively discussing both pregnancy and parenting. As I listened to them talk about the endless planning and organising; the methodical cleaning of bottles; the organising of drawers and baby paraphernalia; the importance of a routine; the adrenaline that carries you through the long nights; the fierce love that makes you so determined to do everything right by your child – I realised a rogue 'I could do this' had swum into my head. I held that thought carefully, like a mystical crystal ball that contained both precious and potentially dangerous insight. Nisha wasn't there and I didn't discuss my revelation with her. At that point, she'd been unhappily single for a long stretch. I didn't want to give her another reason to feel left behind, especially as I wasn't going to *do* anything other than consider this new, possibly mercurial feeling. To be a mother, or not to be a mother – that was now the question.

Since then, I've found myself analysing the reasons I've chosen a child-free life so far. Has my decision been fuelled by fear? Was it simply about timing? Perhaps this new outlook was my biological clock loudly letting me know it was finally the right time. I didn't talk to Rory about how I was feeling; I didn't want to get his hopes up until I was certain.

Now, staring at the pregnancy test, I can't help but wonder when I'm finally going to admit to myself that I *want* this – have wanted this – for some time? The thought is as petrifying as the pregnancy itself.

I try to take long, deep breaths to calm down. I begin to recite Pi again in my head. It is the constant I turn to in times of anxiety or distress. I like the certainty of the endless digits. And that is what I aim for in life – a constant normal. But you can also find Pi in unexpected places, too – how a pendulum swings, in mechanics, cosmology, nature. It was my dad who first showed me how recurring numbers appear in the arrangement of leaves on stems, the branches of trees, petals on a flower or spiral patterns on seed heads. I memorised as many of the reassuring digits of Pi as I could when I was a teen. Right now, like so many times before, it is helping me to calm down, think clearly.

And if I think rationally, then the best possible outcome here isn't just possible but probable.

'Focus on what you know, not what you fear, Sofie,' I tell myself firmly, knowing it's what Rory would say.

Even if I can't necessarily imagine myself being a mother yet, I haven't ever really been able to imagine Rory *not* being a father. What if this is our one chance? What if this baby is – as I know Rory will believe – meant to be? At least I don't have to worry about his reaction. I know he's wanted this for years: he started talking about having children as soon as we were on honeymoon, even though I'd made it clear where I stood on that long before we got married.

'Rory, this is all I want,' I'd said firmly on the first night. 'I'm happy exactly as we are. I love our life and the lifestyle we can have *because* we don't have kids.'

We were sitting next to each other on the deck of our luxury lodge overlooking the sea in Newquay, glass of champagne in hand, bare legs entangled under a rug. A favourite holiday spot of ours, Cornwall was where we'd gone on our first ever mini-break, and was a natural choice for our honeymoon.

I'd hated seeing the disappointment on his face that night as we discussed having a family, even though he'd always known it was how I felt. But this was meant to be the happiest, most hopeful time of our lives, I didn't want to bring the mood down. So I'd added: 'Not yet, anyway. Can't we just enjoy being newlyweds?'

'Of course.' He'd kissed me. 'We'll give it a year and I know by then you'll have changed your mind,' Rory had added, and taken a satisfied swig of his champagne. He'd picked up the bottle to pour us another and I'd stared blankly at the stunning Cornish sunset that had set the horizon ablaze, one question circling my brain like the earth orbiting the sun.

But what if I don't?

The question about my 'readiness' has come up many times over the past three years. On the morning of his birthday a couple of weeks ago, Rory causally asked if I'd thought about coming off the pill.

'Time is going so fast; I'm nearly forty, Sof,' he'd said, looking at the presents on his lap – a jacket, some craft beer and the vintage watch I'd found in an antique shop. I realised then that he thought my gift symbolised something. Perhaps, unconsciously, it did. He turned it over in his fingers, studying it thoughtfully before slipping it on his wrist. 'I just think maybe it's now or never…'

'You're hardly old, Rory! Thirty-eight is still young for a man At thirty-five, it's me who should be worried.'

'Are you?'

'No?' I said defensively, but the way my voice went up as I said the word gave me away.

Hearing my doubt, he slipped his arm around my neck, eyes bright with hope. 'No one is ever really *ready* for parenthood, Sof. And remember, it wasn't that long ago that you thought you weren't ready for a long-term relationship either. Now look at us!' He got out of bed and rubbed his bare, broad torso that had softened in the years we'd been together but which I found even sexier now. The confidence with which he wore the extra weight made him seem stronger, sturdier, more himself somehow. 'I've got a good feeling about this year. I think it's going to be a vintage one, just like when we met.' He tapped the face of his watch, put it to his ear and smiled, unleashing his dimples. 'Because even though you're still the single best thing that's ever happened to me, this old Omega is pretty special, too, and you know what it's telling me right now?'

I shook my head weakly, feeling nauseous.

'It's time for a coffee,' he said gently, dropping a kiss on my forehead and I exhaled in relief. 'Look Sof, you know I'm ready when you are, but if you're not that's also fine. You and I will always come first. Now, shall I get you a latte, m'lady?' I shook my head again, feeling sick at the thought of the bittersweet fluid.

I realise now it's because I was already pregnant.

Chapter Three

Reluctantly, I exit the cubicle into the communal bathroom. I take a sip of the oat-milk latte I picked up from the café before I came to work and had left by the main sinks, then immediately spit it out when I realise I should avoid caffeine now. It's actually a relief: it hasn't tasted right for weeks, but coffee is such a big part of my morning routine, I kept hoping that it would change. It never occurred to me that I might be pregnant.

Anxiously, I look at the door the to check no one is about to come in, then I tip the rest down the plughole and run the water to wash it away, trying to convince myself that this fait accompli pregnancy could actually be the answer after all. I feel my heart begin to race with anticipation.

It's "Kingsmet", Sofie! I hear Rory joke in my head, as he is always the first to make a pun about his surname. I'm suddenly thrown back once again to the day we met.

It hadn't taken us long to realise how many people we knew in common and just how many not-quite meet-cute moments there'd been over the years. Like the fact that we'd attended rival local schools. Whilst Rory had been on every sports team, the only 'sport' I'd played at school was chess. Although I did remember a girl in my year, Imogen, proudly telling everyone she was dating a Year 11 boy from Bournemouth, and he'd confirmed that whilst that was, in theory, him, Imogen had been a family friend's daughter who'd had a crush on him, but who he'd never actually dated.

We'd also discovered we'd both attended Southampton University at the same time – but didn't cross over as he'd just graduated the year before I became a fresher. Apparently Rory had also often been to Mum's café in Swanage, too. Not only that, but he was also best mates with an ex-boyfriend of Nisha's – and had met her several times. We'd even attended the same thirtieth birthday party not long before we met. We just hadn't ever been formally introduced.

'Small world, isn't it?' Rory had surmised happily. 'So, would you say our meeting now is coincidence or luck?'

'Neither,' I'd replied shortly. 'It's probability. We live in the same town in the same county. It's natural we'd have mutual acquaintances and therefore would eventually meet.'

'You might say, we were *meant* to meet…' he'd countered.

I'd pointed to the big marquee in the distance. 'Okay, TV's Rory King, the Cheese Competition is actually happening in the main tent, you might want to take your chat-up lines there.'

He'd tilted his head, shaded his eyes from the sun and smiled at me. 'It's an unfair advantage that you know my name and I don't know yours.'

I knew exactly who he was because Mum watched the news religiously and particularly enjoyed the local-interest segments that Rory fronted. She said watching them helped her know her customers better. I had disliked the local news ever since our family literally had become the temporary focus of it when my dad died. His tragic fall from the cliffs at Durdle Door whilst foraging early one foggy morning had made every report and front page of the paper for days. Watching it always reminded me how magnified our lives become – the joys, sorrows and secrets – when you live in a small community.

'I'm Sofie. Sofie Jensen,' I'd replied, briskly, but I couldn't help smiling back. There was something welcoming about him, something safe.

'Well, Sofie-Sofie Jensen, I'm really pleased to finally meet you.' He said my name softly and slowly, almost poetically, and somehow he'd unintentionally adopted the slow Scandi rhythm and accent which pleased me. I'd noted how alive I felt, standing before him. More present and more seen than I'd felt for a long time.

I'd stood next to the cameraman while Rory interviewed Mum for his segment. I was pretending to watch her, whilst being spine-tinglingly aware of him. I marvelled over how easy he was in his skin; his natural ability to make those around him relax and feel like they'd known him forever. I found myself smiling when he laughed, feeling instantly happier and more hopeful in his presence and like a light had been switched on. It was a thrillingly new, golden feeling. As soon as he'd finished recording, Rory had turned and thanked Mum and, with well-practised charm, told her she was a total natural.

'Nonsense,' she'd smiled, waving her hand dismissively, but beaming in delight. 'You have a way of putting people at ease, Mr King!'

'Please, Angie, call me Rory. Now, could you possibly spare your daughter for a few minutes to come and have a wander around the fair with me?'

I'd immediately felt panic rising in my chest. 'Er, sorry. Mum needs help here.'

'No, I don't, darling!' she'd interrupted cheerfully. 'Midge is on her way; she's just parking the van up.' Midge is Mum's business - and life-partner of fifteen years. They got together sometime after Dad died, although the exact dates on that have never been clear. 'You two go ahead. It's quiet now, anyway, as everyone is off to watch the prize pigs!'

'So, what do you say, Sofie-Sofie Jensen?' Rory asked, one thick, arched eyebrow raised. 'I'd really love some company that isn't of the farm-animal variety.'

'Nice to know you have high standards,' I'd replied wryly. Just then, to my relief, an announcement was made over the tannoy.

'Will the finalists of the Young Pig of the Year Contest please line up for the prizegiving!'

'Ah. That's me,' he'd sighed regretfully.

'Not-So-Young Pig of the Year?' It was an attempt at a joke, but as soon as it came out of my mouth, I felt I'd gone too far with my banter and I blushed. It occurred to me that he made me nervous. Luckily, he didn't seem offended.

'Swine, actually,' he'd laughed. 'I'm the judge. I'm basically the Simon Cowell of the Dorset County Show. Except with rosettes rather than a record deal.'

'The Bacon and Eggs Factor?' I'd replied quickly and he'd laughed. I felt a flush of pleasure and relief rise through my body and take its place, tellingly, on my cheeks. I looked down and scuffed my trainer into the mud shyly.

'You know, Sofie Jensen,' he said, 'I wasn't meant to be reporting here today – my colleague Ian was meant to be on it – but he called in sick. Ian is *never* off sick. He's famously a very fit and healthy man. It seems like fate, destiny, *Kings*met even…'

'Kismet.' I'd corrected, looking up.

'… Kingsmet, kismet whatever you want to call it!'

'I don't want to call it anything,' I'd replied firmly. 'Because it's not a thing.'

'No, it's a *King*.' He'd grinned. '*Kings*met. Get it? Because I consider it *my* good fortune to have met you, at last.'

Since Dad's death I'd reconciled myself to the fact that nothing is 'meant to be'. Life is a series of inexplicable random events. There is no blueprint. No version in which fate has our life mapped out for us.

'I think the only things you're destined to meet today, Rory King, are those pigs,' I'd said and headed off to pick up another tray of coffee.

Undeterred, Rory had followed me.

'One drink, that's all I ask. Make it my lucky day.'

'I don't believe in luck,' I'd said glibly, over my shoulder.

'Luck is just hope, repackaged,' he'd said. 'And you wouldn't deny a guy some hope, would you?'

'I can "deny" a guy anything I choose,' I was painfully aware that I sounded like a buttoned-up maiden in a Sunday-night historical drama. 'The way I see it,' I'd continued, 'hope is what you cling to when you've lost control of your life. As for luck,' I'd added, 'I don't believe in any special force determining our lives any more than I believe in Santa Claus, or the tooth fairy. I study statistics for a living. I make choices, I don't take chances.' I'd been pleased with that line.

He'd put his hands deep in his pockets then pursed his lips to one side, thoughtfully. I didn't know why, but I had an urge to kiss him. I dismissed the thought from my mind, reminding myself that I had no interest in a relationship at this point in my life.

'But isn't chance just a combination of opportunity and possibility?' he pushed back. I couldn't help but admire the strength of his belief system. Even if it was wrong. 'After all,' he'd added, 'if you don't take chances, you never know what might've been…'

'I'm an actuary,' I'd told him. 'I believe in probability, not possibility.' I'd put down the coffees and picked up a tray of muffins and turned to pass some to a couple of passers-by.

'But a life without risks isn't possible!' he'd argued, walking alongside me before cheekily snatching one from the tray for himself and heartily biting into it. 'You take a risk every time you get out of bed, leave the house or cross the road!' He'd waved the cake in front of me. 'Or when you eat a muffin made by a sexy stranger.' He'd grinned. 'So, why not add, "Have a drink with a persistently charming local celebrity you met at the County Fair" to that list?'

I fought back a smile. 'Number one: my mum was the "sexy stranger" who made those muffins. And, number two: some risks are very much avoidable and down to personal choice, not chance. Like, for example, *choosing* not to go for a coffee with you. Even if you are a "local celebrity".'

'But *why* that choice?' he'd persisted. 'At least give me a viable reason.'

I couldn't help but be impressed that he was, at the very least, as stubborn as me.

'Because I'm not looking for a relationship,' I'd said firmly. 'Statistics show that ninety per cent of relationships that start before the age of thirty fail. So, I've sworn off them until well after. Even then, almost half of all marriages end in divorce.'

'Fair enough.' He'd nodded, and I'd been both flummoxed and surprisingly disappointed by his sudden concession of defeat. I'd been enjoying the verbal sparring more than I cared to admit. But he wasn't finished. 'But luckily for you, I'm thirty-one so by your rules, you're free to date me…'

I'd smiled and shrugged. 'And luckily for me, *I'm* twenty-nine, so by my rules, I'm not…'

'Would it help if I told you I don't want to get married?' he'd said.

'You don't?' Now this was interesting.

'No. Well, not yet. Not until after our first date, at least.'

'Urgh,' I'd groaned and folded my arms as I looked up at him, trying not to smile. 'Are you always this…'

'Optimistic?' He'd grinned.

'Persistent.'

'Only in moments like these. Important ones. Life-changing ones. When luck leads me to a girl like you.' The scent of his aftershave was something headily fresh and earthy that reminded me of walking through fields. His lips were curled into a gentle smile, and softly pronounced dimples had appeared in his cheeks like dents in a pillow. He'd swept his free arm around the showground that seemed suddenly to be shimmering in the late golden summer sunshine. Or perhaps it was his reflected hopefulness? I wasn't entirely sure.

'You really don't give up, do you?' I'd laughed, in exasperation.

'No.' he'd stared at me intently. 'Not when I think something is meant to be.'

I'd rolled my eyes again, but annoyingly, my smile betrayed me as it refused to fade.

'Besides,' he'd added, 'we haven't talked about the other ten per cent.' He'd leaned towards me conspiratorially. 'The under-thirties relationships that *don't* fail,' he'd elaborated.

'What about them?'

'Isn't it worth considering that we might fall into that category?'

'It's highly improbable.'

'But still possible … right?' he'd raised his eyebrows optimistically. They were pleasingly thick and irrepressibly arched like golden boomerangs.

'In theory, anything is possible I suppose.' It was proving impossible not to warm to him.

'Exactly!' he'd snapped his fingers. 'Because what do statistics actually tell us about anything, anyway? It's individuals that matter, not data…'

I'd gasped, horrified by this point of view. 'Statistics are what make us see and understand the world clearly; they're how we make discoveries in science! Not forgetting medicine, economics, the environment!' I'd ticked off the list on my fingers without taking a breath.

'In fact, entire government policies are created from them,' I'd finished in exasperation.

'And look how *that* generally turns out.'

'Literally everything important that we humans know is because of statistics,' I'd fiercely countered.

'Maybe,' he'd shrugged. 'But they don't tell us anything about how we *feel*…'

Another announcement for the pig contest was being made on the tannoy. It felt like a sign.

I'd folded my arms and appraised him thoughtfully. 'Okay, Meridien's Rory King, you want a date? I'll give you a date…'

'You will?' he'd said jubilantly, with an accompanying air punch. 'YES!'

I held my hand over my eyes to protect them from the sun as I squinted up at him. 'I warn you, it's rather short notice…'

'No problem.'

'Great!' I'd gestured with my hand towards the pig enclosure. 'It's right now, and it's with local counsellor, fellow judge and local *celebrity*, Mayoress Elsa Owen.' He'd looked at me quizzically. 'They've just called for you again: she's ready and waiting for you – and so are those prize pigs,' I'd added gleefully. 'Good *luck* with your date, Mr King!' I gave him a cheeky wave as he checked his watch and began to back away. 'I'm sure you'll have loads in common with your date!'

'Bye for now, Sofie-Sofie Jensen,' he'd laughed. 'There's a high probability I'll see you again soon.' And he turned his back and strode across the field and out of sight, into the tent.

To my surprise, instead of feeling relieved, I felt like something had been lost.

'He seems a lovely young man, doesn't he?' Midge had said warmly. She'd appeared next to me, perfectly dressed in a crisp shirt, Barbour jacket, jeans and wellies with a scarf wrapped around her forehead, always ready to step in and be by Mum's side and support her. 'Clever, sensitive, funny – not to mention those adorable dimples. Obviously not my type, though!' She'd laughed and nudged me playfully.

I folded my arms and didn't reply. I wasn't sure why I felt so irritated. Perhaps because she was pointing out the good traits of a man

I had so readily pushed away. I stared into the distance at the main tent. I realised that Rory King's absence had made it feel like the dimmer switch had suddenly been turned down on the day.

I throw my empty coffee cup in the bin and prepare to head back into the office. I might not feel like I'm ready for this big life change; but that's also how I felt when I met Rory. I took a chance back then, and six years on, he has made my life better in every way. And perhaps, despite all my fears and anxieties, there is every possibility that this baby will do the same.

This Wasn't Meant to Happen

Seven and a half months later

The room is bright, white and still. Too bright. Only the intermittent beeping of the monitor and my quiet moans overlay the silence. I'm made up entirely of this pain, unable to move beyond the now and the life-changing experience it contains.

As my contractions intensify, I close my eyes. I recite Pi. I know that giving birth is natural; women have done this for centuries; 1600 babies are born every single day in this country, that's one birth every 54 seconds... I just didn't think my experience would be like this.

3.14159...

Nine months of pregnancy – and thirty-six years – to get to this moment. There comes the sudden deep, desperate, primal urge to push. I shout at Rory to get the midwife and he obediently rushes towards the door.

'Don't leave me, Rory!' I scream shrilly and he hovers momentarily in the middle of the room, like a confused, cartoon meerkat. When I cry out again, he's by my side in a heartbeat. He presses the button by my wrist for help.

Sara rushes in with another midwife: she begins to examine me whilst the other one – Maria I think her name is – stands by her side.

'Your little boy is being good,' Sara, says from between my legs. 'He's ready. Are you?'

I nod fearfully. It's happening quickly, just as I had hoped. It occurs to me now that I may come to regret that wish.

As the next wave of pain builds and I feel the need to push again, I look for reassurance from Rory. Our eyes are fixed on one another's, searching desperately in them for a memory to transport us back to another place and time. To when there was only us.

'I love you, Sofie,' he whispers. 'You can do this.'

I push with all my might.

I feel the baby's head begin to crown and I flit madly between wanting it to be over and hoping that it'll never be.

Rory's eyes are telling me to be strong; be brave; have hope. 'Best possible outcome', that's what my endlessly supportive and naïvely optimistic husband always tells me to believe in. It's what he believes in, after all.

I wonder, slightly cruelly, if he'll still be peddling that myth after this experience. After all, not many births are quite like ours, just one in 225. 0.44 per cent. Rory would probably say that just shows that we – and our baby – are special.

Not lucky. Special.

Chapter Four

This pregnancy is a happy accident, I tell myself as I apply some blusher in the mirror in an attempt to put some colour back in my cheeks, like when Rory and I bumped into each other on my thirtieth birthday, just two weeks after the Dorset Show. Could it be that this, like then, is just the gentle little push I needed. The extra step I would never have taken myself...

On second thoughts, perhaps that's a bad example because I still suspect that our second 'coincidental' meeting was a fix. It was too convenient, how Rory suddenly appeared at my side. I can still remember how I felt the warmth of his smile before I saw it.

'Hi, Sofie-Sofie Jensen.' He'd grinned, leaning his elbows on the bar. 'Fancy seeing you here! Can I get you a drink?' Rory managed at once to get the bartender's attention, which I had been failing to do for the past ten minutes, whilst somehow also focusing entirely on me. His smile was a spotlight; his body turned towards me, hand lightly touching mine, like we were bound together with invisible strings. None of this was done possessively, or arrogantly. It felt magnetic, how we were drawn to each other.

'She'd love one!' Nisha had shouted over my shoulder, gleefully, before I could answer. 'Champagne, if you're offering!' She'd come down from London as she had a rare weekend off from work. 'It's her thirtieth birthday today, you know!'

'Woohoo!' Emma had cheered next to her, in perfect chorus with Inge and Sal. We were in that stage of life where the big girls' nights out of our twenties had tailed off, as serious relationships and our careers had taken over. On the occasions we did go out together, it was to celebrate a milestone moment. Emma, a primary-school deputy head teacher, still loved nothing more than letting her hair down when she could. Her thirtieth, just a few weeks before – the one Rory had also attended – had been raucous. Not for me, though. I'm always the one who stays sober and in control.

'*Really*,' he'd smiled in response to Nisha, his eyes firmly on mine, and I felt my insides unexpectedly flip as I remembered our conversation about relationships. 'What are the chances of that, eh?'

I'd smiled at him, unable to look away but not wanting not to let on that I knew that was his catchphrase. I'd watched him religiously every day for the past two weeks.

It had started the evening after the Dorset show: I'd gone back for dinner at Mum and Midge's, in the sweet little cottage in Corfe that she and Midge bought together about ten years ago. I slumped down at the kitchen table with a glass of wine, turned on the TV and switched straight to the news. As soon I saw Rory smiling into the camera lens, I was surprised to feel another pang of regret. From that night on, I found myself switching on the TV every night when I got home to my flat after work, just so I could see him. I wouldn't even take my coat and shoes off; I'd just come in and perch on the sofa, waiting for his segment. Before long I'd picked up on his mannerisms – the way he squinted his eyes thoughtfully when he was interviewing people; how he'd run his hand through his hair before taking on a challenge; or shift from one foot to another when he was cold. And of course, his catchphrase.

'*Now, what are the chances of that?*' he'd say after interviewing a local who had bought a pizza from Tesco Metro that looked exactly like their cat, or some other local story of uncanny resemblance.

His surprise arrival had made my thirtieth celebration feel special, elevated the night to never-seen-before levels of joy, anticipation, *desire*. The evening had taken an unexpected turn, and rather than being fearful of it, I was enthralled. Entranced. And I wasn't the only one he'd charmed.

'We like,' Sal had whispered approvingly at one point. It was true, he was great company, full of interesting anecdotes, a good listener. He asked all the right questions and made thoughtful, pertinent, funny observations. The Rory Show was, I had to admit, a highly entertaining one. He was completely tuned in to me, turned towards me so our legs were always touching. He'd occasionally brush my hand with his, gaze at me while everyone else was chatting until I made eye contact and then reward me with the brightest, most guileless of smiles. I loved how adorably and sexily dishevelled off-duty Rory King looked. It felt like he was having too much fun in life to worry much about anything, let alone being camera-ready.

Later that night, as the girls prepared to leave, he'd asked if I'd like to take a walk along the beach. I knew Nisha had been about to say yes for me, but I'd got there first. I'd hugged her as we said goodbyes outside.

'Happy Birthday, Sofie,' she'd said loudly, winking at me and then Rory. Then she'd leaned in and hugged me, whispering, 'You're welcome!' like she'd gifted him to me herself. I'd pulled away and eyed her suspiciously, and slightly tipsily.

'Did you have something to do with this?' I'd whispered back accusingly. She'd shrugged innocently in response, laughing as she walked away. Nisha has always believed that she knows what's best for me. I also knew that she'd been intrigued when I'd told her all about him and that she had, in fact, met him a couple of times. Because of that, his Socials would have been very easy for her to find.

So, Rory and I had left the bar together that night. It was the kind of balmy, late September evening that makes you feel that summer would last forever. We'd taken off our shoes and walked barefoot along the moonlit beach for a while before sitting down on the sand, talking companionably and passionately over the lapping waves about our careers, our dreams, our families. Being with him felt familiar – safe, somehow.

When he'd unexpectedly leaned in and kissed me, I realised I was helpless to resist him.

'There's something about you, Sofie-Sofie Jensen,' he'd murmured, when we'd eventually, reluctantly, prised ourselves apart. 'I could fall in love with you…'

This Wasn't Meant to Happen

'Aaand that's my cue to go.'

I'd scrambled to my feet and begun to walk away, panic already rising in my chest like a wave. I'd *promised* myself I wasn't going to fall in love with anyone and he'd just made me realise I could come dangerously close to that.

'Would it be so bad? To fall in love?' he'd called, grabbing his shoes and jogging after me.

'Not for you, perhaps,' I'd replied. 'Definitely for me. I've made the choice to sail solo.'

'Some would say that's the most dangerous way to travel.' He'd had to take big strides through the sand to keep up.

He'd grabbed my hand to stop me. 'What are you so scared of, Sofie?'

I looked at him and momentarily got lost in his green eyes. The wind had picked up and it suddenly felt like the waves were dangerously bigger than they were before. I didn't want to push him away, not really. There was something about him that felt different, something that I was drawn to. He made me want to take a chance. He made me feel that anything was possible, rather than probable. He made me feel that with him, I could be adventurous and safe, excited and calm. Loved, not lost. But then I reminded myself that love could be as incalculable and changeable as the sea. I couldn't risk it.

'*Everything*,' I'd replied. I'd walked away, head into the wind, as quickly as I could.

'Okay, forget love,' he called above it. 'What about One Fun Date? That wouldn't be scary or dangerous!'

'That depends.' Each time my feet sunk in the soft sand they slowed me down.

'On what?'

'The date. Like…' I'd struggled to think of an example. 'A date climbing a mountain would be dangerous, for example.'

'Luckily, I'm more of a bouldering guy myself.'

'What's that?'

'A type of rock climbing.'

I'd stopped, turned, shuddered as I'd stared at him. 'Rock climbing? Well, that makes my answer to One Fun Date an even harder No.'

'Okay, no bouldering. Just a non-dangerous drink, I promise.'

'What if it leads to more?'

'More drinks or more…?' His eyes had sparkled with amusement as he'd stepped towards me.

I'd turned, begun walking again.

'Okay! Okay! You win. No drink, just good old-fashioned fun.' He'd caught my elbow gently with his hand and gazed at me confidently. 'I warn you, though, I bet after One Fun Date with me, you'll definitely want a second.'

I'd stared at him, at the unfeasible length of his blonde eyelashes, the verdant green of his eyes threaded with flashes of gold that made me want to just give in to whatever this moment was. 'Actually,' he'd added, 'I'm going to punt my luck on a third, too.'

'Betting is for losers,' I'd mumbled, even as my mouth disloyally curled into a smile of admission. I couldn't help but be charmed by him.

'That's just the "Shape of My Heart",' he'd crooned then in a gruff, raspy voice, whilst playing air guitar.

I'd stared at him, head tilted in curious interest before guffawing with laughter. 'I-I'm sorry, what was *that*?!'

He'd grinned without embarrassment. 'One of Sting's best solo songs. He wrote it about a poker player who gambles not to win, but to find the answer to the mysteries of the universe.'

'And does he?' I'd asked.

He'd shrugged, grinning. 'The lyrics are a bit ambiguous to be honest. Maybe he found it in some "Fields of Gold"?'

'Or in a "Message in a Bottle"?' I'd shot back, quick to pick up on the game.

'Sting fan, too, are you?' he'd said, reaching his hands around my waist and moving his lips towards mine.

I'd pushed him away. 'Don't Stand So Close to Me!' I'd joked. It had felt like his laugh had echoed across the entire beach and it thrilled me to have that effect on him.

'It was actually my mum who was the real fan,' he'd admitted as we picked up our shoes and began to walk barefoot along the shoreline.

'Was?' Had he lost a parent, too? Was that why I felt such an immediate, strong connection with him?

'She might still be, to be fair, but I wouldn't know. My mum isn't really in my life anymore. Not by my choice – she left when I was about three. I found some Police albums in a box of her stuff when I was a teenager, and it led me to investigate his solo stuff. Let's just say I played "If I Ever Lose My Faith in You" on repeat for quite a while.'

'I'm so sorry, Rory.'

'Honestly, it's okay,' he'd said brightly, though his crumpled brow and uncharacteristic solemnity told a different story which made my heart ache for him. 'She did me a favour, really.'

'Taught you never to trust anyone again?' I'd asked sympathetically.

He'd looked horrified. 'No, made me appreciate how lucky I am!'

Whilst his optimism in the face of abandonment confounded me, I liked how easily he shared a fraction of his past and welcomed me into it. And that he understood the loss of a parent, how deeply it embeds itself in the fabric of your being.

'So, about this date…' We'd stopped, the sea curling seductively around our ankles. Pulling us in. Pulling us closer.

One date couldn't hurt, could it?

I'd appraised him thoughtfully. 'Do you promise not to sing again?'

'Scout's honour.' He'd said, holding up three fingers.

'Of *course* you were a scout.' I'd laughed. 'Okay. One date, that's all.' I'd formally offered my hand for him to shake, but instead he'd pulled me towards him. As he lowered his lips to mine, I gave myself entirely to his kiss, telling myself as long as I was careful, I could be in control of whatever this might become.

That's what I told myself then and that's what I tell myself now: I can be pregnant *and* totally in control … can't I?

Seven and a half months later

I feel another, uncontrollable urge to push and I cry out again – not in pain, but persistence. I feel the mound of our baby's head pressing against my flesh, turning me inside out. I squeeze Rory's hand so tightly it seems to me like our skin has been permanently welded together. Fingerprints indelibly marked on mine. Genes fused in a way that will never be broken. Except we already are. Broken, that is. But while the pain feels almost impossible to bear, I don't want it to end. It is my biggest act of love so far. Here, in this moment, this room, this life: it's just me, Rory and our baby.

As I prepare to push once more, fear gnaws deep in my belly clamping my insides as tightly as my contractions. I squeeze my eyes shut to try and visualise Pi, but instead of numbers I see stars. An entire galaxy sparkling behind my eyelids, lifting me up and lighting the way. I can see myself holding my baby boy in my arms at last, but the image implodes, the fractures falling like meteors before vaporising into nothingness. I cry out, but I make no sound. With a final silent push, I let go of the fear and the pain — and him, too. His little body slides silently from mine. He's not here, though. His soul is, perhaps, already light years away from here. I wish I were, too.

I'm disconnected from everyone and everything, including myself. Rory's next to me, weeping noiselessly. The two midwives are working efficiently and tenderly with our lifeless baby as if they did this every day. Which, as a profession, they do.

One in 225 pregnancies ends in stillbirth in the UK. That's seven stillbirths every day. Over 2,600 last year. And now we're part of that statistic. We — our boy — is that one.

Our baby boy, gone before he was ever here, asphyxiated in my womb by the nuchal cord which became wrapped around his neck, as discovered by the consultant when I came into hospital just thirty-six hours ago. The life source I provided for him both his beginning and his end.

Chapter Five

I quickly dive back into the toilet cubicle just as someone comes into the bathroom. I'm not ready to see anyone in close personal quarters. I sit down quickly, shuffle my feet, cough and pull at the toilet roll so it sounds like I've just finished. I don't want anyone gossiping about the length of time I've been in here. Although, for us actuaries, gossip is a low priority: we're more interested in reality than rumour.

Besides which, there's only two other women that work in the actuarial department and they're both in their early twenties and completely wrapped up in their own lives. Lives that couldn't be further from pregnancy. They're too busy having fun.

'Fun'. That's how this all began.

'A *fun*fair?' I'd said somewhat incredulously when, a week after my birthday, Rory had revealed our One Fun Date. My heart had sunk as he gestured for us to walk down Bournemouth Pier. 'I didn't think you'd be quite so literal.'

'I'm a news reporter,' he'd grinned. 'It's my job to be literal.' He was wearing a white shirt with blue jeans, scuffed brown boots and a green bomber jacket. He'd told me he'd come straight from doing a report on a magician from Poole who'd set a new Guinness World Record for doing the most magic tricks in one minute. 'If I promise fun, I'll bring you to a funfair. So, here we are. I mean,' he'd waved his hand at the rides, 'what could be more fun?'

'*Literally* anything.' I'd replied shakily, trying to block out the noise, the bright flashing lights, the sweet, sickly sugary smell of candyfloss, and the screams of joy and fear that put me instantly on edge. 'I hate heights, avoid adrenaline at all costs and steer clear of danger. This, Rory King, is my nightmare.'

'You just haven't been to a funfair with *me*. I promise, there's nothing to be afraid of. Come on!' He'd taken me by the hand and made me run down the Pier approach to the arcade, where he quicky reminded me of 'Kingsmet' by winning a cuddly toy from the first grabber machine he tried.

'How did you do that?' I'd gasped.

'Just lucky, I guess!'

'I bet you say that to all the girls.'

After winning prizes on most of the arcade games, he begged me to brave a ride with him – his choice. This turned out to be a small, slow, caterpillar roller-coaster aimed at toddlers, who all looked at us in confusion as we queued up. Not helped by the fact that Rory then screamed so loudly on the gently undulating insect, it made me laugh so much I practically fell out of the carriage when the ride finished. Afterwards, candy floss in hand, he asked me if I trusted him enough to go on the Ferris wheel.

I'd studied him for a moment as I plucked some spun sugar from the bag and popped it into my mouth, where it melted deliciously.

'I can't stand heights, but weirdly, I do,' I'd replied.

Whilst the wheel was gently rotating up to its full 100-foot height, I'd gripped onto Rory's hand for dear life. With my eyes squeezed shut, I'd asked him about his childhood. Mostly because I needed a distraction.

He told me how his mum had been a talented dancer, the kind who took part in competitions all over the country and won national championships. She spent every spare hour of her childhood – and every spare penny of her mum Sandra's hard-earned money, according to Rory – on lessons at her local dance academy. Sandra worked three jobs to support her daughter's hobby. But then, Nikki hit her teens; she became interested in boys, not ballet, dancing in clubs, not on stage. She started hanging out at bars in Bournemouth and by the time she turned seventeen, she was pregnant. Three years after having Rory, she left.

Another example of how people you love abandon you unexpectedly, I was tempted to say.

'I'm so sorry, Rory. That must have been incredibly hard,' I'd said, stroking his hand in sympathy.

'No, not at all,' he'd said decisively. 'As far as I'm concerned it all worked out for the best…'

I'd stared at him inquisitively. 'How so?'

My stomach had flipped like a pancake in fear as we rose higher in the air. I'd felt breathless as the sand, sea and sun encased us in an iridescent, golden miasma. I took deep breaths to calm myself as we reached the top.

He'd gazed unseeingly to the horizon. 'She was young, not ready to be a mother. She was brave enough to bring me into the world, but also astute enough to know that she couldn't guide me through it. I understand why she chose to leave, and I respect her decision now. I don't see that she abandoned me, because she actually did the right thing for my future. And she left me in the best possible hands.'

I was in awe of his levels of both acceptance and forgiveness. I'd never met anyone like him before.

'You weren't angry?'

He'd shaken his head. 'I was too young to know how to be. She stayed in sporadic contact over the years. Occasionally, she'd come back to Bournemouth for my birthday or Christmas, or a brief after-school visit if she needed money from my gran. But when I was about thirteen, she remarried and went on to have a couple of children by this rich, older guy. Then, the visits stopped. When I was fourteen, I went to London to try and reconnect with her. She was living in this nice, detached house in a leafy South London suburb, four-by-four parked outside. She made it clear on her doorstep that she wasn't interested in a relationship with me.' He'd paused then. I could tell from his expression how much it still hurt, but he quickly moved on, like he wanted to wipe clean his memories. 'Her new life had no place for a spotty teenage son who lived on an estate. I admit I lost the plot a bit then, went off the rails, you know?'

'I do.' I was taken back in an instant to the dark months after my dad had died.

'You, too?' he'd smiled, eyebrows raised in interest as he turned to look at me. 'You don't seem the type... What was your poison?'

'Studying,' I'd replied. 'I mean,' I'd added quickly, 'there was a brief period of partying just after my dad died, but I soon swapped that for schoolwork. Maths, specifically. I was obsessed with numbers.'

'Woah, craaaazy!' He'd thrown his head back and laughed. 'The risk-averse actuary, a secret off-the-rails *maths* junkie – I don't believe it!'

I'd laughed then, too, enjoying being teased by this sweet, sensitive, sexy man about something I had always taken so seriously.

'What about you, then, rebel boy? What did you do?' I'd teased, in return.

'Oh, the normal stuff,' he'd said flippantly, a smile playing on the corner of his lips. He squinted up at the sky and started a list on his fingers. 'Theft of various vehicles, beachside violence, drug dealing ... murder.'

I must have looked so horrified that he quickly said, 'Not in real life! When I was fifteen, I lost about six months of my life to *Grand Theft Auto*'.

I'd exhaled in relief. 'So, you were about as rebellious as I was,' I'd pointed out teasingly. 'But you were a gaming geek, instead of a maths one.'

'Well, *my* addiction caused me to fail most of my GCSEs,' he'd said faux competitively. 'I bet yours had a more positive outcome?'

'Fair point, you win.' I'd conceded. 'But why gaming? Why not girls or drink or drugs?'

'It was the ultimate escape, I guess,' he said thoughtfully, 'Instead of being the victim, I could be the hero. Whether that was a perky, heroic plumber in *Super Mario*, or a highly focused, murderous *Street Fighter* – neither of which I would ever really want to be. Especially the plumber, because that guy deals with *really* dangerous shit.' I'd laughed again. 'I was playing all night and barely able to drag myself out of bed in the morning. I just didn't want to be in my life anymore. Gaming numbed my pain by turning it into pixels. Instead of feeling it, I could shoot it, fireball it or even…' – he paused – 'Super Combo Crazy Buffalo it.' He'd raised an eyebrow and his smile lifted further with it. 'You'd know what that meant if you'd spent your misspent youth playing *Street Fighter*. I may have still been a virgin, but I had *all* the moves.'

'Me too. But in chess.'

He'd laughed again. 'I bet no one has ever worried about you having a dangerous addiction to *that*.'

'True,' I'd grinned. 'So, what made you stop?'

'When I failed my GCSEs, Gran read me the riot act, took the PlayStation away and sent me to counselling. But mainly, she showered me with love, belief and positivity when my self-esteem was so low that I didn't believe I was good enough for anything. I went back to school, repeated the year and got the grades I needed to do my A levels. I actually wrote a *Grand Theft Auto* inspired play for my Drama GCSE practical, based on *Romeo and Juliet*. So, you could argue, I was actually learning all the time.'

'Your gran sounds like an amazing woman. You're lucky to have her.'

'I am,' he'd replied then paused and eyed me intently in a way that made my knees go weak, and not just because we were dangling in the air. 'Hang on,' he'd smiled and put his arm around me. 'I thought you didn't believe in luck, Data Girl?'

The wheel had stopped at the top of its climb, the sky a lilac wash around us. I realised that suddenly, inexplicably, I felt safe.

'I don't.' I paused for a moment before I spoke again. 'At least, I didn't.'

Rory had lightly removed a strand of hair from my lips, blown there by the wind. I gazed into his eyes as his fingers brushed against them and then he pulled me close. In the moment before his lips met mine, I felt this enormous sense of being vulnerable but *with* someone rather than alone, so that together our vulnerability became a strength. Then, gently, with the wheel slowly descending back down to solid ground, he kissed me and I leaned into it in a way I'd never done with anyone before.

It occurs to me now that I can lean into this pregnancy the same way – with my whole heart. With that thought, I decisively head out of the bathroom and towards my desk in our basement floor office. Ready for another day, predicting risk. And a new life, as a mum-to-be.

Seven and a half months later

I'm watching everything from my elevated Royal-box style seat up here near the ceiling. Here, but not here.

'Would you like to cut the cord?' Sara the midwife says to Rory.

When he replies, his voice is a soft wah wah wah, like something from a Peanuts cartoon. I watch from above as he shakes his head.

You can do this I want to say, but no words are available to me.

Rory's down there, but I can't reach him. I can see our baby, too.

His face is pale, like his dad's, and also like my dad's, and like the moon, which is glowing ethereally outside the small hospital window on this darkest of mid-February days.

Everything is quiet, except the melody to 'Moon River' that's playing in my head. I feel like I'm drifting away from myself, higher and higher, towards the same rainbow's end as my baby and I'm glad. But I stop suddenly and for a moment it feels like I have a choice. If I just snipped the invisible string tying me to this world, I'd float away. But as soon as I have that thought, I feel myself plummet. Down, down, down. And as I fall and flail, an unfathomably loud wail thrusts me mercilessly back into the room, shattering the silence like glass. It takes a while for me to recognise the noise has come from me.

'Do you want to hold him?' the midwife asks me, her face full of kindness, comfort, but also, neutrality. I gaze at her dumbly. I wonder how many times she's had to witness this tragic scene before – a woman delivering a baby she knows is already gone; who will never breathe, never live beyond her womb. I want to know what it feels like for her when she delivers a healthy, living, breathing baby. What does her expression look like then? What will she feel when she walks from this room today? Will she remember me once we've left here? Will she remember him?

I look down at him then. Our baby. And realise she's expecting me to answer.

How can I hold our dead baby?

But then again, how can I not?

This Wasn't Meant to Happen

'You don't have to decide right now,' the midwife says gently. 'We can give you some time. If you want, we can take him away, clean him up, swaddle him up, dress him.' She nods at the knitted yellow baby blanket I brought that's neatly folded on the chair in the corner of the room, with matching knitted hat and mittens resting on top.

'No! Don't take him!' I croak desperately. 'Please don't take him away.' I start to sob, then. 'I want to hold him, please. Please can I hold my baby...' She presses her hand lightly on my arm and smiles benevolently down at me.

'Of course you can. Here, careful, he's heavy.' I look up at Rory in wondrous fear, my head exploding with the enormity of all we've been through in the past thirty-six hours. And all that is still to come. He just stares back at me.

I'm shaking uncontrollably as I hold out my arms and our precious boy is passed to me. He's now wrapped in the buttery yellow blanket I bought especially for this moment but also, for one completely unlike this. And I feel moored. I draw him close to my chest and Rory envelops us both with his arms. A never-ending circle of love.

Pi. To infinity.

Chapter Six

Later that afternoon, I extricate myself from work early citing a headache. My head feels like it might explode with the magnitude of my secret and my growing excitement at the thought of telling Rory. But how to do it? I step out into the warm July day that's been sweetened by a light afternoon shower.

The sky is the perfect shade of periwinkle; pink-tinged candyfloss clouds are floating overhead, like ballerina tutus. It feels like I'm looking up at a new, bright, baby-focused future – entirely different from the one I'd previously mapped out.

I'm pregnant. I'm pregnant. I practise the words in my head as the bus moves towards Southbourne. I need to constantly remind myself that this accidental occurrence is real and permanent and not the strange, ephemeral circumstance it feels like.

Uncharacteristically for me, I have no plan, no list, no script for a big, romantic, pregnancy reveal. I'm just hoping I'll be able to control my natural catastrophising nature enough to tell Rory the news without adding, 'But it's early days so we shouldn't get our hopes up just yet.'

I clutch my work rucksack tightly to me and raise it on to my shoulder ready to disembark the bus. Carefully, like I'm carrying a very fragile object (which I realise I am), I get off at my stop and begin the short walk home, stopping for a moment to take in the view of the glorious coastline that I'm lucky enough to call home. I take in the beach that connects Boscombe to Southbourne and stretches east to the claw-shaped peninsula of Hengistbury Head, all the way round to Mudeford Spit.

Across the sea lies the shadowy silhouette of the Isle of Purbeck where I grew up. Sometimes I feel like living here means I'm torn between two versions of my life: Before Dad, and After Dad. I often wonder if he'd be surprised at the risk-averse, work-addicted, home-loving woman I've become, so far removed from the wild, nature-loving, swimming, fishing, foraging girl that he was proud to call his. I turn away quickly, not wanting to answer that question and hurry home, the relief flooding over me as soon I see the familiar, friendly shape of our house, and the small-but-content life I've boxed up safely inside.

I remember the day Rory and I came to view it, not long after we'd got married. We couldn't believe we'd found one in our budget in such a desirable area. Like much of Bournemouth's housing, our street is a jigsaw of architectural styles: a bungalow next to an Edwardian house with curved gabled facades; an Art Deco apartment block, a Guest House alongside ex-council flats.

Our home is a detached 1960s brick-fronted house complete with kitsch mock-Tudor detail. We both found the aesthetic confusion of the house charming, like an adorable kid who might wear a tutu over a swimming costume and accessorise with welly boots. It needed work – a loft conversion and kitchen extension were essentials – but whilst Rory wanted to put in an offer right away, I was solely focused on the maths. What mortgage could we get? Could we make a profit if we sold it once we'd done the extension? Rory told me not to worry, it would all work out. But I wanted to be in control of the numbers.

I couldn't deny I'd completely fallen in love with everything about the place, from the small, manageable garden to the spacious, beautifully light main bedroom with its front-facing balcony doors, and the magnolia tree that stood proudly outside it framing the sea view beyond. From those same balcony doors, I could see the shadowy, comforting silhouette of Purbeck, my childhood home whilst standing in the very solid presence of my future.

And so, apparently, could Rory.

'This would make a great room for a baby, don't you think?' He'd called, gesturing at me excitedly to come and look at the light, airy spare room with its surprisingly high ceilings and big dormer window.

'If we have one,' I'd replied quickly, surprised that I hadn't just said 'no'. The no both he and I were expecting.

He'd immediately thrown his arms around me in delight. '*If? If!* I'll take *if*!'

Since then, Rory has never let go of that 'If'. An 'if' that has now become a 'when'.

I stare up now at the same spare room window, soon to be a baby's nursery – just as Rory predicted. There's a climbing, flowering shrub that's experiencing a late-summer bloom (I know the feeling) but whose name momentarily escapes me, tickling the edges of the window frame with its delicate clusters of lilac fronds. Delicate clusters – like the new cells forming in my body.

Wisteria, that's it. Part of the pea family, actually.

'Hello, pea,' I say to my belly, then. 'Hello my sweet, sweet pea.'

Seven and a half months later

'Do you have a name for your sweet boy?' Sara asks. I look down at his shock of golden, Viking hair and his chalky, protruding lips. Rory's about to answer but I get there first.

'Leo. His name is Leo.' His name is like a breeze on my lips. There all too briefly, then gone.

'That's lovely.' Sara says. I look up at her and the midwife she's training, who's doing her best to remain impassive but is not quite able to make eye contact. I can see the tension in her body, can feel how desperately she wants to escape this room. I don't blame her; I feel guilty, for what I've done to her. Her dream job of delivering babies is meant to be about life, not death. I wonder if, when she chose this career, she realised this horror would be part of her experience, too?

It occurs to me that I could ask myself that same question. Of course, I've always known the statistics. One in four pregnancies ends in miscarriage. I just allowed myself to hope and believe that I would not be the unlucky one.

This Wasn't Meant to Happen

Sara and Maria retreat respectfully out of the room and we are left alone, silently looking down at our eternally sleeping baby boy in my arms. Rory reaches out to touch my hand and I look at him, then quickly away. The probability that I could be lucky, that this unexpected gamble, which Rory made me believe was a safe bet, would pay off, had never been a certainty at all. The promise that I would never lose someone I loved again has been obliterated and all that's left are the shattered pieces of my heart.

Chapter Seven

The hours between me getting home and Rory coming back at seven-thirty feel excruciatingly long. I busy myself with admin, going through the bills and our finances and replying to a text inviting me to Inge's little boy's and Sal's son's joint fifth birthday at the weekend; and another reply to Emma, who suggests meeting up for lunch with her and baby Fergus beforehand. I find I'm already excited for the moment that I'll get to tell them that I'm joining their mum club. Emma will be over the moon, I know. She's still on maternity leave from her teaching position and has always said she feels a bit envious that Sal and Inge were able to navigate the baby days together. I feel lucky that the majority of my close uni friends chose to stay in Bournemouth after graduating. If only Nisha would move back here it would be the icing on the cake.

I do my daily financial admin: move money between our accounts, check in on various savings, ISAs, premium bonds, and the mortgage rate. I switch energy providers to get the best deal, check Martin Lewis's website and read the most recent financial news. Rory is not a money man. Or much of a domestic one. He's a dreamer more than a doer. I don't mind. We're both used to me being the practical one – juggling a big job with running a tight ship at home. I sort the bills and admin and we share the rest of the domestic load. Rory also brings the fun, energy and positivity. He's the life of the party when we're out, and the light relief I need at home: he books the holidays, organises our social life, ensures we spend time with my mum, Midge and his nan. He makes me relax, makes me laugh. Don't get me wrong, sometimes he maddens me with his laid-back nature, but mostly our relationship proves the age-old 'opposites attract' theory.

I keep glancing up at the clock. The house always feels quiet without him, yet even when he's not here I feel encased in our shared happy memories. Now there's a new energy, a little person who will join us in a few months' time and will no doubt bring untold chaos to this orderly, controlled calm. Not to mention an abundance of delirious, overwhelming love and awestruck laughter and the possibility of a whole new life stretching forwards together. There will be anxiety, hope, fear, gratitude, frustration, love – the endless, infinite love everyone talks about – and I'm not naïve enough to think there won't be challenges along the way. Rory may have quit his bouldering hobby for me, but I know that becoming parents will feel like climbing a rock-face. And we'll be doing it without safety ropes. Feeling a flicker of panic re-emerge, I start folding and putting away laundry in the utility room to calm myself. Then I clean the downstairs bathroom and the kitchen. Wiping the surfaces urgently, I long to call my best friend, the person who has guided me through the best and worst times of my life. I pick up my phone, scroll through my contacts and my finger hovers over Nisha's name. But then I remember her last visit just a few weeks ago, when she was staying with her parents for the weekend, and she came over to ours for dinner.

The three of us had been in the kitchen. I was cooking, Rory and Nisha were chatting.

'Oh, for God's sake, put each other down!' Nisha said suddenly as I placed some poppadom's and homemade mango chutney and raita in front of her and Rory on the island unit.

'What?' I'd protested. 'We're not touching each other!'

She'd rolled her eyes and tilted her head, her sleek, black bob brushing her shoulders. 'You just brushed Rory's bottom with your hand when you put the dips down. He did the same when he passed you to get the wine from the fridge. Before that, he kissed your neck whilst you were stirring the curry.' She tapped a finger for each occasion. 'You squeezed his shoulder when he was opening the wine. He kissed you after he poured you a glass. And that's just in the past few minutes. You do it so often, you don't even notice.'

'At least we're not snogging in front of you.' Rory had grinned, wrapping his arms around me and nuzzling my shoulder.

'Thanks,' she'd drawled, then. 'Oh, ignore me. I'm just jealous.' She'd reached over and checked her phone, which she'd been doing all night.

'How's it going with Andy?' I'd gone to pour her more wine, but she'd put her hand over her still full glass. She'd been seeing a guy from work for a few months who she was clearly infatuated with. He was a few years older, in his forties and a senior consultant. Nisha seemed to have high hopes for him because, as she put it, 'He isn't emotionally stunted, like most men I've been with.' I, however, was reserving judgement until I met him. I wasn't sure what was taking her so long.

'How come he didn't come this weekend?'

'He had a family thing.' She'd said, through a mouthful of heavily-dip-loaded poppadom. Rory had retired to the lounge with his phone, where he was no doubt scrolling through his socials.

'Seeing his folks?' I'd asked.

'No.' She'd paused to finish her mouthful. Swallowed. 'His kids.'

'You didn't tell me he was a dad!' I'd gaped at her as she'd taken a sip of wine, mainly to avoid looking at me.

'He's married, too,' she'd said briskly. 'Separated, though. Well, he will be. Soon.'

'Oh, Nish!' I'd groaned.

'I know, I know,' she'd said edgily. 'I don't need the "Don't risk your heart on someone who isn't going to look after it" speech. I'm aware it's a less-than-ideal situation…'

I'd raised my eyebrows. 'That's an understatement.'

Her dark brown eyes were pleading, swimming with contrition.

'He's telling her he wants a divorce this weekend.' She'd glanced at her phone again. 'I wouldn't be in this if I didn't think it was long over between them.' Then she'd looked up. 'I'm in love with him, Sof.'

I'd nodded and looked away, busying myself with refilling the dips. Nisha has a bad habit of falling for unsuitable men.

I knew her well enough to keep my counsel as she told me how kind, clever and sensitive he is, a great guy and a wonderful dad. That he was trying his best to do what was right in a difficult situation.

Right for himself, my lips were clamped firmly shut, but my thoughts were having a free for all.

'He just doesn't want anyone to get hurt.'

Doesn't want his wife to find out.

'I don't *want* to be seeing a married man,' she'd said, defensive, even though I'd not said a word. 'It's as miserable, lonely and exhausting as being single was. But you know what they say, you can't help who you fall in love with!'

I couldn't let that statement pass without a response.

'Of course you can. It's a choice, Nisha, and you have to ask yourself if it's a good one.' I'd paused from stirring the lentil dhal I'd made and turned to look at her. 'Because you *can* choose to step away, not only to protect yourself, but also the other people you're hurting, who don't deserve to be treated like this. If Andy's the one and if you honestly believe his marriage is over, I'll support you. But don't say you have no control over it, because you do.'

She'd looked wounded. 'Not all of us are as lucky as you and get handed love on a *plate*. My options are more limited, these days.'

I'd softened my tone then. 'I'm only lucky, Nisha, because *you* encouraged me to make better choices.' I'd watched as she picked up her phone to check it for the millionth time. 'But you have to ask yourself, if it's so right, should it be this hard? And should it make you feel this anxious?'

The rest of the evening had been tense. Nisha headed off straight after dinner, and I've not heard from her since. That was three weeks ago. I know I should have texted her to check in, but work has been so busy, this pregnancy has consumed me, and part of me felt like I needed to make a point. I don't *want* to support her in this, because I think she's going to get hurt. I wish I had at least phoned her now: it feels wrong to do so just to tell her my news. Talk about rubbing salt into the wound.

At six-fifteen, I go into the lounge and turn on the news so I can watch Rory, a habit I've maintained since we first met. I know he has a pre-recorded report from a Willy Wonka room at The Chocolate Box Hotel in Bournemouth. As I watch my husband on the screen, I can't help but laugh as he showcases the lickable wallpaper, finishing his report by submerging himself, fully dressed, in a chocolate bath.

'This is Rory King, reporting from a real-life chocolate bathroom *sweet*. What are the chances of guests liking it a *choco*-lot!'

Rory bounds into the house forty-five minutes later, like a whirlwind, kisses me, deposits his bulging, half-open rucksack on the island, paperwork spilling out of it. He removes his jacket and chucks it over a kitchen chair – it misses and falls on the floor – then starts to pull off his trainers, one by one. I watch him, silently from my position on the bar stool.

'Are you okay?' he asks.

'I'm pregnant.' The words spill out as messily as his bag contents before I can stop them. I've spent the last two hours practising various ways to tell him. None were quite this direct.

I wait and watch as my husband takes in my bombshell. He freezes in the most precariously balanced position, head bowed over his bent legs, one in a kind of demi-plié, the other foot crossed over his knee, his hands holding on to his second trainer which he was attempting to remove when I made my surprise announcement.

I stare at the top of his head, the soft swirl of his double crown and shaggy russet-gold mop that's more Southwest surfer than serious news reporter and a symbol of his prolonged youth (thirty-eight going on twenty-five, that's Rory). He wobbles suddenly and looks at me in a perfectly captured Polaroid of stunned happiness.

'Are you sure?' he says, kicking his shoe off and coming towards me. He clearly doesn't want to have his hopes raised prematurely. 'But, when? How?'

'Well, Rory, there's this thing we've been doing for a while now called sex. And you know, when the man puts his pe—'

'You're on the pill!' he interrupts.

'Remember that stomach bug I had a few weeks ago? Well, it affects how the pill works. I did the test at work…' I hold it up for him as proof.

Confusion makes way for instant joy as a full-beam smile floods his face, cheeks punctuated by deep, cushiony commas, accompanied by hashtag lines of happiness around his eyes. Rory's emotions are a gallery of impressionistic delight; the brushstrokes of his facial expressions make it abundantly clear to me exactly how he's feeling at any given moment. How he manages to remain neutral when he's doing serious reports, I'll never know.

'Holy SHIT!' he says and whoops as he leaps across the room towards me. 'I'm going to be a dad! You're going to be a mum...' He pauses and lets this thought wash over him. 'We're going to be *parents*!'

'What are the chances of that, eh?!' I laugh weakly, momentarily caught up in his complete and utter joy.

'And ... you're okay with it?' he slides his arms around me, his face suddenly uncommonly solemn and full of concern.

I pause for a moment and look at my husband, joy and optimism, hope and gratitude radiating out of him like a rainbow. 'Well, it wasn't planned, so that must mean it's *Kingsmet*, right?' I smile.

'Oh, wow,' he exhales, looking at me. 'Sofie.' He puts his hands to his face and wells up then. 'Is this actually happening? I'm so happy. This is the best news, *ever*. I can't wait to tell—'

I put my hand up to his mouth to stop him. 'Can we wait until we've had the twelve-week scan? Just to be on the safe side? It's still very early...I don't want to jinx anything.' I thread my arms around him. 'I also love the idea of this just being our secret for now.'

'Secret. I can do secret,' he says, opposing the statement by looking like he might explode with the news. 'I *love* secrecy, it's very ... sexy.' He grins and then kisses me. 'Although,' he adds as he pulls his lips away, 'that sounds like a line Randy Andy would pull on Nisha.'

We laugh together then, in the way only a smug, happy couple can do, but I stop when a sudden flood of accompanying guilt hits me. It feels like we have just won the lottery without ever buying a ticket. And whilst we both appreciate how lucky we are, I also know that to some – to Nisha - it will just seem supremely unfair.

That night, Rory and I lie in bed contentedly spooning. I feel submerged in love, luck and happiness. I turn over in bed to face him, wind my arms around his waist and pull him close, so our stomachs are touching. I imagine our tiny baby cocooned safely between us. I stare at Rory's peacefully resting face.

'Rory. I can't sleep…'

He opens his eyes, used to this sentence. He pulls himself up on one elbow and I know he's about to give me one of his customary pep talks to curb my anxiety. 'Sofie, you have nothing to worry about. We are going to make the best parents; we'll be the greatest team. This baby will be the luckiest kid alive. Even *more* loved, even *luckier* because we didn't expect him or her. I mean, how hard has this little one fought already to get this far? All you need to focus on is growing this baby and trust me on everything else. Because everything *is* going to be okay. More than okay, it's going to be *amazing*.'

'I know that,' I say, laughing. 'You didn't let me finish. I can't sleep because I'm so *happy* for us.'

'And that', Rory replies, blinking with emotion, 'is the best news ever.'

I stare at his freckles that merge into each other along the bow of his upper lip, his cheeks that remind me of Purbeck's undulating hills when he smiles. As I thread my arms around him, I feel a shimmering sense of being both at the start of something and at the centre of it. I'm buoyed by possibility and purpose. A new life exists for us both because of this new life of ours inside of me.

How *lucky* am I to have this life, this love, this man, this … *family*, which I was so sure would be out of my reach? And how did I convince myself for so long I didn't even want this experience, when now, within the space of a few hours, the idea of *not* having this baby feels incomprehensible?

'What are you thinking, Sofie?' Rory asks, then puts his finger up before I can answer. 'No, let me rephrase that. What are you feeling?'

'I feel…' I pause, think, smile. 'I feel like I've got everything I didn't know I wanted.'

Chapter Eight

It's an unfeasibly hot September morning and I'm lying on the bed in the scanning room at Poole Hospital. Rory's on a chair next to me, his hand squeezing mine as the sonographer rubs jelly on to my exposed tummy. In her mid-to-late fifties, with unruly grey hair and piercing blue eyes, she reminds me a little of Mum. I feel a stab of guilt that I haven't seen her for weeks. But I know I couldn't see her without telling her our news. And I only want to do that once I'm sure everything is okay. I feel another stab of guilt when I think about Nisha. She texted me two weeks ago to say that she needed to talk, then briefly explained that Andy decided to give it another go with his wife. There was no more detail other than that. I texted her back, told her how sorry I was and that she deserved so much more. I've texted her a few times since then, to check in, but I haven't phoned her yet. Not because I don't want to; I just don't know *how* to, without telling her I'm pregnant. Nisha is the one person I'm used to sharing everything with. She has always been the first person I go to with my anxieties. I'm still coming to terms with this new version of our relationship, where we have secrets. Especially as this one of mine I know will be painful for her. It's bound to compound her sadness over the loss of this latest relationship and what she saw as the first step towards having the family she longs for.

Luckily, so far, this pregnancy has been textbook. I've felt tired, nauseous and bloated, broken out in teenage acne and have an unhealthy obsession with oranges and Jacobs crackers, but I've welcomed it all because they are markers that all is well in this strange, long trimester of waiting. This isn't our first scan. Thanks to my private healthcare I had one at six weeks. But this dating scan is the more important as they measure the fluid at the back of the baby's neck to defect any chromosomal abnormalities. It is one of the peak-anxiety moments of pregnancy – and one that would usually be leveraged by Nisha's practical advice. I wish she was here, now.

But as agreed, Rory and I have told no one. And to my knowledge, no one has noticed any changes in me. Rory marvels over me daily, telling me how beautiful I am, how much he loves the small mound of my belly, my newly swollen boobs. And to my surprise, I do, too. I feel like my body has a purpose. I'm aware of every part of me secretly working hard to create something miraculous. I feel like a superhero – my true secret identity hidden beneath my clothes.

There's a conflicted sense of keeping this precious secret only for us, whilst also wanting desperately to shout it from the rooftops.

I study the sonographer's face with the intensity of a stalker now. I know most mums-to-be at their twelve-week scan are probably entirely focused on their bump and the ultrasound screen, but mine is on her. She has our future in her hands: my belly is her crystal ball.

When she asks me if it's my first pregnancy, I give a brisk affirmative. I don't want small talk. I just want to see our baby.

'Well,' she says with a warm smile, 'I can see you're anxious to get going, so we'll put baby up on screen as soon as possible. Just try to relax. Now, let's take a look at your little one.' She picks up the doppler and turns her back to me.

I close my eyes to gather myself. I can't believe we're here at this pregnancy milestone. I'm so happy and relieved that after this, I'll be able to tell the people I love this new, unexpected joy of ours.

'Did you know that at twelve weeks the baby is the size of a plum?' Rory says from where he's reclined on a chair next to the bed – the picture of a laid-back dad-to-be.

'Yes,' I say, not taking my eyes off the monitor, 'because you're obsessed with telling me each week.' Rory has bought every baby book going and downloaded every app, updating me on the baby's size and development constantly. Once a news reporter…

'By forty weeks, it'll be the size of a pumpkin!' Rory exclaims. 'I read that a mum recently gave birth to a fourteen-pound baby close to Halloween! What are the chances of that, eh?'

'Rory!' I groan.

The sonographer sits back on her stool and removes the probe she was about to put on my belly and snaps her fingers.

'I thought I knew you! You're Rory King.'

'I am.' Rory gives her his toothy TV smile. He loves the local fame that comes with his job.

'Autographs later, can we focus on this please?' I plead.

'Of course, sorry!' she smiles.

I gasp as the cold probe touches my skin then slides around on the gel like my belly is an ice rink. Swirls of grainy black and white particles on the screen come into focus as the sonographer moves over the little mound of my stomach, searching for our baby. I inhale sharply as a shape comes into view. Time stops, oxygen disappears as I wait for the sonographer to speak. I stare at her shoulders, her neck, try to look for any clue, any sense of tension or strain.

'There you are!' the sonographer confirms, then. 'Do you see? What a lovely strong heartbeat! Oh look, I think your baby is giving us a wave!'

I turn to Rory and with bright eyes he leans down and kisses me.

'Look, Sofie,' he says with delight. 'Our baby is doing their first proper broadcast!'

I watch in silent awe at its arms waving enthusiastically as it bounces up and down like an astronaut let out into orbit for the first time. To be honest, I feel like doing the same: defying gravity and floating up to the ceiling with unexpected joy. I feel like I'm in an unfamiliar place, but with someone I've known forever.

It's you, I think. It's *you*.

Looking at our baby, my world has instantly grown bigger and more beautiful. I'm no longer just Sofie King: wife, daughter, actuary, colleague, friend. I'm Sofie King, mum-to-be. A mum to this little *being* who is reliant on me for everything. And by some miracle that thought doesn't terrify me like it should.

'Well,' the sonographer says at last. 'From the measurements I've taken, your little one's due date is February 21st.'

I stare in wonder at the grainy image, overwhelmingly thankful for this unexpected gift. How lucky am I?

Chapter Nine

Saturday morning, the day after our scan, is already saturated in the kind of summer sunshine that makes it feel like the whole world is both glowing and growing. The hedgerows are green and abundant with cowslip and common centaury. Dorset Heath has become a magical purple kingdom, with swathes of bell heather everywhere.

Rory and I are bypassing our usual brunch and driving over to Swanage from Southbourne to see Mum. I know she'll be surprised – usually, we only ever visit on a Sunday. Mum and Midge are always busy at the café on other days, and Rory and I have certain rituals we won't break for anyone. Saturday morning brunches are sacred, as is our Thursday movie-and-curry night. We're not *un*sociable, but aside from my morning swims and since Rory gave up bouldering, it takes quite a lot to get us out these days.

Neither of us can wait a moment longer to share our news. After Mum and Midge, we're off to see Rory's Gran, Sandra. I'm desperate to tell Nisha, too, but I've realised I need to do it in person after trying and failing to do it on the phone last night.

'Hey,' I could tell immediately she was upset with me.

'I'm so sorry I haven't called, Nish. It's been a crazy couple of weeks! I—'

'Yep. Same.' Her tone was cool, detached.

'How are you? I've been worried about you.'

'Exhausted. Devastated. Humiliated. Trying to throw myself into work but it's impossible as he's always there.'

'It'll get easier, Nish. I know how hard this must be for you, but the right person is out there, I promise.'

She didn't reply.

'When do you think you can come down next?' I'd asked then. 'I'd love to see you. And I have some news…'

'I'm working a lot of weekends through to November,' she'd said curtly. Her voice had softened, then. 'You could come here though? I'd love to see you.'

'I… well, it's a bit … difficult right now, work is really busy and…'

'It always is.' Her tone had cooled again. The conversation had ended shortly after that.

I hate the idea that she feels neglected. I hate that I couldn't tell her the real reason I couldn't come. Right now, this baby is my number one priority. I need to rest and keep my anxiety in check, and that means not being far from home. Or Rory.

Rory is expertly navigating the gorse-laden roads. The clouds in the crayon-blue sky are moving quickly, mixing with the pom-pom like puffs of smoke from Swanage's famous steam railway. Dew is glistening on the scrubland and water meadows beyond, like sequins. Above us, the late July sun is a bright yellow paint splodge. It's like a child has deliberately upended a craft box in order to create a picture of joy.

Resting my free hand on his thigh, I look out the window as we drive through the pretty, parish village of Corfe, full of centuries' old cottages. On the hill, Corfe Castle sits proudly, like a decrepit old king overseeing his domain.

I spent many hours up there after Dad died — trying to come to terms with what had happened to him and, by default, me. I found it hard to be at home. Midge was always there and was more of a comfort to Mum than I could ever be. She tried to reach out to me, too. But I just couldn't let her in. Or Mum, in fact. So I'd go to the castle alone, when everyone else was at school and, sometimes, go back after dark. It was Nisha who discovered me there one night the

This Wasn't Meant to Happen

week of our mock A levels, drinking, hanging out with a group of disreputable local teens.

I can still recall blearily watching her clamber up the side of the hill as she yelled my name. I had a bottle of vodka in my hands, a boy was pawing at me with his.

'Sofie,' she'd said, looming over us unapologetically. 'This isn't the answer.'

'Fuck off, we're busy,' had been the lad's offensive retort. I'd pushed him off me forcefully, angrily, then. Somehow, Nisha pulled me to my feet and helped me stagger down the hill.

'You mum is worried sick, Sof. We've been looking everywhere for you. This isn't you; this isn't how your life is meant to play out. What would your dad think?'

I'd cried the first real tears since hearing the news then. I'd been in a kind of stupor before that moment; in shock and denial, then submerged in an oblivion brought on by binge drinking.

To begin with, I'd enjoyed how it felt. I'd liked being so different from the person I was before dad died: the good girl was gone. The sense of release that the drugs and alcohol gave me was liberating; the attention I got from the opposite sex was welcome. Sexual attraction wasn't sympathy; it was baser than that. It grounded me in something that wasn't pity, but I'd begun to realise, was also burying me in shame.

Even before Nisha's appearance, I knew that I was taking it too far. I too was on the edge of a cliff, and in danger of wilfully going the same way as Dad.

Once Nisha got me home to Mum, she stayed over, lying on a camp bed next to mine which we kept for our regular sleepovers. She'd reached up and held my hand when I said I didn't know how to deal with the pain.

'By making it the thing that fuels you, let it drive you to be the best version of yourself,' she'd said in typically simple, direct Nisha fashion. 'That way, your dad will always be a plus in your life, even if he's not here.'

The next morning, we were playing chess and she reminded me that I could find calm amongst the chaos of a challenge, that I knew instinctively how to strategically work my way across a difficult board.

She told me that *this* was the version of me that my dad most admired and that leaning into that would honour his memory. She reminded me of how much he admired my work ethic; that it reflected how hard *he* worked as a fisherman. His version was when he out at sea, combing the ocean, or foraging the land for the answers of how to live simply and well. Mine was finding the answers in sums, strategies and then, eventually, statistics. That became my safety net.

So, I don't say it lightly that Nisha saved me.

I gaze down at my barely-there bump and rest my hand protectively on the slight curve of it. It feels like a lifetime since I was that broken, confused kid up on that hill. I look back out of the window, so very thankful, once again, to be where I am right now.

I'm excited about telling Mum our news today – but at Rory's behest we've parked up in front of the beach on the main road and have walked to Swanage Pier. We're now standing under the white and cobalt blue arch that marks the entrance.

'What are we doing here? I thought we were going to see Mum.'

A smile slowly spreads over his face as the morning sun casts its light over the weather-beaten boards beneath our feet.

Rory and I got engaged here, almost on this very spot. It has always been a special place for us.

'What have you got up your sleeve, Rory King?' I say, narrowing my eyes and prodding him in the chest.

'I just thought it would be nice to come here first,' he says, grasping my hand as we begin to walk.

I look down at the wooden boards and the small letterbox-size plaques that have been placed here by hundreds of people as a homage to their loved ones. Countless messages celebrating engagements, weddings, births – and honouring deaths. There's the one for Dad right near the end of the pier, which we placed after we scattered his ashes. It simply says:

'Per Jensen. Fisherman. Father. Husband. Friend. Always Loved. Forever Missed.'

Whilst Mum and I scattered Dad's ashes at sea, we also laid this plaque – our version of a gravestone. It was a place he visited often, to see his fishermen friends, to scuba dive, set off for foraging hikes and cliff climbs, or to moor his boat.

Rory proposed here then revealed the plaque he'd had made which he'd arranged to be laid next to Dad's. It had that day's date with the words 'Sofie Jensen, Marry me?'

He'd said doing it there was his way of asking Per's permission.

I had no doubt then that I had to say yes to this incredible man who had turned my life upside down in the very best way, but also made the ground beneath my feet feel as solid as these precious metal memorial plaques.

'I wanted to come here today before telling your mum because I thought your dad should be part of this, too.' He glances down and it's then I see another plaque.

It simply says Baby King, followed by the baby's due date.

'We can replace it with their name and official birth date, when he or she arrives,' he says.

'Rory King,' I say, swiping my eyes. 'How do you always know what I don't even realise I want?'

Then, with the backdrop of the pier stretching back behind us, he puts his hand on my bump and with the other holds his phone up high to take a selfie of us.

'The first picture of the three of us,' he says. 'The first of many.'

Chapter Ten

Standing outside Per's Place I'm flooded with a memory of my dad swinging me around the day he got the keys, laughing wildly while Mum looked on. I can almost feel the whip of the wind, the warmth of his embrace, the strength of his arms, the brush of his beard against my cheek. I was thirteen years old, and it felt like life was beginning again after a difficult couple of years. As I understood it, Dad had become frustrated because Mum wanted him at home more, not out on the boat at sea, climbing mountains or hiking for miles. This café was their compromise. It was a dream he'd had for a long time, made real by Mum inheriting a large sum of money from her parents. Per's Place was to be a business they could call their own, where Dad could plant his feet on terra firma and still have the freedom of being his own boss. His vision was a simple seafront café for his fellow fishermen, coastguards, sailors, lifeboat volunteers and hikers to get good, fresh food and hot drinks. Mum's hope was that it would make him happy again.

Mum – a secondary-school maths teacher and private tutor – had always liked to earn a monthly wage. A natural saver and worrier, she admitted to Nisha's mum Sita one evening when he was out at the pub, and I was eavesdropping, that she was concerned this was another whim of his and that eventually Dad would feel confined by the café. But she wanted him to be happy and agreed to support him and the business as much as she could.

Despite everything since then, she's kept her promise. She's worked tirelessly, giving up the career she loved and her social life to keep the café open. All in memory of a man she'd been separated from for months before he died and who had left us facing financial ruin.

Mum has always said it was lucky for us that Midge was already in our lives when Dad had passed. Eighteen months earlier, Midge had been new in town and had put an offer in to rent the studio flat above the business, after Mum and Dad had decided to let it after a tough third year at the café. Prior to that, Dad had used it occasionally when he had to get up early for fishing trips, or when he was working late at the café. I suspect he also liked having a place he could be alone.

Midge's long-term partner, Carole, had recently died of cancer, and Midge, being Dorset born and bred, had decided to move back here after twenty years in London. She yearned for community, for fresh sea air and the big horizons of her youth. She wanted to rent somewhere temporarily until her London home sold. Mum liked her immediately, said there was a warmth about her that made her feel like she'd known her a long time. Dad was less welcoming towards her.

I remember lots of heated late-night conversations between Mum and Dad about it. Mum said they needed a tenant for the extra money but Dad said he'd changed his mind, that the café was doing fine, and Mum had nothing to worry about. Mum stood her ground and Midge moved in a month later, and she and Mum became firm friends.

It wasn't long before Midge (an accountant) took over doing the books, too. The year had been a particularly difficult one for the café and it transpired that Dad had got into some trouble with the tax man.

'Just a bit,' he'd said vaguely, when Mum had challenged him on what we owed. 'Nothing I can't work out.' I'd been listening outside the closed kitchen door. 'Remember, Angie, one penny on land is better than ten at sea.'

It was one of the many Danish proverbs that he'd often throw into conversation and, on this occasion, I could hear it only infuriated Mum.

'Christ, Per, what does that even mean?! Just tell me how much.'

When he admitted it ran into the thousands, Mum immediately enlisted Midge's help, without discussing it with Dad. This started a whole new raft of arguments between my parents.

Looking back, that was the tipping point in my parents' marriage. Dad became more distant, more introverted. He was at the café less, hardly ever at home. Most days, he'd go out on long walks – which started at lunchtime and invariably ended when the pubs closed. At first, Mum was wild with worry, but then we all became accustomed to this new normal. As he withdrew, so did we. Me into school, my friends and my teenage angst; Mum into her new friendship and the day-to-day running of the café which she'd taken on, having left her teaching job to cover his many absences.

Midge had become a full partner in the café by then, having invested some of her money into the business to help save it when Dad lost interest. She said she'd always dreamed of having a little business by the sea. She started working at the café too, to help Mum.

A year later, Mum finally told him to move out. Dad had nowhere to go. She suggested that he move in to the flat, instead of Midge. Then she moved into our spare room.

'Just until she completes on her house,' Mum said. Midge had found a property to buy in Swanage, right in the centre of town. But then it fell through.

When Dad died just a few weeks later, we discovered he'd failed to renew his life insurance. Because they weren't yet divorced, their financial lives were still tangled up together. On top of that, he'd convinced mum to remortgage the house in order to buy the café. To realise the full extent of the financial mess he'd left us in was devastating. We had to sell our house and move into a Park home in Wareham.

The first Christmas I came back from university in Southampton – studying Actuarial Science – Mum bashfully explained that Midge was still living with her as her house had fallen through, and they were now sharing a bedroom. I was blindsided. It felt like no one had been truly honest with me for years.

Over lengthy chats, Mum told me that falling in love with Midge had been as much of a surprise to her as it was to me. I put aside my own pain and sadness that somehow Dad was being replaced and did what I could to accept Mum's relationship, I wanted her to be happy, after all. By the time I graduated, she and Midge were co-owners of their own home in Corfe. They've been together in the café and cottage – and happily so – for fifteen years now. Almost as long as Mum was with Dad.

But I have never really believed the trajectory of their friendship-to-relationship path was quite as Mum made out. I think she wanted to believe that there was no link to her and Dad's separation, and even perhaps convinced *herself* because so much about that and his subsequent death was complicated. But I've always believed that her and Midge's romance bloomed before Dad died. I've tried to let go of those thoughts because deep down I know she deserved this second chance. I loved Dad, but he made life so difficult for her, and he is no longer here. I understand that Midge brings stability to her life where before there was chaos. I also respect the fact that Midge is, like me, considered, sensible, risk-averse. I'm not sure I'd have gone to university without knowing Mum had someone in her corner. But that doesn't mean I have to be close to her.

When Midge and I talk now we're always kind, interested, polite. But I think we're also both fully aware that our relationship is driven by our mutual love for Mum. Sometimes Midge will surprise me, by bringing up a happy memory from our past, or a surprisingly accurate observation about my personality. Then, as if worried she's overstepped somehow, she'll quickly return to our common ground of Mum again. I know Midge would love us to be closer after all these years, but the wall I've built to keep a healthy distance between us is to protect my dad's memory. Anything else feels disloyal to him, somehow.

'You ready?' Rory slips his hand into mine.

'I am.' Coming here is a comfort. A place where dreams begin, not end. I can't wait to share this news with Mum.

We walk into the café only to find it completely empty. Not only of customers – which is worrying on a Saturday morning – but of Mum and Midge, too.

'They must be out the back,' I say.

I hear laughter from the kitchen and Mum and Midge emerge, both looking surprised but pleased to see us.

They're dressed in matching outfits of jeans and Breton tops, but they couldn't look more different. Ironically, Mum is much shorter than Midge (Midge being short for Margaret, not short for 'short'). Her outfit is baggy and crumpled, her cheeks rosy, face free of make up. Whilst Mum always looks to me like she's weathered several storms, Midge is by contrast tall, neat and beautifully presented – like an elegant vase.

'Sofie, Rory! What a glorious surprise! How long have you been here? We didn't hear you come in.' Mum draws us in warmly for hug. She looks tired, I note, as I lean awkwardly into her embrace. Her wild, silvery hair is limp, and there are dark smudges beneath her cloudy blue eyes.

The café hasn't changed. It still has the same L-shaped counter Dad made; the rustic, whitewashed walls he stripped himself; the wooden floor he painstakingly laid. The same noisy, temperamental coffee machine stands on the counter in front of the back wall. Above it, the reclaimed oak shelves are stacked high with simple white enamel mugs and plates. Six, long rectory-style tables stand in the centre of the room, with two more down each side. Mum has also added a long bar table with stools in front of the windows which gives customers a glorious sea view. The only other real change Mum made was to introduce a 'Fry-ups and Fresh Coffee' menu. A shelving display made from old pallets – another of Dad's builds – lines one wall and is filled with locally made chutneys, sauces, and cordials.

I don't know if she's done it for herself, for me, for him or all three of us, but as well as keeping the name 'Per's Place', there's a display of Dad's fishing paraphernalia to one side of the counter next to a big photo of him on his boat, *Sofie's Choice*. His beaming face is turned directly to the camera, biceps bulging, beer in one hand, the other holding three-year old me on his lap. In this photo, he was thirty-six – the same age I am now. He never saw fifty; he died one month shy of that landmark.

'Hi, Angie. Hi, Midge.' Rory leans over and kisses them one by one. Both Mum and Midge wrap their arms around him, then Midge and I exchange a brief embrace whilst somehow barely touching each other.

'You look really well, Sofie,' she says politely.

'Thank you, Midge,' I reply. 'So do you.'

I think they both look exhausted, but I don't want to be rude.

'I'm sorry to spring a visit on you like this. We should have warned you we were coming.'

'Can I get you all a drink?' Midge offers with her best hostess smile.

'Fizz, please!' Rory says, warranting a sharp nudge from me in his ribs.

'Coffee please.' I say brightly. 'Actually decaff,' I add, trying not to blush as I'm sure this alone will give our news away.

'So, to what do we owe this pleasure?' Mum says.

'We have something to ask you, actually Angie.' Rory nudges me. I clear my throat, suddenly feeling awkward about how we've planned our big reveal.

'What would you like to be called?' I say stiffly. Mum stares at me, somewhat bewildered.

'What, love?'

'What *name* would you like us to call you?' I repeat. This plan of Rory's suddenly feels awkward and staged. I have half a mind to just pull out the scan.

'Would you prefer to be called Grandma, Nana…?' Rory smiles, putting his hand on my tummy.

'Granny or Nanny?' I add, smiling now.

'Or *Nan*gie,' Rory finishes proudly, having clearly taken some time to come up with that.

Mum looks at me, then at Rory, then at my stomach.

'You're *pregnant*…?' she exclaims just as Midge arrives with our drinks. I feel inordinately annoyed by her timing. I wanted this to be a moment just with Mum.

Mum pushes her chair back and brings her shaking hands to her mouth. She looks more stunned than happy. Understandable, given my previous stance on not having children. Midge presses her hands against her carefully painted coral-pink lips in a prayer position. I'm sure I see a shimmer of tears in her eyes, which surprises me. I thought she'd be more emotionally removed from this.

'This is q-quite a surprise!' Mum stutters. 'I-I didn't think you wanted to have children, Sofie? I mean…' she trails off. 'You've always been adamant about that.'

'Well, sometimes life takes an unexpected turn.' I look at Midge, then back at Mum, to make my point.

I pick my bag up off the floor and take out the scan, pushing it across the table with a smile. Mum stares down at the little folded envelope, before opening it. She stares at it in silence.

'What wonderful news, Sofie!' Midge exclaims, clapping her hands loudly as if to drown out Mum's prolonged silence. 'You must be so thrilled!'

'We're over the *moon*.' Rory replies with a beaming grin.

Midge gets up and hugs both me and Rory then quickly steps back to make way for Mum. But she hasn't moved. She's just sitting, staring at the scan.

'Mum? Are you okay? Are you happy?'

She looks up then and her gaze seems to swim between Rory and me before settling on me.

'I'm sorry. I-I'm just in shock. I just didn't think… I never expected… I mean, I'm so happy for you, Sofie. For you both. *Obviously*, I'm happy! How many weeks are you? Do you feel okay? Is everything okay? How long have you known?' Her sentences are fired with urgency.

'Twelve. Yes. So far, so good. Seven weeks and we wanted to wait until we'd had the scan before we told you.'

She nods, still staring at the printout.

'More drinks, I think!' Midge says suddenly. 'Rory's right. This is an occasion that requires fizz. I'll get some of our lovely sparkling elderflower for you, Sofie.' She moves away, clearly thankful to have found a role. Rory follows her.

'Can I?' Mum says tentatively, nodding at my tummy. I nod and push back my chair. She stands up, leans over the table and presses her hands lightly against my middle. She has a faraway, whimsical look on her face.

'How are you feeling?' Mum asks when she pulls her hand away.

'Happy, but also scared. Petrified, actually.'

She nods, expecting this reply. 'It's completely normal to feel like that, Sofie. Everyone does.'

'Did you?' I press. 'You've never talked much about your pregnancy. Did you feel ready? Did you have an easy or difficult time? Any problems during the birth?' It's my turn for quickfire questions.

'Oh … it was so long ago I can barely remember, darling! But I do remember that my labour was so fast, I gave birth in Per's fish van. You shot out…'

'… as fast as a needlefish before we even got to the hospital.' I finish. This part of my birth story, Per's description of the event, is family folklore. I've been told it so many times I can deliver the punch line myself. 'But what about your pregnancy?' I say, leaning in, eager for any information I can get. 'Did you have any sickness or cravings? Were you anxious?'

'Sofie,' she interrupts firmly, putting her hand over mine. Her grey-blue eyes, usually so open and easy to read are suddenly oblique. 'Let me give you one bit of advice. Try not to worry, just *go with it*. You're at the beginning of the most wonderful journey and all you can do is lean into it. You have everything in place to make a wonderful parent. And I can't wait to be a *granny*.'

'Not a nangie, then?' I smile, choked up.

'Definitely not,' she laughs. 'Sofie,' she says softly then. 'When this baby comes, I'll lean into my new role, too, with all my heart.' She kisses my forehead tenderly just as Rory and Midge come back in with a new tray of drinks. Rory pops the cork on the fizz, pours them each a glass and hands me my sparkling elderflower.

'To our family and to the future,' he says brightly, raising his glass. Everyone smiles and clinks. Behind Mum, I see Dad smiling in the photo. And in that moment, our family finally feels whole.

Chapter Eleven

'Congratulations! Can I say that?' My boss, Ed, pulls at his tie to loosen it then smooths his thinning hair. 'Hard to know, these days.' He clears his throat, clasps his hands on his desk formally. 'And do you give consent for me to share your news with the whole department?'

'You can.' I say equally formally and awkwardly, but also with relief. I'm so happy that I can finally relax.

We had our twenty-week scan yesterday and I didn't want anyone other than family and close friends to know until we'd reached that safe milestone. Luckily, I only really started showing at seventeen weeks and even after that, I've been able to conceal it well.

Ed taps his pen on the desk nervously and slightly adjusts the angle of his framed family photo. His two sons also work at Prospect. One in underwriting, the other in accounts. I briefly imagine the family photo that'll one day be on my desk.

'Best thing in the world, being a parent,' he says. 'I mean,' he adds quickly. 'That's not to imply it's better than *not* having children. To each their own and all that! No judgement!' He looks at the door, as if wishing to escape through it. 'So, anyway, we do have … er, a maternity package in place, although I'm not too familiar with it. I know we have two other women alongside you in the department, but you're the first pregnant one! I'll have to contact Marjorie in

This Wasn't Meant to Happen

HR to find out what happens next. I'll … er, start looking into it all now.'

He looks at me to indicate the conversation is over. It's a relief. I'm not keen to continue the awkward exchange either. 'And these risk-limitation reports aren't going to write themselves!' I say, jauntily.

'Don't forget the three Ps, Sofie,' Ed calls as I head for the door.

'Protect, Product, Profitability!' I parrot.

I realise there's a fourth P in place now. My pregnancy. Will it change how Ed and the rest of the department see me? My career is so much a part of who I am. This is all I've ever known, all I've ever been focused on. Not to mention that I'm the main breadwinner in my household.

When I get to the cluster of desks and people that make up my team, I'm distracted by my phone pinging with individual messages from Emma, Sal and Inge. I had messaged the most recent scan pic to all of them just before I went in to see Ed.

I told them all about my pregnancy the weekend after I'd told Mum. We'd met up for coffee in a Starbucks and I put the twelve-week scan on the middle of a tray of coffees before carrying it back to our table. Emma was breastfeeding Fergus and the other two were trying to stop their two boys fighting under the table, so no one noticed at first. I sat down and waited.

'OHMYGOD!' Emma exclaimed. 'Whose is that?' She'd studied each of our faces with shining eyes, expertly shifting Fergus to her other boob then picking up the scan and brandishing it like a flag.

I'd slowly raised my hand.

She'd gaped at me, her generous lips stretched into her character-istically wide smile, messy red hair seeming to glow with joy from the follicles to the tips as she cradled Fergus's head. His hair – I'd realised – was the exact same shade of russet as hers. I'd wondered, would our baby have red hair, too? Rory was what he described as 'strawberry blonde', but I'd seen photos of him as a baby and he was ginger. 'Probably why my mum scarpered,' he'd joked, when he'd shown me his gran's albums after we'd been together a few months.

'SOFIE!' Inge and Sal gasped in unison. 'That's amazing news!' They'd both got up and hugged me tightly, so I was in a sandwich.

'Don't squash the baby!' I'd laughed.

'How are you feeling?'

'What made you change your mind?'

'When are you due?' They'd shot their questions at me one after another.

'Wonderful. It was kind of a happy accident. Twenty-first of February.'

'Ooh, Pisces!' Sal said knowledgably. 'A water baby, of course!'

'I know,' I'd said with a smile. I don't follow horoscopes like Sal does but I'd looked it up as soon as we got our official due date and was inordinately pleased. A keen swimmer myself, I imagined going to baby swimming classes with him or her. I'd already mentally framed one of those underwater photos of our baby, just like the album cover of *Nevermind*.

'Here, take Fergie, will you, Sal?' Emma had said, pulling him off her boob, pushing up the flap of her bra and fumbling to rebutton her top, whilst cursing under her breath. 'Oh Sof!' she'd said at last as she embraced me. 'I'm so happy for you, you have no idea!' Then she'd pulled away. 'What did Nisha say?'

'I haven't told her yet.' Sal and Inge eyed each other uncertainly. 'I want to do it in person, so can you make sure you keep it to yourselves for now?'

Logging back into my laptop, I see that Ed has sent the all-office round robin announcement of my pregnancy as we discussed. It feels real, all over again.

There's a sudden slew of 'Congratulations!' emails in my inbox, though none of my colleagues look up from their screens or come over to see me in person.

Apart from Tarun, that is. He's a relative new starter. Unlike Kate and Lena, the juniors in my team who match him in age and experience, he came straight in as Senior Actuarial Associate. He's also made it clear he has designs on a management role. Specifically, mine.

'Huge congratulations, Sofie!' he says brightly, engaging me in intense eye contact. 'I bet you can't wait for a year-long holiday.'

This Wasn't Meant to Happen

'I'm not sure keeping a tiny human alive day and night can be classed as a holiday, Tarun.'

'You'll obviously take full maternity leave, though, right?' he probes, resting his bottom on my desk. I have an urge to shove him off.

'Oh, I still have a way to go before I even need to think about that.' I smile benignly, but I'm furious that he's asked me.

'Well.' he grins. 'It'll come along before you know it. It's so important, the role of a mother, isn't it? You want to be present as much as possible. Congrats again!'

He strides off then, stopping to chat to each member of staff like he's the boss.

Just then an email arrives from Joe. At forty-two, Joe is a few years older than me. He's a naturally morose Scot but he's also unerringly kind and has the kind of dry wit that means we've always got on well – drawn together, I think, by our similar, somewhat serious outlooks.

From: joe.schwartz@prospectlife.co.uk
To: sofie.king@prospectlife.co.uk
Subject: Plus one

I would have come over in person, but you were being hogged by Tarun the Twat. You sure do know how to shock! Big congrats. So happy for you and Rory. When are you due?

J

I reply quickly, feeling a surge of guilt for not telling him first, but I didn't quite know how. Like Nisha, I know that my baby news will undoubtedly be painful for him. His wife, Rachel, died of breast cancer three years ago. I know they had been hoping to start a family before she was diagnosed, because Rory and I had become good friends with them both. Sadly, she entered a hospice two weeks after our wedding in September and passed away peacefully just as autumn came in earnest. She was only thirty-six. Joe has thrown himself into work ever since and become more withdrawn than he used to be – even with me. He's always at his desk early and stays late, long after everyone else has gone home. I get it. My own experience of long-term grief after the initial shock was to laser focus on my studies.

I email him back.

From: sofie.king@prospectlife.co.uk
To: joe.schwartz@prospectlife.co.uk
Subject: re: Plus one

A shock to us too, Joe. Baby is due in Feb, so a way off yet.

From: joe.schwartz@prospectlife.co.uk
To: sofie.king@prospectlife.co.uk
Subject: re: Plus one

You and Rory will be a great team. The baby is lucky to have you. You and Rory are lucky, too.

I take a moment before I reply, the guilt and sadness of what Joe has lost overwhelms me.

Thank you, Joe. I know.

Chapter Twelve

Nisha has come down to visit her folks and we're meeting for lunch. When she suggested getting together, she said she had something to tell me. Two weeks after my twenty-week scan and four long months after finding out for myself, I'm also, finally, going to tell her I'm pregnant.

She pulls down her sunglasses and takes a sip of the large glass of Sauvignon that's just arrived for her. The UK has been experiencing a seemingly endless Indian summer that has somehow stretched into early November. It's hard to believe these beautiful days will ever end. Even harder to believe that we're on the cusp of winter, the season that I'll be a mum.

'So. What's new?' Nisha says, stabbing a bit of salad with her fork. Her sunglasses are on, but I know that her make-up will be immaculately applied beneath. It still amazes me how my once-geeky school friend – who loved science, chess and studying in that order – transformed into this sleek, stylish woman.

The atmosphere between us is expectantly charged.

'You first. You said you had something to tell me?' I ask, stalling as much as possible.

'Oh…' she says with a dismissive wave of her hand. 'I need more of this first.' She lifts her wine and takes another long sip.

'We… we haven't really talked properly about what happened with Andy, either,' I say, addressing the elephant.

She looks somewhere beyond my right shoulder. 'It's difficult to talk about. I know you didn't approve…'

'But I also know how upset you must be and it doesn't change me wanting to understand what you've been through.'

Nisha tells me that after she went back to London, he told her that he and his wife were only on a temporary break and that he'd realised how important his family were to him. He thanked her and said that he hoped she wouldn't make it awkward at work.

'What a dick,' I say angrily. She looks surprised, I don't usually get so het up. Obviously, I can't tell her it's my hormones. 'If it's any consolation, I think you've had a lucky escape.'

She shrugs and takes another slug of wine.

Silently, we push food around our plates. I feel awful that I haven't been there for her. I miss her. Secrets aren't good between best friends. I have to tell her why I've been so distant.

'Nish,' I say putting down my knife and fork. 'I know this might not be the right time…' She looks up, pushes her sunglasses on to her forehead and looks at me quizzically. 'I have something I want to tell you, but I wasn't sure how, when, or if I should…' I stop. I look down at my plate, at the salad I've been only playing with.

Nisha puts her cutlery down too and leans forward expectantly, taking my hand.

I take a deep breath, like I do before I'm about to push off in the pool. 'I'm pregnant.' I exhale loudly in relief at expelling those words.

Not a ripple of response. She just stares at me. Eventually, when she speaks her voice sounds thick, unfamiliar.

'I thought you were going to say you'd got a promotion.' She laughs, but it is forced.

'I guess I have. A promotion to motherhood!' I say with a weak smile.

She pulls her sunglasses back down and lets go of my hand, drinks more of her wine. 'Are you okay? Is this what you want?'

'Yes,' I reply, honestly.

'Really?' She hides neither her surprise nor her concern.

'Yes, Nisha,' I say again and smile as if to prove my point. 'I'm … happy.'

'Happy.' she repeats. 'Sure. But mostly scared … anxious? It's okay,' she adds. 'You can tell me. I know you better than anyone.'

'I promise you, Nisha. I'm happy. Honestly.'

She studies me then as if to confirm I'm telling the truth.

'Okay. Then I'm happy for you,' she says finally, without emotion. 'Still surprised, though!' She takes another sip of wine, sunglasses still firmly in place. 'When did you decide to start trying?' she asks lightly. 'I had no idea you were thinking about it. You've always said you didn't want kids.' There's an edge to her voice.

'We *weren't* trying. It just sort of … happened. It was a surprise.' I pause. 'Another surprise was that once I was pregnant, I wanted it so much more than I'd ever wanted to not be. Does that make sense?'

'It does,' she says. Her voice comes out almost as a whisper. 'And how's Rory?'

'Well, you can imagine *his* reaction.'

She smiles weakly. She's had front-row seats to Rory's enthusiasm and optimism for years. She swipes away a tear I know she won't want me to acknowledge.

I stare at the view ahead instead. At the families gathered on the beach on this strangely unseasonal day: flying kites, walking dogs, building sandcastles. The thought that before long, Rory and I will join them fills me with quiet joy.

'So how far along are you?'

'Nearly twenty-two weeks,' I pull my bag on to my lap to get out the scan. She stares at me, jaw agape.

'Bloody HELL, Sofie!' Nisha peers round the table. 'How have you kept that a secret for so long? I've missed half your pregnancy already!'

'I know, I'm sorry.' I remove the bag and open my coat, which has been concealing my still-small bump. Nothing to worry about, so I've been told. The baby is measuring well, and Mum has told me that she didn't really show until her third trimester. 'I found out around the time Andy broke it off. I know you must have felt like I wasn't there for you, but we decided not to tell anyone until we were safely through the first trimester. And then I wanted to wait until I could tell you in person.'

She shakes her head in disbelief. 'I still can't believe it.'

'I know. If it's any consolation, neither can I.' I lean forward. 'Can I tell you something else?'

'Jesus, it's not twins, is it?' She takes another slug of wine.

'God, no!' I laugh. 'No, the truth is, I haven't bought *anything* yet for the pregnancy because I was paranoid of jinxing it. But now I'm over the halfway mark, I feel like I can start.'

'Are you seriously telling me that there's no week-by-week spreadsheets of essentials to buy? No immaculately organised nursery with fully Marie Kondo'd drawers? No garage full of baby paraphernalia?' She looks over the rim of her sunglasses. 'Are you *actually* Sofie King or a pregnant imposter?'

'Oh, there's definitely spreadsheets,' I laugh. 'I just haven't actioned most of them. I'm pretty sure Rory has bought half of John Lewis already, though.'

I roll my eyes but truthfully, I love how enthusiastically Rory has leaned into his role as father-to-be. He's researched the best prams and already worked out the right car seat to buy. At my behest he's also bought top-of-the-range safety gadgets to help ease my anxiety once the baby is here.

'Okay,' Nisha says suddenly. 'We're going shopping. I'm taking you to Castlepoint right now. H&M have a great maternity section. You don't have to spend a lot to look good, you know.'

Nisha knows I'm not that into clothes or spending money on myself, I prefer to save. But I'm excited to have my best friend's help on how to dress my bump, rather than hide it.

She pays for lunch, and I dutifully follow her out of the café.

'I've missed you, Nisha,' I say suddenly.

She stops, turns, grasps me tightly by the arms. 'You've got this, Sof.'

'I know,' I say certainly.

She looks surprised. I'm only just getting used to it myself, this feeling that everything is as it should be in my life.

I look away again as another tear slides down from behind her sunglasses.

This Wasn't Meant to Happen

It's only when I get home a couple of hours later, laden with bags, that I realise we'd never discussed her news. I phone to ask her when she's on the train back to London.

'Oh, don't worry, Sof,' she says, her voice low, hoarse and muffled by the noisy train. 'It's not important. Your baby is all that matters now.'

Chapter Thirteen

I stagger in out of the downpour, letting the warmth of my house envelop me. I love living by the sea, except when heavily pregnant in the depths of winter. I don't love the rain pelting my body like bullets, the bitterly cold wind that claws at your skin, the thrashing waves that climb the sea walls higher each year. It's cold, grey and miserable, but thankfully, the twinkling fairy lights around the streets and shops provide a glimmer of comfort and joy. Christmas is only four weeks away and then, it's the New Year. The year Rory and I will become parents.

I put my bags and keys down and take off my ankle-length hooded puffa coat and gloves – shaking the water off them as I do so.

'I'm home!' I call. Rory's currently decorating the nursery. He's been up there all weekend.

I've just come from my Sunday-morning pregnancy yoga class. The concept of taking time out of my busy to-do list before now to breathe and stretch used to be alien to me. I've always preferred swimming, slicing through water every day, focusing on my bi-lateral breathing whilst actively ticking off the lengths. But I know how beneficial yoga is for both me and the baby. Plus, I wanted to meet other local pregnant mums, which I have. Now there's a chance our baby will grow up with friends they've known their whole life. A support system.

This Wasn't Meant to Happen

Nisha hasn't, as promised, been in regular contact. After our lunch last month, our relationship has gone back to an occasional flurry of friendly but distant texts. When I phone her, it goes to voicemail. I understand. I feel disloyal to have found new people to share this experience with, but for the first time in years I need something else more than I need her. It doesn't mean I don't miss her, though.

There's a small group of five of us at the yoga class who are all due around the same time. I'm the oldest of the group by a few years. I don't have a huge amount in common with them other than our pregnancies, but we started going for a coffee after class (decaf, of course) and I *like* that they're different. I like the admiring glances we get when we're together, the affectionate smiles towards our growing baby bumps. Being with them feels like being part of a special club.

Today, I got talking to another girl who was new to the class. At twenty-nine weeks to her fourteen weeks, I felt like an old hand. Tall and almost awkwardly angular, she'd positioned herself at the back. I remembered how intimidating I found it at first so introduced myself, but she seemed reluctant to talk.

'It gets easier in the second trimester,' I'd said, which I hoped was helpful. 'Third, not so much!' I'd exhaled comically as we'd lowered into downward dog, but she hadn't responded, other than with a polite smile. She'd already left the class before I got the chance to ask if she wanted to join us for coffee.

I've been seeing lots of Emma and baby Fergus, too. She's been sharing her own pregnancy tips and was the one who told me about the yoga classes. I can't believe that in just a matter of weeks, I'll be bringing my baby to our meet-ups too.

I smile to myself as I hear Rory singing along to the radio upstairs. I grab a fresh towel from the pile of folded fresh laundry in the utility and dry my face and hair. Then, I head into the kitchen, flick on the coffee machine, enjoying the gentle *phut-phut-phuuut* sound and the heady aroma as it delivers the dark liquid into Rory's special 'Dad ... LOADING' mug. He gifted it to himself a few weeks ago, after our twenty-week scan. He'd bought one for me, too – it has *Mum-to be!* emblazoned on the front.

As I pour milk into Rory's coffee and hot water into my herbal tea, I still find it hard to believe that there could have so easily been a different version of our life without this baby.

I head upstairs with our hot drinks, excited to see how Rory has been getting on turning the spare room into a nursery.

I open the door, preparing to bear witness to Rory levels of mess and chaos. On one hand, I'm right: there are ladders, paint pots, kitchen roll, newspaper, old mugs and plates everywhere. But I also feel like I've stepped into a room of sunshine.

Rory is up a ladder jiggling precariously along to the music whilst brandishing a paint roller covered in 'Dayroom Yellow', putting the finishing touches to the final coat.

He descends quickly and comes over, fussing over me and the bump.

'Perfect timing. I've just finished! Come on, sit down with me and let's take in the view. This time tomorrow, we can bring in the furniture.'

'And in just over two months' time we can bring in a baby.' I sit down slowly, cross-legged with my back against the wall, and rest my head on Rory's shoulder.

I can picture it all: the ocean-grey curtains and seagrass rug I've bought to cover the natural oak floorboards. The mid-century vintage Danish wardrobe that used to be in my childhood bedroom and that I've taken everywhere I've lived since. The 1970s Ercol chair I've had reupholstered with pale grey striped fabric that I'll use for nursing. The adorable ocean mobile I bought on my shopping trip with Nisha and which I plan to hang in the nursery window. Suddenly I'm struck by a vivid image of me scooping our sleepy baby into my arms.

I begin to sing a Danish lullaby, 'Bjornen Sover', under my breath: 'The Bear is Sleeping'. It's one that Dad used to sing to me. I'd be the bear curled up in a sleeping ball, then I'd uncurl at the end and roar before collapsing into giggles as he tickled me.

Two months is too long. I can't wait for the day when we'll bring our baby home and I can sing this song every night at bedtime.

Chapter Fourteen

After lunch the rain stops, and the wind dies right down in a typical Dorset weather style. At my suggestion, Rory and I drive to Lulworth, a place that holds complex memories, adjacent as it is to Durdle Door and the place where my dad died. Singing that lullaby has made me think of Dad and I had an urge to feel close to him, so Rory suggested we come for a walk here. As we exit the car, I see that the sun is trying desperately to push itself through the thick, dense cloud. Perhaps nature is always a metaphor for birth and death, but it takes being in one of these life stages to notice how we are surrounded by reminders of the inevitability of both, every single day.

Since I've been pregnant, I've been thinking a lot about Dad, about the man he was – the father he was. I can't help but wish he was here to experience this. He would have made a wonderful grandad; he would have shared his love of nature, the earth and the sea, gone for wonderful walks with his grandchild, taken him or her on exciting foraging adventures, cooking up their finds together after, just like he used to do with me.

Even though this place took him from me, I feel an urge to be here, as it also once gave so much to him. For some reason, this pregnancy has made me feel braver, bolder and closer to the adventurous child I was before Dad died than I have been for years.

Holding hands, Rory and I slowly, carefully walk the mile-long path that showcases the Jurassic Coast's famous limestone cliffs, shingle beaches and clear blue sea from Lulworth Cove all the way over to Durdle Door, stopping briefly so Rory can take a photo of me and my bump. It feels like a pilgrimage. An opportunity to confront death with new life.

Just as we're beginning the decline, a group of retirement-age hikers recognise Rory, calling out *'Now, what are the chances of that?'* to great hilarity. Rory's as obliging with them as always, and they, gratified by his attention, immediately start telling him their fascinating local tales. Usually I stand back, invisible to Rory's fans. But today, they notice me. Or rather, my bump. They're both surprised and delighted to discover that Rory's a dad-to-be. It's news to them because I haven't let him announce it on TV or social media. Rory accepts their back slaps and congratulations with unmitigated pride.

They offer to take a photo of us but Rory declines, knowing I won't want them to. 'Let them,' I say, to his surprise and mine. 'It'll be nice to have one of the three of us.' We stand with Rory behind me, his arms circling my bump, framed by the great arc of the 200-foot limestone arch of Durdle Door. It stands as a sentinel in the sea, a gateway to the past and also a symbol of the new future we're about to enter.

When they're done, they hug Rory and give us both their best well wishes. Then we make a slow, careful descent down to the beach.

Swirling rose-gold ribbons of sunshine move across the sky. The sea is a perfect aquamarine; the rugged, crumbling cliffs flank us far enough away to feel protected rather than at risk (I'm always, understandably, anxious around them), whilst the gentle, undulating green duvet of the Purbeck hills snugly brings it all together. In this moment, I feel held by the landscape.

I look at Rory next to me who is scrolling through Instagram, no doubt wanting to post a picture of this view. He's always enjoyed engaging with his followers on social media. I don't really use it, myself. I have a profile, but I'm more interested in protecting my life than sharing it with strangers. And Rory's job means I've always preferred to keep my life offline.

I can see Rory looking at the shot of us the hikers took.

'You can post it, if you want,' I say.

He looks at me in astonishment. 'Really? Are you sure?' His reddish-blonde hair is messy underneath his beanie hat, sunshine catching the smattering of sandy-coloured stubble on his chin. He'll be clean shaven again before his next news report tomorrow, hair wrestled down with hair gel, outdoor activewear replaced with a smart coat and a scarf looped neatly around his neck. Right now, he's just my husband and my baby's dad-to-be. And I want everyone to know it. I'm ready to share our excitement with the world.

He turns back to his screen and begins to write the accompanying post.

'Went to Durdle Door and got the first pic of our baby in a frame before it's even born! #whatarethechancesofthat #dadtobe #comingsoon #ITVmeridienwest #localnews #durdledoor #dorsetlife #luckyman #nofilter

It's so Rory. He doesn't care who knows how happy he is or what people think, because he just wants to share his joy with the world.

'Can you ping that photo to me?' I ask him.

I open up Instagram and upload the bump picture that he's airdropped. It's been over a year since I last posted anything. I've never posted a photo of myself before. But I want to mark this happy moment in a place where for years I've felt only grief.

I pause to think, before writing a simple three-word caption.

'Best Possible Outcome.' #thirdtrimester #solucky

I look up to see that Rory has welled up because he understands what this means. This pregnancy has finally made me believe in what he's tried to convince me of for years.

I hit Share. But in that moment, my joy is sapped slightly: will sharing the news of our baby jinx us somehow? After all, there's nothing certain about hope: it can't be measured mathematically; it can't be controlled. It can be added or subtracted, until it's either there – or gone.

We walk back up the incline-steep cliff path – with me on the far inner edge. I still fear the sheer drop, the lack of fencing, and can't believe the ease with which other people stop to take in the view, often far too close to the edge.

Sensing my discomfort, Rory squeezes my hand tightly. I'm determined to not stop until I reach the top. When we finally do, me panting with exertion, we pause, kiss, embrace – me, in relief. As we turn our heads, we see a glorious rainbow has sliced through the ancient arch of Durdle Door.

I look down at my bump that's sandwiched between us.

The pot of gold.

Chapter Fifteen

The baby kicks sharply into my ribs and I prod it gently back, then immediately mark the moment down in the pregnancy journal Emma, Sal and Inge bought me along with some beautiful flowers, the day after I told them I was pregnant. Here, I also note the amount of Kegel exercises I've done, how much water I've drunk – and it's where I've written our baby-name list and my notes from the antenatal classes we've been going to.

I love these little silent conversations the baby and I have on a regular basis now, connecting, communicating – just the two of us. I rearrange myself in the car seat to try and give the baby more room. Tricky, now that I'm thirty-three weeks. I already feel huge, even though I have over six weeks to go. I can't believe it's already the beginning of January.

'You okay, Sof? Do you need to stop, have a little stretch? Do you want some water?' Rory asks, glancing at me anxiously. Funnily enough, *I'm* the relaxed one now. He constantly asks if I'm all right, if I'm comfortable, if I need anything.

'I'm okay,' I smile at him reassuringly. 'It's just the baby, using my organs as punchbags again. Cut it out, champ!' I exclaim as the little one delivers another right hook. 'Strong as a lion, this one.' I laugh.

As I say those words to Rory, a name occurs to me, one that isn't written down on our list.

'What about Leo for a boy?' I say to Rory.

Rory tilts his head for a moment, thoughtfully, then tests it out. 'Leo. Leo King. I like it! A lot.'

'Me, too.' I smile. 'Now we just need to decide on a girl's name.'

'Nearly there,' he says as we turn the last corner.

'In more ways than one,' I reply, stroking my bump.

We make our way through the picturesque village of Corfe and arrive in front of Mum and Midge's sweet Dorset-stone bungalow. Mum throws open the front door, steps out and shuts it quickly behind her without letting us in.

'Well, look at YOU!' Mum says uncharacteristically loudly. 'You're HERE!'

'We are,' I say uncertainly as I take in her strange, rictus smile. Rory seems unperturbed.

'Ange, is it okay if I head straight into the kitchen and grab myself a beer while you two are chatting?' Rory says, adding equally loudly. 'I'm GASPING!'

'OF COURSE!' Mum says, too loudly, too brightly as she opens the door a slither and lets Rory inside. 'We'll be right behind you! I just want a quick word with Sofie first!'

'GREAT!' he calls back loudly from behind the closed front door. I look at her suspiciously. Mum immediately pulls me into a hug.

'Sofie, I'm so glad you're home, love!'

'Mmm,' I reply, noncommittally. Whilst I like her house, this has never been home for me. I understand Mum wanted to leave the Park home that defined all she had lost when dad died and start again with Midge. But it was where she and I had lived together. It was the place we muddled through in those years before I went to uni. By leaving it, I feel like we lost a part of what connected us to each other in our grief, too.

'You look glorious, Sofie,' she says as she takes me in, her eyes filling up as she looks at my rounded stomach.

'Or, like a human Christmas pudding,' I smile, rubbing my protruding belly. 'Shall we go in?'

'YES!' she says loudly, smiling with barely contained excitement as she dramatically swings open the lounge door and we step inside. 'She's here!' she calls loudly, as if announcing my arrival. Which, I realise she is when a loud 'Surprise!' echoes loudly around the cottage.

'HELLO BABY!' reads the giant banner on the back wall, framed by a huge, beautiful, pastel balloon-arch and a sea of smiling faces.

I don't have to fake the shocked smile that's spread over my face, happy tears of unexpected delight spring into my eyes as Mum points over to Rory and Nisha – clearly the key conspirators – who are standing together at the back, near the kitchen, grinning and waving at me. Sal and Inge are here, too, waving madly, clearly excited to have some kid-free time, as they're each clutching a glass of prosecco in both hands. The girls from my pregnancy yoga class are here – since last week we've all been going to the same antenatal classes, too. It's been nice as Rory got to meet their partners. Obviously, he immediately charmed the girls and got on brilliantly with the guys.

I wave at Emma; she's cradling Fergus and looking a little stressed as he is crying. Midge is standing straight and tall next to her, smiling brightly as always. Nearby is Sita, Nisha's mum. Rory's gran, Sandra, is sitting by the table, legs splayed in a relaxed fashion, glass of fizz in one hand, head tilted with perplexed confusion as she studies the elaborate nappy cake arrangement made from nappies and baby socks, which is perched on the glass dining table. A table which is also heaving with food, a cupcake tower and presents. Sandra is barely five foot and has the same russet tint to her hair as Rory, albeit dyed these days. People are often fooled by her diminutive stature, but she has the tough, determined survival streak of a woman who has been let down in her life more often than she's been lifted up, with a soft maternal side she reserves only for Rory. He, quite rightly, adores her. I'm just relieved she deems me good enough for her beloved grandson.

'Right, everyone,' Nisha says loudly, clapping her hands together. 'Let's start by cracking open some fizz – alcoholic and non – and let Sofie get over the shock!'

'Nisha,' I say, approaching her first when everyone relaxes and starts chatting. I give her a hug, but she is awkward and stiff in my embrace. 'This is so wonderful.'

'It was nothing,' she replies shortly.

'Don't be modest, it all looks amazing!'

'Midge did it,' she shrugs. She oversaw decorations.'

I glance at the table which is covered with delicate quiches, beautiful salads, plates of rainbow crudités and homemade dips, and even a beautifully presented cheese-grazing board.

'And the food,' she adds.

So much love and attention detail has gone into it, it makes me weepy.

'I devised the games, though,' Nisha blurts out, clearly worried she's upset me. 'And Rory, well he just had to ensure you didn't find out. Which was a concern, obviously.' We both laugh, then. Rory is notoriously terrible at keeping secrets.

'Well, even though I hate surprises, this is the nicest one I've ever had. Aside from this pregnancy!'

'You handled it like a pro. Not the socially awkward actuary we all know you are.'

'That's rich, coming from a physically awkward science geek!' We laugh again, both relieved to have broken the ice with gentle banter.

'Sofie!' Sita sails over towards us, resplendent in olive silk trousers and a matching embroidered top. She looks just like Nisha, with the same high brow, aquiline nose and precisely cut bob – but with the addition of elegant, silvery streaks that complement the diamond piercing in her nose and the chunky silver necklace and bangles she always wears. 'Let me look at you, Sofie. Oh, you look gloriously *abundant.*'

'Thanks. I think?' I say, mouth twitching with suppressed laughter. This kind of flowery comment is typical of Nisha's mum.

Sita thrusts the tray of canapés she's carrying at Nisha and wraps me in a gigantic hug, the familiar waft of her jasmine perfume immediately evoking childhood memories of long afternoons spent at Nisha's house after school.

'It's a compliment Sofie. Look at you! You're a goddess of glowing joy and fertility! May I?'

I nod and smile politely as she gestures to my bump and then places her hands gently on it. At least she asked before manhandling me. Most people don't. 'Oh, you clever girl! You must be so very excited. And Angie,' she turns to Mum who is hovering behind me, 'you must be desperate to meet him or her!'

This Wasn't Meant to Happen

'Well, the baby isn't due until February!' Mum says carefully. I've been surprised how restrained she's been about this pregnancy. She hasn't gone overboard fussing, like I thought she would. She's phoned occasionally to see how I am and if I need anything, but she hasn't started knitting like a maniac or gushed to everyone about how wonderful it will be to be a grandmother. I've seen less of her, actually, as I haven't always had the energy to go and visit on a Sunday.

Sita grasps her hands to her chest as she gazes at her. 'You must be *elated*! I know *I* would be if Nisha told me *she* was pregnant. Obviously, we'd like a wedding first…' Her heavily lined eyes close briefly as if to imagine such a scenario. She opens them a second or two later. 'Sadly,' she sighs, 'family life still eludes her for now. And time is marching on, is it not?'

I glance at Nisha who is starting determinedly at the ceiling, pretending not to hear.

'I had my daughter when I was twenty-three and that was considered *old*,' Sandra offers then, her West-country accent coming out strongly in the sentence. Rory still has his, too, although it is less pronounced. His soft regional accent is one of the many reasons viewers love him. 'Youngsters these days think youth is something they get to keep, not borrow! And', she adds, 'some try and keep it for longer than they should in my opinion. Although,' she adds proudly as she looks at Rory, who has a group in thrall with one of his stories, 'my boy has mastered the secret of being young at heart whilst mature in spirit. It's hard to find a man like that these days. Sofie, you're a lucky girl!'

'You know I don't believe in luck, Sandra, just good choices,' I say. But even as I say it, I realise that thanks to this baby, I no longer truly believe it.

Sita sighs, then. 'I can only hope that Nisha meets a nice Indian man.'

'Or just a nice man, Mummy. Let's widen the field shall we, seeing as I'm apparently running out of time?' Nisha rebelliously grabs a glass of prosecco from the table behind us and raises it to Sita. In Hindu culture, alcohol isn't permitted. Nisha turns then and walks over to where Emma, Sally and Inge are standing.

'She works too hard, that child, that's the problem,' Sita sighs. 'I blame myself. I taught her she could have it all…'

I smile politely at Sita and Mum, grab a flute of sparkling elderflower and follow my best friend. As I make my way to where she is, I see everyone is cooing over a delightfully chubby baby Fergus, now almost nine months old, who is spreadeagled asleep in his pram, hands opening and closing like a lotus flower.

Emma is in the middle of relaying her birth story again to some new listeners, which I already knew involved a hideously long thirty-six-hour labour, forceps and then an emergency C-section.

'It was *amazing*,' she says now, sighing as she gazes down at Fergus. 'Honestly, worth every second. I'd do it again in a heartbeat.'

'*Really?*' Nisha scrunches her nose up in disbelief. 'It sounds like hell.'

'You'll understand one day, Nish. Won't she, girls?" she adds, turning to Inge and Sal. Their eldest girls started school this year and their boys are now two and at nursery together. Fergus stirs awake and cries, and I glance at Nisha. She's stepped up and is rocking the pram back and forth to try and get him back to sleep, while Emma talks to me.

'Oh, I can't wait for you to have this baby, Sofie!' Emma says. 'I can show you the ropes, take you to all my baby groups and introduce you to my NCT chums. Our babies will only be a school year apart! I've already started researching catchment areas for the best ones. It's never too early to start looking. I'll email it to you…'

'Great!' I say, not wanting to tell her that I can barely get my head around giving birth, let alone the idea of having a school-age child.

I turn around to give Nisha a 'help me!' look, but she's disappeared. Just then I see Rory coming through the door carrying what looks to be something large and heavy.

'This gift arrived for you from work. Delivered personally by someone you know…' Joe appears through the door, practically bent double carrying the other end. He looks weirdly out of place, like a chess piece on a Monopoly board. I wave at him, but I can't take my eyes off the beautiful curved, Scandi-style cot that they're carrying. It's perfect.

It's all completely perfect.

This Wasn't Meant to Happen

The baby shower is a joy. I feel lifted by all these people I love, all of whom have made such an effort. It's funny to watch Mum and Sita get involved in the silly party games. The two of them are in their element, showing off their knowledge. I spot Midge – the happy observer – standing at the edge of the room and head over to talk to her.

'Thank you for all this,' I say, as I stand next to her.

'For what?' she smiles, not taking her eyes off Mum.

'The food, the beautiful decorations – you've put in so much effort.'

'It's my pleasure, Sofie.'

We watch the games for a bit longer, laughing alongside each other.

'You don't fancy guessing which melted chocolate bar is on the nappy, then?' I ask, as we watch Mum sticking her finger into the middle of a big, brown sticky blob and licking it. 'Or guessing the flavour of the puree in the jar?'

'I'm happy to just watch.' Midge smiles. 'My knowledge of babies is pretty slim.'

'Mine, too.' I glance down at my bump. 'Which might be problematic.'

'You'll work it out, Sofie,' she says. 'You always do. I've no doubt you'll make a wonderful mum.' I find myself unexpectedly teary at her words.

'Motherhood wasn't for you, then?' I ask. I realise I've never asked her.

She smiles and shakes her head. 'It didn't really feel like an option for me, given my … preferences. Things were different in my day…'

'Do you ever wish…?' I trail off. I don't want to upset her or offend her. 'Sorry, it's none of my business…'

She places a hand on my arm. 'No need to apologise. I don't do regrets, Sofie,' she says. 'You can make all the plans you want in life, but then it has a funny way of forcing you to throw the dice in the air and see where they fall.'

I look down at my enormous stomach and then back at Midge. 'Don't I know it.'

When everyone has gone home and it's just me, Mum, Midge, Sita, Sandra, Nisha and Rory I open my gifts.

Mum hands me two wrapped presents.

'Oh, an expectant grandmother's excitement!' Sita says clasping her hands together.

'More fizz, anyone?' Nisha asks, standing up.

Sandra thrusts out her glass and grins.

I unwrap the paper carefully and pull out the most beautiful homemade quilt of pale lemon, white and green squares.

'Mum!' I gasp.

'I just patched together some of your old Baby-gros,' Mum says modestly.

'It's beautiful – perfect,' I say, choked. The quilt is embroidered with daffodils and daisies on alternate squares. She's left several squares blank at the top.

'I went with a spring theme – and used yellow, because I know it's the colour of the nursery. That space is for the baby's name when we know it,' she says. 'I can embroider it on once he or she arrives.'

I can't speak. I'm too overwhelmed. I look back down at the beautiful quilt. In each corner is a square of faded leafy-green corduroy. In the bottom right-hand, a boat has been lovingly sewn on. When I look closer, I realise that the square is a pocket. Mum gestures at it to get me to look inside.

I tuck my fingers in the pocket and pull out a tiny photograph. It's me as a baby, on a fishing boat. I'm maybe nine or ten months old, small, chubby and red-cheeked and beaming at the camera as the wind blows my hair into a Mohican and Dad gazes lovingly down at me.

'The material is from your dad's favourite pair of trousers,' Mum says now, voice thick with emotion. 'I used the rest of that material on the next gift.' She gestures at me to open it.

I swipe away a tear and open the second present. I pull out a little green dungaree romper suit made from the same soft, worn, faded cord and instantly press it up to my chest to hug it.

Lost for words, I hug her tightly too, not wanting to let go.

'What did I miss?' Nisha says as she comes back into the room.

'Just the loveliest mother and daughter moment I'm honoured to have witnessed.' Sita says, wiping away a tear.

For a moment, I think Nisha might walk out again.

'You know,' I say, 'I think I could do with some fresh air. Nisha, fancy joining me?'

Chapter Sixteen

Nisha and I are sitting outside on Mum's swing seat. It's one of the only things she brought with her from my childhood home to the Park home, and now to the cottage. Nisha and I spent many happy hours on it as kids, playing chess, talking, laughing, planning, dreaming.

The darkness wraps itself around us like a blanket now. Above, a glorious spray of stars arcs majestically across the sky.

Nisha pushes her feet against the ground, and we rock back and forth gently. It feels like with one swing, we could travel back in time and her denim-clad legs would be replaced by bare, skinny, bruised, nut-brown ones, fringe grown out and hair plaited down her back, face free of make-up, nose in a book.

I glance at her, waiting for her to speak but she doesn't. 'You okay?' I say at last.

She exhales and nods. 'Sorry. I should have prepared myself for that. Being a highly regarded doctor with letters after my name just isn't enough for Mum. And it's not like I'm trying *not* to get married and have children. Quite the opposite.'

She looks up, her long, dark eyelashes seem to sweep the sky as if combing for clues to the secrets of the universe.

'Your mum means well, Nisha,' I say carefully. 'You both want the same thing.' She doesn't answer. 'Have you talked to her about how you feel?' I ask gently.

She huffs in tearful frustration. 'And allow her to lecture me that because I didn't just marry a nice Indian man when I was 21, I've willingly sacrificed my chance to have a traditional family unit?' She skids her feet on the floor, scuffing her perfectly polished, expensive-looking boots. 'She's probably right. I'm thirty-six. I can't see it happening now, to be honest.' She blinks, looks up again then turns to look at the sea.

'Nor could I, Nisha,' I say softly. 'But it has.'

'Not all of us are as lucky as you, Sofie,' she says edgily. 'Some of us endure loads of crap Tinder dates and meet a stream of unsuitable men before we think we've found one that's right. And then, we get our hearts broken,' she adds, looking away. 'Sorry, I don't mean to snap. I'm just starting to accept that it's not necessarily going to happen for me.'

The silence stretches a long way between us.

'I know your break-up with Andy was tough.'

'You have no idea,' she laughs, blinking rapidly.

'I also know I was too caught up in my pregnancy to check in on you and I feel terrible about that, but Nisha, he wasn't right for you. You've had a lucky escape.'

'Or perhaps certain paths just aren't meant to be,' she says quietly.

Nisha glances at my protruding stomach and then looks away. She thinks I can't understand. She thinks my life is all neatly wrapped up and I might as well stick a big fat bow on my belly and be done with it.

'You know what Rory would say? Luck isn't down to experience; it's not even a circumstance. It's an attitude. I like to think of it as more of an equation, though: belief plus possibility equals hope.' I take her hand. 'And there is no one I believe in more to achieve what they think is impossible than you, so I will continue to have hope, enough for us both, no matter what you say.'

Her eyes shimmer with tears and she swipes them away.

I put my arm around her, and she leans her head on my shoulder. Nisha's dark hair drapes over her eyes as rogue tears continue to fall.

Slowly, hesitantly, she stretches her hand out and puts it against my stomach. It's the first time she's done so, I realise. It's not long before the baby obediently obliges with a gentle press of its foot. She immediately gasps and puts her hand to her lips. Then she lifts her head up and looks at me. Her brown eyes seem threaded with gold as she smiles with genuine delight.

'Hello, baby,' she says softly. 'I really hope I'll be able to have a friend for you one day. If not, I'll just have to make sure I'm the best one I can be to you and your mummy.'

Just then a shooting star soars far over our heads, and we watch it together, in awe. When we look at each other again and I see Nisha's eyes, now sparkling like stars themselves, I know that we both wished for the same thing.

Chapter Seventeen

It's Valentine's Day and the end of the first week of my maternity leave. But most importantly, at thirty-nine weeks exactly, it's also the day I'm finally classed as 'full term'. Despite the first two trimesters flying by, recently it has felt like I'd never reach this point.

The novelty of this pregnancy wore off around week thirty-five, just after the baby shower and around the time the three Hs (Haemorrhoids, Braxton Hicks and Heartburn) arrived. It was a relief to finish work and be able to just … relax.

Not that I've slowed down much. I've been in full nesting mode to ensure I'm one-hundred per cent ready when this baby decides to come.

This morning, Rory presented me with a beautiful gold, charm bracelet, a Valentine's gift, with two initials already on it – mine and his. 'The third initial is to come very soon, once the baby's born!' he said. He never ceases to amaze me with his thoughtfulness.

And I also have a last-minute lunch with Nisha to look forward to today. She phoned last night – she's been back in Bournemouth a couple of times this month and when we talked, she told me she had exciting news.

'I can't tell you yet, though, as I don't want to jinx anything.'

I grill her as soon as I sit down at our table.

'You can't keep a heavily pregnant woman in suspense a moment longer. It's unfair on me and the baby, right, champ?' I give my bump a little prod but the baby remains stubbornly quiet.

'Okay.' She claps her hands excitedly, eyes shining brightly across the table. 'I've been offered a senior position in paediatric neurology at Southampton Hospital. I had my interview a couple of weeks ago and was offered it yesterday!'

'Nisha! Does that mean…?'

'I'll be moving back here!'

'Oh, my GOD! I had no idea it was something you were even thinking about!'

'Now you know how I felt when you told me you were pregnant!' She laughs. 'No doubt Andy will think it's because of him but, to be honest, it's something I've been considering for a while. I want to make some changes in my life, get some more balance, settle down. Once I sell my flat, I can afford a good-sized house in a nice village in the New Forest – halfway between the hospital and here. I want to be close to my folks, especially now that they're getting older. And I want to be somewhere I can imagine raising kids someday. I'm also hoping there'll be more men in the Southwest dating pool than there are in London. Or at least,' she adds wryly, 'more single ones…'

'It sounds like you've really thought this through.'

'You know me. I like a strategic plan. London is like an exhausting merry-go-round these days. And something else is pulling me here too…' She smiles, then and presses her hand to my belly. 'I want to be here to experience *this* ride, with you.'

We spend the rest of lunch excitedly planning where she'll live and how often we'll see each other. It feels like the old days. Before I was pregnant. Before I was married, even.

After lunch, Nisha heads to Boscombe to meet the others at Emma's – and tell them her news. I've had enough excitement for one day, so I head home.

I know I should rest, but my nesting urges won't allow it. Instead, I sit on the floor in the nursery surrounded by neatly arranged piles of baby vests and Baby-gros, booties, scratch mitts, baby blankets and muslin squares. Then I have all the nappies, cotton wool, sanitary towels, giant knickers, nursing bras, breast pads, nipple cream and pyjamas which I pack and re-pack into my hospital bag for the third time.

In between practising my breathing and trying to imagine my uterus opening like a flower, I've spent the past week scrubbing the entire house from top to bottom. I've also emptied, cleaned and reorganised every single cupboard and have re-washed and re-ironed all the baby clothes. I've batch-cooked meals and put them all in the freezer alphabetically. I've sterilised bottles just in case I can't breastfeed, and I've even cleaned all the downstairs windows.

Everything's in order, which makes me feel calm and happy – and, suddenly – exhausted. I feel completely drained: it's a tiredness that seems to emanate through my bones and there's a new, persistent dull ache in my back. I make my way to our bedroom to lie down and, without fighting it, I fall asleep.

By the time I get up, it's gone 5pm. Groggily, still disorientated from my nap, I glance into the nursery on my way to the stairs, look around and smile. The Ercol rocking chair is in place next to the Danish cot with a canopy hanging over it, the shelves are all stacked with classic baby books. Everything's as it should be.

'I'm ready.' I say out loud and I feel a flash of adrenaline that feels almost euphoric. The ache in my back is still there and seems to have spread, but I'm used to these pregnancy twinges and pains that come and go. Unless, I suddenly think, it's *not* just a twinge, but the beginning of a contraction? How are you meant to know? The most anxious part of this pregnancy is waiting for labour to begin. Not knowing what it will feel like. This can't be it, can it? I need a sign. An obvious sign.

'Come on, little one, time to wake up!' I say to my tummy. I give it a little prod. I feel the years fast-forward and can imagine waking up my child for nursery, for school, after a teenage night out. When you're pregnant, people talk about the difficult sleep-deprived months to come, but I can't help but think about the joyful years stretching before me, too. Of waking my child and preparing them not just for each day, but for life.

I rub my tummy gently again and then stretch my hand over to my side, pressing my fingers where I know it's bottom is, because doing so always guarantees a response within moments. I wait for the familiar gentle push of a hand or foot or tightening of my tummy as the baby shifts slightly with what little room it has in there now. But there's nothing.

I give another gentle prod. Still nothing. And then comes the sudden, sickening realisation: I can't remember the last time I felt my baby kick.

I scramble in my mind for a memory, but the only movements I've consciously noticed these past few hours have been made by me: Fold. Pack. Roll. Stack. Repeat.

What about the kicks?

Heart racing, I sink to my knees in the nursery and reach for my hospital bag. Unzipping it, I hurriedly pull out the notebook in which I've religiously noted down every movement since week eighteen. To my horror, there's nothing recorded today since 11:30am – just before I met Nisha. That's over five hours ago. Perhaps I didn't write the next ones down?

I look at the Kicks Count app on my phone and feel my panic rise when I see the last entry is also just before midday. Perhaps I forgot the others? I quickly go through my day in my head. Packing the bag. Rory's various phone calls. Lunch with Nisha. More organising. My nap.

I realise with a sickening jolt that I've been so happy and relaxed, so lost in the preparation of what is to come, I haven't been focused on the baby today. Not at all.

The disbelief, nausea and light-headedness come at once. Familiar sensations from panic attacks past that I haven't felt since the aftermath of Dad's death, but today, there's something more. A deep-rooted confirmation of what I know to be the improbable, but possible. The unthinkable, but feasible. I try to banish the statistics about pregnancy loss that have already started scrolling through my brain at an alarming rate. Facts and figures that once made me terrified of stepping foot on this path in the first place, but that I've managed to lock out of my brain for the past nine months. Now, they come flooding back in.

I resolve to stay calm. Be positive. I tell myself I'm just being over-anxious. I've been worried about the baby's movements so many times over the last few months and Rory has always reassured me it's fine. If I go and see Sarah, my midwife, now she'll just tell me the baby's movements are slowing down in preparation for birth. They do that, don't they? Don't they?

Best Possible Outcome.

That's what Rory would say if he were here now.

In his absence, I say it to myself, instead.

Chapter Eighteen

I phone Rory, feeling winded as it goes to voicemail. I try to imagine what he'd say to comfort me, even as I'm scrolling back through my contacts, to Nisha's number. I think of our lunch, of how quiet the baby was.

I look at my smartwatch. 5:15pm. I flick to the Kicks Count app, still positioned stubbornly at two. I look at my watch again. I usually have at least ten episodes of movement in a single day.

I phone Nisha. I hear people talking in the background. Cups and glasses clinking. Laughter. Normality. I imagine her, Sal, Inge and Emma all sitting round Emma's kitchen table, wine in hand, putting the world to rights. I know Nisha will do the same with me now, stop this catastrophising brain of mine in its tracks, and the thought immediately calms me down.

'Hey Sof, what's u—'

'Nisha,' I interrupt, unable to wait. 'The baby isn't moving. It hasn't for a while. I know it's fine, but you know what my brain is like – instant freak-out!' I force out a what-am-I-like? laugh.

I wait for her to reply. I know exactly what she'll say, though.

'*There's nothing to worry about. This is entirely normal.*'

I just need to hear someone else say it.

'Okay, Sofie, take a breath…' Her voice goes muffled and I can hear Emma asking if everything is okay. When Nisha comes back

This Wasn't Meant to Happen

on the phone, her voice is as calm and reassuring as I expect. I instantly relax. She's not worried. It's just me catastrophising, as usual. 'How long has it been since you felt the last period of movement?'

'A few hours, I think,' I say tentatively. 'Earlier this morning, and then a big movement about an hour and a half before lunch. It's normal, right? A sign I'm getting ready for labour.'

'Have you called Rory?' she says, her tone is light and breezy.

'He's not answering.' I glance at my watch. 'He'll be preparing to go on air. He's doing a live report at 6pm. Shall I call the midwife or—?'

'No,' Nisha interrupts, and I exhale. 'Call the hospital,' she says, then. 'Tell them as much detail as you can about when you last felt the baby move and say we're on our way.'

My heart thunders so loudly I can hear it in my ears. 'Don't you think I should wait for Rory?'

'No,' she says firmly. 'We're not going to wait, Sofie. When you get off the phone from me, call the hospital and tell them you need to come in. Then call Rory back and leave a message telling him to meet us at the hospital. I haven't had any alcohol so I can drive, don't worry about that.' She knows me well. 'Get your hospital bag and notes and I'll meet you outside your house in my car. Have you got all that?' Nisha is no longer my best friend, but calm, authoritative Dr Nisha Shah. 'I'll be there ASAP. Everything is going to be okay. Emma, Sal and Inge all send their love.'

'It's going to be okay,' I repeat under my breath, like a prayer.

I ring Rory but it goes to voicemail again, so I leave a message sounding as calm as possible. I don't want to worry him unnecessarily.

'Rory, can you come straight to the hospital when you get this? Nisha's taking me. See you soon. Love you.'

Everything's going to be okay.

I hit call end. I rub my stomach, willing for movement, hoping for any familiar press of a hand, knuckle or knee, a stretch of the leg or kick of its foot to tell me it's okay. But there's just a dull ache in my back that's getting stronger. Maybe this is what a contraction feels like? How am I meant to know?

I squeeze my eyes shut and breathe, trying to focus on what I've learned in the classes I've been to. I resort to an old habit, reciting Pi.

Struggling with my coat and hospital bag and with my phone pressed against my ear, I head out of the front door. I step blindly into a world suddenly shrouded in thick fog. A heavy, gloomy darkness wraps itself around me and holds on tight.

I stare blindly at the sliver of the moon as I wait for the maternity unit to answer. I notice with a degree of distance that it's snowing. My breath mists in front of my face, my brain has frozen in its own fog.

I recite Pi out loud.

Three…

Three – Rory, me and the baby.

3.1415…

Five – the hours since I last felt my baby move.

3.14159…

Nine – the months I've been growing our baby inside me.

3.141592…

Two – the number of movements I've felt today.

At last, they answer. I speak. Answer questions. I hear my words echo in my head. 'Thirty-nine weeks… No movement… Five hours.'

Five hours. How did I not notice?

My voice sounds slow, deep, like a record put on the wrong speed. I long to rip it off the turntable, break it over my knee and fling the pieces far, far away. The receptionist tells me to come directly to the hospital.

Nisha arrives moments later. She doesn't get out; she just opens the passenger door.

'Your carriage awaits,' she says brightly. She doesn't make eye contact with me.

I get in, put my seatbelt on and stare out of the windscreen as we drive through what's quickly become a snowstorm. Small clumps of white flakes cling desperately to the glass like a baby's fist holding on to its mother's finger. I watch as they're swept away by the wipers.

I silently will this baby to move as Nisha accelerates onto the A338, past Boscombe and Bournemouth, towards Poole. I think of my hypnobirthing CD, use my breath to stay calm and focused on the baby's safe arrival.

'Do you want to phone your mum?' Nisha asks, glancing at me in concern.

I frown. Shake my head.

'There's no need; everything's okay.' I stroke my belly gently as I speak, talking to my baby as well as her. Nisha nods and I see her hands tighten on the steering wheel. I keep staring straight ahead at the white storm we're driving into.

'Repeat this after me,' I say quietly to Nisha. 'Best Possible Outcome.' She glances at me, smiles weakly and nods. 'Say it!' I prompt fiercely.

'Best Possible Outcome.' Nisha says, and she grasps my hand without taking her eyes off the road.

I've decided that any other answer will not be part of this equation.

Chapter Nineteen

St Mary's Maternity Unit at Poole Hospital looms up out of the thick fog. The snow's falling more heavily now; the roads quickly became treacherous on the way here. Even though Nisha kept her cool, at times it felt like we were skating on thin ice.

'We're here.' Nisha screeches into a parking spot and unstraps herself quickly. 'Let's go.'

I go to open the car door, but my body has frozen as well as my brain.

'I'm scared, Nisha,' I whisper.

'Sofie, I'm a doctor,' she says taking my hand. Her brown eyes are pools of professional calm and determination. 'You're on my turf now and let me tell you something, hospitals are magical places. Hope literally lives here, okay?' She runs round to my side of the car and gently eases me out. As I stand up, I'm convinced that I just felt something shift inside me.

'Nisha! I ... I think I felt the baby move!' My breath weaves white in front of me like a ghostly apparition.

'Oh, thank God!' Nisha's palpable relief shocks me. It feels disproportionate both to her previous calm and immediately pierces the balloon of hope I've been clinging to. If Nisha thinks there's really something to worry about, then there must be. I put my hand on my stomach and will the baby to do it again. Nothing.

'I … I thought I did. But I don't know…' I feel sick with fear.

'Let's get you in, Sof,' she says gently, easing me towards the front door. With limp limbs I allow her to guide me like a marionette. I pull out my phone – there are three missed calls from Rory.

'I'll call him back,' Nisha says, taking charge. 'Just sign yourself in at reception.'

I'm almost blinded by bright light when we walk inside, immediately sickened by the sterile smell. I cradle my tummy as Nisha leads me to the reception desk. I stand, mute.

My baby isn't moving.

A floating face greets me. Sharp, inquiring eyes and a painted-on smile behind a plain wooden desk and plastic screen. I can hear Nisha behind me, pacing the floor as she tries to call Rory. He obviously hasn't picked up. Perhaps he's already on his way.

Please let him be on his way.

'Can I help you?' the floating head says testily. Her voice is on the wrong setting. It's like I'm hearing it from underwater.

My baby isn't moving. The words still won't come.

Nisha strides up, business-like in her camel coat, and stands next to me. I'm clinging tightly on to my pregnancy notes. My hope.

'You should be expecting us. My friend is thirty-nine weeks pregnant and hasn't felt her baby move for several hours,' she says briskly. 'Her name is Sofie King.' She leans on the desk, asserting her authority.

The receptionist bristles in response. 'We *expect* a lot of people here today. Every day, actually. This *is* a hospital you know.'

'I'm aware,' Nisha says coolly. 'I'm a doctor. Chief Consultant Paediatric Neurologist at Southampton Hospital, as of next month. With outreach clinics here.'

The receptionist has the good grace to blush. 'Oh, right. Let me just have a look.'

Just then the doors burst open, and Rory appears, almost tripping over his feet, wrapped up in his smart coat, black scarf and beanie hat covered in snow, desperately looking left and right.

I try to call out, but my voice doesn't work. He sees me and practically skids across the floor.

'Thank God I'm not too late! Are you having contractions? Is it time?' He is breathless with excitement.

I stare at him, the lump in my throat ballooning until I have no oxygen.

'Rory,' Nisha says quietly. 'Sofie hasn't felt the baby move for several hours. We've come to get her checked out.'

'Oh, I thought she was about to give birth!' He exhales in visible relief, missing the point Nisha is trying to make, so convinced is he that nothing can possibly go wrong. I study his face forensically for signs of anxiety, but there's none. If he's not worried, then I shouldn't be. Rory wants this baby so much and he *always* gets what he wants. Here, right here, is the hope I needed. I lean into him then, wanting to exist only in the circle of positivity he's wrapped me in these past nine months, past six *years,* actually. Of *course* everything is going to be okay; how could I possibly have doubted it? I'm a King now.

'Rory,' Nisha pulls him away and whispers to him urgently. He glances at me and smiles but, like a kaleidoscope, the pattern of it has changed. I see fear in his eyes, which makes the ground beneath me suddenly tilt. I close my eyes. Darkness descends.

'Sofie!'

When I open them, Nisha and Rory are holding me up and the floating face from reception now seems more willing to cooperate. She hurriedly gestures towards the antenatal-clinic waiting area where a sea of blue chairs is neatly arranged. As she retreats, she tells us we'll be called very soon.

The room is filled with pregnant women of varying stages, some with their partners, some alone – a few with small children. Somehow, my legs carry me to a spare seat. Or maybe Rory does. I can't be sure. Fingers of freezing fog have followed me inside, caught my body, brain, heart. I could speak but I know no one would hear me. I can move, but if I do, I might break. Crack.

I close my eyes again to block everything else out, repeating the three words that have become my mantra.

Best Possible Outcome. Best Possible Outcome.

'Sofie?' Rory asks in concern. 'Are you okay?' His face looks stretched, spectral almost.

The noises in the waiting room have become a deafening

cacophony in my head. A blonde, heavily pregnant girl no older than sixteen is pacing the room in a dressing gown, her slippers slapping rhythmically against the grey lino floor. *Slap, slap, slap.* She stops every so often, her face contorted into a grimace, and groans loudly. Another woman, with a bump that seems to be pointing directly downwards, leans against the wall and moans, at the same octave and with additional vibrato. A lady in her second trimester laughs companionably with her partner as they flick through a trashy magazine, their light-hearted joy like a tinkling percussion accompaniment of bells. *Ha ha he, ha ha he.* Opposite them, a woman cradling a large bump sporadically snaps at her young child when he starts running around, a loud, cymbal crash of 'Stop moving and behave!'

Start moving and behave! I will our baby. I press my hands against my tummy, feel Rory rest his on top of mine.

A nurse calls my name, and the entire room turns to stare at me accusingly. We might have been fast-tracked to the front of the queue, but I'm quietly petrified of what it might mean.

Nisha grasps my hand before I get up, and squeezes it tightly. Her tawny skin has paled significantly and when she lets go, she goes back to picking the skin around her manicured fingernails like she used to as a teen.

Rory takes my other hand. I have to focus on how to walk as my body has forgotten. Nothing's coming naturally. Everything is forced. But forward means finding out our baby is okay.

Everything is okay.

That's what I keep telling myself.

And if I say it enough, maybe it'll be true.

Chapter Twenty

A white room. A monitor. A midwife. Rory. Me. Our baby. A calm, reassuring voice. Blood pressure taken. Gel applied. Then foetal doppler. It's so quiet. I sit up slightly, straining to hear the pounding hooves of a heartbeat; the speeding train announcing the presence of my baby's life force.

Silence.

'Don't worry!' she says with a smile as she moves the doppler around silently, eyebrows knitted together. 'Baby must be in an awkward position, this often happens!' She moves the doppler into a few different spots, then puts it down. 'How about you pop out for a quick walk and maybe get yourself some chocolate and try to wake this lazy baby up?' she says brightly. 'There's a vending machine outside. Just come straight back when you're done!'

We sleepwalk out of the room, back down the corridor. The vending machine is in the reception waiting room. Nisha's there, her back to us. Head lowered over her lap; hands clenched.

Rory hands me a Dairy Milk from the vending machine. I stuff a piece in my mouth. It's like eating tar.

We walk up and down the corridor a few times in silence; I jiggle, prod with ever more urgency. Rory is silent. When we go back in, she's waiting, smile fixed on her face. Someone else is with her.

'A second opinion,' she says, still brightly.

This Wasn't Meant to Happen

I smile at the new addition. He's noble-looking, like a bird of prey. Grey hair sprouting out of the side of his head, a hook nose and a thick monobrow that sits heavily on his large, furrowed forehead. He nods at Rory and me and tells us he's going to do a CTG scan.

I wait for the words of kind reassurance. They don't come.

Rory grips my hand tightly. Mine remains limp. A minute, five minutes or an eternity passes, I don't know which. The consultant asks us to move to the ultrasound room.

I'm lying on another bed. I realise it's the same room where we'd had our dating scan. I rewind in my head to that day. I remember the joy of seeing our baby wave at us. I feel like I'm looking at a split screen of those two moments in this room. Then and now.

But now the screen is turned away from us.

My breath shallows. Fear constricts my stomach, my heart, my chest as I watch the consultant's face, waiting for it to change, soften, smile. Say everything is okay. My baby is okay.

Please say it's okay.

No one speaks. When I inhale, it sounds like I'm emitting a death rattle. It echoes around the room into the silence.

I gaze desperately between the consultant and the midwife and then at Rory. My normally verbose husband hasn't said a word.

Why won't anyone speak? Just two words, that's all!

Time has slowed to a standstill. The bird-man consultant turns his head, his hooded eyes and lowered brows don't move, nor do they mask his sorrow.

'He's gone,' he murmurs under his breath to the ultrasound tech. But to me, his words seem to yawn in the silence of the room as if through a loudspeaker, the syllables stretching, morphing, distending.

He. A boy. Our boy. We didn't know that he's a boy.

'Your baby has died,' he says to me, then. 'I'm so very sorry.'

Those words are as sharp as knife and they slice through the silence, slashing my entire universe to pieces.

They've made a mistake.

I look at Rory. He'll tell them.

Tell them they're wrong. Why isn't he saying anything?

'NO!'

One word. The final, fatal stab of a broken dream. It takes a moment to realise that it didn't come from me.

It's Rory's roar of pain. His visceral, vocal embodiment of horror and despair that rips through the room. His legs that collapse beneath him as he sinks to the floor. From where I'm lying on the bed, belly exposed and still shimmering with ultrasound gel I look down at the back of his head that's now bowed over his knees. Stare at the bottom of his shoes. I remember the policeman's shoes on the day they told Mum and me that Dad had died. I'm now watching this moment from a great distance. From the past. There, I'm not and have never been pregnant. My unborn baby is not dead. It's happening to someone else. This horror is unfolding, from afar.

I want to reach out to Rory, cling to him, comfort him, tell him it's okay. *My* baby isn't dead. But I can't. Because I'm not here.

I close my eyes; the shoes disappear and so do I. I'm a void. I'm the space around my baby on the ultrasound screen. The fathomless black that's carrying him has now enveloped me and we're both lifeless within the vast ocean that is my body. Floating headfirst in this room. My womb.

A boy. Our boy.

'My boy,' I whisper. No one hears me.

'I don't understand!'

I lurch back, eyes open as Rory speaks. He's looking up at the consultant from his kneeling position beside the bed. He looks like a knight, brought to his knees by the cruellest of swords.

'How can he be gone? How can this have happened...' Rory sobs.

You said this wouldn't happen, I think as I stare at the top of his head.

'My boy,' I say again, louder this time. 'I want to see our boy. Please.'

The consultant looks at me unflinchingly. 'Are you sure?'

I nod.

Slowly he turns the screen and I see our baby curled up inside me. The consultant points out the cord that appears to be wrapped around his neck; the place where his heart should be beating; the limbs that hang limply. I gaze at the gentle slope of my boy's brow and nose and see a slide at the play park I'll never take him to. The perfect petals of his lips in profile: a bud that'll never bloom into a smile. He's there, but not. Both in front of me and in the future that I'd imagined for him, but also gone.

I hear the murmur of voices as the consultant talks to Rory, but I can't make sense of what they're saying.

Nothing makes sense. And yet everything does. I know it's true with the kind of innate certainty that I've spent my entire life trying to avoid. Loving something so much only to have it cruelly snatched from me.

Why did I believe Rory when he said it would be okay? Of *course* this was going to happen: my worst fear imagined, finally made real.

It's then that I clutch my belly and scream into the room. Into my womb. The consultant glances at the midwife, turns the screen back around, but all I can see are stars that exploded millions of light years before. Stars that once existed. That were, not are. Past not present. A future that once felt within my reach. Now, no more.

Chapter Twenty-One

Gently, we're led out of the room. A smiling mum and dad-to-be are walking down the corridor towards us.

I can tell from the size of her bump and naïvely excited expression that she's here for her twenty-week anomaly scan. We lock eyes and she immediately stops smiling. She looks at Rory and I think for a moment she's going to say, 'What are the chances of that?' But it's a recognition of a different kind: someone coming face to face with horror. She squeezes her husband's hand tightly, his expression morphs into one of alarm and they both look down at the shiny, hospital floor as they pass.

I know then it has already begun. We've become the faces no one wants to see, the nightmare they don't want to begin to imagine. I look longingly at their departing figures, wanting to swap lives even as we're ushered quickly into a room.

Four lime green tub chairs have been placed in pairs opposite each other in a garishly decorated room, a table in between them. 'The Bad News Room' I mentally name it, when I see the prominently placed box of tissues in the middle of the table. As soon as the door clicks shut behind us, Rory and I collapse into each other.

'I'm sorry. I'm so sorry. I'm so sorry…'

'It's not your fault. It's not your fault…'

Our words are like trains speeding past each other. I can't distinguish anything other than the rattle in my own head, the echo in my shattered heart. He strokes my hair as I repeat my apology into his chest. His heartbeat is fast and strong and all I can think of is the little one inside me, now still. The hours I didn't notice the baby moving. The kick that could have been his final one. A silent cry for help.

'You didn't do anything wrong,' Rory says. I hear it, but don't believe it.

'How do you know?' I say, accusingly.

I think back to earlier today and all this week: to the hours I spent sorting and tidying when I should have been resting. I think of the exercise, the yoga and swimming. What about the lengths I'd swum? Only twenty a day, but that's 100 a week. How much would that add up to over seven and a half months? Plus, the six weeks when I swam 100, without realising I was pregnant. I quickly do the maths. Over 3,600 lengths. Was it that?

I think of the days I pushed myself to go into the office when I was knackered because I was so controlling about my job; the late maternity leave I took – just two weeks in the end – in order to get as much time with the baby when he or she arrived. Was it that?

I go further back still, to the day when I did the pregnancy test. When I wasn't even sure I *wanted* the baby. Is this my punishment for that initial doubt? Did my baby pick up on those fears? But I *did* want him. I *do*. More than anything. I want him so much.

'I'm sorry…' I cry again, my apology a rasp in my dry mouth.

'It's not your fault,' Rory repeats. 'It's not your fault…'

I only hear the echo.

Your fault your fault your fault.

Dark thoughts invade my brain like detectives investigating a crime scene, trying to find evidence of neglect. Why, after all these weeks and months of careful engagement and the extra scans. Why, after noticing everything about the pregnancy, recording every kick, every flutter, every hiccup, every gentle mound of its bottom, the feet, elbows, knees, pressed against my stomach; me watching, fascinated, as it morphed into strange shapes on an hourly basis. Why, *why* did I lose focus at the last hurdle?

It's my fault. Me. My body. My brain. My fault.

We sit and wait, staring blankly into a future submerged in darkness. I look out of the small window and wonder how the clouds are still moving across the sky; why the news reel on the mute TV on the wall is still rolling. Why I can still hear people talking normally outside this door. Surely the whole world has come to a complete standstill?

Finally, the consultant comes in. For a split second, I imagine he's going to tell us that he was wrong; he made a mistake. Doctors *can* be wrong, after all. Even Nisha says so. I cling on to this hope for a split second, like a safety rope. It's quickly snatched from me as he begins to speak.

He explains gravely what he pointed out during the scan, that the umbilical cord is wrapped tightly around our baby's neck which cut off the blood oxygen flow to the brain. He adds that it might also have been compressed against itself, reducing the flow of oxygenated blood through the nuchal cord. He stresses that, from the scan, he can't tell if our baby had other issues, says we'll have a better chance of knowing the cause of death by having a post-mortem after he's born. Whilst this wouldn't necessarily identify a clear cause, it might rule out what didn't cause the death. He adds that, as this was our first child, this would be especially important when considering any pregnancies in the future.

I stare at him without saying a word. How can he talk about the possibility of another baby when I'm still carrying this one inside me?

But I have no oxygen to give life to those words. All hope is gone. Obliterated. I exist entirely in here now. In this hospital, this horror. And yet I'm also not here. I'm with my baby. Carrying him, loving him, wanting desperately to save him.

I stare out of the window again. The consultant informs us that because our baby has passed away inside me, I can either go home and wait for my labour to begin naturally or they can induce me now. He says there's no medical need for me to deliver immediately. It's up to me.

'If you decide to be induced now, you'll be given two tablets to be taken twelve hours apart, which will bring on contractions. I can give you one to take now and another at home in twelve hours' time.

This Wasn't Meant to Happen

Taking them means you'll deliver within thirty-six to forty-eight hours.'

The words swim around my head like globules of liquid mercury, pulling apart, moulding together, reforming into a bigger shape. Too big to comprehend.

I must deliver my baby.

'Sorry, what?' Rory says, then. 'Surely you can't expect my wife to go into labour and give birth naturally to this baby?'

Not give birth, Rory. Deliver death.

'I can assure you, Mr King, it's the safest way,' the consultant replies.

'What about a C-section?' Rory asks.

'C-sections are high-risk operations,' he explains, making eye contact with Rory, not me. 'It's always our preference to opt for a natural delivery, if the circumstances allow for it.'

He crosses his legs, coughs, looks down at his notes. I wonder then how many times he's had to do this? Have this conversation. Deliver this news.

'I can't,' I say then. My voice is raspy, unfamiliar, alien. 'Please,' I beg, staring at the consultant. Willing him to look at me. 'I can't…' I start to cry again, imagining the pain of labour – already scary enough – now with the added horror of knowing that our baby is dead. I bury my face in Rory's chest, feel his heartbeat against my cheek.

'She can't,' Rory says firmly, rubbing his forehead with his thumb and fingers.

'A natural delivery is the preference,' the consultant repeats. 'We don't want to put your wife through high-risk surgery unnecessarily,' he explains. 'In most cases, C-sections are done only if the mother has a pre-existing condition where her health is at risk, like placental abruption or pre-eclampsia, or if her waters have broken and we had to….' He coughs awkwardly then, and looks at his clipboard as if the right words might appear before him.

'Had to what?' Rory prompts.

He looks up but doesn't look either of us in the eye. 'Perform an emergency operation in order to protect the life of the baby.'

'Hold on,' Rory says, shaking his head like it's a snow globe. He stares, waiting for the words to settle as I stare blindly at the snow still falling outside the window. 'Are you saying that because our baby has already died and there is no *life* to protect, my wife isn't allowed a C-section?' Rory's voice is seething with shock and fury.

'Mr King…' The consultant looks at a point somewhere past us both. 'As I said, C-sections are very complex operations and are not undertaken unless in extreme circumstances…'

'If this doesn't count as extreme, then what does?' Rory says in exasperation. He leans over and cradles his head in the curve of his arms. I press my hand down on his back.

'Mr King,' the consultant says again gently, 'I understand this is hard to take in. It's a shock on top of what is already truly terrible news. But I hope you trust me when I say that we only have your wife's health in mind. A natural delivery is far safer for her and will allow for a swifter recovery.'

The consultant's eyes swivel quickly past me to his clipboard. Can he see me? Am I even here? Or am I just words on his to do list; another patient to tick off on a rota of many?

My baby has died, and I've disappeared. I no longer exist. Doesn't he realise there is no recovery from this?

Fleetingly, I wonder if he has a wife, children? A grown-up daughter perhaps? In the same situation, would he expect the same of her?

'It's too much … too much,' Rory murmurs.

My hand creeps on to his lap and rests there limply. I continue to stare out of the window. I'm rigid. Mute. One continuous, hellish sentence reel plays in my head.

I have to deliver my baby.

Eventually, we agree I'll be induced. The consultant passes me a packet of two tablets and establishes what I need to do: take the first of the tablets now, go home and rest. Take the other tablet and come back into the hospital once the contractions start.

He repeats how sorry he is and says that a bereavement counsellor from Spring – Poole Hospital's charity to support parents through baby loss – will be coming shortly to talk to us. He gets up to leave, but before he does, he says one more thing.

'I know the thought of this seems impossible right now but in my experience of this situation – which I'm sad to say is vast – you might find you feel differently in the future. I hope it might be an experience you come to cherish, one day.' He's respectful enough to look down, then. 'I really am so sorry for your loss.' he adds before he retreats out of the door, leaving Rory and me alone.

Chapter Twenty-Two

We walk out of the Bad News Room with the leaflets given to us by Alice, the bereavement counsellor from Spring who came to see us after the consultant had left. We were barely able to take in what she was saying, let alone converse with her or process what must come next.

Rory's clutching the stack of leaflets so tightly his knuckles are white. Alice suggested we spend the next hours thinking about the delivery. Whether we'll want to hold him, name him, bring in an outfit or a blanket for him. Will we want a photo taken of him, a lock of his hair, footprints, handprints?

How can I think about any of these unfathomable things, while I'm still carrying him inside me?

'Perhaps, you'd like a memory box?' she'd suggested kindly. A box for our baby who will also be put in a box. A coffin.

It all feels so unreal, I can barely take it in.

We walk into reception now, past all the pregnant couples waiting for scans to where Nisha is still waiting. She senses us, turning almost in slow motion. In a millisecond, she presents an entire silent-movie reel of emotion from anticipation, hopefulness through to anguish, despair, helplessness. Silently she stands up, reaches for us wrapping us all tightly together. None of us say a word. There are none that can make sense of this. We stumble out of the doors like a six-legged

This Wasn't Meant to Happen

creature into the Christening-cake, fondant-icing covered world. Then she squeezes us both tightly, wraps her scarf around her face and just … melts away.

Rory and I sit in the car in darkness for a long time before he starts the engine and makes the journey down the endless levels of the multi-storey hospital car park like we're descending into hell itself and out into a world I no longer feel we belong in. I look out at the white, wet, falling snow that I know will soon enough melt into nothingness, as if it were never here. Our baby is here but will also never be here, too. I wrap my arms around myself and fold myself over him. I want him to stay with me forever.

When we arrive home Rory and I sit in the driveway. If the hospital is the ocean where our ship sank, this house is now the unhospitable island we're stranded on where we have to come to terms with surviving without him.

'I can't do this,' I whisper. 'I can't.'

'I know,' Rory replies.

Eventually, we go inside and are immediately faced with the black shadow of the pram in the hallway, like a hearse. I collapse then, my legs no longer able to hold me up. Somehow, Rory lifts me and our baby in his arms like we're nothing (are we both already ghosts?). Effortlessly, he carries me into the lounge.

I stare around blankly at my home, where I do not belong. This, calm, meticulously ordered place with its Danish furniture, wood-burning stove and simple décor: it all feels offensively normal.

It feels far too light in here, too hopeful for the darkness I'm now encased in. My eyes fall on the driftwood frames featuring photos of Rory and me on our wedding day and on honeymoon in Cornwall. The most recent – the one of the two of us on Swanage Pier when I was twelve weeks pregnant – taking pride of place in the middle of the mantlepiece. I don't know whether I want to hug it tightly to me or throw it across the room. I think of the photo we'd taken just a few weeks ago, at Durdle Door, and how that night the *Evening News* anchors had announced our pregnancy to the entire County by putting the photo of us that the hikers had taken up on screen. I remember watching as they linked to Rory on his outdoor broadcast in Christchurch, already a proud, beaming dad.

By the time he got home, he'd been flooded with hundreds upon hundreds of messages of congratulations and support on social media. New followers for a new life.

A lifetime ago, now. Our baby's lifetime.

Rory lays me down on the sofa, covers me with a soft blanket and draws the curtains. He puts the TV on. *Garden Rescue*. Except … it's about spring planting; the hardiest perennials; how to prevent plants from dying. I close my eyes and begin to sob while Rory hurriedly switches over, then over again, before giving up and switching off the TV entirely.

'I'm going to call your mum and Gran.' They're the only people I've agreed to tell.

I hear Mum cry out at the news as he explains that our baby has died and then tells her what will happen next. I don't speak to her, I can't.

'Tell Sofie I love her,' I hear her say. 'And I'm sorry. I'm so very sorry.'

Chapter Twenty-Three

It's happening.

Thirty-one hours after learning our baby has died, we're on our way back to the hospital so I can deliver him. The weight of shock, grief and fear in the car seems proportionate to the ominously black sky, eerily white blanket of snow and the empty roads. It's a source of small comfort that it feels like the entire world – not just our baby – is in a sleep that feels like death.

I'm a shrivelled silhouette of my former self, just like the trees we pass. Gnarled, bare, devoid of life, clinging on to this baby like a lone leaf I don't want to let go of. I tried so hard to keep him safe, but I failed. I've lost: this life, this luck, this baby, this version of myself.

The contractions are coming every eight minutes now. Rory puts on the radio to break the silence. Radio 1, is, for some inexplicable reason, playing 'Circle of Life' from *The Lion King*. I begin to weep; it's so unusual for the station's playlist that it feels it's being played just for us. For him. Our baby boy who we're about to meet.

Leo. Our little Lion King.

Rory fumbles to switch it off. As he does, I put my hand on the dial to stop him. He looks at me queryingly. I want to hear it. Even though I can't fathom how I'm meant to deliver him and let him go today, I want to listen to this message that feels like it's from the universe to us.

We arrive at the labour ward and are ushered brusquely to the busy waiting room. The same one we were in two days ago. I sit, bewildered, hospital bag on my lap as my contractions intensify. Around me, women huff and pant, all clearly in different stages of labour, all waiting for beds so they can give birth. All appear to be – like me – carrying full term babies. But there's one huge difference.

In the distance, I can hear a baby cry. Then another, and another until all I can hear in my head is crying babies. Blindly, I put my hand out to reach for Rory, but it connects with an empty chair. I hear a raised voice, a tone of uncharacteristic fury. Rory, I note from somewhere inside my brain. Suddenly he's next to me again, ushering me up, with Alice from Spring on the other side. I recognise her voice from the phone calls she has made to us in the past two days.

'I'm so sorry, Sofie,' she sounds appalled. 'You shouldn't be here. The receptionist didn't read your notes. I have a special suite to take you to. It's quiet and private and you can stay there as long as you need. Come with us.' I look up and see there's another young woman by her side that I recognise. My midwife, Sara. I cry out in relief, and pain.

'Take my arm, I've got you,' Sara says. She leads us from the ward, down a corridor and towards another room. 'I'll be here with you, every step of the way, Sofie. And I want you to know we'll do everything we can to make you as comfortable as possible, and to give you as little or as much space as you need. We'll look after you. And your baby boy, too.'

I weep then, at her kindness and because she's talking about him as if he's still alive. As if he's still a part of our family equation. Three units of a sum we'll never be able to make sense of.

$2 + 1 (-1) = ?$

Mine + Us = Minus.

Part II

We find a place for what we lose. Although we know that after such a loss the acute stage of mourning will subside, we also know that we shall remain inconsolable and will never find a substitute. No matter what may fill the gap, even if it be filled completely, it nevertheless remains something else.

Sigmund Freud

Chapter Twenty-Four

It has been an hour since I gave birth to our baby boy. The midwives have just left us alone to have some time together. I look at Rory now, who stares unseeingly back at me. Like me, Rory's a ghost. We have no idea what to do next. Like any new parents we're filled with love and pride for our baby boy. But our baby is dead.

None of the questions I've been asked since Leo arrived have been covered by my birth plan. Instead, we've been given a whole new set:

Are you going to name him?

Would you like to have a post-mortem to find out the cause of death?

Would you like to have footprints and handprints of your baby or a lock of hair, so you can have mementos of him?

Would you like some photos taken?

Would you like to bury or cremate your baby?

Would you like for the hospital to organise a funeral service for you?

I look down at him resting in my arms, wrapped snugly in his blanket, little knitted hat covering his brow. His sweet, round face is the only part of him exposed. The bluish moonlight glow of his skin mirroring the sky beyond the hospital window. I study the spidery veins on the closed crescents of his eyelids; the feathery sprays of sandy lashes that rest peacefully against the soft domed dunes of his cheeks. His gently parted lips are the deep lilac of crocus buds. As I gaze at him, I feel a flood of love far greater, lighter and deeper than the abyss I'm in.

All the fear, pain and distress I felt giving birth to him has gone; the panic I felt at the thought of holding him replaced by a strange calm. I'm with him, and that's all that matters.

The consultant was right. However hard the idea was, delivering him is the best thing I've ever done in my life. He may not have lived, but at least I experienced every moment of his arrival. It feels like the first and last true act of grace, love and sacrifice I'm able to give him as his mother.

I close my eyes. I'm not surprised to find that his face is wrapped behind my eyelids like a shroud. I know that I'll see him there forever.

I open my eyes. I want to commit every part of him to memory while I can. With a shaking finger I stroke the creamy skin of his cheek; it feels cold and waxy to the touch. His wispy, sandy mullet and his skin remind me of Rory, but he's gossamer pale, eyelids almost translucent, too-dark petal lips parted as if preparing to whisper the secrets of the universe to me.

I feel serene, like this is completely normal. I'm a normal mother who has just given birth and is proudly holding her perfect baby. Like any proud new mum, I long to show him off to the world; tell everyone I have a son. But I also want to keep him close, too; to not have to share a moment of him. I know Mum and Nisha are waiting outside – Rory called them to let them know I was in labour – but I need more time for just me. I begin to sing 'Bjornen Sover' softly to him. The Bear is Sleeping. My voice cracks with emotion when I get to the part about there being nothing to be afraid of.

I can feel Rory's nerves pulsate through the air. While I'm gratefully holding our baby, Rory hasn't made a move to hold him – in fact, he's keeping his distance. I want to tell him that cradling Leo like this has made me calmer and more complete than I've ever felt.

'Isn't he handsome?' I smile through my tears as I pull the blanket back a little from Leo's face to show Rory. 'Look, he's strawberry blonde – just like you.'

'And your dad,' Rory says hoarsely. 'He's got his Danish genes.' He stretches his quivering hand towards our boy's head and strokes his sweet, cold face and caresses his well-defined nose. He sobs then, emotion coming in unrelenting waves, head bowed so that his tears fall on to our boy's pale cheeks.

With father and son's heads almost touching, I realise it's not me or Rory I see in his sandy hair or his sturdy shoulders. His sloping brow and proud nose like the curve of a cliff are all my dad.

I'm still holding him when Sara arrives and asks if they can take him so they can do his hand and footprints, lock of hair and photos – all of which we decided we wanted in the minutes after the birth. I couldn't imagine *not* having them. I glance at Rory, fear apparent on my face.

'Don't take him, please! I'm not ready to say goodbye…'

'Don't worry, Sofie,' Sara says gently. 'We'll bring Leo back to you in his CuddleCot.' We must look puzzled because she gently adds. 'It's a refrigerated cot made for special babies like Leo – to keep their bodies cool so parents like you can spend as much time together as you need. You can bathe him, dress him, have visitors. You can stay all night, if you choose.'

Relief floods over me as I hand him over to her. I can do so, now I know I'll see him again.

'I won't be long. Try and get some sleep while we're gone?' The door clicks shut behind her as she wheels Leo away.

Immediately, I feel bereft. Rory stares at the place where Leo was.

'How about a sleep?' Rory croaks at last. His voice is not his own. It's mechanical, robotic. 'You must be exhausted.'

'I don't want to.' I gasp, shake my head, try to breathe, realise I can't. A sob escapes; unrelenting waves of them follow. Rory sobs, too. We sit, holding each other for what feels like forever. I can't explain why, but his presence makes me want to be alone.

When the crying subsides, I speak again.

'I'd like a shower.'

Rory nods. He dutifully gets my washbag and the towel we packed from home. The new dressing gown I bought. He gently guides me to the ensuite. His eyes are red-rimmed, face chalky white. 'Do you want help?'

'No, thanks,' I croak. He must need a moment as much as I do. I shut the door and lean back against it. I look around the small, sterile wet room, slip off my dressing gown and hang it on a hook. I step forward and stare in the bathroom mirror.

I'm deathly pale; charcoal black smears have besieged my eyes. My blotched, streaked skin is an ordnance survey map of trauma. I lower my gaze, stare with detachment at my body. My boobs hang heavy and engorged, red, swollen areolae glaring at me accusingly – finding me guilty of a crime I had no control over. The skin on my stomach is both painfully swollen and unbearably loose. My lower body is stained with blood that I'm strangely reluctant to wash off because it's part of Leo. I'm so far removed from the presentable person I was – the shiny new mum I expected to become. I'm a tarnished replica.

I step into the shower and turn it on. I stand, turning the hot tap further until the water scalds my skin, the water beating against my back, punishing my body for all it has failed to do. I stagger sideways, slide down the tiled wall until I'm on my knees. Then I curl up in a ball as blood from Leo's birth pools around me.

It's here that Rory finds me a few minutes later. Carefully, he wraps me in a towel, picks me up and carries me back into the room, cradling me in his arms like a baby.

Chapter Twenty-Five

We've been in here with Leo for either a minute or an hour, time doesn't mean anything anymore. The room is heavy with love, his familiar weight now transferred from inside my body to my arms. It's hard to believe he isn't just sleeping. My tummy might be empty, but my heart is full when I'm holding him.

There's a knock on the door. When a head peers around it, I find I'm clasping him tightly and protectively to my chest. Even after Sara told us we could stay as long as we like, I'm petrified that someone is about to say I must let him go.

But it's Nisha. Nisha who has always been here when it mattered. She looks like she hasn't slept. Her usually blunt dark bob is dishevelled, her clothes creased. She looks undone.

'Can I come in?' she says. 'Your mum said she was happy for me to come in first. She just needs a moment.'

I nod, grateful to Nisha for being brave enough to be first. She puts her bag down in the corner and comes straight over to the bed, where I'm lying with Leo. I can tell she's trying to hold back her tears as she looks at us.

'Are you going to introduce me to your baby boy?' she says, voice cracking as she puts her hand on my shoulder.

Rory hasn't shared his name. I'm glad.

'Leo,' I croak. My mouth is dry, lips dehydrated after the birth, but I can hide neither the pain nor the pride in my voice. I pull the blanket away from his face a little. 'His name's Leo. Leo Bear King.'

The bear is sleeping.

'He's perfect, Sofie,' she whispers. She turns her face away from me for a moment and I know she's trying to compose herself. Then she puts her arm around my shoulders and drops a kiss on Leo's forehead. Even though I'm crying, I'm so happy that my best friend is meeting my beautiful boy.

'He reminds me of your dad. Leo has his Nordic nose.'

'We thought that, too!' I cry-laugh.

'Shall I take a photo of you, Rory and Leo?' she asks.

Rory and I look at each other and nod in silent agreement. Now he's with us, there's no doubt in our minds. Leo's our son and we want to have a record of these precious moments with him.

'You hold him?' I ask Rory. I've carried Leo for nine months. I want Rory to have this moment.

Rory hesitates as I lift Leo towards him. The veins in his temples pulse, chin quivering as stiffly, he holds his arms out and I tentatively pass Leo over. Slowly, he draws our baby close to his chest. His face softens from tension to love as he strokes Leo's cheek with the curve of his thumb.

Then he's crying and so am I. And Nisha is taking photos and crying, too, and I'm so thankful that she's here because it means Leo will always exist to someone other than us.

When Nisha has finished taking the photos we want – one of us cradling him, then both our lips brushing the sweet slope of his forehead, and Rory's hands cupping his tiny feet, a close-up of his clenched hand – I ask Rory to call Mum in so she can meet her grandson.

Chapter Twenty-Six

The knock is so quiet it's as if it doesn't want to be heard. Rory opens the door and Mum hovers there on the periphery like a reluctant party guest, blinking at the sudden exposure to the bright, white room. Or perhaps, to us. Leo is now back in my arms. Sensing a family moment, Nisha, once again, melts away.

Midge, as ever, is by Mum's side but all I can focus on is Mum. She retreats almost instinctively when she sees Leo and me, her hand reaching for the door handle. Midge gently intercepts her at the elbow. Mum looks at her desperately and they have a silent conversation with their eyes.

You can do this.
I can't. It's too hard.
You can.
I'm afraid.
This isn't about you. This is about Sofie. And Leo.

I want to tell Mum that she needs to be brave, step up and cherish these precious moments, not for me but for herself. Soon, her time with her grandson will be gone. The all-encompassing fear and sorrow in her eyes are clear, and I understand, I do. But I also know it's my job as Leo's mum to stop her from being afraid. To not see a dead baby, but her grandson.

'Mum?' I say gently. 'Come in … please. It's okay.'

She gazes at me desperately, her pain painted on her face.

'It's okay,' I repeat. They're all the words I have.

'Oh, Sofie,' she sobs, without stepping closer. I know she's afraid.

I want to tell her that this part, this I can do easily. This is natural. Cradling my son, loving him, cherishing each precious moment I get to spend holding him. It's what comes next that scares me.

I want to say all that but 'Please?' is all I manage. I don't want to mourn him yet. I know I'll have the rest of my life for that. The only way I'm coping is to stay focused on this moment, the one where Leo is here in my arms. I want her to do the same. To hold her grandchild; be in this moment so she always has a memory of him.

I lift him a little, offer my arms to her, encouraging her to come closer and, for a moment, she does.

But then she shakes her head. Backs away.

'I'm sorry,' she cries. 'I'm so sorry.' And she disappears out of the room.

Midge gazes at me from her position by the door, her neat brows are curled upwards in empathy like an anchor. She steps towards me quickly, kisses me lightly on the forehead and tenderly strokes Leo's cheek.

'Your mum will be back,' she promises, her voice cracking a little. Then she turns and follows her out of the door.

Chapter Twenty-Seven

I must have napped briefly. I come to, drowsy and disorientated, to the sound of the door opening.

'Leo?' I cry out. I go to sit up, but I'm in so much pain I lie back down again. I vaguely remember Sara coming to take my blood pressure and being so sleepy that she gently took him from my arms, put him back in his cot and told me to try and sleep. I've barely had a wink since we first came to the hospital two days ago.

I feel a flood of relief to see him lying there. I begin to cry great racking sobs of distress, only pausing when I realise I'm being cradled like a baby myself.

'M-mu-mum,' I say, hiccupping through my sobs.

'Shh, there now.' She presses me close to her, the familiar earthy scent of her perfume suddenly under my nose.

I look over her shoulder and I see Rory by the door and just behind him, hovering in the corridor, Midge. I know Mum's here because of her. I blink in silent thanks and Midge presses her fingers to her lips then out towards me. Then she retreats and Rory slips away, too, so Mum and I are left alone.

'Sofie,' Mum says, her voice thick, her arms holding me tight. She kisses my forehead, her tears mixing with mine and rests me back against the pillow, stroking my brow like she used to when I was a child and then as teenager after dad died. She kisses me again then, hesitantly, she walks over to Leo's cot.

'He looks just like you, Sofie.'

'And Dad,' I rasp.

She inhales and lets out a soft, pained sigh.

'He does. May I?' she asks tentatively, holding out her hands as she leans over his crib.

I desperately want him in my arms too, but restrain myself so she can have her moment.

She settles herself down in the chair by the window with Leo and starts singing the same Danish lullaby as I did, transforming in front of my eyes from the mum she's always been to the grandma she was meant to be.

When her last note has disappeared into the ether, she stands up and walks over and carefully hands him to me. Our arms meet and we hover in the passing position so that, momentarily, we're holding Leo together. It's then that I feel the tie between us strengthen, tighten and knot even more firmly in place.

'Mum,' I cry, and she holds me as I hold him.

'My beautiful, brave girl. He's perfect and I'm so proud of you. And I'm so sorry,' she whispers. 'I'm so, so sorry.'

We stay like that for I don't know how long, clinging to each other for comfort but also as if clinging to life itself.

Chapter Twenty-Eight

Rory and I are curled up in the hospital bed together. The pillow is wet with tears. The usual maternity-ward noise is audible from outside: hurried footsteps and chatter of busy staff, the rattle of trollies being wheeled past, machines bleeping. I swear I can hear a baby cry close by. Maybe it's just the echo of Leo's, somewhere in the ether.

To anyone looking through the window of our suite, Rory and I could be any new parents lying next to our sleeping newborn. They wouldn't know he was dead. I almost don't believe it myself, he looks so peaceful, lying here next to us. The thought of him spending the nights ahead alone in the hospital mortuary is unbearable.

I don't sleep. I spend each precious hour of the night watching over my son, while I still can. Just as dawn breaks, sensing that the little time I have is running out, I ease myself out of bed leaving Rory curled up like a baby himself. Then I carefully lift Leo out of the cot and sit in the chair cradling him as I watch the sun rise out of the small hospital window, casting a weak, wintry yellow light over my baby boy.

It's the beginning of a new day, one that will end without my baby in my arms. Despite all we've just been through, I know it'll be the hardest day of our life. And then comes tomorrow. And the day after that…

Chapter Twenty-Nine

Day three. Home. I stare up, counting the bumps in the Artex ceiling above our bed. 'Get ceiling replastered' was one of the house jobs I was annoyed I didn't get round to during my manic, pregnancy nesting. I hate myself for having cared about such trivial things, when all I needed to do was focus on keeping our baby alive.

Leaving Leo at the hospital was the hardest, most unnatural thing I've ever done. Having him, holding him, loving him and then leaving him there on that bitterly cold, bleak February morning was a loss even more unbearable than delivering him.

I haven't left our bedroom since we've come home, other than to go to the bathroom. Doing so involves walking past Leo's nursery.

I glance out of the balcony doors at the magnolia tree in our front garden which, in spring, will burst into glorious bloom. Before Leo, I used to throw these doors open each morning so that I could hear the seagulls, see the small rectangle of glistening sea in the distance. Now, they're shut tight. This room is a vacuum of grief in which Rory and I have been encased for days.

Since Leo died, time stretches, yawns, screams, cries. Every day it swallows me in its greedy, gaping jaws, spitting me out the next morning only to consume me again over the next few hours. Each Groundhog Day of Grief is the same as the next and yet different from any day that has ever come before. Strange to think that out

This Wasn't Meant to Happen

there in the world people are still busy doing their daily tasks. While I'm lying here, useless, leaden, broken.

I glance down. The once crisp, freshly laundered white sheets are crumpled, stained with sweat and blood on my side. I need Rory to change them again, as he's had to do each day since I came back from hospital.

Where is he? I feel the anxiety rise at his absence. I can't be on my own. I need him with me. To stop me from drowning in this grief.

Looking at the clock I see it's almost 11am. 'Before', I'd have been in a meeting with sales leaders, then back to my desk and a stack of assessments. My day was always broken down into predictable hourly or half-hourly increments. I knew what to expect of every single one.

Now, the hours swell and melt, brain consumed only with thoughts of my baby, senses overwhelmed, energy expended just with the simple act of being alive. My body won't stop serving up post-partum hormones that wake me in the night; make me want to eat ravenously and pee continuously, as painful as that still is. This along with the post-birth constipation has made me petrified of going to the toilet.

Everything hurts, inside and out. My eyelids sting so much I close them, but when I do, I see Leo's limp, lifeless body. My heart feels like it resides on the outside of the body – beating still – but exposed, vulnerable. My stomach is a soft, sad, painful pouch that's a constant reminder of my baby boy who less than a week ago lived and died within me. Inside, I'm swollen, sore. Tight corkscrews of pain like mini contractions punish me mercilessly; there are even moments where I think I can still feel him move inside me. My boobs are rock-solid (my milk coming in was a shock that happened yesterday). The final act of indignity, grief and degradation is my body's refusal to accept that my baby is gone.

I'm a sleeping, walking, weeping mess of fluid that seeps from every orifice. I feel like I'm made up of liquid fractions rather than a whole: one quarter blood, one quarter milk, two quarters tears. Sometimes, in my fitful hours of sleep, I have such vivid dreams of Leo that I wake up believing he's still here. I dreamt that, like *Alice in Wonderland*, I'd cried so many tears that I was drowning in a river of my making. Except in my version, I was in a place called *Wondering*

Land, sucked into a whirlpool of 'how?' and 'why?' before being spat out into a sea of breast milk, drowning in the very thing my body produced to keep my baby alive.

I thrash my hands against the mattress, my head against the pillow and cry silently into it. Where's Rory? I feel bereft without him; like the tsunami that hit us both has swept me away and he's somewhere far from me, on dry land.

'Sofie? Sofie, hey, shh … I'm here. I was just cleaning the bathroom.'

He slides back into bed. I cling to him, the words registering. I've never known him to clean, ever. His domestic skills involve telling me to get a cleaner.

He curls his arms around me. 'It's okay. I'm here. I'm not going anywhere. It's okay.'

I stare at him, then close my eyes.

It's not, I want to say. *It won't ever be okay again.* But I don't because I can't speak. I'm numb. Null. Void. An erased version of the woman I used to be. A mother without her baby.

Chapter Thirty

Day Five. I stare at the ceiling. I have no idea how many minutes or hours have passed, only that they have. The bed suddenly feels like a vast vessel that I'm sailing in alone and that might capsize at any moment. I feel Rory's absence in this bed now as keenly as Leo's absence from my belly.

From the moment he came to the hospital, Rory and I have been inseparable. We've laid, curled together; conjoined in our grief just like we did in the hospital bereavement suite. Our world entirely removed from anyone else's. On pause. Stopped.

And yet *he* hasn't stopped. As well as dealing with his own grief, he's been looking after me. He's the one who gets up when I need to eat or drink. He takes me to the bathroom. Changes the sheets: I hear the washing machine going almost constantly on a spin cycle just like the images of Leo in my head. Rory has stayed by my side whilst continuing to do the necessary daily tasks: telling his boss, answering calls from the hospital, ordering a food shop, paying bills, cooking dinner, doing the dishwasher. All I have done is lie here. Silent. Numb. MIA.

Missing in Action. Mother In-Active.

All day, I stare at the ceiling silently, lie limply in his arms, or listlessly watch daytime TV gameshows – the only genre of programme guaranteed to not feature death, hospitals or babies. I realised this after foolishly watching daytime TV on my second day home, only to find that the day's main discussion on a lunchtime magazine show was a US celebrity's stillbirth. At least I know I'm safe with *Tipping Point*, or *Countdown*. Not that I'm even watching them really: all I see when I stare at the flickering TV screen is my internal TV show – Leo bouncing around in my tummy during the scans, holding him in my arms, on my chest. And, then the last shots before the credits roll, Leo in the cold cot, wrapped in his yellow blanket, knitted hat sitting snugly on his head.

Meanwhile, Rory has fielded calls from the bereavement counsellor, from my mum, his gran and Nisha. They're still the only people – other than Rory's work – that we've told. I know Sandra wants to come visit, but I can't face her just yet. She's very … forthright. Thankfully Rory has put her off for now.

Somehow, Rory has been able to anticipate my every want or need without me saying a word. He's had to, I guess. I've barely spoken since we got back from hospital. It seems I haven't just lost my baby, but my voice, too. And myself. I feel like a half-folded bit of origami made by an enthusiastic amateur but abandoned before it's properly finished. A shape that once had a purpose, now a crumpled mess.

I glance across at the space next to me, the sheets smooth on his side, pillows uncharacteristically plumped by him – and with seeming finality. This morning, Mum rang Rory and told him she was going to leave Midge in charge of the café and would be coming to stay with us for a few days. I could hear the relief in Rory's voice as he gratefully accepted her help. She said she was already on her way.

When he got off the phone, he was unrecognisably efficient. He collected all the mugs from our room, and when I protested, firmly but kindly told me he had to get up and start dealing with life again. I begged him not to, cried even as he pulled on his clothes. He stroked my head, said it was time for him to handle the reality of what had happened, not hide from it. He added that there were things he needed to do. 'For Leo.'

I wanted to say surely the only 'thing' we needed to do was work out how to go back in time and stop our baby from dying. I also wanted to add, '*and FYI, Rory, I'm not hiding. You can't hide from something you're actually in.*' But I didn't. I just turned my head and stared at the wall.

Perhaps it doesn't matter that he's not here. I'm not here either. Not really. I'm drowning deeply in my memories; living and reliving the horror of the last few days.

It doesn't matter if I'm asleep, staring at the ceiling, the walls or the TV; I'm constantly submerged in every single moment that led me here; trying to work out how this happened.

Sometimes I go back further. I see snapshots of my pregnancy, from the shock and instant overwhelming anxiety I felt the moment I saw the two lines on the pregnancy test, to my scans, baby shower and beyond. I gasp as if winded and sob into my fist. My brain let him down long before my body did. Now he'll never know how much I love him.

I fast forward, to all the other ways I might have failed him. Did the nuchal cord get wrapped around his neck because of a position I slept in? What if I forced him to move when he didn't want to with those little nudges I gave him? I vividly remember the feeling of pressing my hand to my belly as I pushed against his foot, or elbow, or knee, or bottom and waited for his response.

Come on, champ, I'd laugh. *You can do better than that!*

I hold my empty tummy and writhe with agony at that memory now.

I lean my head back on the pillow and look at the ceiling. Even if I didn't actively cause him to get tangled with the umbilical cord, then my lack of attention at the end didn't help him. What if I'd alerted the hospital sooner? Could they have saved him?

I rewind, replaying that entire day differently. Waking up, trying to engage with Leo, realising quickly he wasn't responding, getting straight in the car and driving to the hospital, calling Nisha on route to say that I was sorry, I couldn't make lunch. Her meeting me at the hospital instead. The consultant saying something like: 'The baby is experiencing reduced movement, but there's still a heartbeat. We need to get you to surgery as soon as possible and get this baby out!' Then all action emergency stations like something from *Grey's Anatomy* before he is born, the cord untangled. His little life saved.

I can see it all in an alternative universe out of my reach. Gone, just like him.

I only realise I'm wailing when Rory comes in the room and gathers me in his arms.

'Hey, Sofie. Shh, it's okay, I'm here, it's okay…'

'But … it's … not … is … it … Rory?' I manage this series of staccato words just about through my dry heaves and death rattle gasps, infuriated by him trying to sugar-coat this horror. 'It's not okay and it won't ever be again.' I push him away, turn over and bury myself in the pillow and duvet. I know I'm being unfair; I know we're in this together and he's hurting, too. But in this moment, as much as I blame myself, I also blame him. The truth is, I just don't trust his judgement anymore.

Chapter Thirty-One

As I lie in bed, staring listlessly at the chips of paint on the wall, I can hear Rory pacing the hallway downstairs. He's having another muffled conversation on the phone. It can only be Mum, Nisha, or Sandra. He's under strict instructions to not tell anyone else. I'm not ready. Once the news is out in public, we'll have to share Leo. Then, he'll become something other than my beautiful baby boy. Something tragic, ugly even.

It takes me a moment to realise Rory's on the phone with the hospital. One of the many incredibly hard decisions we had to make in the hours after I delivered our son was whether to have a post-mortem to get an official cause of death. We were told it could take up to twelve weeks to get the results, and that even then it might be inconclusive. As far as we're concerned, we have a valid cause of his death ('nuchal-cord asphyxiation') confirmed upon his delivery. Whilst a post-mortem might uncover other issues, it's unlikely. Up until that day, in my thirty-ninth week, I'd had a healthy pregnancy. There were no other problems.

Of course, another reason to have a post-mortem would be to identify any issues in future pregnancies, but as I can't contemplate that, the decision was simple for me. Rory was torn, but ultimately didn't want to delay putting Leo to rest either. The hospital said they'd organise the cremation, I'm sure that's why they're ringing. But

I'm not ready. I can't make any more impossible decisions about our baby.

Downstairs, I hear Rory turn on the hoover in preparation for my mum's arrival – joining the dishwasher and washing machine he seems to have constantly on the go. I'm sure I heard him out in the garden with the leaf blower earlier. Another way in which our lives have been upended since Leo died is this role reversal of ours. Now, it staggers me that I was ever concerned with such arbitrary things: how can orderliness, tidiness, cleanliness ever be made from the mess that is our lives now? Wouldn't it be better if, just as we must accept our baby's death, we accept the unfathomable fucking mess that is life?

If I could find it within myself to get out of bed, I'd break every plate, cup, glass, ornament, every single *thing* we own, so it needn't be tidied or dusted or washed or dried again. Just like my baby will never be bathed or dried. *Everything* should be as ephemeral as his life was. We can eat off paper plates and throw them away. Live in an empty house. It's what we're going to do now, anyway. Now our baby has died.

The light has grown dim. It must be late afternoon as I can hear children from the local school, their laughter and chatter taunting me. From my submerged fugue of grief, I can hear the doorbell ring. I immediately panic. Mum couldn't get here that quickly, and we're not expecting anyone else.

I hear the click and creak of the front door and immediately cower under the covers at the sound of a loud, unfamiliar, *cheery* voice.

'Hello there! I'm Janine. You must be Dad? I'm here to see how baby and Mum are doing?'

I sit up quickly and wince, both at the pain of the simple movement and the presumptive words that slice through my insides like a knife.

In response, Rory's hushed voice, sterner than I've ever heard him. I can't make out exactly what he's saying, but the hurried, high-pitched hum of a chastened apology from the stranger is enough for me to know he's told her our baby died.

It goes quiet. I hear more murmured talk and then the soft click of the door being shut. I presume Rory has done his job. Sent whoever it was away. I pull back the covers feeling sick with relief. A moment later Rory's head appears floating around the door, his face tight with anxiety.

'Sofie, I've got the community midwife downstairs. She needs to examine you, check your stitches.' I shake my head desperately. He comes and sits on the edge of the bed and takes my limp hand. 'It's just a quick visit; we need to be sure that you're healing properly.'

Another trauma of the birth is that I needed an episiotomy to help get Leo out. It feels symbolic really. I've literally been torn apart by his death.

I nod, almost imperceptibly. Visibly relieved, Rory helps me sit up in bed, then he disappears for a few minutes before he gestures her in with a curt command, rather than a welcome.

She is small, in her mid-sixties, with a pinched face and small beady eyes. She says hello almost patronisingly kindly, tells me how sorry she is without making eye contact. I stare beyond her vacantly as she goes through her list of medical questions, nodding or shaking my head at appropriate moments. I weep silently as she examines me.

Once she's ticked everything off her list, she leaves. I turn on to my side slowly, feeling the now familiar rush of blood in my giant post-birth pants. Even though I want to hide back under the covers, I have to change my maternity pad. I call for Rory, but no sound comes out.

Rory comes back up after seeing her out. He sits on the edge of the bed, smooths the duvet down with his hands, subconsciously rearranging the toppling tower of books on his bedside table into a neat pile, before scooping them into his arms and trying to hide their covers. But I know them off by heart, having seen them there every day for seven months. *What to Expect When You're Expecting. Pregnancy, Birth and Beyond. The Positive Birth Book.* Oh, how I long to throw them all across the room.

'I told her to read her notes next time she does a home visit.' Rory rubs his head then his eyes, visibly distressed.

'I think I'll have a shower,' I croak, my voice sounding like fingernails against sandpaper, so rarely have I spoken these past few days.

'Okay,' he says looking up. I know he's surprised that I've shown an interest in getting out of bed. 'Perhaps you could come downstairs after?' he adds hopefully. 'I could set you up on the sofa in the lounge?' He puts the books outside the bedroom door, unhooks my dressing gown and slips it over my arms. I bought it to wear in hospital after having Leo. It was meant to keep me warm during night-feeds at home. I start crying again. He looks bewildered; I know he's wondering what he's done wrong. The answer is nothing.

Still weeping, I take Rory's arm and shuffle slowly towards the bathroom, deliberately turning my back on the nursery that looms to the left.

'Do you want me to come in with you? I could wash your hair, massage your back?' He strokes me tenderly on the shoulder. I immediately stiffen.

The last thing I want is to be touched. I don't want kindness. I don't deserve it.

'No, thank you,' I say politely. As I shut the bathroom door, his drawn and anguished face disappears. And I'm relieved.

When I make my way back to the bedroom, the books are gone.

Chapter Thirty-Two

I wake with a gasp from a half-sleep. Same day or a different one? I was having a dream. A dream of a different day. A different life. A happier one. I was on a beach, basking in sunshine and happiness with Rory. There was a baby, but he got swept away by the sea. I can't keep him, even in my dreams. I clutch my tummy and look out the window. I see a rainbow – a fleeting one. I turn away. There's no pot of gold at the end.

I curl into the foetal position, arms and duvet wrapped around myself. My sleep pattern – once variable at the best of times – now consists of falling into a deep coma at 8pm and not waking for at least twelve hours. It's a sleep that is almost like a death. In many ways, I'd prefer to *not* sleep. Part of me is scared that when I go to bed I might not wake up.

Or is it more that I'm scared I don't want to?

I blink as a knock on the door reverberates in my brain like a drill. I look up at the ceiling and wait for Rory to come in.

Mum appears, face etched with grief and worry. She must have arrived when I was asleep. I want to cry with the guilt of taking her back to 'Grieving Daughter in Bedroom' mode. A state she's all too familiar with. She's holding a cup of tea and wearing an apron and slippers – her role as matriarch, housemaid and cleaner immediately cast. I feel a sudden wave of jealousy because my role is unclassified.

I'm a mother without her baby. There's no title, no job description that exists for that.

She sits on the edge of the bed, strokes my forehead gently, which again makes me want to cry. I want to speak too, but I can't. I don't know what to say. Sorry, mostly.

I lean back against the pillows, and she slides up on the bed next to me without saying a word. Stiffly, I allow her to hold me again, just like she did in the hospital. Even though I can't help but ache for my own baby, I find comfort in this moment: it's just me and Mum once more.

She begins humming, rocking a little as she holds me. It's the Danish lullaby we both sang to Leo in hospital. Hearing it somehow soothes me and makes me feel close to Leo and to Mum and to Dad. An invisible thread that ties us all forever. Tears fall on to my cheeks and it takes a moment for me to realise that they're not mine.

'I'm sorry,' I sob, then.

'This isn't your fault, Sofie,' she says, her voice querulous with emotion.

Whose is it, then? Who else can I blame?

We sit there for a while together. Eventually, I sink down under the duvet and she tucks me in, and even though I feel like I'll never sleep again, my eyelids grow heavy; my useless body becomes limp.

In my sleep, I dream of Leo.

I know I always will.

Chapter Thirty-Three

My bedside alarm clock is a blur of neon numbers in the darkness, like motorway floodlights on a wet windscreen.

It's 5.47pm. I slowly edge my legs out of bed. Downstairs, the clink and clatter of the dishwasher being emptied, again, cupboards opened and shut. The same hushed but urgent tones, now louder as along with Mum and Rory, I can hear Nisha's voice, too. She must've arrived when I was asleep.

I need the toilet. I shuffle out into the hallway and stare at the nursery. I try to imagine going inside. Just the sight of the door makes me dizzy with grief. How can the room be there but not him?

I make it to the bathroom. Stare at another wall while I pee. A mixture of blood and urine and clots expelled, I pull the chain. Replace my pad. Shuffle back to bed, eyes averted from the nursery as I pass.

My phone on the bedside table pings urgently; it's lit up with messages and notifications. I know what they all say. There has been a constant flow these past few days. As far as our friends are concerned, I'm fast approaching my due date: 'Any news?' 'Time for a curry?' 'Get on the Pineapple Express!'

My phone pings twice more and I want to throw it against the wall. I know I should feel grateful that so many people care about us enough to check in, but each thoughtful, enquiring message is like a dagger to my heart.

Only my uni friends' WhatsApp group has remained silent. I know Nisha has told them. I know because they have all messaged me individually today to share their shock, their sorrow, their condolences. I have yet to reply to any of them. I will, but right now I just don't have the words.

I sit up, lean over and watch as another message appears, grimly fixated on the ever-growing collection of unopened WhatsApps and texts, like backed-up cars in a traffic jam. My eyes fall upon a particular chat group: 'Feb Yoga Babies'. This thread has been particularly active over the past couple of weeks as we shared our fears and excitement for reaching our birth month – and started celebrating the babies who have already been born. There was just three of us remaining, waiting to give birth. I will be waiting forever, now.

I stare at the message for a moment, the words blurring. I can't read it. I just can't. Immediately, the phone pings again and again. I don't have to open the messages to know what they say.

For a moment, I consider making my announcement. Get it over with. After all, at some point, these blissed-out new mums are going to be forced to witness the aftermath of our car crash. But not yet.

I pick up my phone, click on the group and scroll back past the proliferation of excited 'Congratulations!' to the announcement itself.

> We're so happy to announce the arrival of Ivy Josephine, born this morning at 12:07am and weighing 7lbs 8oz. We're completely in love and can't wait for you to meet her!

The announcement is accompanied by the classic trio of new baby photos: newborn baby resting on Mum's chest, who is gazing adoringly down at her. A pair of tiny feet nestled in Dad's hands. And finally, the new parents sat up together on the bed, beaming as they present their baby. The same photos Nisha took of Rory and me except … spot the difference.

I study them for longer than necessary as if to punish myself. Then, I lob the phone with all my strength at the chest of drawers in the corner, causing a collection of framed photos from our wedding day to topple, crash, crack.

I hear Rory coming up the stairs again, taking them two at a time.

'Sofie, are you all right? What happened?' He's panting, breathless, his face red and panicked, shaggy hair plastered against his forehead – so different from his on-screen news reporter quiff that it makes me want to cry. Is he coming undone, too? He takes in the phone on the floor, the broken photo frames, shards of glass.

My phone screen is also smashed and splintered.

'I want him, Rory,' I manage through my gasps. 'I want Leo.' I wail then – a banshee-like sound that is animalistic, primal and that comes from the very core of me. Rory wraps me in his arms like he'll never let me go.

'I know,' he says, his voice low and soothing. 'I know. We need to tell people.' He says decisively, rocking me gently. 'You'll feel better once it's out in the open.'

I shake my head, angry that he's suggesting anything could possibly make me feel better. Doesn't he realise what'll happen once everyone knows? Didn't it happen to him when his mum left, just like it did when my dad died? The onslaught of over-interested attention; the constant invasion of our grief for gossip; that public pity only serving to make my pain worse.

I stare out of the window to the blackness beyond, remembering how Dad's death was all over the local news. Our roles as Tragic Widow and her Daughter were thrown at us; subsequently avoided and gawped at by our community in equal measure.

In life, Dad had always been an integral part of the landscape and community, but by falling from those cliffs he became fossilised in death, too. He saved lives himself, in his role as volunteer for the RNLI. Ironically, he'd often be called to help with cliff rescues. It helped that their station was next to the café on Peveril Point. It was a small comfort to us that it was his RNLI friends who recovered his body when he slipped from the cliffs near Durdle Door. But it also made me aware of how easily a rescuer can become a victim.

So, what I *want* to say to Rory is, no, it won't make me feel better. Telling people will make us Bad News personified – especially with Rory being a locally famous news reporter.

I don't want to open condolence cards where, *I'm so sorry this happened to you*, will turn into, *I'm so glad this didn't happen to me*, by my grief-stricken brain.

I don't want my memories of Leo's birth to be pulled apart and reconfigured in other people's eyes as something ugly, when there was so much beauty in it that I can't begin to convey. How can we possibly articulate the immense pain, pride, trauma, gratitude, sorrow, loss and love Rory and I felt that day? The infinite love that now defines our loss.

'Sofie?' I look at Rory and realise he's still waiting for my answer. 'We have to tell people. I can't keep avoiding our friends and family. They deserve to know. It'll help, I promise.'

I almost envy his naivety.

'I'm not ready, Rory.'

'Okay,' he expels the word as a gentle sigh and gets up off the bed. 'I'm going to make some tea.' He kisses me before he leaves the room and in that kiss I can feel the heaviness of all he's carrying in it, see the weight pressing down on his shoulders and the guilt on mine. I have done this to him.

'Nisha's downstairs,' Rory says, turning back. 'Can I send her up?'

I nod in acquiescence.

That, I do want.

Chapter Thirty-Four

Nisha is tucked neatly up in my bed next to me. Her black hair fanned out perfectly on the pillow, arms folded across the smooth flat of the duvet. We're both staring at the ceiling. In the room. The hole. Once again. She's been here before with me, after Dad died.

I can't remember a time when Nisha wasn't next to me, when I needed her. She was there after Dad died and I didn't know who I was meant to be anymore. It was Nisha who'd stopped me hanging out with the wrong crowd up at Corfe Castle. She was the one who encouraged me to go back to school. To go to counselling. To focus my mind on my studies.

I can't believe I'm back here, again. Without my dad. And now, without my baby, too.

She's bought a stack of sudoku books with her, and a chess set which remains unopened. I have no strategy for moving forward right now.

I have no one to blame but myself. It *is* my fault. It must be: not only did my body fail our baby, but my brain and my heart did, too. I can't forget that when I took that pregnancy test, I wasn't sure if I wanted Leo. That will stay with me forever.

In the silence, Nisha reaches over and takes my hand. 'It's not your fault, Sofie,' she says softly. 'It's not your fault.'

She gets her bag, pulls something out and tentatively gives it to me. It's the photo she took of me, Rory and Leo at the hospital, in a little mother-of-pearl frame. I cry so much when I look at it that she tries to take it away again. But I cling on tightly.

'I'm sorry,' she says gently. 'Let's put this away for now shall we, Sof?'

I shake my head, press it against my chest.

I want to tell her it's the most beautiful present she could have given me, but I don't have the words.

Then, she opens her bag and brings out a bottle of white wine that I don't want and a family pack of giant chocolate buttons that I do. I eat every single last one. One after another. I count them as I swallow. Twelve, thirteen, fourteen, fifteen… Each consecutive one claggier, harder to swallow. But I can't stop.

Nisha lets me sob on her shoulder like I've done so many times before. She doesn't even mind when I get a mix of tears and chocolate dribble on her beautiful, emerald-green silk top. I try and rub it off with my hand and only succeed in making it worse. I let out a strangulated laugh, which causes a bubble of snot to shoot out of my nose. I immediately feel guilty. How can I possibly laugh at anything ever again?

I don't know how she can be here, when she should be in London. When I ask, she says she's taken some extended holiday.

'Worst holiday ever,' I manage.

'I want to be here, Sofie. I'll be here as long as you need me.'

She turns on the TV and we watch *8 out of 10 Cats do Countdown* and even though she's highly competitive and the only person I know who can ever do the maths round faster than me, I work it out first.

'I must really be in a bad way,' I say hoarsely, 'if you're sacrificing a win out of sympathy.'

'It wouldn't be a pity party without me indulging the patient a little.' She turns the TV off and rolls over in bed to face me.

'You know, I told the uni girls yesterday? They were so worried after you called me when I was with them, they knew something was wrong. They want to see you.'

'I'm not ready.' I'm glad she's told them, so I don't have to but that's enough for now.

This Wasn't Meant to Happen

She adjusts her head on the pillow, flattens her hair underneath her ear. Neat and tidy, tidy and neat, I think. Sita and Mum named us Little Miss Neat and Little Miss Tidy when they visited us at our unusually spick and span student flat in Southampton. Now, I'm more Little Miss Big Old Mess.

'I know you've been getting lots of messages wanting to know how you are. So has Rory.'

'Has he put you up to this?' I slide down in bed on my back, fold my arms across my stomach protectively.

'He may have said that it was proving tricky to field the daily enquiries,' she replies, leaning up on one elbow. 'He needs some support, Sofie. He can't do this on his own. You have to tell people eventually, why not now?'

'It's too soon.' My throat throbs at the thought, a cold hand clenches my heart until I can't breathe with the pain.

3.1415926535...

Five days. The last time I was asked to do something unimaginably awful. Only five days. Give birth to my dead baby. Then name him. Then hold him. Then say goodbye to him. Next comes choosing when to cremate him. Horror after horror.

897932384...

'You can't stay in this limbo forever, Sofie.'

Forever? Try not even a week! I turn and look at the wall.

'Hiding from the world is only a short-term solution. You know that,' she says gently. 'And it would release some of the burden from Rory...'

She pauses, lets those words settle.

Burden? Is that what I am? I listen to the rain drumming on the window outside like impatient fingernails. The last thing I want is to inflict more pain on Rory.

I close my eyes and pretend to go to sleep. I hear her slip out of bed quietly. Go downstairs. Hear the murmur of concerned voices. The front door opening and closing. As soon as she's gone, I go into the bathroom and throw up, acrid bile mixed with watery chocolate until my throat burns and tears stream down my face.

Chapter Thirty-Five

It's 5am. Unusually, I've woken up early. Rory is already out of bed. Or perhaps he was never in it. While sleep is like death for me, it seems to be completely unattainable to him.

I want to find him, but that involves leaving the bedroom. He must be upstairs in his attic office. I know he goes up there: I hear him, climbing the stairs as if somehow needing to be further from me. Sometimes I hear the whir of the rowing machine. Other times it's eerily quiet. I wonder what he's doing but don't have the energy to investigate.

I pick up the sudoku book that Nisha brought round. I find the simple act of placing numbers in the boxes cathartic, temporarily preventing my brain ricocheting madly with guilty, grief-ridden thoughts and paralysing pregnancy memories. I like that there's a place for each number; a small sense of calm and order regained by putting each unit in the right place. Everything boxed up neatly.

As I pencil in the last digit the temporary bliss disappears, in its place comes abject guilt. How could I think of anything other than him?

I stare at that final number. Three. The magic number: the number our family should be now. The first number in the sequence of Pi.

But there is no order, no sequence, no rule for this.

I tear out the page then and rip the finished puzzle into tiny pieces. I throw the book across the room.

I stare at the wall for a moment and will myself to move. I can't stay here forever. I want Rory. I want to be with him.

I slide out of bed, gasping as my feet press against the cold floorboards. I shiver and pull my dressing gown on. I make my way around the bed and open the door. The corridor is dark, but there's a slither of light coming from the nursery.

I stand still, feet frozen, body pulled towards the light, drawn to it but fearful of it, too.

How can I enter the room that we decorated with so much love, excitement and hope? A room that just a week ago held the promise of the lifetime of days and nights we'd have with our baby. I don't want to see the collection of little soft toys we chose for Leo – now missing the one toy I wish we still had. The small cuddly lion with impossibly soft fur that Rory bought from the hospital shop on the day he was born. Leaving it there with Leo at the hospital was far worse than the moment – just thirty-six hours earlier – when they told us he'd died. At least then when we went home, our baby was still with us. Part of me.

I don't want to see the carefully chosen classic books I'd lovingly placed on his shelves. *Guess How Much I love You. Peepo. Lost and Found.*

Once upon a time, when I briefly believed in a happy ending, I couldn't wait to read these to my baby.

I don't want to go in, but Rory is there and suddenly, more than anything, I want to be with him. I *need* us to be in the room together, like we were in hospital and when we first came back home. I don't want to be alone anymore.

I open the door and to my surprise, rather than descending into darkness it feels like stepping into heaven. The room is bathed in warm, buttery light from the night light reflecting off the pale-yellow walls into the still-dark morning. Whilst my feet sink into the Berber rug which feels like a cloud, the boot of grief on my chest presses down heavily when I see Rory fast asleep on the floor clutching the quilt my mum gave me at my baby shower.

I look around and realise that the room has changed since before Leo was born. On the wall over the nursing chair now is a framed print of a lion with a pale orange mane that I've never seen before. Underneath it says: 'L is for Leo' and his birth date. Rory must have ordered it after we came back from hospital and hung it up without me knowing.

I tiptoe softly over to the cot as I spot something else. Stifling a sob, I lean over and pick up the lion – the same one we left with Leo.

I hold it against my chest and suddenly flashback to leaning over Leo's hospital cot that night, watching our baby boy whilst Rory dozed, trying to commit every part of him to memory. When Rory eventually woke up, he disappeared out of the room to get some coffee. I was upset at the time. I didn't want him to leave Leo for a second and it felt like he was gone for ages. When he eventually came back, he was clutching a little toy lion. He came over to me, to the cot and gazed down at Leo.

'I bought it from the shop to take with us, to remember him. But now I think I want him to have something to cuddle when we're not here. I don't want him to be alone in the mortuary, Sof. I don't want to leave him alone.'

Then he'd sat on the bed and, cuddling the lion to his chest, he'd cried.

We'd tucked it into Leo's little cot with him before we left the room. Left him behind in the hospital forever.

Rory must have bought another one, especially for Leo's room.

The love I feel for my husband in that moment, for all the little things he's done since Leo died, is tinged with a deep shame that I've neglected him. As well as losing his son, Rory has now faced the Worst Possible Outcome and had his own belief system destroyed, too. And yet he continues to give me and Leo all his care, thought and love.

I look at my sleeping husband just as he shifts, tilts his head the other way, hair flopping down over one eye. Quietly, I sit next to him and gently nudge his knee with my hand. Rory opens his eyes.

'Sofie?' he blinks and shifts, immediately sitting up, rubbing his face, brushing back his hair – physically pulling himself together for my benefit. 'Are you okay?'

'What are you doing in here?'

'I wanted to be near him,' Rory says simply. 'You?'

This Wasn't Meant to Happen

'I want to be with him too,' I say. 'With both of you.' I lie down facing him, curling my arms around his body and he pulls the tiny quilt over our arms.

'I love you, Rory,' I whisper. But he's dozed off again. I stay, lying there, pressed up against him and staring at the face that used to shine with positivity, but which has paled and aged in the past few days. His eyebrows, even in repose, are pulled together in pain.

I watch him – just as I watched our baby – until dawn breaks and the sun sends an unexpected shaft of spring-like light into the room.

'Let's tell people,' I say softly to Rory as he opens his eyes. 'I want to tell people about our boy.'

Chapter Thirty-Six

Lunchtime. Bed. Rory's downstairs, texting people, as he's been doing all morning.

I close my eyes, turn up the volume on the TV to drown out the noise of my brain but the doorbell rings loudly – an alarm in my head.

Wah wah wah! Danger! Imposter! Pull up the drawbridge. Fire the cannons.

I want the world to know that my boy arrived. That I'm a mother. But I'm a mother who is without her baby and who, honestly, just wants to be left alone.

My ears strain to hear voices. I'm grimly intrigued to know who's first in the queue at the Circus of Grief.

'*Roll up roll up everybody,*' I long to shout. '*Come into the House of Horrors! Witness the Incredible Lactating Lady who gave birth to a dead baby, but whose body still thinks her boy is alive!*' Carefully, I swing my legs over the bed and strain to hear the conversation Rory's having at the front door. But it's too muffled. I get out of bed and shuffle slowly to the landing. I lean over the banisters at the top of the stairs.

It's Sandra, Rory's gran. Rory has folded himself into her arms, finally getting support, rather than giving it, I suppose. I can see the pram has gone from the hallway, packed away, no doubt, with the other baby items we bought. Fleetingly, I wonder where he's put them. In the garage, gathering cobwebs? Has he sold them? Taken them to a charity shop?

I tentatively descend a few stairs, but the last one creaks loudly. I freeze and stare down as Sandra looks directly up. Black spots appear in front of my eyes. I wobble precariously and feel the steep drop loom up to greet me.

What if I fell?

The thought curls seductively into my brain just as my hand grabs the banisters for support. I'm annoyed that now I *want* it to, my body doesn't fail me.

'Sofie? Is that you love?' Sandra says loudly.

I stagger back upstairs, desperately hoping she doesn't follow.

I can barely hear Rory's response, but I know what he'll be saying: Sofie's not ready for visitors.

'Nonsense,' I can hear Sandra loud and clear, as if she has a megaphone. 'I'm not a visitor; I'm *family*!'

I huddle under the covers and close my eyes. Perhaps if I pretend to be asleep, she'll go away.

She doesn't even knock. She just walks in, opens the curtains letting in blinding, bright sunlight which burns behind my eyes.

'Sofie, it's Nanny Sandra.' This is the name she gave herself for me when Rory and I met. I couldn't believe how different she was to my own gran – my mum's mum – who lived in Ireland and whom I only ever met twice before she died.

I open my eyes. She sits heavily down on the edge of bed and stares at me intently with her cornflower-blue eyes, bluer thanks to the heavily rimmed horseshoes of eyeliner she always applies thickly under the lashes.

'You're awake,' she says in her soothing West Country burr. 'You do know it's the middle of the day? Let's get you downstairs. Do you the world of good, it will.'

'I-I'm not really up to it, Nanny Sandra.'

'Of course you're not!' she says, briskly empathetic. 'Understandable, with what all you've been through. But I know what it's like to have to get up and face the world, love, after your heart has been broken. That I do.'

How can you? I want to scream. *You've never lost a child!*

Then I remember in a way she has, and I feel deeply ashamed.

'You've got to get used to being around people at some point – tragedy makes everyone come out of the woodwork. They'll all want to know your business. What happened, how, when and why. You might as well start by getting used to being around me.' She puts her hand on my arm and rubs it gently. 'Now, I'll need your help getting down the stairs. My hips are not what they were.' She doesn't give me an option to refuse.

'I'm not in such great shape myself, to be honest, Sandra,' I say, wincing as I pull my legs over the side of the bed.

'You've been through it and then some, poor child. But you can't stay up here forever. The world keeps turning, whether you want it to or not.'

She takes my hand, pulls it encouragingly and I put my feet on the floor because I don't seem to have another choice. I try to locate my slippers. I can't bend down because I still feel sore from my stitches. I blindly shuffle into them like an old woman.

Once I'm standing, Sandra slips my dressing gown around me, links her arm through one of mine – more to support me than the other way round, I think – and leads me gently.

I feel like an invalid. I consider that word, let it roll around in my head, like a marble about to drop down in the complex spiral run that is my brain:

Invalid.

In valid.

I'm not valid.

I'm not a valid mother.

A mother brings life to their baby.

My body caused my baby to die.

My baby is in the hospital mortuary, a tiny body waiting to be buried.

The thought causes my legs to buckle beneath me so suddenly I almost fold in half. Sandra grips on to me tightly.

'I can't,' I cry.

'You can,' she says firmly. 'I'm here; Rory's here and your mum is, too. We'll hold you up. That's what we'll do. Hold you up. Come on, left and right that's it. One step at a time, that's all, dear. One step at a time.'

Chapter Thirty-Seven

Six whole days without my baby. Today – the twenty-first of February – would have been his due date. I feel like I've slipped through a vortex into a nightmare.

In another version of my life, one where he lived, I might have woken up today, gone into labour, delivered my baby boy and brought him home. Texted everyone to let them know. Instead, I'm messaging the yoga WhatsApp group. It is the one message I feel I must send out myself. I take a deep breath, close my eyes and hit send. I feel a wave of nausea as I do so. I put down the phone, slide down in bed.

> Sorry for the silence. Leo Bear King was stillborn on February 15th, weighing 7lbs 3oz, with sandy blond hair and the sweetest face. I will miss him forever.

Sending it feels like losing him all over again.

I'm staring at the ceiling once more. My phone rests on the table, so inactive that I wonder if it has died too. I reach over, pick it up, check to see if my message has sent. It has. I notice from the ticks that it has been read. I feel like I've given something precious to people and I don't know what they're going to do with it.

I'm on the sofa in the lounge, which I've frequented in daylight hours since Sandra visited yesterday. Rory is in constant contact with the hospital who want to know if we've made any decisions about his cremation. They tell us there is no hurry but seem to phone daily. I want him to tell them to leave us alone. Give us time. But I know I can't put it off for much longer. I feel the pressure of that next step as keenly as I felt the pressure to tell everyone. Another too-high hurdle I'm expected to jump over when I'm still face down from the ones that came before. As Rory would be too if he just stopped for a moment.

He's busy sending texts, emails and messages on social media to the friends who contact him and to whom he feels compelled to reply, one by one. I know everyone is being kind, asking first how I am. But I never hear them checking in on him. I'm not sure which is worse: his manic cleaning, or the frenetic messaging. It's exhausting for me to watch and for him to deal with.

I want to turn the volume down on the world. Or better still, put it on mute. Change the channel. Switch it all off.

It's amazing how *noisy* grief is. Even though I'm barely able to say a word – sentences, small talk lost to the chasm of sorrow – the voice in my head telling me all I did to deserve this is on full volume and can't be lowered.

Outside of *that*, the world is painfully deafening, too. I hear car engines rev from outside the window, babies crying in their prams and seagulls piercing my ears with their cries. The letterbox bangs and the doorbell rings relentlessly. Delivery upon delivery of cards and flowers flooding through the front door. Rory doesn't bring them in here. He knows I don't want to see any of it.

I can hear the vans arriving outside, though – they're so regular that I can identify the slam of the van door now, the heavy footprints. The regularity means our neighbours will know something has happened. Even with our curtains firmly drawn, I can practically see theirs twitching.

I know that the people who love us want to let us know they're thinking of us. But for me, the endless supply of dying blooms isn't a comfort. For Rory, their continuous arrival has also made for awkward conversations with the delivery people.

'Celebrating something, are we mate?' one guy loudly said first thing this morning at the front door.

I didn't hear Rory's mumbled reply. I feel guilty that I'm still in this bubble of sorts, protected, to a degree, from everything. Until today, I've barely looked at my now repaired phone. I haven't replied to any texts, unless they're from Mum or Nisha. I start them, on occasion, but find I either don't know what to say, or I can't stop typing, giving people way more detail than necessary, because if they want to know, they need to know *everything*. Then I delete it all. Because how do I convey the most painful but most cherished experience of my life in a simple message.

Only Joe's message a couple of days ago warranted a reply.

> I heard from Rory that your baby boy Leo died. I'm so deeply sorry for your loss. I can't begin to understand what you're going through and there's no need to reply to this, but please know I'm here for you both. J x

To my surprise I quickly tapped out a response.

> Thank you, Joe. To be honest, I have no idea how to get over this.

Seconds later, his reply came in.

> There is no over, only through.

While that small exchange brought a moment of comfort and connection for me, I can see Rory is drained from having to repeat our tragic tale over again and answer questions about how I'm doing. Obviously, he only delivers the glossy version of our grief that's suitable for public consumption:

'She's as okay as can be expected,' I hear him say on the phone every day, several times a day. 'Sofie's being incredibly strong,' followed by, 'We're so grateful for all the love and support.'

What if he *were* to give them the real version, I wonder? That I'm so obliterated by the pain and loss that I don't know how or if I'll ever recover?

And what if they were to ask him how *he* is? What would he say?

I look down at my phone. It has been almost an hour and not one person from the yoga group has replied.

Chapter Thirty-Eight

Late afternoon. I'm staring at the TV blankly.
My phone beeps – a WhatsApp message. It has been over an hour and a half since I messaged the baby yoga group.

I grab it, look at the screen hungrily. It feels like I'm pressing my face against the windscreen of the wreckage I'm in, trying to get the attention of other drivers on this road who speed unseeingly by.

> Sofie! We're so sorry to hear your terrible news! Please know we are all thinking of you. We can't imagine the pain you're going through right now and understand if you want to remove yourself from this group in case it's too triggering. Please let us know if there's anything we can do. Take care, Love from us all xxx

I put the phone down slowly, numb with disbelief. I read it again. It's a message that has clearly been composed privately by everyone in a newly created group where they will have freely shared both their horror at my news – and relief that they are Not Me. I can imagine the messages now.

Setting up a new group to talk. Has everyone seen the message in the Feb baby chat?!!
 – *OMG! Poor Sofie. Should we go and see her?*
Seeing us will be much too painful. It's best we keep our distance.

Anyone else holding their baby so closely right now?
I'm never complaining about a night feed again!
We are so lucky!
I'll never take motherhood for granted...
How should we reply to Sofie's message, then?
Hang on – just pumping. God, I hate expressing!
Sorry, Ivy just woke up from her nap! Be right back.
We should make it as easy for her as possible. Give her the option to leave, or let the group go dormant and keep the baby talk here.
Agree. It's the kindest thing to do.
Poor Sofie.
I'm devastated for her.
Can't stop crying. Imagine if it had been one of our babies?

The door opens and I quickly hide the phone, sit up, wipe my eyes. Rory peeks around it and smiles at me hopefully. Always with the hope.

'You're awake.' He comes inside, tentatively sits on the sofa next to me. He's subdued; he seems to have shrunk in the past few days, weighed down with all he is carrying. His stubbled jaw is tight, he barely moves his lips when he speaks. Sometimes he disappears up to his office. I see him passing often, carrying parcels. I'm not sure what they are. I presume they're condolence gifts he doesn't want me to see. Once up there, he stays for at least an hour. Possibly letting out some stress on his rowing machine. Anything to not have to sit in his grief. I want to tell him that all I want is him, my husband, here with me. I wish he'd just let go of his contained grief, stop the incessant tidying up, so I could feel more comfortable with how unravelled I am.

'Can I get you anything?' he says with whispered politeness.

I shake my head.

He takes a deep breath like a nervous child addressing a parent; it makes me suddenly angry. 'Sofie, we need to talk. About our plans for Leo's cremation...'

Like a child myself, I turn up the TV so I can drown out what Rory is saying. How can he think about cremating our baby when I have barely made it past the moment I delivered him?

'Okay.' He sighs. 'I can see you still don't want to discuss any of that right now. Shall I send your mum in, to keep you company? I love Angie, but I've spent quite a lot of time with her these past few days… I could do with a break.' He smiles weakly. I look out of the window. Resentment and bitterness darken my thoughts. Why does he keep asking so much of me?

He retreats, head lowered.

When he's gone, I feel ashamed, guilty, bereft. I'm a terrible wife. I'm not supporting him the way I should. I want to call out, ask him to stay with me here, in this room, just for a while. But he's long gone.

No doubt gone to talk to other people about our baby.

Chapter Thirty-Nine

Nisha has come over and brought her chessboard again – the same one we played on after Dad died. Nisha would carry around a travel board, so we could play it anywhere, whenever I needed to ground myself.

Clearly, she thinks the same tactic will work again. Instead, it feels like I'm in a strange time vortex: same game, same reason for playing, different grief. Can't she see that I have no strategy this time? No way of deciding what's next? I'm only capable of 'What if...'

Nisha has finished work and is spending more time in Bournemouth, staying with her parents whilst she's house-hunting. She starts her new job at Southampton Hospital at the end of March and tells me excitedly that she's just put in an offer on a three-bed house in Brockenhurst, a beautiful village in the New Forest, about forty minutes from here and twenty minutes from the hospital. Everything is working out for her.

I try to show my excitement, but I can barely manage a smile at this news. I know I'm terrible company: self-pitying, self-absorbed, self-flagellating. It has been ten days since Leo died. Ten days of staring at the walls; feeling intermittently numb then angry but mostly mute and helpless. Sometimes, in my darker moments, I wonder why Nisha bothers with me. Is it loyalty? Duty? Guilt? And what about

Rory? He's out seeing friends tonight. I know he needs to see people, but I can't help but feel … abandoned.

We make slow progress with our game. She talks more about the house she's found, speculates about her job. Finally, she asks if I've heard from work. It's like she's been building up to it all night.

I shrug. I've no idea if anything has come from the office or not. Rory is Chief Condolence Card Opener.

'It's worth thinking about,' she says. 'At some point. When you're ready.'

'Ready for what?' I frown.

'Going back to work. It'll be good for you.' I must look so horrified that she hastily adds. 'Studying was like therapy for you when your dad died. Work would provide the same distraction.'

'That was different.' I say tersely.

'How?' She looks up at me, her head tilted.

'My baby *died*, Nisha.'

'I know, Sof. But life goes on. Like in chess, the game continues until the last piece is played. Even if you don't want it to, *especially* when you don't want it to, that's when you have to get back up and keep moving. It's the same advice you gave me recently.' Her gaze is distant, like she's not talking about me at all.

'I know,' I say, my voice is thin, reedy with hurt. Did she really just say life goes on? 'But this is different from being dumped by a married lover. You didn't lose a baby.'

My spiky response sits like a barbed-wire fence between us.

'Right, I've just realised I need to be somewhere.' She swallows, attaches a smile to her face. She gets up, picks up her bag and coat. Well, good. Let her go. She turns. 'Can I just say one thing? You're not the only person this has ever happened to, Sofie. You're not alone. And you've got so much love and support, you will be ok, I promise.' She looks at me then, with a strange mixture of sadness, pity and … something else I can't place. Her expression makes me want to curl up and not see anyone ever again. Because if my best friend doesn't understand, who will?

I don't even say goodbye when she leaves. Doesn't anyone understand that I don't *want* to distract myself from the pain of losing Leo, when my grief is what tethers me to him? It is all I have left.

Chapter Forty

Evening. 8pm. I'm in bed. Rory's upstairs, working in his loft office. He's slowly easing back into work. No reporting, no live TV, just some researching and drafting upcoming segments.

I know he has no choice: his two weeks of bereavement leave is up. I just don't understand how life is meant to go back to normal.

Mum's still here – a sure sign that we remain in emergency territory. I haven't spent this much time with her for years. Not since I moved in with her and Midge the summer after I left uni, working at the café until my graduate placement at the insurance company started that September.

It was a difficult time in our relationship. Aside from the fact that Mum had never shown any previous interest in women, I couldn't work out how I'd missed their relationship growing into something more. I knew Midge had been a great support to her after Dad died. She understood grief, having lost her partner a few years before. But I thought that was all. I kicked myself for being so naïve and for being so caught up in my university studies that I'd taken no notice of *my* absent love life. Let alone Mum's very present one.

I wondered what else I had been missing. How long had they been involved? When she and Dad were at crisis point, I'd supported Mum in her decision to ask him to leave. I thought that she'd put up with enough. His absences – both emotional and physical – his increased drinking, self-absorption, stress, anxiety and depression meant that she had no other option. I knew the pressure she'd felt running the café alone while he was out with his fishing boat, or on hikes, or climbs. I knew he'd gradually left the day-to-day running to her, even though she had her own work as a teacher and private tutor to juggle. When they eventually split up, they called it a 'trial separation'. Two months later, he tragically died.

Where once I felt grateful for Mum and Midge's 'friendship' that blossomed even more after his death, when they officially moved in together and then fell in love, I felt a bit betrayed. Like they'd been hiding in plain sight from me all along.

'What is it about the relationship that upsets you so much, Sofie?' Mum had said that Christmas break, when Midge had gone out to her book-club's festive drinks. 'Is it because she's a woman?'

I'd found this offensive, of course I didn't mind that she was a woman. I minded that she wasn't my dad. 'No, Mum. I'm open to the idea of you falling in love with whoever you want. I just wish the person you chose to have a relationship with wasn't someone that you met when you were still married to Dad, who you kicked out of the family home in order to move her in!'

'It wasn't like that, Sofie…'

'No wonder Dad didn't want her to rent the flat. Did he suspect something even then? Was there an instant spark between you?'

'No! He just hated anyone getting too close to me. You know he didn't like me having friends. Male or female…'

'Well, clearly he was right to be suspicious.'

Mum had exhaled wearily. 'Sofie, you're wrong. Your Dad died three years ago. And I won't apologise for this friendship … no, this *relationship* I've been lucky enough to find since then. Midge makes me happy. And when you're my age, you'll learn that you have to grab it when you can, because neither happiness nor time is guaranteed to anyone. And if you took some time to get to know Midge, I think you'd realise you two actually have lots in common.'

'Really? That's funny. *I* haven't broken up any marriages recently,' I'd said petulantly.

I knew as soon as I'd said it, I'd pushed it too far.

'That's enough, Sofie!' Mum snapped.

I'd dropped my head shamefully.

'I won't have you slandering Midge when all she's ever tried to do is help this family. We'd have lost everything without her!'

I'd looked up, then. Clearly, she had no idea how I felt.

'I *did* lose everything, Mum,' I'd said, my voice shaking with emotion. 'My dad died. And unlike you, *I* can't just replace him.' Then I'd stormed out.

It had been months before we'd seen each other again.

When we did, it was tentatively awkward. Occasionally, I'd arrange to see her on a Sunday and Midge would make herself scarce. Mum and I would cook, chat, sometimes have lunch with Sita and Nisha because we found we were more comfortable together if we had company. As the months passed, Midge would join us. Begrudgingly, I admired her softly, softly approach: she didn't try too hard; she knew when to give me and Mum space and she didn't demand anything from me. But I quickly countered that it was probably because she felt guilty.

Our relationship only found balance when Rory came on the scene a few years later. Mum and Midge both loved him and he encouraged me to spend more time with them both.

'Most people only have one mum you know, Sof. You're lucky, you've got two!'

'No, I don't.'

He'd shrugged. 'Well, you could have, if you wanted. Which, trust me, is preferable to none,' he'd replied.

There's a knock at the door and Mum comes in. She's keeping busy in the house so Rory can be up in his office. Often for hours on end, late at night.

She has visibly aged these past few days. Like Rory, she seems to have shrunk into her shoulders, which are permanently hunched with concern.

I look out of the window vacantly as she takes my hand. I know it has helped Rory immeasurably to have Mum here. He doesn't really know how to deal with this new, numb version of me who can't function at the high level I used to. Who can't cope with functioning on *any* level.

I hear Rory moving around upstairs and I realise how far away he feels from me. He never used to spend this much time up there. He always wanted to be with me.

Mum's presence has given him a reprieve – not just from the constant chores, admin, the phone calls and emotional grunt-work placed on him over these past days – but from me. While she's with me, he doesn't have to be.

But her presence, whilst a comfort, is also a reminder that the role of mother is one that has been cruelly stolen from me: my baby isn't here for me to look after. And he never will be.

'Will it always be this hard, Mum?' I rasp, my voice unused to speaking. 'You haven't ever lost a baby but...' I trail off, unable to finish my sentence.

She looks at me, head tilted, eyes cloudy with both pity and pain.

'Your dad used to say, "Though it is hard to imagine being in another person's shoes, we should always try."'

Dad and his Danish proverbs.

'Grief is something you'll always wear,' she continues, gently tucking a piece of hair behind my ear. 'But whilst it might feel like a suit of armour right now – protective, but heavy to carry – in time, it'll become a superhero's cape. The thing that reminds you of just how strong you are.'

My throat swells until I can barely swallow. 'Another of Dad's sayings?'

'No,' she says, 'that one's all mine.'

'Did you blame yourself? After he died?' I ask, suddenly. I've been thinking about him a lot. It's as if my new wound has knocked off the scab of the old. I miss him more because I realise Leo was also a part of him. I feel like I'm in twice as much as pain.

'Yes, of course,' she says, her voice distant, a hushed whisper like she's far away.

'Do you still miss him? Mum?'

'Hmm?' It feels like she's drifted away from me.

'Do you ever wish you'd been there, that morning?'

She's back in the room. She stares at me searchingly. 'Yes... Yes, of course,' she says carefully. 'But I always come back to the fact that it wouldn't have made any difference. There were too many factors out of my control.'

'Like what?' We haven't talked about his death for years and I'm hungry for information, but she's shut down again and I'm left with my own recollections of the build up to that day.

I'd barely seen him in the weeks before he died. I'd been angry at him because – typical teenager – I believed their separation affected *me* the most. He'd failed *me* by failing in his marriage. I kept refusing to see him when he turned up at the house.

'Be patient,' I'd hear Mum say to him when I refused to see him. 'She'll come round eventually. She just needs time.'

But I was stubborn. And at seventeen, I'd no idea that time was something you should never take for granted.

After he died, I had no one to blame but Mum. She readily accepted that blame, too – I think to stop me apportioning any to myself. Is that what mothers do? Try to protect their child from pain, even if it makes life more painful for themselves? I think of Leo. I would have done that every day of his life, if I'd been given the chance.

'Your dad was … a complex man,' Mum says at last. 'He loved us, but the man I'd fallen in love with, the father you grew up adoring, was gone. Walking, foraging, fishing – that was what made him happy in the end. He died doing what he loved.'

'I was horrible to him…'

'Sofie, show me a teenager that *isn't* horrible to her parents. He knew it was a normal part of growing up. He also always knew how much you loved him. And you were his proudest achievement. The gift he said he'd never take for granted.'

'I blame myself,' I whisper then, voice hoarse, as I began to weep. 'For Leo dying.'

'Oh Sofie, no don't-'

'Who else is there, Mum? I interrupt. 'My body equals my fault.'

'Sofie,' she says with a fierceness that surprises me given she's walked on eggshells around me for years. 'Life isn't an algebraic equation. Things happen in life that we have no control over – the variables, you'd call them, right? Looking for a reason why Leo died won't bring him back.' She takes my hand. I cling to hers like I'm a child again. I can't remember the last time we did this and suddenly I wonder: when did I stop? Did I let go of her, or did she let go of me? Does being a mother mean having to let go of your child, regardless of whether they live a long life – or don't get to live at all?

'Do you know what I've realised over the years?' Mum says now. 'That the guilt I feel about your dad's death is just proof of my love for him. Grief is the price we pay for it, isn't it? That's what the Queen once famously said, God rest her soul.' She makes a quick sign of the cross – once an Irish Catholic, always an Irish Catholic – and cups my face with her hands and looks deep into my eyes. 'I couldn't have stopped Per' – she falters for a second trying to find the right word – 'falling. Nor could you have prevented Leo from dying. Sometimes things happen that are just out of our control. There's no one to blame.'

'But what if—'

'What ifs can't help us,' Mum interjects firmly. 'Here are the facts: without you, Leo would never have existed at all. You overcame your fears just for him. You did everything by the book from the moment you found out you were pregnant. You had nine wonderful months carrying him. Then you bravely delivered him. You couldn't have done any more, Sofie. Leo was so *lucky* to have you. You were – you *are* – a wonderful mum.'

I let those words settle around me, like a warm blanket on a cold day. *Lucky to have you.* And me, him.

He may not be here, but I'm a mum, still. A mum to a stillborn baby.

'What if…' I begin. 'What if … I wanted to find a way to honour that?'

She smiles and take my hand. 'Now that's a "what if?" I'll allow.'

Chapter Forty-One

It's Monday morning. Mum went home yesterday. She has staff shortages to sort, coffee to brew, pies to make.

Pi. Just like the mathematical constant, the days since we've been home from hospital have been an endless sequence, all leading back to the same place.

I know it makes Rory happy for me to be downstairs. He thinks it's progress, but I've simply carried my grief to another room. On the rare occasion I'm not lying on the sofa, I move slothfully around the house, like an animal in quicksand. I'm disappearing, and the worse thing is, I don't care.

I hear Rory on the phone now, discussing our baby's cremation. I know I need to be involved. I have to do what's right for our little boy and say goodbye properly. Honour him, like I said to Mum. I've started writing a plan, including a list of songs I'd like to play. It's the least I can do.

The door creaks open and Rory peeks around it, a smile plastered on to try and mask the permanent worry etched on his face. He's gripping his phone tightly like it's a lifeline. Sometimes it feels like he needs it as protection from me. This busyness of his has become a barrier between us.

He's holding a small, handpicked bunch of flowers in his free hand. He looks gaunt with grief. His days' old, burnished stubble has grown into a red-blonde beard that makes him look strangely familiar. Like my dad, I realise. 'Sorry the call took so long. We're very popular right now,' he says ruefully.

It's true. Tragedy does make you surprisingly popular: new friends, old enemies, distant family, close bystanders and online observers, all want a piece of it.

'I always hoped it would be due to my shining personality or personal achievements, not my baby dying.' I force out a laugh – my first attempt. I ruin it immediately by bursting into tears. 'Sorry,' I manage through my sobs. It's the word I must have said more than any other in the past two weeks.

Rory strokes my short, straggly, greasy hair as I try to catch my breath. I feel ashamed, not just of how I look, but that I'm doing such a terrible job of hiding just how terribly I'm doing.

'Speaking of work,' Rory says uncertainly, 'some flowers arrived from Prospect?' He's so tentative with me, everything he says sounds like a question.

I glance at the small bunch of bright spring flowers that Rory's clutching uncertainly – a burst of brightness in a world of black – and find I can't take my eyes from them. Unlike the lilies and roses filling our house with the scent of death, this little cluster of spring blooms are a welcome sight because they make me think of Leo. Daffodils, which tell of fleeting joy and bright hope after a winter of darkness. Snowdrops, as white as Leo's skin. And vivid violets that remind me of the dark inkiness of my baby's softly parted lips. I reach out, take them and bring them up to my nose, inhaling their sweet scent.

'They're lovely,' I croak.

'These are from our garden. I went out early this morning and picked some. I … I thought you might like some in here. I'll always think of daffodils as—' He stops.

'Leo's flower,' I finish for him. I can't remember the last time he said our son's name apart from discussing the cremation.

He nods once, blinks as if to compose himself. 'Your boss sent a big bouquet of roses and calla lilies,' he adds. 'They're in the kitchen. They must have cost a fortune.'

'The death package,' I say wryly. I allowed Rory to send a

message to my work telling them what had happened, when he shared the news with our friends and extended family.

I stroke the golden daffodil trumpets Rory picked for me that seem suddenly like little loudspeakers to my love and loss.

'This card came with the flowers.'

With Sympathy it says on the front.

Dear Sofie,

Sending condolences and reassurances that everything here is in hand. Your job is here for you should you want to return, but Tarun is ensuring everything is running smoothly so feel free to take your time coming back.

Best wishes,
Ed & the team

'That's nice,' Rory says, reading it over my shoulder.

'Mmm.' I feel choked, a flash of jealousy of how little I'm needed, but also like a hand has crawled out of the envelope and is trying to drag me back into my old life.

'Nice of them to reach out, I mean.' He pauses, glances at me, then down at the floor. 'I guess it's something to consider, too.'

'What is?'

'Whether you do want to take your time, or if you want to consider going back earlier than planned. I hate the idea of you being here alone once I'm back at work full-time after the funeral. It would be good for you to get some normality again.'

I feel a rushing in my ears, like when you put your head underwater. First Nisha, now Rory. He must understand that normal is now like a star that will forever be out of my reach. *My* normal exists with Leo, on the infinite edges of my universe, not in an office looking at statistics, mortality rates and risk models. None of that matters anymore. My work is pointless. Death is death, whether you have financial security or not. How can I offer protection now, when I know first-hand your world can self-destruct in a second – no matter what you try and do to protect yourself from it? How can I care about financial loss, when all *I* care about is the loss of my baby?

And how can I face everyone at work? I have no idea who I am now that I'm a mum to a baby who hasn't lived. I know I'm not the person I once was. I'll never be that person again. Do I take six months off work for maternity leave as I'd originally planned? Or do I not go back to work at all? Do I change my life entirely because it has, against my will, already changed beyond comprehension?

I suddenly feel guilty that I have a choice.

I think of the countless women who don't have that luxury, who have a miscarriage before twelve weeks and have to continue as normal even though their world has imploded. Or like me, have a stillbirth or late miscarriage but who, financially, can only take the minimum bereavement leave and then have no other option than to go back to work after a matter of weeks.

Why should I have it any easier?

'No need to decide now,' Rory continues quickly, sensing my rising panic. 'Perhaps we could start by going for a walk today? It's been over a week since you left the house, you know.'

'I know how long it's been,' I say sharply. 'My baby died. People stay in bed for far lesser things, Rory: flu, a stomach bug, a bad back.'

'*Our* baby,' he corrects.

I look away.

'Okay.' He sighs in response to my stubborn silence. 'I'm going to go upstairs to my office. I've got some stuff to do.'

'What's so important, anyway?' My tone is snider than I intended.

'Just some … admin. I can stay here, if you want?' He says this less than enthusiastically.

I slump back on the sofa, turning my head away. 'I know I'm terrible company.'

'Sofie…' He reaches out, touches my arm. I shrug him off, wrap my arms around myself.

I pretend to go to sleep even as he sits there, deepening my breath purposefully until I hear him creep quietly out of the room. The creak of the stairs and floorboards directly above telling me exactly where he is.

A long way from where I am.

Chapter Forty-Two

Day fourteen.
    3.14...
The first of March.
3.141...
I stop, my mind unable to focus even on Pi.

A new month. I know I should be relieved to say goodbye to February – the worst month of my life – but in doing so, I must let go of Leo's birth month forever.

I stare out of the car window like a prisoner on day release. Another first today – my first trip out of the house.

The sky is veiny blue, sickly-looking with smears of whitewashed clouds daubed everywhere and a pale, jaundiced sun behind them. The streets – familiarly wide and lined with blossoming trees – feel foreign. Ahead of us, the French-inspired turreted building that is the town hall looms. It looks the same as it always did. Everything's the same, but I'm different. Why isn't everything different?

The sun bursts through the clouds suddenly: a taunting beam of light shines directly on the town hall, like an arrow from the sky. I'm too angry at its ruthless vitality to consider it a sign that I made the right choice to come here.

I'd come downstairs this morning to find Rory smartly dressed, car keys in hand, the kitchen so tidy that I wanted to escape from it

This Wasn't Meant to Happen

immediately. I longed to see the kind of mess that, in another version of our lives, should be there: baby bottles on the surface, abandoned dinner dishes by the sink, a trail of discarded baby clothes.

I'd looked at Rory standing in his coat and felt instantly unnerved: we'd had one argument, and he was leaving? Apart from popping to the supermarket once or twice, he's been with me for the past two weeks. Not in the same room – but he's always been *here*.

'Tea?' He didn't kiss me like usual; he just turned and opened the cupboard to get a mug without waiting for my answer. I saw him hurriedly trying to push the *Mum-to-be* mug to the back of the cupboard which clearly he'd forgotten to remove. The rest of the house has been completely cleared of baby paraphernalia, not just the pram in the hallway. It is another thing he has quietly dealt with. Nevertheless, I had a sudden urge to throw the mug against the wall; then smash every other one in that cupboard into smithereens too so there'd be no more cups of tea. No more pretence that the insipid hot drink we're so bloody obsessed with has the power to solve something like this.

I'd been thinking about Rory's comment all night: about how going back to work would be good for me.

'Will you be okay if I pop out for a couple of hours?' Rory said as he put the milk back in the fridge after pouring it in my tea.

'Where?' It was less a question, more an interrogation.

He'd rubbed his forehead. Closed his eyes.

'I … I have to be somewhere. I have an appointment.'

'What for?' My voice was cold, accusing. I was angry now. At him, at myself. At the world that demanded so much from him. What could be so important?

He'd looked up at me from under his eyebrows which were tightly sewn with sorrow.

'I'm going to the town hall to register Leo's death on the stillbirth register,' he'd said. 'Having the certificate will allow us to go ahead with his cremation. I know you can't face it but we need to put our boy to rest for his sake … and for ours. I can't leave him any longer, Sofie. I won't.'

Rory's firm resolve was a coat I hadn't seen him wear before. Underneath it, I realised he looked defeated, drained, not just by the death of our baby – but by *me*. Suddenly, I wanted to be there for Rory. Help him through at least one of the many impossible things that *he's* had to deal with since Leo died.

'I want to come with you,' I was surprised to hear myself saying.

'What?' Clearly, Rory was too.

'I want to come. I'm Leo's mum. I should be there,' I'd felt a little of myself return with those three words.

I'm Leo's mum.

I'd seen a little of Rory return, too. Hope shone in his eyes, just like it used to.

'It won't be too much for you?'

'I want to do the things that other parents get to do for their baby. I want the certificate that'll prove that he did exist, even if he didn't live.'

Suddenly, I was more certain of this than I'd been of anything else.

'And I want us to do that together.'

When I'd come downstairs a bit later, fully dressed, albeit in an old tracksuit and wearing the barest amount of make-up I could manage to make myself look human, Rory had smiled with such relief, love and hope it made me want to break down all over again.

We park outside the town hall now, and gripping each other's hands tightly, we walk in and sit in the waiting room. I stare ahead, paralysed, numb.

Two other couples are there. I know they're registering births as they have their babies with them, nestled in their little Maxi-Cosi car seats like the one we bought for Leo but never got to use. Rory squeezes my hand.

'Are you okay?' Rory whispers. 'You don't have to do this, you know. You can wait in the car, if you prefer?'

'I want to stay,' I say firmly.

I want to take my rightful place as Leo's mother. To have it acknowledged in a public place and have lasting official documents that prove that even though he isn't with us, he was here. He made us parents.

I've spent every waking hour imagining what the last few days would've been like if he'd lived. I've also had moments – in that mystical place between my dreams and reality – when I've woken up and it didn't immediately register that he's dead. For a few sacred seconds I've blissfully believed that I was still pregnant, that his death was a nightmare I'd just woken up from. And then, when it hit me, I've been unable to fathom that I'm still alive to experience this level of unrelenting grief. That this pain, loss, trauma and shame – this living nightmare hasn't ended me. Life does indeed go on, even if you don't want it to. In a funny kind of way, I'm proud of myself. After all, the worst has happened and so far, I've survived.

Is there something in that, I wonder? That Leo has gifted me a free pass from fear?

There's also a part of me – the self-punishing one – that wants to test myself. To see how much more I can endure. I mean, if I'm still standing after giving birth to my dead baby, surely being among these living newborns can't hurt me.

For a moment, as we sit patiently in the waiting room, this seems possible. Everything is calm. Rory and I sit holding hands. We're not exactly at ease, more on high alert. Rory is emitting an air of thankful disbelief that I'm up and out and being normal.

It's the conversation that does it.

My ears prick up as the two new mums opposite me begin cooing over one another's babies sleeping peacefully, tiny, knitted hats pulled down over their heads, eyes shut tight, perplexed frowns hovering on their sloped brows, lips parted just like Leo's had been.

And yet I can see from here they're also very different. There's no pale grey tinge to their little faces, no purple stained, cracked lips forever waiting to exhale. Their fingers twitch involuntarily; their chests heave with life in a way that Leo's never did. I watch, ghoulishly fascinated, as the women's husbands nod at each other in solidarity while their proud wives chat. They don't notice Rory and I staring at them. We're invisible. Ghosts.

'What's your little one called?' says the petite blonde, wearing wide-legged trousers, bright white trainers and what looks like a cashmere jumper. Just a few days post-partum, she's as shiny as a pound coin – she even has lipstick on. 'He *is* a boy, isn't he? I only ask because everyone keeps mistaking our Artie for a girl!' She laughs with the smug confidence of someone who believes only their baby could possibly be so beautiful.

'Artie? What a lovely name!' says the other one. She's a redhead, curvier than her blonde counterpart; softer, more homely looking. 'They all look the same at this stage, don't they?' she laughs. 'Like little baby birds! This is Elijah.'

'He's *gorgeous*,' the blonde enthuses.

To be honest, I think he looks exactly like the scrawny bird of his mother's description. I continue to watch them, like I'm a referee at a tennis match.

'Thank you. Not so cute when he screams all night!'

'Is he your first?' The petite blonde enquires.

A proud nod in response.

'Artie is, too.'

'When was he born?'

'February 16th,' she says, beaming with maternal pride.

I can't breathe. I feel like I'm subsiding. Sinking. Drowning.

The redhead gasps in surprise. 'So was Elijah! What time? We were probably at the hospital together! How *funny!*'

How funny, I imagine myself adding. *I delivered my baby on the same day, at the same hospital, too – but dead.*

I feel Rory giving me a gentle squeeze of reassurance, which becomes more like a gesture of physical restraint as I lean forward, towards them. I see his sideways glance of concern, hear him call my name as I get up.

'I'm ok, Rory.' *I just want to see their babies, the living ones. Like Leo should be.*

I walk slowly, deliberately across the room towards them. I see their look of surprise as I get close, stare down at their babies. I can sense they're uncomfortable. I want to reassure them; let them know that I'm just a new mum, too. I'm in their gang.

'February 16th is my son's birthday, too!' I say, peering down at the baby closest to me. Artie, I think it is? I can't take my eyes off his tiny little fingers, the perfect white crescents of his impossibly small fingernails. It takes all my willpower not to reach out, touch him, feel the warmth of that grasp and allow myself to imagine it's Leo.

'Oh, really?' one of them says with an instantly inclusive smile that momentarily warms me. 'What's his name?'

The sweet joy of the present tense.

'Leo,' I say, wishing his name had more syllables so it would linger on my lips and in the air between us for longer. 'Leo Bear King,' I add, for my benefit not hers. 'Born at 6:17pm on February 16th. Weighing six pounds, eleven ounces with sandy hair and … and…'

Rory has appeared by my side. I feel his arm wrap around me.

'Sofie,' Rory murmurs softly. 'Come on, let's sit down.' He tries to pull me back to the other side of the room, but I shake him off. I'm enjoying talking about my baby. For the first time since Leo was born, I feel like a normal mum.

'That's a lovely name,' the redhead says kindly. Her smile seems a little forced. I see her glance nervously at her husband. 'Is he at nursery today?'

I frown before realising that she's assumed Leo is an older child, as he's not here with us.

'No, he's—' I stop and stare at the floor, not knowing what to say. I want to prolong this conversation, the one where she thinks my baby is alive and well. I consider saying that he's with his grandparents. For a moment, I wish I had brought my phone so I could show them the photos we have of him on the day he was born. The same day as their babies.

'Sofie, please.' Rory steps forward and slips his arm around me again. 'I'm sorry.' He turns towards our seats as he addresses his apology back to them. 'We're here to register our son's stillbirth,' he tells them matter-of-factly over his shoulder, so used is he to sharing the news. Their faces instantly take on a look of abject horror. 'Our baby died,' he adds unnecessarily.

'Oh!' Artie's mum gasps in distress and puts her hand over her mouth. Her expression is one of pity. Pity and horror.

Both my baby and a normal version of motherhood gone again – just like that. Rory leads me back to our seats. The 'Death' side of Births and Deaths now.

'I … I'm so sorry for your loss,' the blonde says from a safe distance across the room, obviously emotional. 'I can't imagine what you must be going through!'

'Thank you,' Rory says politely.

I don't respond. All I wanted was to feel part of their circle, to imagine just for a moment that I was someone they might have bumped into at the same coffee shop, frequented baby groups with.

Artie cries then, and I watch as she fusses over him unnecessarily protectively whilst Elijah's mum plucks her baby out of his car seat and looks at me pityingly, as if holding him close will stop us tainting them with our tragedy.

I don't want their pity. I just want inclusion in their New Mum Club. I'm a new mum, too after all. I stand up again determined to be a part of their gang, just for a minute. I walk quickly towards them and feel my arms involuntarily reach out towards the blonde's baby.

The dads close ranks, then. They put their arm around their wives. One instinctively reaches forward and clasps the handle of the Maxi-Cosi car seat and brings it closer, too.

It's then that I realise how they *really* see me. Not as a grieving mother they empathise with, but someone dangerous, desperate. Who might try and damage *their* baby.

Black patches form over my eyes like a hastily sewn quilt, one after another after another until I can't see or breathe.

I'm falling.

I feel Rory catch me, then nothing.

Chapter Forty-Three

That night, Rory and I lie in bed wrapped in the warmth and security of each other's arms, silence shrouding us. It feels to me like the memories of today are swirling between us like a mist amid the weight of our grief. As much as the experience of collecting his death certificate was painful, we've been brought together because of it.

Leo, Artie, Elijah. The names circle in my head, echoing like the distant singing of children's nursery rhymes and added to the list of other babies my boy will never get to know.

Ring a ring a roses…
Atishoo atishoo we all fall down
Twinkle Twinkle little Star
How I wonder what you are…

I close my eyes and imagine him lying next to those babies on mats at a Baby Massage Class. I see him and Fergus crawling around with push-along-toys at a Drop-in-and-Play session. I imagine him at nursery; at birthday parties; on his first day at primary school. Secondary school. Football matches. Scout camp. Movie nights. Prom. Graduation. Wedding day. In an alternate universe – one where Leo had lived – this would have been my reality.

'Sofie?'

I open my eyes and look at my husband's face on the pillow next to me. His eyes are wide open, but unusually distant. I wonder if he's imagining an alternative future for our boy, too. Is he consumed with thoughts of what life would have been like if we'd been registering his birth today, instead?

Am I destined to always be defined by my most loved one's deaths? Dead Dad Girl, now Dead Baby Mother?

There's a rushing sound in my head, like I'm on a waltzer and I feel my brain ricocheting between the two worst experiences of my life until they're all I'm made up of.

'Sofie?' he repeats. He eases up on one elbow and rests his head on his hand.

'Mmm?' I lift my lips to his. At least there is still him. Still us. Certainty. Stability. Love. We kiss for a long time. We kiss like we are trying to forget. Briefly, I feel myself leave my brain and the pain of my body behind and I'm able to focus only on the moment.

Even though it was hard, maybe today has led to a small amount of acceptance. Perhaps this is a turning point not just for me – but for us both. I know I've been distant; not known how to reach out to Rory, only lean on him. I'd like that to change. I allow my hands to travel down under the covers to Rory's waist; my fingers graze his stomach and continue their sudden, urgent journey down. I'm desperate to be released from this pain, to find pleasure again. I slip my fingers under the elastic of his pants, trying to find the smooth, thick arc of him. I want to hold Rory, cling to him like a safety rope.

I'm surprised when he draws back and opens his eyes.

'You know, Sofie,' he murmurs, 'seeing those babies today really made me think about—'

'Me, too.' I tuck my forehead in the place between his jaw and chin, rest my free hand on his chest and brush my fingers through the fine golden curls of his chest hair, marvelling at how my body fits so perfectly against his.

'Really?' I look up and see surprise has spread over his face.

His relief confuses me. Why would he think they *wouldn't* make me think of Leo?

He pulls himself up to sitting.

'I haven't wanted to say anything, Sof,' he says. 'I know it's not the right time and I know it's way too soon. But since this afternoon, it's all I keep thinking about. And I was so worried you wouldn't feel the same way, you know, about us trying for another baby one day…'

I roll away immediately. Pull the duvet up around my chest.

'I've been thinking what life would be like if Leo was still *here*. Not what it would be like to have another baby.' My voice is dull, distant. I feel like I'm underwater again and I've forgotten how to swim.

'Of course.' Rory rolls towards me, puts his hand on my arm. I stiffen. He rests his head next to me, his hand travels down my arm. I fight the urge to fling it off. 'Me too. It was just… Seeing those parents in that waiting room with their babies, it made me think… It made me think I still *want* that for us one day. I know we've just been unlucky…'

Needles prickle the back of my throat; my breath vacuums back into my chest so that even as I try to speak, only one word comes out as a thrust of effort.

'*Unlucky?*'

'Yes! The chances are…'

I swing my legs out of bed, my back turned to him.

'I don't want to take any more *chances*, Rory. We rolled the dice and lost, okay?'

Rigidly, I walk to the bedroom door, get my dressing gown and put it on whilst still talking. 'Every possible outcome – good, bad, or tragic – has the same chance of occurring again.'

'Maths doesn't always provide the right answer, Sofie,' Rory says quietly.

'No?' I laugh bitterly. 'Well, nor do your pie-in-the-sky philosophies based on random chance. At least I have actual *reasoning* to back this up. Do you know all the countless ways that you can experience pregnancy loss, Rory? You can't just order a new healthy baby. No one is magically immune from the worst outcome. There's no 'luck', only calculated risk. And losing Leo—' I stop and gasp as my breath shallows and the boot stamps down on my chest again. '—Leo dying,' I carry on, determined to get my point across, 'has proven to me that best thing to do is take *no* risks at all.'

'But if we'd taken no risks, we'd never have had him!' Rory counters, desperately. 'And I'll never regret having Leo.' He slumps back against the pillows. I lean against the doorframe then, suddenly unable to hold myself up, I begin to weep.

'Sofie.' Rory scrambles out of bed and wraps me in his arms and I lean limply against him.

'I don't want another baby, Rory. All I want is Leo. All day, every day I think of him. I even dream about him. I imagine what he'd be doing now if he was alive. How many hours he might be sleeping; what it would be like to breastfeed him, to take him out in his pram, watch him sleep. It was *Leo's* face I saw on those babies, Rory. Only him. There will only ever be him for me now, and if you can't cope with that, then perhaps you need to be with someone else.' I try to take another breath, but it rattles in my chest relentlessly until I begin to sob.

'Sofie, don't ever say that. I love you. I only want you…' Rory says softly.

I hear those words but don't believe them. I turn away from him. Not only have I failed Leo as a mother, but I'm also failing Rory as a wife. Because the difference between Rory and me is that all *I* want is Leo.

Chapter Forty-Four

It's Saturday night and I'm going out for the second time this week. Not content with going to the town hall to register my son's death, Nisha and I are in a cab on our way to meet Emma, Sal and Inge in a cocktail bar by Bournemouth Pier. We're celebrating both Emma's birthday and Nisha exchanging on the house she saw in Brocklehurst. I'm only going because Nisha said it would be good for me. She, Rory, and even Mum think I need to 'see people', or, specifically, 'see friends.'

To be a better friend, wife, and daughter, I said, 'Okay'. Perhaps if I say the word enough, I might eventually feel it?

Today, I also said, 'Okay' to this Friday, the sixteenth of March, for Leo's cremation. Exactly a month since I delivered him.

I want it to be just Rory and me at the crematorium. It's probably selfish, but I don't want to share a minute of our time with Leo. We've promised Mum and Nanny Sandra that we'll invite them to a proper memorial where we'll scatter his ashes, when I'm feeling stronger. But I can't face having to share my grief with anyone else, or to feel under pressure to think of anyone other than Leo.

So obviously, it makes sense that I'm preparing myself for the big event by getting all dressed up and going out on a Saturday night, like normal people do. I'm pretending to be 'okay' even though in six days' time I will have to face yet another unthinkable event and cremate my baby boy.

Rory was surprised (but clearly pleased) that I agreed. He looked at me when I came downstairs, like he did when he first met me. But then, when I looked closer, I realised that there was a new distance in his expression now.

I left him in the lounge, head bowed over his phone. Face lit by the blue, ghoulish glow of the virtual friends on Instagram that have done a better job of keeping him company recently than I have. Comforted him. Lifted him up in a way that I've not been able to.

Last weekend, Rory asked me if it was okay if he sent an Instagram post, sharing the news of Leo's loss to his 11,000-plus followers. Just a photo of Leo's footprints with his name, birthdate and three words written in the post:

Stillborn, still loved.

There were no hashtags, no other details.

I made it clear I didn't love the idea.

'We can't hide it,' Rory had said. 'The channel announced our pregnancy by sharing the photo of us at Durdle Door. When I was on air the day you went to the hospital, I told people we were due any day now. People will be wondering, Sofie. They'll ask…'

'I don't want you to tell strangers, Rory, like you'd broadcast any other local interest news. Leo, our experience, he's—it's private.' The air between us had become thick with tension.

'I won't *broadcast* it, Sofie. I won't give any personal details or share photos of him. I just need to do this before I go back to work so I don't have to deal with random people coming up to me on the street and asking me about the baby.' He'd looked so exhausted, so broken by his role as Chief News-breaker, Chief Caregiver, Chief Survival Officer that I'd acquiesced.

'Okay,' I'd said. The now familiar word reluctantly exiting my mouth. I can't work out if Rory is always asking too much of me, or if I'm always giving him too little?

He posted the picture Nisha took of Leo's feet cupped in his hands. From the moment he did, his phone began lighting up every two seconds like a laser show. He was flooded with likes and sympathetic, supportive comments.

'See?' he said, showing them to me. His face had brightened; his mood lifted by the comments, which clearly made him feel vindicated. That people were inherently good and kind supporters. Rather than, as I believe, inherently nosy voyeurs.

He spent the evening refreshing and replying to each comment whilst I stared at the TV waiting for him to be back in the room with me. Eventually, I gave up.

'I'm going to bed.' I reached over to kiss him, but he barely looked up from his phone.

'Night, Sofie!' His cheeks were flushed, eyes bright, he sounded almost *high*. The act of reaching out and sharing our son's death had done this. It had unleashed a new life in Rory. It both sickened me and made me curious. Maybe I should share more, too? Look for connection instead of severance, risk moving my boundaries for once. Let people in instead of keeping them out.

And so here I am. On my way out – of my head and the house. I'm going to talk. Drink. Share. Cry. Laugh, even. Perhaps that will make me feel, if not better, then more ... normal.

As soon as Nisha and I walk into the bar I know I've made a huge mistake. I feel panicked and out of place. It's so brightly lit I feel like I'm centre stage. I know immediately that no amount of drink is going to make me feel like I can blend in. If this is normal, I'm far from it.

The place is packed with people dressed up to the nines. Not at sixes and sevens, like I am. I feel old, bruised; both conspicuous and invisible at the same time. I tug self-consciously at my black top and too tight jeans that Nisha assured me were fine to wear for a night out in town. I notice a stain on my crumpled top and rub at it half-heartedly. I scrunch my toes in my old strappy sandals and notice how tacky my carelessly painted toenails look. Who am I doing this for? Certainly not me. My phone pings just as Nisha spots the girls at a corner table. I pull it out of my bag and read the message from Rory.

> Have fun! Rx

My fingers hover for a moment, thinking of all the things I could say. That this is the opposite of fun; the concept of fun died when my baby did. I don't say that. Instead, I type two letters.

I stare at the text, hit send and put my phone back in my bag.

Nisha firmly guides me towards the table. Emma smiles warily as we approach and then turns and says something to Inge. Sal has a rictus smile plastered on her long, pale face.

'Are you okay?' Nisha murmurs as we approach the table. They're all holding a glass of prosecco, the oxygen in the room dissipates and I have to clutch on to Nisha's arm as I gasp for air. 'It's going to be fine,' she says.

'Okay,' I manage obediently as we continue our approach, but then I stop and try to turn back to the door.

Nisha takes my hand with her free one and squeezes it. I look at her desperately and she stares steadily back at me, her perfectly lined eyes unblinking, like a cat. 'Sofie, it's just the girls. It'll be fine.'

'Okay,' I say again, plastering on a smile as we head towards the table.

Chapter Forty-Five

Emma greets me first. She gets up, opens her arms, edges around the table and hugs me so tightly I can barely breathe. I want to lean into it, but my body just stiffens.

'I'm sorry,' she says, wiping her eyes as she pulls away. 'I swore I wouldn't do this. I just— it's so awful. It was such a shock.'

'I know; it's okay,' I say.

'You shouldn't be comforting me. I'm so happy you're here, Sof,' she says tearfully.

I nod, too choked to speak.

I turn and say hello to Inge knowing I'll be in safe hands with her. Inge is always the life and soul of the party. The one to crack inappropriate jokes. The wild card.

But she just smiles rigidly at me. 'Hello, Sofie. I'm so ... glad ... you could ... come.' She speaks in staccato, like she's learned a script. 'I can't imagine how hard this is for you.' She steps back, her lines in this tragic play clearly over. Frankly, I'd have preferred a joke.

I swallow, smile. Move on. Sal doesn't speak at all she just waves awkwardly from a distance then sits down hurriedly.

How did Nisha convince me that coming to a bar to meet my friends for the first time since Leo died was going to be anything other than excruciatingly awkward? I can see with almost X-ray vision what they're thinking. They have no idea what to say, how to be around me. They just want to get this over with. I don't blame them.

They've all done their bit over the past few weeks. They've texted me their condolences, sent cards and flowers, they've even asked to visit. Emma even turned up on the doorstep one day. But I wanted to see them only when I could smile and say with some truth that I'm doing better. Wear my grief with an element of dignity. But now I realise that it is way too soon for any of that. I shouldn't have come. I'm not fit for social interaction.

And yet here I am.

Nisha and I sit down. Emma pours us both a drink. We all hover our glasses in the air awkwardly for a moment before we clink.

'Happy birthday!'

The words pierce my heart, the high-pitched but celebratory sound of the toast is as discordant as my presence at the table.

Happy Birthday.

It will never have the same meaning again.

Conversation quickly segues to Nisha's new house.

'Cheers to moving in day!' Inge says and raises her glass. I take a huge swig.

There's an awkward lull in conversation when Nisha goes to the bar to buy another bottle.

I down all of my prosecco, feeling the bubbles burn in my throat. I empty the rest of the bottle into my glass, filling it to the top without offering it to anyone else. Eyes shift. The tension is thick. I drain this second glass quickly, too: I want that hit of warmth, then the welcome blur that I remember so well from after Dad died.

I drink half the next glass, wait for someone to speak. I look around at the varying vignettes of people having A Good Time: laughing, drinking, flirting, kissing. It feels a world away. A different universe.

Should I talk first? Show them a photo of Leo? I scrabble in my bag for my phone.

'It's so good to see you, Sofie,' Emma says. I look up at her, phone in my hand, with Leo's photo as my screensaver. I look down, then back at her. Her smile is frozen on her soft, rounded face as she holds tightly to her glass. She hasn't taken a sip from it; her eyes are darting around the room, looking for an escape.

I want to show him off, let her see how perfect he was – how *real*. But I realise it's not socially acceptable to present a photo of your dead baby in a bar.

So I slip the phone back in my bag and ask her about her baby. About Fergus. But as soon as I do, her face turns taut. She flushes red. Emma glances at the girls, puts down her still-full glass of prosecco.

'Sofie, I … well, I have to tell you something. I'm pregnant again.'

Both boots of grief. A full fucking stampede.

I'm cremating my baby next week and Emma's going to have another one.

'Oh, that's wonderful news,' I manage, in monotone. 'Congratulations.' I want to feel happy, I do, but it just hurts.

'I'm so sorry, Sofie,' she says, clearly upset. 'I didn't know if … *how* to tell you. If you'd be okay…'

'Of *course* I'm okay!' I enthuse, my voice louder than I expect it to be. 'I'm so happy for you, Emma!'

So happy for you. But also, really fucking sad for me.

'I don't want this to be a problem with us, you know?' She tilts her head to one side, takes my hand, draws in her eyebrows. 'It happened once; it'll happen again for you Sofie. I know it will. You're meant to be a mum.'

I don't know how to unpick all that she's said. As if Leo was just a stepping stone to success. *It didn't work out, but hey-ho! You can try again.*

Just then Nisha comes back with another bottle of fizz, and I raise my glass instantly so it can be filled.

'Just in time, Nish! We're celebrating! Emma's pregnant again! Isn't that wonderful? Isn't she lucky?' My voice is too loud. Too high. Too forced. Nisha glances at me with concern, then turns to Emma and hugs her.

'To luck!' I say. 'May you be blessed by good, not broken by bad.' I down my glass of prosecco. Then, I pick up Emma's glass and down that, too.

One for each of her babies. And then one more for mine.

Emma and the girls leave quite quickly after that, saying they need to get back for their babysitters.

'Lucky you!' I slur into my glass.

Nisha and I make our way out of the bar not long after, me staggering whilst she tries to hold me up. The blast of cold air nearly knocks me over. Streetlights orb brightly against the rain-soaked streets making my eyes squint and my head spin.

'I'm so sorry, Sofie, I shouldn't have left you alone like that,' Nisha says as I sink to the ground. 'I didn't know about Emma. I'd no idea... Oh, Sofie.'

I lean over, vomit, then begin to cry.

'I'm a mess,' I sob.

'You're human, Sofie. And being human *is* messy, full of pain, but also full of love.'

I shake my head, sniff, wipe my streaming nose. 'I'm a horrible person, Nisha. Selfish, mean, angry. So fucking angry, Nisha! I don't know what to do with it. I didn't deserve to have Leo. I don't deserve to have Rory, or you...' I'm sobbing again.

'Shh, now,' Nisha says, holding back my hair. 'That's not true.'

'It is,' I say quietly, tears rolling down my cheeks. 'I'm a terrible person who doesn't deserve any of what I have.'

'You're right, you don't, Sofie. No one deserves what you are having to go through. Not this much pain, it's not fucking fair. And I wish it hadn't happened to you.'

I wipe my mouth, hiccup, shake my head. 'But it has. And it'll never be okay again.'

'I know,' she says tearfully.

'No, you don't.' I stretch my legs out in front of me, feet encased in the strappy sandals, now swollen, red with cold. Stupid me for thinking I could be normal. Nisha takes her shoes off, stretches her legs out next to mine. She turns and looks at me.

The stars above us blur and stretch so Nisha seems to be bathed in a spotlight.

'I do know, Sofie,' she says then. 'I do.'

I stare at her in disbelief as a dense stillness expands between us.

Nisha's eyes are pools of black. I reach out and hold her hand. Squeeze it tightly. I'm aware we must look ridiculous, two grown women slumped on the cold, wet ground, oblivious to everything around us.

'Nisha?' I croak. 'What are you saying?'

She stares at the ground. 'I found out I was pregnant, just before Andy broke up with me. He was horrified. He told me it was a mistake and that I should get rid of it. That he had no intention of having any more children and had already decided to go back to his wife.' She sticks her chin out defiantly and stares out ahead towards the sea in the deeply veiled distance.

'Oh, Nisha. Why didn't you tell me?' I think of the long period of silence after she came to dinner with Rory and me. I didn't call her, because I was too busy judging her for her affair. I had no idea she was going through all this. I feel awful.

'I was too humiliated; too ashamed. I knew that the relationship was wrong, but the baby ... it was everything I wanted. And then, by the time I saw you for lunch in Bournemouth ... when you told me your news. Well, I was no longer pregnant by then.' Her voice is thin, discordant, reedy, an instrument that hasn't played this tune before.

'What happened?'

She blinks, looks up at the sky. 'Andy tried to convince me to have an abortion, but I refused. I didn't care that he didn't want me. I resolved to love the baby more, be more to my child than he could have ever been. For a few short weeks, I felt stronger than ever. Able to face the world head on, now there was two of us. I wanted it so much. But then...' she pauses. 'I began bleeding when I was about eight weeks. I was at work, and I knew straight away. I went home. Passed these clots—' She stops. Breaks down.

'Oh, no, no. I'm so sorry, Nisha,' I say at last, squeezing her hand tightly. 'I'm so sorry.'

She sniffs, wipes her eyes. 'It's nothing like what you've been through...'

I take her by the shoulders, look her in the eyes 'Nisha, never say that. Your baby died, too.' I hug her then and she begins to sob. I can't bear just how much I have let her down. She was protecting me. Like she always does. And what have I done for her?

'You haven't told Sita and Arj?' She shakes her head. 'Anyone?'

She shakes it again. 'Nisha, if I'd known I'd have come to London. I'd have…'

'If you'd known,' she cuts in determinedly, 'your pregnancy would not have been the calm, beautiful journey it was. For the first time in years, when you were carrying Leo, your life was driven by hope, not fear. I didn't want to take that away from you. Look,' she smiles bravely, her eyes glistening still. 'You don't have to worry about me. I'm made of tough stuff. I just wanted you to know that I understand the pain of a friend telling you their happy news unexpectedly.'

I put my head in my hands. 'You sat there and listened while I told you I was pregnant. You even took me maternity shopping…' My head spins as I recall that day. Her shock. The secret tears behind her sunglasses. The pain she buried to protect me and my baby.

'I did it because I could be happy for you and sad for me at the same time. And you know I'd do it again,' she adds, her dark eyes flashing like the stars above us. 'Even though it was hard, your pregnancy gave me hope, too. Both our babies have made me even more certain that this is what I want. I've decided I'm going to do it alone. I've started looking into sperm donation. I want to be a mum, Sofie, and I'm going to do everything I can to be one.'

A silence falls between us again.

'That's so brave of you, Nisha.' I suddenly feel so exhausted I can barely hold my head up. 'I have to bury my baby this week.'

She strokes my hair with her spare hand. 'I know. Come on, let's get you up and home.'

She manages to get me on my feet again. It's raining harder now. Nisha spots a glowing light through the rain and she raises her hand to flag the taxi down.

The cab pulls up and we climb in. I rest my head on Nisha's shoulder as we head home, our fingers locked tightly together. For the first time in years, we're completely in the same place.

Chapter Forty-Six

The Gothic-style chapel at Bournemouth crematorium is a sombre grey sepulchre against the forget-me-not sky.

A starry runway of daffodils lines the path to the chapel. It's a bitterly cold March day – six days since I went out with Nisha and the girls. I sent a message to them afterwards. I was completely honest, explained it was too soon for me. I even shared that Leo's cremation was coming up. I've realised after talking to Nisha that I have nothing to hide; nothing to be ashamed of. I don't have to go through this alone. I'm sick of hiding my grief and I want all my friends to know that, one day, I'll be strong enough to be around them all again. Just not yet.

I also sent a little pregnancy pamper package to Emma congratulating her, with a long note telling her how much I'm looking forward to meeting her baby. I wrote that I hoped she understood if I keep away for now. That as happy as I am for her, I'm still sad for me and I need to just work my way through that. *I'll get there, though*, I wrote. *I promise. It's just still such early days.* A package arrived from her this morning – a beautiful, scented candle with an L on for Leo. She said she thought perhaps we might like to light it in the chapel at the crematorium, or back at home. She said she'd be thinking of us and Leo. And that when I'm ready, she'd love to hear more about him.

The thought of seeing her, so I could talk to my friend about my baby boy made me feel so briefly, unexpectedly happy that I cried.

I cling tightly to Rory's arm with one hand now, the other is thrust firmly in my pocket for warmth. I'm full of trepidation, but also desperate to be near Leo again. It's a small comfort to know that after this ceremony, he will be home with us, once and for all. No more hospital rooms, no mortuaries, no more coffin. Eventually, we'll bury his ashes somewhere. We just don't know where that will be yet. I'm learning that these decisions become clear, in time.

We're greeted at the door by a man who gives us an order of service with Leo's name and birth date, the date of the service, the location and the lyrics of the songs that will be played during the service. The hospital organised most of it, but the songs are all my choice. We chose to not have a vicar or registrar. The man smiles kindly and says he'll be upstairs in charge of the music. He says to take as long as we need.

The room is small, but Leo's tiny coffin – which I can see ahead – is still swallowed by it. I cling to Rory's arm with my free hand, and he steadies me. He is staring at the coffin. For a moment, I'm uncertain if either of us will make it as far as Leo. But we've done harder things. I'm just thankful we don't have an audience. Rory is worried that it looks like we're freezing our family and friends out, but this service will be one of the scarce moments of being his parents that we'll have, and I want to be fully present for him. Not trying to hold ourselves together in front of others.

I'm wearing my work uniform of white shirt and black trousers because I couldn't face buying anything 'special'. Rory's wearing black jeans, a dark polo-neck jumper and his navy wool, double-breasted coat. A camel scarf is looped around his neck and his sunglasses are clutched so tightly in his hand his knuckles have turned white. We've learned the hard way that they're a necessary accessory for any trip in public, regardless of the weather. He's also wearing a daffodil from our garden in his lapel. I can also see, on top of Leo's coffin, the halo of white narcissus that bloomed in our garden in the last few days and that we picked for him. This trumpet-like flower that appears briefly but abundantly at this time of year has become

Leo's emblem: the impression they make on the world is immense, but they're gone as quickly as they came.

Just as we were leaving to come here, Rory handed me a box.

'A gift,' he said. 'For today. Well, not just today…'

Inside was a simple gold necklace with a round, spinning pendant. In the centre, on one side is a tiny version of Leo's footprint, the *Infinity* symbol is etched in italic underneath. On the other is his name and birthdate. I'd cried as Rory had clasped it round my neck. Then Rory had handed me a piece of paper. It was a certificate of a star he'd named after Leo, the nearest one to his constellation that he could get.

I press one hand against the necklace for strength as we begin the walk towards Leo's tiny coffin. I'm shocked by its insignificant size. How can it be so small when I feel like Leo's presence filled my entire universe?

I stumble a couple of times, vision blurred from my tears. Each step takes me closer to Leo and for that I'm grateful. 'Circle of Life' from *The Lion King* is playing. His song.

We arrive in front of the white casket just as the chorus hits. I knew it would be emotional, but I didn't anticipate Rory's loud sobs, his body convulsing with raw, pent-up grief. I realise then that he hasn't prepared himself for this moment. Rory doesn't have a blueprint for death like I do. It's a cruel fact that his first funeral happens to be his baby son's. He also hasn't spent the last few weeks consumed by grief, crying continuously and staring blankly into the distance like I have. He's had to 'man up', 'be strong', 'keep it together' – not just for me, but for every single person who has called, or messaged, or come knocking at the door.

I put my arm around Rory, holding him up for a change. I feel calm, peaceful, determined to be strong for my boys. Rory has taken out a piece of paper, but he seems frozen, unable to open it, let alone read the words.

I reach for it. At the top, in his generous, looping handwriting is written, 'The Little Prince'. It's from the same book that he's holding.

'I'm sorry…' he sobs.

I don't know if he's talking to me or to Leo.

'I'll do it,' I say, my voice quiet but strong. He nods, his shoulders shaking as I slip my free hand back into his and begin to read the passage about all men having stars.

At the bottom, Rory has written:

Goodnight our precious little star, sleep tight, shine bright.

We love you and will look for you forever,
Mummy and Daddy xxx

Still clutching the piece of paper, I rest my hands on the casket and lower my head to kiss it and it's then that my tears silently fall on to the smooth, white wood. My necklace dangles against it, knocking gently against the surface. Rory's hands curl round me and he pulls me back and I allow myself to be held by him. I take out the daffodil from his lapel, and gently place it in the centre of the other cloud-white daffodils.

A few minutes later we turn and retreat out of the chapel, two lost vessels sailing side by side through a storm, not knowing if we will ever reach dry land again.

Chapter Forty-Seven

That night when I get into bed, I don't immediately turn away from Rory to stare at the wall until sleep comes, which has been customary over the past few weeks. Instead, I curl up against him, my eyelashes brushing against his cheek.

Other than my brief fumble, which ended with Rory asking about trying for another baby, we haven't attempted sex. The advice from doctors after you give birth is to wait four to six weeks – but what about when your baby has died? What then? When the place that used to be about love, intimacy, passion, *life* has become a graveyard? No matter how much I may want to, I don't know how to turn our bed into a place of pleasure again.

Rory lifts his hand and caresses my cheek, drops his hand to the necklace he gave me, lowers his lips and kisses it and the skin of my decolletage. I realise now how much I've missed the feel of him. Like a cat, I stretch out alongside my husband. Feet touching feet, knees touching knees. Thighs. Stomach. Chest. Lips. And being there, like this, with him, I feel … better. I acknowledge this small degree of happiness, surprised that this is an emotion still accessible to me. It makes me wonder what else I might be capable of, with a bit of effort.

Rory moves, twitches slightly, almost imperceptibly. His breathing grows heavier with held back intent. He moves his hand slowly, lifts it to my forehead, gently brushes my hair from my forehead and his fingers lightly trace down the outline of my face. After a moment's pause, he tentatively lowers his lips to mine and lightly covers them with his.

'I love you, Sofie,' he murmurs, then pulls away. He's letting me know that there is no pressure, no expectation for anything more.

But I find myself wanting more. I raise my lips and kiss him again, pressing them against his with strength. Surprised, he opens his eyes. Kisses me back. It is so gentle, so uncertain but also so full of love, it makes me weep silently. As my salty tears gather in the parting of our lips. I realise I'm trembling.

'Sofie,' Rory murmurs then, saying my name like a prayer.

I feel a deep yearning to let go of the pain. To be a part of each other again. One plus one instead of minus one. But I'm scared. Petrified, actually. My body has been like an abandoned puppet for weeks, limp with a lack of desire for life, let alone sex. I want to connect to it again. Connect to him.

Tentatively, I draw my arm up and across Rory, so that my hand is resting lightly on his chest, my head in the nook of his shoulder and neck. I let my lips brush against his skin and breathe in the familiar, musky scent of him. I feel cossetted by the warmth of our bed and our bodies. I'm acutely aware that even though our world has collapsed in on itself, by being together like this we might just be able to lay the first foundation of something new.

I close my eyes and allow myself to drift away from the memories of the last few weeks. From Leo, even. Focusing on the moment and the memory of what I used to do and how good it used to feel, I lift my head and cover Rory's mouth with light kisses and he warily accepts them. Where once this act was fluent, natural, now it's stilted, reticent. I know I have to lead; let him know this is what I want not what I think he wants. I allow my tongue to caress his upper lip and he responds by welcoming it with his.

'Please,' I say softly when Rory tentatively pulls away again after a minute. 'Please don't stop,' I urge. Obediently, he kisses me again and I allow my hand to travel down his chest, into his pyjama bottoms. His eyes display a mixture of longing and apprehension. He moans as my hands find the smooth shaft of him.

'Is it okay if I touch you, too?' Rory murmurs, as his hand slips underneath my T-shirt.

Even as I will my brain to want this, my body involuntarily tenses as he touches me. I can't stop thinking that what comes next will involve him touching the places that most recently belonged to Leo: my breasts that were full of milk for him, my vagina that delivered him.

I try to relax, close my eyes to concentrate on the sensations, but all I see is the bright, white hospital room; feel the bed beneath me where I laboured; hear my cries as I give birth to our sleeping boy. I open them again, but it's only Leo's face I can see, not Rory's, the contours of his perfect profile pressed against the back of my eyelids like a flower in a scrapbook. I *want* to feel desire. I *want* to separate sex with my husband from the trauma of our loss. I *want* to be a wife again – in all senses of the word. I want to, but I can't.

I try to allow my lips to respond to Rory's, but the guilt, shame and pain flood in at the same time. I feel myself drifting away to a distant shore.

'Sofie?' Rory pulls his lips away and strokes my hair tenderly. 'It's okay, let's just lie here together. Honestly, it's okay.' I look up at his face in the half light and feel myself crumple at what we've lost. Not just Leo, but part of us.

My face wet with tears, Rory murmurs messages of love and comfort in my ear, spooning and gently rocking me as I turn away from him. He tells me that it's okay, that it's still early days. He tells me that he loves me and is proud of how brave and strong I am. But as I lie here, tears wetting the pillow as they have every night since Leo died, I don't feel brave and strong, I feel bereft. And I can't help but feel that Rory deserves more than this. He deserves more than *me*. Just like Nisha deserves a better friend, my mum a better daughter. And Leo deserved a better mum.

I wait, not moving at all while Rory holds me. He does so until he thinks I'm asleep, then he lets go gently, slowly rolls out of bed. I don't move a muscle as he opens the door, creeps out the room and goes upstairs.

I lie alone, staring at the wall and thinking about the wall that divides us now. And I have no idea how to break it down.

Part III

maggie and milly and molly and may
Went down to the beach (to play one day)
and maggie discovered a shell that sang
so sweetly she couldn't remember her troubles, and
milly befriended a stranded star
whose rays five languid fingers were;
and molly was chased by a horrible thing
which raced sideways while blowing bubbles: and
may came home with a smooth round stone
as small as a world and as big as alone
for whatever we lose (like a you or a me),
it's always ourselves we find in the sea.

E.E Cummings

Chapter Forty-Eight

'What are your plans for today, Sof? A beach walk perhaps? Coffee with a friend?' Rory makes these suggestions hopefully. Always hopeful, that's my husband.

'Maybe,' I reply, clasping the cup of tea he has brought me, between my palms.

'I was thinking, why don't we get away this weekend – just for a night? We could stay in a hotel; a change of scene might do us the world of good. And it would be a nice way to celebrate my first week back at work.'

Celebrate?

I don't reply; I just stare into the brown murky liquid swirling in my mug. Rory is at the foot of the bed, feverishly tidying my discarded clothes into neat, folded piles whilst also getting dressed for his first day back, putting on his jeans, hopping into his socks and pulling on an impeccably pressed shirt, whilst I lie here with this cup of tea.

The doorbell rings then and he dashes downstairs, coming back with three large parcels, which he starts to carry up to his office.

'What are they?' I ask.

He turns, looks down at them and then at me. 'Oh, a little treat I bought myself. It's some new gaming stuff. I've set up an area upstairs in my office. It's just something to … you know … take my mind off things.'

I nod, understanding. I don't begrudge him needing an escape.

I also know he has no real choice other than to go back to work. The TV station has already kindly given him extended compassionate leave until after Leo's cremation. I just don't understand why passing that milestone means life is suddenly meant to go on as normal? This isn't going to suddenly get easier.

I look out of our balcony doors at the magnolia tree. The scale of my daily achievement over the past week has been obsessively watching it slowly come into flower. Each bud like a baby swaddled in its own pale pink petals. Sometimes petals will brush against the window, plucked mercilessly from the tree by the wind so early in their already brief life.

It's Monday 26 March, ten days since Leo's cremation. Just over five weeks since he was born. Outside the world is coming out of a long winter; the days are stretching; leaves are growing; buds are forming. New life developing. The world is waking up.

Everyone – including Rory, it seems – expects me to come out of hibernation, too.

Rory's doing his hair in the mirror now. It has been newly cut. When did he get that done? I know that last night he shaved off his straggly, overgrown stubble. His grief uniform of tracksuit bottoms and T-shirt have now been put away. It's like he's slowly transforming, too. He looks almost exactly like he used to before Leo died. He's wearing the same air of childish excitement, too.

'Don't go,' I say then, under my breath. Then louder. He turns to look at me.

I beg him to stay; tell him my fears that if he leaves, something might happen to him, too. Why wouldn't it? It's what happens to people I love. In response, Rory rubs his forehead and face which makes his features elongate so much it's like looking at him in a Hall of Mirrors.

Roll up, roll up again to the Circus of Grief. Meet the Incredible Stretching Man whose wife causes him such worry and exhaustion that his face is made of rubber!

'Sof, we've talked about this.' He walks over and sits on the edge

This Wasn't Meant to Happen

of the bed. 'This kind of irrational catastrophising isn't healthy.' He pulls a card out of his pocket. It's for the counselling service at the hospital. 'There's support and help out there. I think you need to start using it.'

I take it, limply. How am I being irrational when every fear I've ever had has been proven by Leo's death? Surely now Rory must see that my belief system has always been the right one.

Taking my silence as acquiescence, he kisses me on the forehead like a child and tells me to have a good day. Then he strides out of the bedroom and down the stairs. He's out of the house moments later. I look at the clock – 7:45am – after I hear the front door click. Rory's calm and orderly early exit is a departure from his usual whirlwind of snooze buttons, staggered dressing and hurried breakfast. Even though I'd always left long before him to go for a swim and then to work, the evidence of his morning routine was there in the tornado of mess, unmade bed, trail of crumbs and half-drunk cups of tea in the kitchen that greeted me in the evening when I got home.

I get up as soon he's left as if to prove that I can. When I make my way downstairs, it's like he's never been here at all. The Scandi-style kitchen is completely immaculate. I glance at the vast dining table, empty save for the spray of eucalyptus in a ceramic vase in the middle. Why does it seem much too big for us now, even though Leo never came home? I go into the hallway. For once, he hasn't pulled every one of his many coats off the hooks and thrown them on the floor to get to the one he wanted. Or left a trail of rejected shoes and lace-up boots in his wake for me to put away.

It's as if Rory's never even been here. It's how I felt when he removed all the baby paraphernalia, too. Strangely, I long for the mess back. To have my old husband back, the one who promised me everything would always be okay. And the naïve version of me that believed him. But mostly, I want Leo back.

I eat breakfast without tasting a thing, shower without feeling the water, get dressed in clothes that finally fit my body and just want to rip them all off as they no longer reflect me.

Outwardly, I look 'normal'. My milk has long since dried up; my tummy is slowly shrinking so it just looks like I'm carrying a little extra weight rather than a pregnancy bump and my stitches have healed. Inside, I'm unrecognisable.

As the morning passes, I find I'm relieved to have the chance to be on my own with Leo. I spend most of the morning in his nursery, holding his little urn of ashes, which we're keeping on the mantlepiece until we work out when and where to scatter them. Only the bright, lunchtime sun streaming through the window encourages me to go downstairs and out into the garden.

Once out there, wrapped up in my coat, I notice that the tulip bulbs have pushed their way through the ground. Bright daffodils border the garden like a halo. I close my eyes and allow the sunshine to warm my face. I've brought the urn outside, not wanting to leave Leo for a second. I hug him to my chest, thankful he's with me.

Looking around, I notice some wild chickweed growing over our small veggie patch. I remember how Dad often used it in curries and decide that I'll cook one for Rory, just like I used to.

My phone pings and I pull it out of my pocket, expecting it to be Rory. But it's Joe.

> At work and just wanted to check in. Thinking of you both. Hope you're finding a way through.

I think for a moment, before typing.

> Surviving, thank you for asking, Joe. How's everything there?

Thirty seconds later, Joe replies.

> Tarun the twat is making you look even better at your job on a daily basis.

I smile, grateful for the support and reassurance that Joe keeps providing from a distance, reminding me about my life before.

I look down at the chickweed in my hand and have a sudden, visceral memory of Dad and I, out for a walk in the fields and woodlands of Purbeck the summer before he died. We hadn't gone foraging together for years, partly due to my teenage hormones, which meant I mostly wanted to be either on my own or with my mates, but also because Dad was barely there. He'd leave the house long before I got up. In the evenings he'd walk, too, stopping only to eat dinner before he was off across the fields without a backwards glance. On this day, I'd woken early, anxious about my looming GCSEs. Dad had been in the kitchen, staring out the window into the dusky pink morning light. I'd walked up to him and, for some reason, slipped my hand into his. When I'd seen his foraging basket, tools and boots all there and ready, I'd asked if I could join him. Suddenly I wanted nothing more than to be the kid that went out walking with her dad.

Ten minutes later, we were striding through fields and forests together, feet wet with dew, golden, morning light guiding us, binding us together again. As I recall, we didn't talk much – Dad wasn't much of a communicator – but I felt like my world was balanced when I was with him like this. This version of my dad was the one I wanted. Not the quiet, distant one. Or the drunk, maudlin one.

I remember now how we happened across a large, soft carpet of chickweed dotted with tiny white flowers.

Dad had bent down and grasped a bunch tightly, his arm muscles twitching as he plucked and pulled it up to his nose, triumphantly breathing it in.

'Chickweed, the spring tonic,' he'd said in his soft, stilted Danish accent. 'It grows in groups and is delicious in salads, vinegars and curries. It can clean and boost your immune system. You can make it into an antiseptic salve. But, Sofie, like all plants, it can also teach us how to live and survive in balance with both ourselves and with others.'

I'd gazed at the plant he was holding, with its stringy stem and symmetrical opposing leaves and tiny star-like flowers. Dad told me they only lasted a few days.

'Even though chickweed looks like it grows in clumps,' he'd told me, 'it allows plenty of room to grow whilst maintaining a close relationship with other plants around it. He'd looked at me then, his sea-glass eyes opaque. 'We can learn so much from trees and plants. They don't have limits; their focus is always on personal growth. They react to the environment around them and adapt to the changing seasons. They know there'll be challenges ahead and adjust themselves accordingly. When a tree is exposed to the elements alone, it grows thicker roots, a thicker trunk. It becomes stronger to face the storm, Sofie.'

Remembering that conversation feels like a message in a bottle, found long after it has been sent out to sea. There was much to read into it.

Still thinking about his words, I take the chickweed, go back in the kitchen and start rummaging through my cupboards, getting old spice mixes and whatever ingredients I can find that will work in a curry. I make a batter with some chickpea flour, sliced onion, curry powder, water, egg and baking powder, then stir in the chopped chickweed leaves and cook them until crisp in hot oil. I add some green beans and other veg from the fridge. Then, I whip up the rest of the chickweed into a pesto – replacing my normal basil with it. The smell that lingers in the house is like taking a step back into my childhood. And just like that, for the first time in weeks I lose myself for the entire afternoon to something other than my grief for Leo.

Rory and I are sitting at the table eating the curry, to all intents and purposes like a normal couple. He's telling me about his day at work; I'm still thinking about his Instagram post that I saw before he got home.

I stare at the pakora curry that I put so much effort into making this afternoon and that gifted me rare respite from my grief. I scoop some curried chickweed into my mouth and feel a little of that same calm settle inside me.

'So, what have you done today?' he asks. 'Have you been anywhere?'

'I went in the garden,' I offer. 'Made this dinner.' Both feel like huge achievements to me. Clearly, Rory doesn't agree.

'Sofie,' Rory says gently, putting down his cutlery and staring at me with concern. 'It's not healthy cocooning yourself away. Why not ring Emma, or Nisha? See if they're free to meet up tomorrow? It'd be good for you to get out, to be with people, talk…'

'I'm okay here,' I reply stiffly. Most new mums struggle to get out

This Wasn't Meant to Happen

the house and don't feel like socialising. Why should I be any different just because Leo died?

And why is it that he thinks my wanting to spend time here with Leo alone, to make room to just sit with my grief is unhealthier somehow than him throwing himself into work and sharing everything on social media with strangers? Who decided *that* was a more acceptable grieving process?

Since he announced Leo's death, he's posted every day about Leo. So much for just sharing him once, to let everyone know what's happened. He hasn't put up a photo of him, or me, or the three of us together – I know he wouldn't do that without my permission – but earlier, he put up a photo of Leo's footprints that we were given for his memory box. He'd posted the quote underneath the picture: *There is no footprint too small that it cannot leave an imprint on the world.* He'd followed it up with a caption about how important it was for him to return to the world of work, to find a way to be with people again after being wrapped up in grief.

I find it hard because every feeling he shares with his followers, he fails to share with me first.

'I saw your post today. I thought you were only going to do one?' My voice is tighter and more strained than I intend.

Rory's chewing slows and he looks over at me, somewhere over my shoulders just like the consultant did that day. And the community midwife. Am I now invisible to my husband, too?

'I know you don't like social media, Sof, but it helps to share what he means to me. And I don't really have anyone else I can do that with.'

Me! I want to yell. *What about me?*

'Blokes aren't so easy to talk to, you know,' he continues. 'It's not the sort of thing you bring up at the pub. But here...' He looks down at his phone which is flashing with notifications. 'It feels good to connect with other people who understand. I'd like to share more. I hope that's okay?'

He starts telling me about the bereaved fathers he's started following, who have found him on social media. He explains how they've contacted him by DM to offer advice and support. He says he follows all the baby-loss charities: Sands. Tommy's. Saying Goodbye. He tells me our experience is shared by so many people and that talking to them helps him not feel so alone.

As Rory talks, I observe him. For the first time in weeks, I can see a glimmer of his old self back. Something has returned to his eyes – something that looks familiar. He's been lifted by these people, these strangers. They've given him back his positivity, his belief system. His hope. All things I have destroyed for him. How can I deny him this?

'Okay,' I say.

That word again.

He smiles at me with a full-watt Rory King smile, full of love and gratitude and positivity.

I look back down at my dinner and push it away, my appetite gone. Whilst I've missed the old Rory so much, I'm scared that if he's back and I'm not – where does that leave us?

Chapter Forty-Nine

Saturday night. Rory has completed his first week at work. He has been cycling there and back each day, like he used to. He's upstairs now, probably playing with this new gaming kit, add-ons of which seem to arrive daily. He said he wanted to give Nisha and me space to talk.

We are currently curled up on the sofa in the kitchen, drinking herbal tea to combat our post-takeaway bloat. A chess board sits between us. Nisha left London a couple of weeks ago and is staying temporarily with her parents until the small renovations are done on her new house. Each time she comes over, she forces me to play. It's like she thinks she's still dealing with seventeen-year-old me.

Back then, playing chess with her felt like getting a gentle push in the right direction. Now, it feels more like a shove.

'How are you doing, Sof?' She says now as she moves her white king's pawn forward two spaces, attacking the centre. 'Rory tells me you're thinking about going back to work. That's good.'

I look up at her in surprise. I mean, she's right – sort of. Not that I've had much chance to think about it. It was a conversation Rory broached with me only last night. I can't believe he's already talked about it to Nisha. It feels like a betrayal, but also, once again, like he's pushing his agenda for our future: *he* thinks it's time; therefore, it must be. The same way it was 'the right time' for us to meet; get married; have a family. Look how that worked out.

'I think it'll be good for you,' he'd said to me over dinner. 'It's really helping me to be back doing something I enjoy. Please just think about it, Sof. You loved your job.'

What would be good for me, I wanted to say as I watched him shovel down the veggie chilli I'd spent all afternoon making, *was if my baby hadn't died*.

'Okay,' I said instead. Meaning, '*Okay, I'll pretend to think about it.*'

'Really? I wasn't expecting you to agree so easily!' he'd said. 'That's great Sof! I honestly think it'll be for the best. Why don't you email HR tomorrow?'

I stare at him, open my mouth to protest but give up.

'Okay,' I say instead.

Agreeing seems much easier, these days.

I didn't email today, though. And I'd hoped Rory had forgotten because he didn't mention it again. But clearly, he's gone for the two-pronged attack instead and got Nisha involved.

'Rory thinks it's a good idea.'

'Yes, well, Rory also thinks having another baby is a good idea, too.' I move my black pawn in front of hers in defence. A closed game.

Nisha looks up. 'Maybe it is.'

'Not you, too!'

'I know you're scared, Sofie, but just because Leo died it doesn't mean it'll happen again.'

She moves her knight to f3. I move my black knight into the same opposing position.

'What if it does? There are no guarantees.'

She moves her bishop next to c4, next to my pawn. I do the same.

'Rory just doesn't want to give up hope of having the family he's always dreamed of. Your turn,' she says then, as she moves another pawn. 'You can't stand still in this game, you know that, Sof. You must keep moving.' She looks innocently at me through her long, dark eyelashes then down at the board.

'Grief isn't a game, Nisha,' I say edgily. 'Besides, any move I make at the moment feels wrong.' I move my other knight in defence to g6.

She immediately makes an unexpectedly modest move, pawn to d3. I stare at the board for a moment. I was expecting her to move it to d4, taking a more central, attacking position. I don't know what her strategy is now. She seems to be slowing the game down, but I can't work out why. I consider my options: none of them are good.

'Zugzwang,' she says.

'Bless you.'

She sits back and looks at me intently. 'You must have heard of zugzwang?' I shake my head. 'You haven't? Well, in chess, zugzwang is being stuck in a position where you feel that any move you make will be a bad one. Personally, I think it's the time when you can be your bravest. After all, you've nothing left to lose.' She pauses, looks down and starts nervously picking at the cuticles around her perfectly painted merlot-coloured nails. 'It's why I've made an appointment to start investigating the IVF process using a sperm donor. I'm following your advice: belief, plus possibility equals hope, remember? Perhaps you should do the same.'

I get up then and stand with my back to her facing the patio doors, looking out to the pocket handkerchief garden beyond. I'm sick and tired of people telling me what to do. Of expecting something – anything – from me.

'I've been brave, Nisha. I had hope, and look what happened.'

'You can't just give up in the middle of a game, Sofie. You have to keeping making your way across the board as best you can. And maybe Rory is right; perhaps that means going back to work, maybe even trying for another baby one day.'

I turn, angry at her now. I'm furious, actually.

'Look, Nisha, whilst I'm happy for you that you're making this choice, my situation is different, okay?'

'That's not what you said before,' she says gently. 'It's still a loss; that's what you said.'

'Well, I was wrong,' I shoot back defiantly. I turn away, close my eyes. I regret the words as soon as they come out of my mouth.

'Nisha, I'm sorry I—' I turn round to find she has her back to me and is putting on her coat.

Her face is impassive when she turns around. 'I know you're hurting, Sofie. And I understand, I do. But it's not the first time you have been dealt an unlucky hand and had to find a way through it. I— We all want to help you, but first you have to let us.'

I put my hand up to my chest, find the necklace engraved with Leo's footprint and hold it between my fingers for strength.

The sky is clear; the stars are out. I crane my neck, push my nose against the glass to look for Leo's constellation. I wish Nisha would just go. I don't need to be told what to do. *I'm* the authority on my grief, not her.

'You didn't die, Sofie,' she says softly, then. 'You can find a way through this. Not over, but through. If not for you, or Rory, then for Leo.'

'What if I can't?' I say, looking at her desperately. 'Getting up, going out, going back to work – none of it will help! Nothing will take the pain away.'

'It will get better, in time.'

'But I don't *want* it to, Nisha!' I cry. 'This pain is all I have of him now.' I swipe at my eyes. 'Maybe,' I say, turning round to face her, feeling defiant, 'maybe *you* just want me to feel better quickly to make yourself feel better.' I pause. 'So you can stop feeling guilty about how much you resented my pregnancy.'

The words fall fast, landing heavy; there's no stopping them once the avalanche has begun. I feel ashamed at what I've just said, then bold. Who cares if her feelings are hurt? She can't possibly be in as much pain as me.

It feels like a long time before she speaks again.

'I was sad about my own miscarriage,' she says quietly. 'My feelings about your pregnancy were about *my* sadness, not your joy. I may have been shocked by your news; I may have wished things had been different for me, but I never resented you or your pregnancy. You're my best friend and I've only ever wanted you to be happy.'

Shame and sorrow quickly replace the anger. I put my face in my hands and sob. I know it's me who is being bitter, resentful and ungenerous, not Nisha.

'I know you think that since Leo died, I've pushed you to do things you're not ready for and maybe you're right,' Nisha says with her hand on the lounge door handle. 'I've always tried to be there for you, but can I ask you something? Do you honestly think you've been there for me when I've needed you?'

'I'm not in a fit state to be anything to anyone!' I sob.

'I'm not talking about now,' she says evenly, and I look at her blearily. 'Where were you when Andy dumped me? I was devastated but you didn't even come down to London to see me because you said you didn't want to get on a train. And why do you think I didn't tell you about my own miscarriage in the first place? Because I knew it would trigger your anxiety levels. I've spent the last twenty years protecting you, trying to help you, Sofie, but I can't do it if you won't help yourself!'

'That's not fair!'

'You're not the first person to lose a baby and you won't be the last.'

I turn away. I'm too hurt to look at her. But she's right: I haven't been there for her like she has for me. But I don't want her version of 'being there' if it involves this.

When she speaks again, her voice is softer. 'You've been through something truly terrible. I know that. I can't imagine how much you miss Leo and I'm not going to begin to try. But he's not here and Rory is. Your mum is. And I am. And we will keep being here no matter how much you shut down or try to push us away. We love and need you, too, Sofie.' She pauses, looks down, takes a deep breath. 'There's something I've wanted to talk to you about, but I haven't known how.' I turn, wipe my eyes, intrigued – but also triggered by a memory of me saying the same words to her. Is she going to tell me she's *pregnant*?

'This probably isn't the right time, either.' She looks up, defiantly. 'I've got an appointment at a private fertility clinic in Bournemouth in a few weeks' time. And I wondered if... I wondered if you'd come with me?'

I stare at her, bewildered, trying to take in her request, whilst dealing with the wave of relief that her news wasn't what I thought it was. I don't know what to say. I've never seen Nisha look so vulnerable. Not as a teenager, at school, or at university. Not when she was a junior doctor, or a locum. Not in a relationship. She's always seemed to walk through life with such confidence: in her body, her brain.

Always laser-focused on how she wanted to live her life. But now she just looks … scared.

'I know it's a big step, but I've been thinking about it a lot. I've only found the strength to do this because *you* helped me realise that I need to take control and do something proactive about my situation. I know, from being pregnant so briefly, that I want a baby. And I don't want to have to wait for the right man to come along, in case he never does. I want to be in control, this time,' she continues passionately. 'At your baby shower you told me I shouldn't give up just because I've had some setbacks and I realised you're right: I can't give up before I've even tried. I *have* to believe this will happen for me because it's all I've got.'

I stare at her for a long time. That phrase is the last one I want to hear right now. 'I'm sorry,' I say eventually, my voice shaking with emotion, 'I can't help you, Nisha. No matter how much I want to, I … I'm not the person you need.' Best friends are meant to do anything for each other. But I can't do this.

'You're my best friend, Sofie,' she says, her voice breaking. 'You're the *only* person I need.'

I shake my head, tearfully, I try to explain. 'You need someone to hold your hand and tell you that everything is going to be okay. You need someone to say that of *course* you'll find a sperm donor; of *course* your IVF will be successful, you'll become pregnant and have the baby you dream of! But I can't be that person, Nisha, because I don't believe it anymore. I'm sorry.' Tears are streaming silently down my face now, and down hers, too.

'Leo *died*, and you're right, it didn't just happen to me. Babies die every single day, Nisha. There are over two thousand stillbirths a year in the UK alone. In England, fifteen per cent of all pregnancies – that's over 100,000 babies – are miscarried. But even that statistic is underrepresentative because so many miscarriages are unreported. Globally, the number reaches over 23 million miscarriages occurring each year.

'What happened to us happens to so many women, year in year out. And I don't want either of us to experience this kind of pain and loss ever again. I can't risk it.'

There's a long silence and for a moment I think she's got it. She understands.

'Can you answer something for me, honestly, Sof?' I look at her tearfully. Her dark eyes are sombre and serious. 'Do you ever wish you hadn't had Leo?'

I feel myself reel from the audacity of the question. I shake my head in shock. But then I do it again, because I realise that is also my answer.

'Is that no?' she asks softly.

I nod, feeling the familiar swelling in my throat.

'So, in spite of all the trauma you've gone through, that experience of carrying him, of being his mother, delivering him, those are experiences you'll always cherish?'

I close my eyes, feeling the room spin as I'm taken back to the moment when I held him in my arms. I nod, fervently.

'And it has changed you?' she presses. '*He* has changed you?'

'Yes,' I manage. 'Immeasurably.'

'So,' she presses thoughtfully, 'even though you've become one of the statistics you most feared, the one in four women who experience miscarriage or stillbirth, you don't regret being pregnant? You just wish the result was different?'

I manage a nod.

'So you can understand why I'll do whatever it takes to have that, too?' she asks quietly. 'Even if it's a risk. Even if I might have another miscarriage, I have to try, Sofie, because the loss will be even greater if I don't.'

I'm too choked to respond. Nisha steps forward, reaches out and takes my hand.

'When you were pregnant, you were at the very best I'd ever seen you: you were happy, confident, brave, secure, strong. *Leo* made you all those things. I know you feel broken by what happened since, but those qualities are all still inside you. They were Leo's lasting gift to you. For that reason, I refuse to let you wallow in your grief and not also feel gratitude. Because I think you *are* lucky. And the best way to honour Leo is for you to realise that.'

It's then that I truly break down, sinking to the floor in equal parts agreement and anguish. Nisha stays by my side, like she always does. She holds me as I wail.

In that moment, with my best friend holding me, I feel that, perhaps, being in pieces is good. Because pieces can, eventually, with time and patience and determination and support be put back together.

'Will you come, then?' she asks at last, when my sobs have subsided. 'To my appointment?'

I'm still trying to catch my breath through my tears. I look up at her and I know she sees fear in my expression. I know because I can't hide it. I want to tell her that I'd give anything to be there with her at her appointment, to hold *her* hand for a change. But I just can't. Not yet. It's too soon. I hope she can understand that.

'I'm sorry,' I croak. I wait for her say 'it's okay'. But she doesn't. She just looks down at me sadly, then gets up slowly off the floor, and leaves.

Chapter Fifty

With Nisha gone, I go out into the darkness of our garden, still edged with the perfect display of spring flowers, up-lit and phosphorescent like unwelcome ravers at an illegal house party. Neat lines of white narcissus, like the ones on Leo's coffin, are flanked by acid yellow daffodils and limp, drunk-looking purple-faced crocuses.

I run across the small lawn and begin pulling the flowers up, not carefully or delicately, but with wild angry abandon, crying so hard that I'm doubled over.

I fall to my knees, rip more from the soil; wanting to break up this party that they've dared to throw without my consent. I'm calling it off.

Everything should be called off. Spring. Beauty. Life. Hope. All of it.

Before long, a pile of forlorn purple and white heads lie on the grass next to me. The soil collects under my fingernails as I pull more up, ripping at their roots, unearthing them from their home. As I do, I find myself remembering the trips I took with dad, foraging for plants and flowers that would feed us, heal us with their magical, medicinal offerings. It feels like a different life. But as I kneel here, it also feels like a life I belong in far more than I do this one.

I stop, panting heavily as I wipe my eyes. I look at my dirtied hands and then at the pile of violet and white corpses. I realise there isn't a single daffodil amongst them. Subconsciously, I've left those bright evanescent survivors who only fleetingly grace the world with their beauty, but whose bulbs remain firmly rooted in the earth they grow in.

Rory eventually comes down from the loft and finds me there, still on my knees, crying into my muddied hands. He picks me up, carries me inside and takes me up to bed. But he doesn't get in with me; he doesn't stay, and I don't ask him to. He slips from the room and I hear him go downstairs. As soon as I hear the kitchen door click shut, I clandestinely slip out myself, to Leo's room. The only place I want to be.

This is my temple now; it holds my once-cherished hopes and dreams for him. I don't believe in God, or any sort of hypothetical paradise, but I like to imagine Leo is in a better version of this room. The pale yellow of this paint casting a warm, golden glow like sunshine on sand whilst miles of heavenly green hills reminiscent of Purbeck's roll endlessly around him, sea creatures swimming in circles in the blue water beyond, like the mobile that hangs over his cot.

Once I'm in here, all thoughts of life without my baby fade away. I go to his drawers, pull out a carefully rolled Baby-gro and clutch it to my chest. Here I don't have to deal with what's going on with me and Rory, or me and Nisha. Leo's little urn is still on the mantlepiece in here – I can't imagine him anywhere else.

I go and pick him up, but jump guiltily as the nursery door creaks open and Rory's face appears unexpectedly with two cups of peppermint tea. I close the drawer realising too late that I still have the urn in my hands. I feel like I've been caught shoplifting and quickly put it behind my back.

I glance at him guiltily, but he looks similarly flushed and guilty, too. His phone is, as ever, in his spare hand. I see him glance down at it as it buzzes with yet another notification.

'Is everything okay?' Rory looks dubiously around the room. His eyes widen in alarm as he takes in the baby-changing table. Earlier today, I laid a nappy, some wipes and an outfit out. *Goodnight Moon* is lying open on the nursing chair.

'Sofie,' he says, stepping towards me and gently taking the urn from my hands. 'Please can we chat about where to scatter his ashes?

We can find a lovely place, somewhere we can both go and visit him—'

'I want him here,' I say firmly.

'Okay, we could scatter them in the garden, or … or plant a tree for him?' Rory continues as if he hasn't heard me. 'I'd love to have something that will grow for him; a place we can visit, spend time with him … *together*.' His eyes flicker uncertainly around the room, and he adds, 'Somewhere … outside. We could plant some spring bulbs, some more daffodils to go with the ones that are left, that will flower next February, in time for his birthday—'

'And what if we move one day?' I interrupt, heart racing, breath shortening in panic. 'I don't want to bury his ashes until we can be sure they're somewhere we'll always be able to go. I can't leave him again, Rory.'

Suddenly everything seems so ephemeral. Not just Leo's life, but ours. This one here. The one that used to feel so safe and stable. I can't see anything lasting forever anymore. I think about Nisha, about our lives, our losses, our friendship that I thought would weather any storm. I think of Mum, Dad. Rory and me.

'I just want us to work out where the best place for him is,' Rory continues. 'We could have a little memorial. Invite some family, close friends…'

Your Instagram followers?

'I want him here with me, Rory,' I repeat.

'Okay,' he sighs. 'I understand you're not ready.' He gently takes the urn from me and puts it back on the mantlepiece. 'Shall we go to bed?' he asks, hopefully. I look at the urn just behind him.

'I'm okay here, thanks,' I say, unable to meet his eyes.

I feel Rory stare at me for a long time. Then he walks out, shutting the door so firmly behind him that the floorboards beneath me shake as he treads heavily upstairs.

Chapter Fifty-One

Sunday. Dappled sunlight is streaming into our bedroom. I'm watching the magnolia tree that has bloomed fully in recent days, its baby-pink petals now cupped to form the shape of hearts.

Spring – the season of rebirth – has arrived in all its restorative, rejuvenating glory, but my grief is having none of it. The way I see it, it's simply nature's way of redecorating: papering over the cracks of winter, just like everyone wants to paper over the cracks left by my baby's death. As far as I'm concerned, spring can fuck off.

I turn my back to the view, but as I do I notice that a single bright yellow daffodil in a vase is on my bedside table; a card is propped against it. It's then that I remember which 'Sunday' it is.

Mother's Day.

I sit up and take the card as ever-present tears threaten to spill.

I'm a mother. I know that with more certainty with every day that passes, but I'm also facing my first Mother's Day – the first of many – knowing that my child will never tell me he loves me, press a paint-splattered hand to a piece of card for my benefit, or draw a stick person that's meant to resemble me.

I open the envelope. Rory has turned a photo he took of the sunrise on the day I had Leo into a card. In it, he's written:

This Wasn't Meant to Happen

I promise there will be brighter days ahead.

I love you.
Rory xx

The envelope still feels heavy and when I shake it a small, gold charm falls out. The letter L, the third charm for my bracelet he bought me for Valentine's Day that already has mine and Rory's initials on it. I begin to cry. I bring it to my lips, kiss it, take my bracelet off and connect the charm on.

My phone pings then and I pick it up.

> Thinking of you and Leo, always. Nish x

I stare at it tearfully. Even when I let her down, Nisha is always there for me. She always has been. And so is Rory. And Mum. Even when I try and push them away. Why do I keep pushing them away?

And Leo. Leo is here for me to, in his own way. Like Nisha said, he's still a part of me and always will be. I will never regret having him.

I pick up my phone and message her before I have time to overthink it.

> Thank you, Nish, for everything. And I'm sorry. I know I'm so lucky to have you in my life x

I swing my legs out of bed and resolve to do better for them all.

Chapter Fifty-Two

The morning is bright; the sun casting a pale, lemony glow across the overgrown lawn. Rory is inside making some breakfast before we head off to Purbeck to have Mother's Day lunch with Mum and pop in on Sandra for tea. I bend down and begin plucking some dandelions from the grass, storing them in the pocket of my coat. Dad and I used to make all sorts with them: muffins, beer, cordial, tea. I feel a sudden urge to get out his foraging book filled with his scribblings and recipes.

Rory has of course cleared up the flower beds since the decimation I wreaked on them yesterday. As usual, he did it quietly, without complaint or question. One of the many ways in which, every day, he puts out the little fires caused by my grief.

Today, even the yellow daffodils are looking sorry for themselves. Overnight, their petals suddenly looked brown, brittle, bruised.

With muddy nails and dandelions cupped in my hands I stand in front of the border and stare at the stretch of dug-up earth in front of me. Barren, where once there was brightness. Loss, where there was once life.

But then, in the far back corner, I spot something. A single, glowing yellow daffodil in perfect luminous bloom, golden trumpet still swaying proudly like a kid on the back bench in a school assembly.

This Wasn't Meant to Happen

Hello little one, I find myself saying to the flower, but also to Leo. *I'm so proud of you for being so strong, for doing your best to be with us. I wish you could have stayed. I hope you know that your presence lit up my life. You changed my world. And you changed me. For good.*

And then I stop, because I find I'm weeping. The last two words are echoing in my head.

For good.

I know then that I want— no, I *need* to find a way to be the person he made me. Someone better, braver. Someone changed forever.

Someone changed for good.

Chapter Fifty-Three

Late morning and I'm driving down the familiar winding roads of Studland, taking in the glorious green expanse of hills wrapped around me.

Rory has chosen to cycle here on his own. I told him to; said I'd meet him at the beach where we've decided to walk before heading to Mum's for lunch. I sensed he needed space. And I need it, too. I only have room for Leo today.

He stared at me like I'd been inhabited by an alien. 'But you hate me cycling because you think it's too dangerous – and you hate driving alone.'

The truth is, things that used to make me anxious have been replaced by a new 'fuck it' attitude caused by my realisation that we have little control over anything.

'You've spent too much time stuck with me.'

He'd given me a sad smile. 'No matter what you may tell yourself, Sofie,' he'd replied, 'I never feel stuck with you.'

I arrive at Studland's South Beach after Rory. He doesn't see me approaching as he's too busy taking a photo of the view.

The beach is just down the road from my old childhood home in Corfe, close to Mum and Midge's cottage. I'm glad that Mum is cooking lunch for us today, as I can't face being in public, and Midge generously said she'd cover at the café so we can spend time together.

This Wasn't Meant to Happen

Today, Mother's Day is sitting heavy for so many reasons. Of course, I'm thinking of my own loss, but it's also made me think about Mum and how I was lost to her for a while – during the summer Dad died and afterwards, when I was distant from her for years. I'm also remembering that Rory's mum left him, too: not dead, but still ostensibly, gone.

Every year, without fail Rory sends her a Mother's Day card with a nice message, hoping that maybe this will be the year when she steps up. Gets in touch. I know that this year, he wrote to her to tell her about Leo. I don't know if he has had any response. The fact he hasn't talked to me about it suggests not.

He's always said that hope is an anchor for the soul. It used to sound beautiful to me, but now when I think about it, I think it means hope won't let you sink. You're just stuck floating in one place. That's where he is with his relationship with his mother. Full of hope but stuck in one place because of it.

Rory and I hold hands as we walk silently down the steps to the small beach.

I feel instantly at home here, it's like an extension of my childhood garden – the equivalent of a local playground. As a kid and teen, I used to come here to kayak, sail, swim, hike or forage with Dad, not to mention go wild sea swimming with Nisha on weekend mornings and in the school holidays. I haven't been here for a long time, though. So many happy memories have become tangled with such painful ones.

The sun is floating high in the sky, like a bright yellow balloon being held by a tiny, invisible hand.

It's unseasonably hot for the end of March; the familiar briny, seaweed smell is, surprisingly, comforting and familiar. Rory and I stand and gaze wordlessly out at the sea for a while. To the left, Bournemouth is just visible in the hazy distance. Ahead of us, boats speckle the horizon. We watch as two paddle boarders head back to the shore, their wetsuits shimmering in the warm spring sunshine as they work hard against the tide. A kayak is just heading out towards

Old Harry Rocks and I'm reminded of one of Dad's Danish proverbs.

Don't sail out further than you can row back.

I realise that in getting pregnant, that's exactly what I did.

But I also realise that Nisha's right. I can't imagine *not* having experienced the journey of sailing to this place with Leo. Even if he couldn't stay for the life-long return journey with me.

I sit down in the sand for a moment as Rory walks down to the shore. He picks up stones and starts skimming them across the water and I swear I can see Leo as a child there, next to him. I can see the sandcastles he would have made; his footprints in the sand alongside us. I can hear his squeals of laughter; the splashes as he jumped waves at the water's edge. I blink as sunlight hits the sea and sends jewels shimmying across the water like the stones Rory's throwing. I pick up a handful of sand and watch as the grains slip through my fingers. Each one seems to represent the infinitesimally tiny wonder that is life. Just like Leo was. A grain of sand, a ripple, a wave, an earthquake. Shaking my world. Waking me up.

When I look up, Rory has stopped skimming stones. He's crouched down and is writing something in the sand with a stick, head bowed over his creation. I walk over to him and slip my hand into his, rest my head on his shoulder. I see he's drawn Leo's name, surrounded by a heart. I feel a flood of love that Rory always knows exactly what to do to honour him. I put up my hand to my infinity necklace. I think of the star he named after him, of my Mother's Day card, the L charm, the toy lion he brought home, the daffodils he picked for us to wear to the crematorium. The words he found for Leo's funeral.

Leo might not be here, but Rory is a wonderful dad to him, still. And I want to be the best mother I can, too.

Not only that – I want to be the best wife I can be to my husband.

We stand there together, Rory and me, looking down at our boy's name etched into the ground and for a moment, it feels like he's here, too, holding each of our free hands so we're in a circle. Pi. To infinity. His name in the sand makes his presence more solid. Of course, I know the letters will soon be washed away by the tide. But never our love.

This Wasn't Meant to Happen

We look at his name for what feels like an eternity.

I walk away first, squeezing Rory's hand and reaching up on my tiptoes to kiss him on the lips lightly. We close our eyes and rest our foreheads against each other.

'I love you, Rory,' I tell him.

He nods, clearly choked. It has been a while since I said those words. 'I love you, too, Sofie.'

'Shall we go?' I say, pulling his hand a little.

'Can I just have a moment?' he says, squeezing his eyes shut and rubbing his fist into the space between his eyebrows. I glance at him; it's rare to see this kind of emotion these days.

'Of course.' I begin to walk back across the beach, glancing back over one shoulder to look at my husband, who is still standing still, in the same place.

I feel the gentle rays of sun on my face, bringing light and warmth to what could have been a dark day, and feel a small sense of peace settle within me. Today, in this moment, I feel like I can see how we might learn how to live with Leo, with our grief, together. Forever a family. Minus, but also plus.

When I'm nearly at the car park, I glance back to see if Rory has followed me. I watch him kneel, then sit back on his haunches. He takes his phone out of his pocket, leans over the heart in the sand with Leo's name in and takes a photo. Then another. He bows his head again, this time over his phone. I stand there, watching him as he types, and I feel my heart sink deep down into the sand.

I turn and begin to walk away, quickly this time. As I do, I pull out my phone then click on Instagram. Our private moment honouring Leo has already been uploaded for the world to see and share. There are words to accompany it too – a quote from *The Little Prince* about a landscape where The Little Prince arrives and departs the earth.

A series of hashtags follow the quote #leobear #mothersday #stillbirth #babyloss #nameinthesand #ourlittleprince

There are more, but I can't look at them. The screen blurs in front of my eyes and I realise that despite what we've been through, we're still drifting away from each other. And honestly? I don't know if I have the strength to row back.

Chapter Fifty-Four

The days pass with painful inevitability and solitude. As well as Rory being back at work, even if he's home he's rarely with me. He's either upstairs, or he's tinkering with his bike, ready to take it out again. He goes on long rides first thing in the morning, before work, so I always wake up alone. And he goes to bed long after me, too. Ships in the night. Or rather, I'm a shipwreck, washed up on this island of grief, alone.

Mum phones regularly and pops in at least twice a week, when the café is quiet in the afternoon. She always comes by herself. A small blessing from all this is that we get to spend time together, just the two of us. We go for walks on the beach, the brisk spring winds pulling us forcefully and awkwardly together. She's still so tentative around me, uncertain of what to say or do. I know she's scared that if she says something wrong, I will break. I want to tell her I'm already in fractions – my former self divided into smaller, jagged pieces that just don't fit together anymore.

'I'm worried about you,' she said yesterday as we gazed at the silver-grey plane of ocean, Purbeck just visible in the distance. 'I don't like you being on your own so much. Why not come and work at the café for a bit during the week? Like the old days? Selfishly, I'd love to have you. We need you, actually; we've lost a couple of part-time staff members recently, and Midge and I are run off our feet. We're both exhausted, to be honest.' She smiles weakly. 'If you could help it would be a real lifesaver.'

'I can't face anyone, Mum,' I told her.

'You don't have to, love. You can stay in the kitchen. Just think about it, please? Even if it's just one or two mornings. No one knows the café better than you.'

In the afternoons, when she's gone back to Midge and the café, I cook, strangely comforted by the peace and solitude of my kitchen as I chop, slice, season and stir, turning the reassuring, predictable pages of Dad's foraging recipe book. The clear instructions in his spiky, barely legible handwriting give numerical stages of what to do next.

Occasionally I use plants found on my walks with Mum: sea beet, dulse in a warming broth, sea coriander for a curry.

'It's like going back in time,' Mum said the other day as she stood, huddled up in her coat, snood, hat and gloves, stamping her feet while I was bent over a patch of sea lettuce, plucking it up carefully with my bare hands.

Yesterday, she brought Dad's old basket full of foraging tools, which, until she moved in with Midge, she kept by the front door. It always felt to me when I visited her as if he might walk in at any moment.

'I thought perhaps you'd like to keep them here. You may get some use out of them,' she'd said.

It's 4pm now and I'm lying on the sofa in the lounge, curtains already pulled. Spring showers are streaking the windows with teary trails. *Countdown* is on in the background. I've spent most of the afternoon alone inside – and in my head – and, I realise, I'm over it.

I've been thinking about Mum's suggestion about going to work in the kitchen at the café. When I told Rory about it, he said it was a great idea.

Today, it feels like one to me, too.

My phone beeps and I pick it up, gratified to see it's a message from Joe. He's still been messaging me frequently, checking in from afar. Unlike most people, he hasn't come round unexpectedly, sent flowers I don't want, or demanded anything of me. He just drops me regular, short messages that lets me know that he's thinking of me, that he's familiar with the place I'm in.

We've been playing Words with Friends. It makes a nice change from the sudoku puzzles I now do daily, obsessively, to pass the time. The prerequisite, he said, was that the words we chose all had to relate to grief in some way. He said I'd find it surprisingly cathartic.

In one game the words we had were: *drained, distress, numb, shit, angry, pain, lonely, hard, hell, anxiety, aching, loss.*

Joe was right, in spelling out my feelings on that virtual board with him, I momentarily felt them all a little bit less. He's also been filling me in on the gossip at work. Nothing much has changed there, but apparently there is a new HR manager called Zoe.

I've logged on to my work account today, for the first time since I had Leo, to read Zoe's all-staff introductory email. It was Joe's suggestion. He said she'd already caused quite a stir and is clearly quite a step forward from Marjorie, the old HR manager who had been at Prospect for thirty years.

> *From: zoe.ansell@prospectlife.co.uk*
> *To: All*
> *Subject: Introduction!*
>
> *Good morning,*
> *As your new HR manager, I'm excited to be joining this well-established stalwart of Southwest Insurance and join a team of people who are connected in every department in our desire to protect people, businesses and communities.*
> *It's clear to me that the 'Prospect' of life insurance is about embracing the future, not just protecting it. It's my intention to find new ways to connect with you all and tap into your individual potential through these rapidly changing times: recognising, rewarding and retaining talent, focusing on new leadership and creating an exciting, inclusive culture where diversity is valued, talent is fast-tracked, and your future prospects are cemented. Not because we've stayed in one place, but because we're constantly evolving.*
>
> *I look forward to working with you all!*
>
> *Zoe*

> Wow.

I tap out the word quickly in a message to Joe and hit send. My phone pings immediately with his reply.

> You can imagine what Ed said. 'Inclusivity? We have coffee and decaf in the kitchen, isn't that enough?'

I'd laughed at that, then thought for a second before I replied, quoting one of Ed's most regularly used statements.

> 'Change is an unnecessary risk that I for one am not willing to take!'

> 'Better the devil you know!'

Joe replies immediately with another of Ed's catchphrases

Suddenly, I feel nostalgic for the simple pleasure of my job, one that I know and understand inside out.

And with home feeling so alien, the idea of going back to the office is becoming increasingly appealing.

It'll make Rory happy, certainly, and maybe, just maybe, it'll make me feel … more like me again? It's worth a shot, I guess. Galvanised, I open an email to Ed with the subject head – Returning to work.

Zoe phones shortly afterwards. Ed has clearly passed my email straight on to her. His way of avoiding emailing me back, I'm sure.

'Sofie? It's Zoe Ansell from HR.' Her voice and manner are warm and gentle rather than formal. 'I've just received your email and I wanted to reach out to you personally. I hope that's okay. And please, do tell me if not.'

'I… It's fine.'

'Sofie, I know we've never met, but please can I just say I'm so deeply sorry that Leo died.'

'Thank you,' I manage, shaken by her directness. I'm not used to it. In my experience, people tend to tiptoe around the subject, offer platitudes or avoid it entirely until it becomes the elephant in the room.

'I understand your desire to come back to work, and of course, we would love to have you as I've heard what an asset you are to your department, but I just want to make sure this is something you want, rather than something you feel you should do or must do, financially? You do know that because Leo was born after twenty-four weeks, you're entitled to the full fifty-two weeks leave and thirty-nine weeks maternity pay? And regardless of that, I also wanted to reassure you that your job is safe; you can of course take as long as you need.'

'Thank you,' I say again. 'But I'd like to come back to work.' I don't know this woman and I don't want her to hear my hidden doubts, to know how impossible it is to make any sort of decision about my life now.

'I understand,' she says kindly. 'It's such early days. I want you to know I can put a support system in place, a phased return perhaps. On reduced hours, with whatever time off you need.'

I accept, gratefully, and we agree I'll start in two weeks. Now that I've made the decision, I want to implement it as soon as possible. The lure of losing myself in numbers, spreadsheets and statistics may be strong. But still, the idea of facing everyone is petrifying.

Chapter Fifty-Five

Two days later, I arrive at Per's Place bright and early after Rory drops me off at the car park at Durlston Bay. After making the decision to return to work, it made sense to take Mum up on her offer in the meantime; get used to being around people again.

'I'm so proud of you, you know,' Rory said, leaning over to kiss me as I open the car door. My throat swells. I turn my head quickly, so he doesn't see me cry. In doing so, my cheek receives the disappointed graze of his lips.

I know he's hopeful that this is the turning point that will see the Old Me returning. The one that does more than sit in a room with her dead baby's ashes; watch gameshows; potter around the kitchen and garden, and wander the Southwest Coastal paths.

I want to tell him that I'm trying, desperately, to find myself again. Not just for me, but for him. For us. But I also know that a big part of me was lost with Leo. I think it always will be.

'Have a good day!' Rory says, brightly, then.

'Okay,' I reply obediently. I swallow back my fear as he drives off.

I walk slowly along the path, rucksack on my back, towards Peveril Point. It's a bright, crisp day in early April, with the kind of wispy scattered clouds and determined sunshine that feels mildly hopeful, rather than celebratory. The view is glorious from here and I feel both fearful of it and, yet, connected to it as well.

This coastline, this café is complexly tied up with two strands of memories: both the beauty of my childhood and the pain. The reef knot holding it all together is my dad's life – his hopes, dreams and ultimately, his death.

The café in the distance is a memorial to him, like a gravestone overlooking the sea where we scattered his ashes. The sepulchral white painted exterior perfectly in keeping with the limestone rocks that descend from it to the bright blue glistening sea beneath.

I take a deep breath and head for the front door. I've prepared myself for a Groundhog Day: Mum and I prepping food side by side, navigating grief together, just like we did after Dad died.

But it's Midge, not Mum, who greets me, thrusting open the doors with her arms wide to welcome me as if into her own home. I allow her to hug me but pull away as soon as I can. 'I hope you don't mind,' she says, 'but it's just you and me today. Your Mum's at home, having a rest.'

I turn, immediately panicking. 'Why? What's wrong? She's not ill, is she?'

Midge reaches out and touches my arm gently but reassuringly. 'There's nothing to worry about, I promise. She's just overworked, and I thought it'd do her good to put her feet up, knowing the place is in good hands. Tuesdays are usually very quiet, so we can handle a morning shift together, right? You can be on kitchen duty; I'll be out front?'

As elegantly but casually put together as ever, in a navy sweater, white shirt and tailored slacks with loafers, Midge gestures for me to go inside.

'Right, I'll get the coffee machine cranked up and bring you one in a min. In my opinion, no working day should start without a hot shot of caffeine!'

I head to the kitchen and start dutifully peeling potatoes. Now that Mum's not here, I just want to get this done and go home. The prospect of an entire day with just Midge is daunting. What on earth will we talk about?

'You know, I'm so glad you're here, Sofie,' she says a few minutes later when she comes into the kitchen with two mugs of steaming coffee. 'This is going to be such a huge help. Your mum hasn't had a day off for weeks.' She places them down on the kitchen surface and gets to work peeling potatoes next to me quietly, almost companionably.

'Is everything okay with you both?' I ask. I realise then that I haven't done that – asked about them – since Leo died and I feel ashamed.

'Ye-s,' she says, uncertainly. 'We're just, you know, older than we used to be. And whilst the café isn't exactly hugely busy, it is relentless. We just can't seem to get staff who *stay*. We get by each week, but we're exhausted. And it would be nice to have some time together that isn't spent here.' Midge smiles wryly. 'Your mum won't close for one day a week like I've suggested, either. She still has such anxiety around money, and she worries that if we're not open all the time, the customers will stop coming. Even after all these years, she believes we're always one bad day away from financial disaster. It's preventing her from enjoying the rest of her life.' She continues peeling and suddenly I notice the way her hands are shaking slightly.

'Well, when you've been left with nothing, that fear becomes entirely rational.'

She glances at me, then. 'Sorry, I don't mean to—'

'No,' I interrupt. 'Thank you for sharing, Midge. I've been in my head so much; I've forgotten other people are dealing with stuff, too. I'm so sorry I haven't checked in.'

'It's not selfish, Sofie. It's called survival.' She puts her hand gently on my shoulder. 'You're doing so well.'

I smile weakly at her and stare down into my coffee cup. 'Thank you, but I'm not so sure. I know I've got to try and get back to normal. Get over it. "Move on" as people keep saying.'

'No!' Midge says firmly, which surprises me enough to look at her. Her softly lined face – impeccably made up as ever – is filled with compassion. 'Sofie, you've had a grenade thrown at your life. You're suffering and will be for a long time. There isn't a version of "moving on" that exists when you lose someone you love, only getting through.' She says this vehemently. I'm reminded of when Joe said the same thing when he first messaged me after Leo died. *Never over, only through.* 'Trust me, I know a bit about grief, although I know nothing about your own particular experience of it,' she adds quickly, apologetically. 'Only someone whose baby or child has died can know that. When Carole died, it felt like my whole world had blown up in front of me. But for you, it has done that inside of you, too. I understand that you need to sit with that pain, because it keeps Leo close to you.' She blinks as she looks down, picks up a potato and her peeler again.

'What if the people telling you to move on are your husband, mum and best friend?' I say quietly.

She puts them down again and puts her hand on mine. 'You try to understand they're saying it because they're scared. They're hurting both for you and for themselves, too, but they're not brave enough to sit with it, like you have,' Midge replies. She looks at me when she speaks again. 'Be kind to yourself, Sofie. You've faced the worst and survived; that's enough for now.'

I put my half-peeled potato down too and press my knuckles against the counter for stability. Midge puts her hand on my shoulder, just lightly, but it's a gesture that feels at once healing, supportive, understanding.

I think of her then, in the hospital after Leo died, gently guiding Mum to support me in the way I needed her to. But also, quietly supporting us both for so many years before. Always there in the background, never overstepping, or pushing her way in. Helping Mum handle her grief and in the process, helping me. It makes me wonder if Mum has stayed away today because she wants me to fully experience some of the steadfast support, loyalty and love that Midge has shown her all these years. I realise Midge has been a buoy, keeping Mum afloat.

I put my hand on top of hers in response and squeeze it gratefully. It's all I can manage. I hope it's enough to convey the gratitude I feel.

I spend the morning peeling, chopping, prepping and cooking. I find it both soothing and rewarding to have manageable tasks that I can do; lose myself in the process of making food for people, without me having to see them, or them me.

I find myself remembering fondly the happy hours I spent in here as a teenager, but most of all, I enjoy it when Midge comes in the kitchen and keeps me company during quiet periods. She chats easily about everything and nothing, requiring very little in return from me. I find myself looking forward to the moments when she might come back and fill me on any gossip she's heard from the handful of customers she's seen. But then it's lunchtime and I find myself entirely on my own, focused on getting plates of toasted sandwiches, chips, homemade soup, and fresh bread rolls and baked potatoes out of the kitchen. By 3pm, when I'm cleaning up in total silence, sinking in the experience of being back in my own head, I desperately wish she'd appear again.

At 4pm, surfaces gleaming and feeling inordinately proud of what I've achieved, I seek her out. She's in the makeshift office in a tiny room at the back of the café, next to the toilets, glasses on, frowning at the computer as she does the books.

I walk in and put my folded apron down on the desk.

'How was it?' she asks, taking off her specs and looking up at me with a kind smile.

'I enjoyed it,' I reply. 'I don't know where the time went.'

'Aha, yes, as someone once said "Cookery is like love. It should be entered into with abandon, or not at all!"'

I laugh. 'And what do they say about accounts?' I ask, nodding at her spreadsheets.

'Accounts,' she ruffles her short, salt and peppery cropped hair thoughtfully, but it still falls obediently back into place. 'Let me see. Accounts should be kept on top of like… the lid on a jar of snakes?'

I laugh out loud as she frowns comically. 'Doesn't have quite the same ring to it, does it? Luckily, I like putting numbers in boxes, seeing everything in order, making everything add up. It's not exciting or creative, like cooking is; it takes a lot of patience, but you can also lose yourself in it and the slog is worth it for the sense of achievement at the end. Both those things provide balance for me. That's why I like working here so much. Do you know what I mean?'

I think of my job and why I got into risk assessment. To have some control over my life. And then I think of how much peace and joy cooking has brought me over the years. 'Actually, I do.'

'Especially for those of us who find it hard to have no control over things that happen in our lives, right?' Midge smiles. 'You know, Sofie, I've always thought we have a lot more in common than the fact we both love your mum.'

'Can I ask about Carole?' I say, suddenly. Midge closes her eyes briefly at the sound of her name, then nods. 'What was she like?'

Midge pauses for a moment, staring into the distance as if to conjure Carole up, then smiles softly and with such love I feel like I can see Carole, too.

'Infuriatingly clever, stubborn and unendingly caring. Both impishly naughty and charming.' A smile of remembrance remains at the corners of Midge's lips. 'Everyone loved her. She knew who she was and how to be around people in a way that I just don't, you know?'

I think of Rory. 'I do.'

'But her illness was long and barbaric. I watched cancer take everything from her: her energy, her spirit, her hope. I hate that in those last weeks I couldn't do anything much for her; I couldn't take her pain away; I felt useless. All I could do was be there every single day and let her know how much she was loved.' She smiles with nostalgic, remembered love. 'Your mum is a lot like her, you know. She has the same spirit and natural warmth.'

'Can I ask you something?' I say, then, suddenly feeling the need to know more about this steadfast woman who has been in my life for so long. 'Did the idea of loving someone again scare you? Especially someone like Mum. I mean, it was … complicated, right? There was grief involved. There were no guarantees it would work out…'

Midge's eyes widen momentarily in surprise at my question, then she tilts her head thoughtfully. 'Yes, I was worried. But you know, Sofie, love is the only thing I've ever gambled on. Because it is the one thing in life that I consider worthy of such a risk. Yes, the stakes are high, but so they should be when you stand to win so much. And, in my experience, even if you lose it all, you've always gained much more than you ever expected to. Even in the worst of circumstances, you're never left with nothing.'

My breath disappears suddenly, and I gasp as I nod. 'That's how I feel about Leo. He's not here, but … but … he's given me so much.' I stop, nod again as my eyes fill with tears and Midge clasps my hands and pulls me close into a hug.

'Sweet girl,' she says leaning away to grab a piece of kitchen roll and wipe my eyes. 'You know, there have been times I've been very jealous of your mum.'

'Why?' I ask, in surprise.

'Because she has you. Someone who is part of her, and always will be. The love you have for each other and for Leo is not the love I'll ever get to experience.'

I feel my chest constrict.

'You asked me not so long ago,' Midge continues, 'if I'd ever regretted not having kids. The truth is, I made my choices, and I've always been happy with them. But seeing you and your mum together has occasionally made me question them. Sometimes I find myself wanting just a little piece of what you two have.'

I look at this woman and realise how scared I have always been to love her back in the way she has loved me. Not because I felt it would be disloyal to Dad, but because I was worried that by accepting her fully into my life and family, I might risk losing her, too.

I find myself holding on to her tightly suddenly, not wanting to let go. This the first fully intentional, meaningful embrace of gratitude and love that I've ever instigated. When she squeezes me tightly back, I know she's been waiting to do so for years.

When I leave, the sun's sailing high over the sea, and I stand in front of Per's Place for a moment, breathing in the fresh air and soaking up the panoramic blue and green expanse of the view. Today, like Midge, this place has wrapped its arms around me and lifted me up and out of the darkness.

I look over to Old Harry Rocks, say a quiet hello to Dad, and then walk to the car park. Midge is still inside the cafe. She told me she's going to walk home after she's locked up.

'It's my favourite time of day to walk,' she'd smiled. 'It gives me time to be grateful for all I have now: this version of my life with your mum, in this town, this place.'

I head down the costal path to where Mum's waiting to drive me home.

'How was it?' she smiles as she opens the passenger door.

'It was okay…' I stop, reflect, rephrase. 'Actually, it was wonderful.'

'Same time tomorrow, then?' Mum says softly.

I look out the window as Mum glances in the rear-view mirror at her unexpected love.

'You're lucky to have Midge,' I say.

She nods and puts her hand on mine. 'I'm lucky to have you both.'

I go back to Per's Place every day for the next two weeks, taking it in turns to work with Midge and then Mum so they can both have a break. One day, when Mum pops in to see us, I tell them it's so quiet that they should both go for a walk while I man the fort. It turns out that being needed is just what I needed, too.

Each day after that, I find more of the rhythm of my old life. I arrive in Purbeck early in the morning so I can go for a walk to clear my head. Sometimes I park at the beaches of Studland and walk along the shore, before getting back in the car and heading to Swanage and the café before 8am. It helps that spring has decided to masquerade as an early summer.

I walk along the familiar coastal paths and shorelines that Dad used to take me on, paths I hadn't trod for years but which hold no fear for me now. After all, like Midge said, I've faced the worst and survived. Every step I take from here must be easier, right?

I find myself searching out the edible plants and flowers that Dad taught me to recognise and which are thriving during this warm spring on Purbeck.

I don't feel alone because Leo is with me. In my head, I'm sharing everything Dad taught me as a child with my little boy.

I identify different fungi on the forest beds, enjoying how the encyclopaedic knowledge I received from Dad floods into my brain as I walk, like a long-closed door has been unlocked.

Then I head to the café to spend a soothing day washing, chopping, slicing, frying and baking, putting every ounce of concentration I have into following Mum's simple menu, whilst occasionally adding a twist of my own. Like the wild rosemary I found one morning on a walk that I added to her regular sourdough mix and served with wild-nettle and garlic soup and which sold out by lunchtime. Then there were the horse mushrooms I foraged for the 'Wild Dorset Mushrooms on Toast' that I scrawled on the menu board as a Special of the day.

By the first Thursday, I was serving customers, too, gradually coming out of the kitchen when Midge was too busy to deliver orders; timidly accepting compliments from the diners before I scuttled off.

During the second week, I found myself staying out there a while to chat a little bit with the locals I know. There were moments where someone offered such heartfelt condolences for Leo's death that I wasn't sure I could respond without breaking down, but I managed it.

On my final day, I faced my worst fear: talking to someone who'd heard about my stillbirth and benignly told me that, 'As I always say, these things happen for a reason.'

Midge swooped in quickly. 'Actually, I'd say plenty of things happen for no good reason at all.' Then she'd chatted nonsensically about the menu, the weather – whatever it took to not let the customer get another word in edgeways.

But those comments have very much been in the minority and have even led to something good. A woman around my age who was in the café on her own approached me when I was making coffees.

'I'm so sorry to interrupt, but I couldn't help but overhear and I just wanted to say … it … it happened to me, too,' she said quietly. 'My baby died – just over eight months ago now. His name was Wilf.'

I stopped making coffee immediately and asked Midge to take over so we could talk for a few moments. I found out the woman was younger than me by about five years, a teacher, and recently married. Wilf was her first baby. He had died shortly after birth and had undiagnosed heart and lung defects. She told me she'd spent the first six months after he died not wanting to leave the house.

'I knew I had a problem when *Loose Women* was the highlight of my day,' she said.

'*Tipping Point* for me,' I admitted, with a wry smile.

'Oh, God, that *is* dark,' she said solemnly, and we laughed.

'I'm Sofie.' I smiled.

'I'm Jen.'

'Would you like to exchange numbers?' she asked shyly after we'd talked for a while.

'I love to talk about Wilf to people, but I can't find anyone willing to listen. My friends can't face me, even my family seem to shy away from the subject. They think my talking about Wilf means I'm "wallowing". I think it's "remembering" but, you know…' She shrugged. 'My counsellor told me I need to "Find my tribe".' She pulled a face. 'I think she read a 'How to Speak Millennial' handbook or something before seeing me. She said that there will be people in my position who know exactly how I feel and who won't say the wrong thing. She said they won't mind me making a joke, or that I still cry unexpectedly. I honk loudly when I cry; I'll be honest about that now.'

'Me, too!' I laughed, marvelling at the unfamiliar sound coming out of my mouth.

After an hour, having swapped numbers, we reluctantly said goodbye, promising to make a date to meet at the café for a coffee very soon.

Chapter Fifty-Six

I'm standing outside the door of my department, entry card in hand, sunglasses firmly on. Instead of being out on a morning walk before starting work at the café, this morning, I've been for a swim at my local pool as I used to do every single morning before Leo. I did my customary 100 lengths, but whilst I enjoyed the feeling of being in the water, the act itself felt perfunctory. Pointless. Like I was going nowhere. I wanted to feel space around me, not other people swimming lengths. I wanted to feel the cold – the real cold. The breath-taking, life-affirming chill of open water. I wanted to take a risk, change lanes, change direction, do something unpredictable to break the endless back-and-forth cycle of lane swimming. I wanted to feel waves, be pulled by the current in a direction I didn't necessarily expect to go.

I felt the same on the bus here. I stared out of the window through my tears, breathing in petrol fumes and other people's perspiration until I was spat out at St Swithun's roundabout and arrived at the grey, imposing building that once, unbelievably, used to be home to all my ambitions.

It is hard to believe I'm back here again now. Not pregnant. But with no baby, either.

All I have to do is open the door, walk through it, go to my desk and get back to work like nothing has happened. That's all.

I swipe my entry card like I'm ripping off a plaster and open the door quickly. The stale, familiar office air curls around me. I'm grateful that no one looks up. Each head remains purposefully bowed, except for Joe's. He looks directly at me and gives me a warm smile. He texted me this morning, sending his support and encouragement.

I begin what feels like an epically long journey to my desk. As I near the end of the office, people look up and over their monitors at me and then quickly away, in case they make eye contact and have to acknowledge me. I'm convinced I hear them whispering. I can feel the air being sucked from my lungs. Suddenly, it's like I'm back in the school corridor after Dad died, being stared at by everyone. Back then, Nisha was by my side. I wish she was here now.

I feel my muscles stiffen, my breath becomes short, and my vision reduces to a tunnel of light that gets smaller by the second. Just before it disappears, someone grabs my arm. It's Joe. My knight in shining armour – or rather, shining shoes and smart blazer.

'Sofie!' he says loudly. 'Glad you're back. I've got some questions to ask you about an optimisation analysis I've just been sent. Can I talk you through it?' He then proceeds to chat all the way to my desk, which sufficiently breaks the deathly silence that has swept through the office at my arrival.

No one looks at me as I pass them. I have a sudden, desperate urge to shout Leo's name so that everyone will know that I'm no longer just Sofie. I'm Sofie, Leo's mother. Even though he isn't here, I'm still that.

When Joe and I arrive at my desk he stays for a few moments as I settle in my seat, then with a light squeeze of my arm, he leaves.

I put my bag down and switch my monitors on.

Tarun walks into the office, loudly greeting the room before striding straight over to my desk. He looks affronted that I'm sitting in his place.

'Sofie, hi, you're back! Sorry to hear your time off was cut short.'

I take a deep breath, force a smile. He's made it sound like I've come home early from a foreign holiday, not spent weeks mourning the loss of my baby.

'I think you'll see that everything has been ticking along nicely here in your absence though,' he adds smugly.

This Wasn't Meant to Happen

'Great.' I turn away, preparing to start work. The scent of lilies from the bouquet on my desk are making me feel nauseous.

My fingers move clumsily over the keyboard as I try to input my passwords. My brain is foggy, body uncomfortable – unused as it is now to being behind a desk. I cleared my inbox before I left on maternity leave, but there are hundreds of emails to get through.

The first one I open is from Zoe.

To: sofie.king@prospectlife.co.uk
From: zoe.ansell@prospectlife.co.uk
Subject: Here

Hi Sofie,
Well done for making it here. And I just want to say I'm here if you need anything at all. Remember, you're not alone.

Zoe

I blink, surprised but grateful she's reached out again, relieved she kept it short. In the time I've been reading it another email has pinged through; it's similar in tone.

To: sofie.king@prospectlife.co.uk
From: joe.schwartz@prospectlife.co.uk
Subject: You're back

I'm glad you're back because this place has not been the same without you. I've got your back.

J x

I read both twice, appreciating the careful simplicity of their messages.

To: joe.schwartz@prospectlife.co.uk
From: sofie.king@prospecthealth.co.uk
Subject: You're back

Thanks Joe. I'm kind of in unchartered waters right now TBH. S x

To: sofie.king@prospecthealth.co.uk
From: joe.schwartz@prospecthealth.co.uk
Subject: *You're back*

I read this recently, and it resonated:
'It is not down on any map; true places never are.'
Herman Melville, Moby Dick

I re-read the quote three times. Then I take a deep breath and open a report, preparing to get back to what I do best. Analysing risk. But I have no idea where to start.

Chapter Fifty-Seven

Where I start, apparently, is at an all-department meeting in the board room. Nothing like being thrown in at the deep end.

I stare at the floor while discussions about 'catastrophic loss observations', 'severity distribution' and 'unexpected risk exposure' occur. Each time I hear those phrases I want to scream. I'd no idea that so much of my job would be so triggering.

Tarun takes the floor on behalf of our department. Listening to him, the work feels so pointless. How can any of us possibly know or prepare for, let alone protect ourselves from, what life might throw at us?

Tarun tries to engage me in the updates, but I'm mute. I hate that he's drawing attention to me. I feel like he's purposely putting my liminal state on show for all to see.

Roll up roll up and see the incredible tightrope walking woman, who is balancing precariously on a very thin wire. Can she put one foot in front of the other or will she fall right before your eyes?

At lunchtime, I walk to the café I used to go to every morning to get my coffee, but once outside, I realise that the last time I was here, I was heavily pregnant and I can't face the inevitable questions. I turn and walk as far away from there, and the office, as I can in the time I have.

I return to work an hour later and get in the lift, still wearing my sunglasses, relieved no one else is in it. But just as the doors close, I'm joined by a woman who dives in breathlessly. She's around my age, perhaps a few years older, with wild, curly dark hair and big, almond eyes. She's wearing flared slacks with a stripe down the side, box-fresh trainers and a white shirt tucked in. She's clasping a box of sandwiches.

'Sofie?' The doors have shut, I'm unable to escape. 'We've not met, but I feel I know you. I'm Zoe.' She reaches out and takes my hand and squeezes it tightly. Her warm Galaxy chocolate eyes look deeply into mine and I have the strange sense that instead of seeing through me, she can see inside me. 'I was hoping I'd get to meet you. My door is open anytime, okay?'

Just then, thankfully for me, the doors open at the basement. I smile weakly and bolt out of the lift without saying a word.

Chapter Fifty-Eight

The office is like a prison. Each day I swallow my grief back as I try to put on my old suit – my old *self*. But I've accepted that version of me doesn't exist anymore.

I *want* to lose myself in work again; I want to prove to myself and everyone else that I can go back to 'normal'. Become Sofie King: Senior Pricing and Valuation Manager again. Instead of Sofie King: broken, bereaved mother.

Ed has called me in to his office to chat about targets. It's the first time he's spoken to me directly since the all-department meeting on Monday. He treats Tarun like he's still doing my job, because Tarun *is* still doing my job. There's been no discussion of him stepping down. My team still answer to him. So, it seems, do I.

Ed can barely look at me in our meeting. He doesn't ask how I am, or how I'm getting on. He tells me it makes sense for Tarun to retain responsibility for most projects, at least until I'm back full time.

I know I should feel relieved – there's no way I can work to the high-achieving level I once did. But I also know that I have to find a way to get back to that version of me. Because if I don't have my baby and I don't have this job, then who am I?

When I leave Ed's office, I have to go outside for some fresh air. But there are too many people outside, talking, laughing, having phone conversations. Being *normal*. I walk back into reception. I want to sink to the floor. Lie down. Be invisible. But to also be seen. Have someone recognise that I'm here and my baby was here, but he died.

I walk to the lift and when the doors close behind me, I scream. By the time the lift reaches the basement, I'm composed once more. I walk to my desk and try to focus.

Later on, in a discussion about catastrophe exposure with Tarun, I have to excuse myself suddenly. Just hearing those two words spoken out loud caused the boot to come down so heavily on my chest I can't even breathe, let alone speak.

'Just nipping to the toilet,' I say, a forced smile planted on my face.

I walk into the bathroom, to relieve myself only from the pressure of being in public. Two women from IT are in there, chatting at the sinks. I go straight into the only empty cubicle available, pressing my back against the locked door. It's then that I'm suddenly hit by the realisation that it was in this cubicle that I did my pregnancy test all those months ago. I sink down so I'm sitting on the toilet and put my head in my hands, holding my breath. When I hear the women leave, I pull my knees up to my chest and sob silently into them.

This is what baby loss looks like. It is a woman sobbing quietly, alone, but surrounded by people, perched on a toilet seat, wishing the cistern would open up and swallow her whole.

Chapter Fifty-Nine

At 5pm, I walk out of the glass doors and feel the spring air wrap me up and instantly lift me to a better place. It's Friday. Somehow, I've made it through the week.

I've never been happier to leave the office. I'm sure this primordial urge to get back to my baby is how most new mothers feel after maternity leave; why should I feel different just because my baby died?

I turn away from the building now and suddenly find myself needing to get as far away as possible. To go back to the nursery, be with my baby boy.

I sprint across the car park and run full pelt down the road, taking a left at the roundabout on to Christchurch Road, then a right, then another left on to Boscombe Spa road and then Owls road. With each step, I know I'm getting closer to him. Where I need to be.

Ignoring the curious glances of other pedestrians, I untuck my shirt and unbutton the top buttons. Then I take off my shoes and run barefoot down the road towards East Overcliffe Drive, which will take me the mile or so to Boscombe beach and then on to Southbourne and home. But when I reach Boscombe beach, I stop in my tracks.

I stop because I already feel him here. Not at home, in his nursery, where his ashes are. But here, by the sea. It's so clear that I find myself gasping to take a breath as I'm overcome by emotion. I watch the ripple of gentle waves rise like floating feathers and then fall again to the shore.

A feeling of intense calm overtakes me. I walk from the promenade on to the beach, enjoying the sensation of my feet pressing into the soft, grainy sand.

I look out at the glistening sea, sparkling in the April sunshine and pull out my phone to text Rory that I'll be late home. I want to stay here for a while.

Above, small polka-dot clouds are scattered across the baby blue sky. A seagull gives an exalted cry that sounds like 'Leo!' I repeat his name under my breath. Then again, a little louder so it's carried on the wind.

I imagine Leo's life rolling out in front of me now, like the sea. Endless tides and waves, peaks and troughs, ebbing and flowing from birth to his babyhood, childhood to his teen years right up to adulthood. All the life that would have – *should have* – bloomed from the wondrous, miraculous seed of a chance *he* took. He had everything against him, but still he gave it everything he had for that one shot at life.

And what if he *had* made it? I think, then. My little force of nature? Who would he be? And, I wonder, who would *I* be now? What kind of mother would I have been? Desperately over-protective, always full of anxiety? Always telling him not to fall, not to fail? Scared of letting him out of my sight?

Or would the act of having a healthy child have made me braver? Would I have believed more in the benefit of taking risks? Would my life have been finally led more by hope than fear? Would I have known how lucky I was, or would I have taken motherhood for granted because it had come so unexpectedly and so easily to me?

I stare at the ground at the small grains of sand, that were all once part of something else. Something bigger.

Being pregnant with Leo expanded my world. And suddenly, I know that I don't want it to shrink back to what it was, now he's gone. I don't want to live as I did before. In a box. Constrained by the walls of the office, my home – even my marriage.

Could the act of having Leo continue to change me now? Change my life entirely?

Perhaps it has already, without me even realising it?

I bend down and run my fingers through the sand, feeling the grains underneath my fingernails like earth. As I do, I'm taken back to memories from my childhood, gathering rock samphire from cliff faces in spring with dad because he loved its 'carrots and kerosene' flavour (as he described it) when fried in a little butter. In summer, aged about nine or ten, I remember fervently wishing I could wash off the sticky, uncomfortable heat of a day spent in a classroom, with a sea dip with my dad. And yet, I can't remember the last time I swam in the open sea. I realise I've just been swimming in straight, confined lines for years.

What happened to that wild-living girl? Would having Leo have helped me find that version of myself? The child I'd been. The girl I was before dad died. Perhaps, a lot like the boy Leo would have been...

I leave my shoes on the sand, tucking my phone in one. Then I walk down the beach towards the shore. The water surrounds my toes, tickling my feet and I feel my heart lift at the sensation. I walk further out, even though I'm still wearing my work trousers that I've rolled up over my calves. I find myself wanting to go in further, getting my trousers wet to the knee, then right up to my thighs.

Before I know it, I'm up to my waist. My work shirt is soaking, billowing out around me like a deflated parachute. I'm wearing a camisole vest and bra underneath it, so I take off my shirt and let it float in the water next to me, my arms outstretched. The cold water encases my shoulders. As I submerge it feels entirely natural; the cold seems to waken something inside me. Each lap of the water against my chest seems a call to action: *Make waves!* It seems to be saying. *Live! Love! Risk!*

Crying out with the cold, I begin to swim, just like I used to do as a kid on Purbeck with Dad and Nisha. In this expanse of open water, I feel separate from my body and from the world: there's a peace here in this place, a lightness, a kind of serenity I haven't felt for years. As my arms cut through the water, I allow it to carry my body and I briefly wonder what would happen if I just stopped swimming. Let myself sink. Here I am as close to death as I can be. Which means I'm as close to Leo as I can be.

I take a deep breath and sink down beneath the surface. Submerge. Just to see what it's like. How long I can stay there for. Gasping, I come up for air after a few glorious seconds. Down there, not only did I feel closer to Leo – but I felt like I was part of him, too – and him of me, floating inside me. Holding each other. I begin to swim again, one arm in front of the other, legs kicking wildly like his did inside of me.

And with each stroke and kick, I feel myself carried by the sea that connects him to me and me to him and us to Dad and to this earth. And then my memories take me further back as I swim on, to the memories of a childhood spent right here: swimming, foraging, clambering, digging with my dad. A childhood I turned my back on the moment he died.

I want to go back.

Just a few minutes after I went in, I walk out, fully clothed and dripping wet, with a handful of dulse that I plucked from the shore on my way out, the red rosette of the fronds feels like nature's reward for my wild swimming adventure. I know I must look like a mad woman, but I feel calmer than I have for weeks. Months. *Years,* even. I feel … renewed.

Shivering, I walk along the beach, to collect my shoes, socks and phone. Inside I feel warm. Fired up. Alive.

For so long I've only craved order in my day: routine, safety, predictability. They were my goals after Dad's death. But I'm realising it's in the taking risks where real life is found.

Suddenly I'm reminded of a line from a Mary Oliver poem.

Tell me, what is it you plan to do with your one wild and precious life?

I don't know the answer yet … but one thing I'm sure of is, if Leo wasn't lucky enough to get to live a day on this earth, then it's my responsibility to live mine to the full.

Because today at work, it hit me like a tsunami. My risk-averse strategy for life has failed *spectacularly*. Even though we teach people to live carefully, life insurance itself is a licensed gamble. We might provide a safety net, but we can't *stop* those things happening. So, shouldn't we be helping people navigate them instead? Giving people the tools to deal with the life events that, in all probability, will almost certainly happen to them at some point?

This Wasn't Meant to Happen

I can't stop thinking of the baby-loss statistics now permanently stamped in my head: In the UK, eight babies are stillborn every day. Worldwide that number increases to 5000, or 1.9 million babies each year. That's the equivalent of one stillbirth every 16 seconds. One in four pregnancies ends in miscarriage – that's not one in four women will have a miscarriage, but that in all pregnancies, twenty-five per cent of them will end in grief. Seventy-six women work at Prospect across all the departments, which means that statistically speaking, nineteen women in the company are likely to experience a miscarriage or already have; like me, they'll feel isolated, alone, ashamed, grief-stricken, unsure of how to talk of their loss with friends and family – let alone colleagues.

Now I think of those numbers across the entire female workforce in the UK. Because if having a baby takes women out of the workforce, what does *losing* a baby do?

I've always loved my job, but today I felt like it didn't fit me, and even worse, that I'll have to fight to keep my place. Fight with an energy I just don't have. Tarun knows my position is tenuous: I'm a bereaved woman who has come back early to work. Too early, I realise. And he's made it clear that he's willing to fight to hang on to the position *he* expected to have for at least a year – and try and keep it beyond that.

I thought coming back to work would be the solution. I turn back and look at the sea one more time before heading home, but I can't help but feel that there's a different life for me on the horizon now.

Chapter Sixty

When I open the front door, Rory's anxiously pacing our hall. He looks at me, both aghast and with relief. I'm a mess, my clothes and hair are still dripping wet and I'm shivering uncontrollably. And yet this is the most alive I've felt for weeks; I have the deepest clarity of what needs to come next.

'Sofie? Are you okay? It's seven-thirty. Where have you been?' He runs to get a towel. He looks like I used to feel back in the days when he still went bouldering.

'I messaged you,' I say, grappling for my phone and finding my text to him. Unsent. 'Dodgy signal, sorry.'

'I was really worried.'

'I'm fine, Rory, honestly. I just went for a swim after work.' I'm clutching foraged dulse and some sea kale I found at the beach. On my meandering walk home I'd also picked some wild bluebells, wood anemones and some pastel pink cuckoo flowers.

He studies me for a moment. 'You look … *wild*.'

'I feel it!' I start to laugh. Properly laughing, from deep inside me.

He smiles uncertainly at me. 'Okay, Sof. Let's get those wet clothes off you.'

'I remember when that would have meant something more interesting,' I giggle as he takes off my shirt and rubs me down with the towel. I take off my trousers obediently, almost flirtatiously, but then remember where his expectation of sex always leads. Trying for another baby.

As his eyes graze my semi-naked body, I quickly dart upstairs, put my pajamas on and grab a towel to dry my hair.

'How was work?' he asks, handing me a cup of tea when I come back down.

'Work was okay, thanks,' I say, 'but the swim was…' – I pause, roll a word around in my brain – 'incredible. I'd forgotten how much I used to love wild swimming. I think I'm going to take it up again.'

'Okaaaay.' Rory looks at me, like I'm an alien. I realise he's never known that version of me. She died when dad did.

'I've also decided I'm going to get in contact with the hospital's counselling service.' I say this because I want to do something for him, something that's expected of me.

'That's great news, Sofie!'

I follow him into the spotless kitchen where everything is, once again, tidied neatly away – on the surface, at least. Not for the first time since Leo died, I long for my messy, disorganised husband back.

Rory looks up then as if sensing my sudden discomfort. 'What's wrong?' he asks.

Everything I want to say. *Everything is different. You're not you; I'm not me. Leo isn't here. We don't add up.*

'Nothing,' I manage, shivering as I speak.

He shakes out my wet shirt, then hangs it neatly on the drying rack and I feel an urge to pull it off, crumple it into a ball and put it on again. Backwards. It would represent who I am now much more than the buttoned-up, ironed-out version of me that went to work this week.

I watch as he removes his own his hoodie and puts it on me. I get a glimpse of his body as he does so. His once broad, soft chest has shrunk. His shoulders are rounded with tension, his stomach concave. He leaves the room, coming back with a new top on and helps readjust the towel around my head. When he's done, he stands for a moment, warm breath tickling my neck as if waiting for something, anything. When I feel his lips touch my skin I step away. I don't need to look at him to know he's hurt.

A moment later, he goes to the fridge and returns brandishing a bottle of fizz with a bright Rory King TV smile.

'I got this to celebrate your first week back!' he says. 'Now we have something else to celebrate too. I know counselling is going to be the best thing for you…'

'What about you?' I interrupt, wanting to stop him before he tells me what else I should be doing. 'How was your day?'

Rory immediately turns his back to me as he stirs something bubbling on the hob, uncomfortable as soon as there's any focus on him.

'Fine, thanks. I'm doing a pre-record outside broadcast tomorrow that'll go out on Thursday night. It's a local interest one, right here in Southbourne, so that's good!'

'Is it?' I reply. He turns round.

'Of course!'

'You don't think it might be hard?'

He stops stirring for a split second. He seems surprised by the question. He's not used to having his decisions queried 'No!' he says. 'It'll be fine. It'll be … good.' He starts stirring again. Faster than before.

'Okay,' I shrug. 'So, what's the story?' I say, remembering the guessing game we used to play about his assignments. 'Biggest pizza in Dorset? A fossil that looks like someone's hamster? Bournemouth's oldest living cat?' I see him twitch a little, in admission. 'Aha! It *is* cat based! It's *always* cat based…' I say triumphantly. 'Okay. Let me keep guessing… Is it the fattest cat in Dorset? A cat that thinks it's a dog?'

I walk over to the fridge and get out a bottle of sparkling mineral water and two glasses from the shelves next to it and begin to pour. 'Southbourne's first ever cat burglar wreaking havoc on the neighbourhood?'

'Haha, very funny,' he says. 'And yes, it *is* cat based. You could say it's the "purrfect" reintroduction to local news.'

Just when I feel like we're having a normal conversation, his phone lights up on the kitchen counter. He glances at it as he continues to stir the casserole. Then he picks it up and I see his face briefly lit by the glow of the screen, immediately submerged in whatever he's reading.

'Do you have to do that right this minute?' I ask, lightly.

'What?' he says distractedly.

'We were talking, or at least … trying to.'

'I just need to reply to this DM…' He starts tapping again.

'Do you? Right now?' I'm trying to contain the hurt and frustration I feel.

'I'll just be a minute, it's someone whose baby died a few months ago so—'

'So did ours,' I interrupt coldly. 'But you don't talk to *me* about it.' Another rock, dropped from a great height from an eroding cliff.

Rory turns, phone still clutched tightly in his hand. His jaw is tight, shoulders tense. He looks almost coiled with tension and stress. 'That's not true.'

I gaze at him steadfastly, with newfound confidence in what I need to say. 'It is, Rory. We talk about work, what we're having for dinner, how I need to move on, whether I should have counselling, what's going on with your gran, or my mum. We talk about TV shows, but we never talk about Leo. Not since the cremation. Mostly you share your thoughts about him with strangers. If you're not on your phone, you're up in your office working, or whatever it is you do up there…'

'I work!' he says defensively. 'Occasionally I go on the rowing machine; I game – that's all! Christ! What else am I meant to do to relieve the tension of living in this house? I can't go out because I don't want to leave you; I can't do the hobbies I love because they frighten you. I'm doing the best I can, but clearly that's not enough!'

'I just wish you were with me more…'

'The only person you want to be with is Leo,' he shoots back. 'You're always in Leo's nursery. You won't scatter his ashes; you're not interested in finding a way to grieve for him together, or how to find a way forward…'

'You've made it quite clear you want another baby. I think it's fair that I need some time.'

'I just don't want to be stuck in this grief hole forever, Sofie! I want a purpose! Somewhere positive to put my love and grief. I'd like to get a group of bereaved parents together … maybe organise a cycle ride or a row for charity, something in his memory…'

He trails off and I don't respond. I can see now what he needs to feel close to Leo, in his own way, and I understand why he thinks he can do that on social media. But I'm too full of anger to stop my own trajectory now.

'I just don't understand why you'd want to share something so private with strangers when we're still processing it ourselves,' I say petulantly. 'It's barely been two months.'

'See what I mean? There's the disapproval again!' He rubs his forehead, turns his back to me and takes some deep breaths. 'It helps me to talk to people.' he says finally.

'What if it doesn't help me?'

There's a moment of silence. It feels like the calm before the storm.

He turns then, eyes flashing. 'All I've *done* these past few weeks is try to help you, Sofie! I've dealt with every phone call, spoken to every friend and family member, made every meal, held you while you've grieved. What about what *I* need? Isn't that important, too?

'You've made it quite clear what you need,' I say. 'To pour out your heart online.'

'I'm doing the best I can,' he says wearily, 'but having not been in this position before, I don't always know what that is.'

'Nor do I. But you keep telling me what I should do, anyway!'

'I'm just trying to help.'

'By sharing our pain with the world?'

He slams his hand on the kitchen counter, then immediately puts it up to his forehead alarmed by his own reaction.

'And what's so terrible about that?' His voice shaking with the effort it's taking to control his anger. 'Leo was my baby, too. Do you think that I'm not hurting? That I'm not grieving? Not just for our baby, but for my wife, who I also feel like I've lost…'

That silences me. I feel the now familiar wave of shame and sorrow.

'I'm still here, Rory, just … different.' I look into his eyes and feel like I see in them, a reflection of who we once were. A happy couple on a date at the beach, at the funfair, house hunting, on honeymoon, completely in love with each other and full of hope for the future. A sum of two equals. Not these single units that no longer add up. I desperately want to articulate what I felt at the beach earlier. To tell him all the ways in which I'm slowly re-examining my life, in response to Leo's death. But I don't know how, because I've realised that one of the big things I've been re-examining recently is *us*. Our marriage.

'I want us to go back to how we were before,' Rory says, dropping his head.

'I know,' I croak, taking his hand in mine. 'But we can't. What we're going through … it's huge. We have to work through it as best we can. Not over, but through. That's what Joe said.'

He glances up at me, then looks away. 'Well, I'm sure counselling will help you with that.'

I drop his hand like a hot rock. 'Aren't you going to come, too?'

He looks startled. 'I don't need to, Sof. I'm managing my grief in my own way.' He turns round and continues to stir the damn casserole. I want to throw it against the wall.

'But you keep telling me Leo was your baby, too!'

He turns around, maligned, misunderstood. 'Yes, but I already know the things that help me deal with it and I'm doing them already: working, writing, sharing…'

'"Inspirational" quotes about our son's stillbirth on social media?' I interject, bitterly.

He pauses and stares at me. His lips are unnaturally drawn into a line, like a neat paper-fold. I'm suddenly aware then of how different he looks from the Rory I fell in love with. Hardened. Haunted. He's lost the soft edges that made him, *him*.

'You don't have the monopoly on grief, Sofie,' he says wearily. 'We're meant to be in this together, but apparently only *you* get to make all the decisions – about how we share our grief and what our future looks like.'

Another silence. Another rock crashing into the ocean.

'Is that *actually* what you think, Rory? That I have *ever* got to make decisions about anything in our relationship?'

I can't believe he's pushing me, again. Like he always does. Not allowing me to stand still for a moment.

'It's been two months, that's all. *Two months*,' I repeat quietly. 'I've got out of bed, gone out with friends, gone back to work, like everyone wanted me to. I'm booking myself in for counselling, like everyone wants me to. That's as much I can cope with right now.'

'I know, I know. It's just, I want … I need—'

'You *want* and *need* more than I can give you, Rory!' I interrupt. The words coming faster than I can think. 'You always have done! Why does everything have to be about *your* beliefs, *your* hope, *your* optimism? Your desire for children? Even now, you're pushing for the next—'

'I… I … just know you'll feel differently, in time. This won't happen again—'

I cry out with frustration, then. 'You promised me everything was going to be okay with Leo, but it wasn't!'

I stop then, even though there is so much more I could say. But what I can't say out loud to him, what I can barely allow myself to think, is that I don't need more time to know that I don't want to have another baby. I will only ever want Leo. But I'm petrified that if Rory knows that, then maybe I will lose him, too.

He steps forward towards me, his face wrought with alarm, but I step away. I finally realise how much he *needs* to be a dad again. And that's what has created this chasm between us. 'Sofie, I know you're scared, so am I. But the chances are…'

'The chances?' I laugh through my tears, 'Jesus, Rory! You're talking to an actuary, remember? Statistically, after one stillbirth, we're more likely to have another, not less. The probability goes *up*, not down. Those are the facts. *That* is the maths, Rory, okay?'

'But it was a completely random event, Sofie! We were just *unlucky*; there's nothing to say that we won't bring our baby home next time…'

'And there's nothing to say we will, either! One in four, remember Rory? And just because we've been that "one" once, doesn't mean we can't be again!'

'We'll make sure we're not!' Fumbling, he grasps my hands desperately. 'I promise, we'll do everything it takes; go private; have every test and scan possible, we'll…'

'Rory, will you just *stop*?' I cry as I throw my hands in the air – and his off me. 'Stop pretending that you have some magic power, some heightened state of luck that others don't have. You can't control life and you especially can't control death; you can't stop the people you love leaving you, like your mum and dad did. Or from dying, like my dad and Leo did. You might want to surround yourselves with lots of people on social media and your TV audience to make yourself feel safe and endlessly loved, but the truth is, they'll eventually leave, too!'

He stares at me then, his expression pained. Without saying another word, he walks out of the kitchen and slams the door behind him. I feel the walls shake along with the foundations of our marriage.

I sink to the floor, then. Crying not for me, or for Leo, but for Rory. Because I realise that I've just exposed Rory's biggest fear – being abandoned – and stripped him of his superpower: his hope. And of all the things I've said and done recently, those are both unforgivable.

Chapter Sixty-One

It's Wednesday morning. The middle of my second week back and the end of the first week of May – my third month without Leo. I'm sat at my computer, staring blindly at policy-risk data and sinking with the weight of pretending I can still do my job.

'Coffee anyone?' I ask, grabbing my mug and standing up. Kate's face freezes in horror, her eyes swivel to Lena and she instinctively moves her face closer to her monitor.

'I'll get them!' Lena gets up, grabs their mugs and dashes off, leaving me standing here. Now I'm up, I figure I'll go and run a question past Ed about some proposed government legislation that might impact our own company policies. But when he sees me approaching through the glass of his office, he lifts his hand, picks up the phone and splays his fingers to indicate five minutes. When he swivels his chair so his back is facing me, I know I'm not welcome anytime soon.

I sink back down in my own seat. The more I sit staring at my monitors, with Kate and Lena avoiding eye contact at all costs, the rest of the department pretending I'm not here, and my boss making it clear that he wishes I wasn't, the more I want to scream.

At home Rory and I simply co-exist, retreating to separate places of comfort: me to Leo's nursery or out on a walk, Rory to his phone, or his loft office.

I feel as isolated there as I do here. On the rare occasions we are together, we fall into the careful, considerate camaraderie of new housemates. We muck alongside each other politely, perfunctorily. We talk, but we don't look at each other. Rory brings me a cup of tea each morning, but never has it in bed with me. Each night I cook big, hearty, warming meals, pouring the regret I feel for not being able to give him the family he so desperately wants into those dishes because words aren't enough. We eat the meals in front of the TV so we don't have to look at each other, or even talk.

Each morning, I get up at five because it's already light and go for an early morning swim in the sea. It has become my happy place. Often, the bed is already empty. Rory will be upstairs in his office, or sometimes out for an early morning cycle before work. He even announced he's started going to the climbing centre again. I can't stop him; I don't want to. The biggest risk has already been taken; the greatest loss suffered. Ironically, these daily gambles of ours feel necessary now for our own survival. With my sea swimming, I feel like I've welcomed back a long-lost friend. Something supportive and uplifting that I kept away from because of my own fear and desire for self-protection, something that was just watching, waiting for the right moment to return.

On Saturdays, Rory and I no longer go for brunch. Instead, I help at the café because I've missed it. I've missed the time with both Mum and Midge. I find it a great comfort, the café, and the coastline that bears the prominent footprint of my father, the imprint of my childhood, and that holds immeasurable treasure in the sparkle of the sea and the rolling hills. There I feel both the presence of Dad, and Leo, too.

Once I was back at Prospect, I missed my morning foraging walks, missed tending the kitchen garden. I missed working methodically in the kitchen next to Midge. I missed feeling helpful, being needed. I have so many ideas for the place. So many ways in which I feel I could add value. So much time that I want to make up for. Being there, life glimmers hopefully and reflects a future that is vastly different from the one I expected to be looking at. Without Leo, but also with him. It's when I'm submerged in the vast blue sea after my shift that I feel him the most. Even more so than in his nursery.

Last night, after work, I went to the hospital to see Carrie, my counsellor. I've been a couple of times now, and though it's difficult it feels a relief to have a space to share. Someone who will simply listen, without trying to give me answers or tell me what I should do. Who allows me to simply talk about my baby and my pain; unlock every single grief-loaded, guilt- and shame-induced thought about his death, every bit of sadness and uncertainty about my life going forward. I hope that having someone to listen to me will help me make sense of it; help me feel that this is normal. That *I'm* normal. That the difficulties in communication that Rory and I are facing are *normal*. I don't know if we'll survive it, but at least this way, I don't feel so alone.

Towards the end of my first session, Carrie handed me a piece of paper and pen and asked me to write down what I feel. Within a minute I'd covered both sides of the paper with everything I've held in my brain for the past few weeks, sobbing as they poured out, my hand working without me even having to think. When I was finished, both physically and emotionally spent, she asked me what I saw when I read over the words on the piece of paper.

'Chaos. Confusion. Grief.' I answered, barely able to take in the emotionally fragile scrawl that covered the pages.

'That's interesting,' she said softly as she gestured for me to hand the paper to her, then studied it for a moment. 'Because I see love. Lots of it. Pouring from you as soon as you were given the chance. I see a mother worrying about her baby, missing him, loving him. I see you wondering who you're meant to be, now that your life has changed beyond expectation. Wondering where to put the love you had for Leo because he's not here. It's a lot to hold in, isn't it? To carry? All that love. All that fear. And you know what, Sofie? That's motherhood. That's it in a nutshell. It's endless love and endless fear. But you don't have to carry it alone or be afraid to let it all out. Grief might be love with nowhere to go. But it's also something you can hold on to like a guide rope. In time, love will become your superpower. Because love is the string tying all your emotions together. And it's that single thread that defines your role and experience as Leo's mother, Sofie. Love, not loss.'

I wept then because I couldn't believe that she saw the mess in my head and heart as something beautiful. Something powerful. Something transformative. I was wrong about my grief tethering me to Leo. It is – it has always been – my love.

Each session I've been to has been hard, but ultimately helpful. It's good to be able to let everything out; the only problem is, I have to pack it all up again and carry it around quietly when I'm here at work.

Next to me, Tarun works quickly, efficiently, loudly: slurping tea, talking to clients, tapping out reports. The 'handover' hasn't happened. He hovers here, like a shadow, an iceberg even. Waiting for my boat to crash.

My team seem to be at once on high alert and withdrawn, not knowing who to answer to, Tarun or myself.

'Lena,' I'll say, 'Do you have those reports?'

'Yes, I gave them to Tarun when he asked for them first thing this morning.'

'What about the experience analysis?'

'Also with Tarun.'

Before Leo, I loved that as an office culture, we didn't 'do' personal. It was enough that I was able to help people I didn't know by providing policies that would financially support families. I gave intense focus to data rather than the people around me, because I thought it gave me insight.

But now I know that statistics don't tell us nearly enough. I want to know more about the 'risks' we're evaluating – the people behind the policies. And I want to know more about my colleagues, too. Because how can we understand our clients' lives if we don't even know each other?

I *want* them to know what's happened to me, because then, more people will know Leo. They'll know how important he was. How much he's changed me. But I know that's not what *they* want and so I stay quiet.

I'm working hard to locate the capable, committed professional who believed she could provide protection from the worst that life can throw. But I can't because I don't believe it anymore. In fact, I'm starting to believe that it's only by leaning into the worst times that we can gain something from what we lose. More insight. More beauty. More gratitude. A deeper idea of what life is about.

Chapter Sixty-Two

I'm slumped in the meeting room unable to focus, staring at my notepad which has doodles all over it. Ed has been talking targets for the past ten minutes. Now he's reminding us of Prospect's three Ps manifesto: Product. Protect. Profit.

I write a *P* on my pad. Then more. *P. P. P. P…*

I pause. P for *Pause*, I think to myself. I write another *P*, followed by an *i*.

Pi.

3.1459

P. I try to think of more P words. Pregnancy, obviously. I write it down.

Pregnancy.

3.14159265…

P.

Parent.

3.141592653589…

P.

Pain.

3.1415926535897932…

'The Board are panicking…' Ed says.

I write the word '*panic*'.

'… about the company's struggle with growth and profitability over the past few years. It seems from research that potential new customers…'

People, I write. Then, *Potential.*

'… question our value proposition and are more likely to take out policies with insurers who offer…'

I look up in time to see him make bunny ears with his fingers:

'… a more "engaged wellness ecosystem" within the life-insurance remit.' He rolls his eyes. 'Apparently, health trends are changing and so, too, must the face of insurance. Customer insight shows that Prospect is now considered a data dinosaur in a digitalised world that's moving away from using more generalised mortality statistics, to more innovative product solutions that tell us more about *individuals.*' He says the word like it's a dirty one.

'Like smartphones and fit bits!' Tarun calls out confidently.

'*Exactly!*' Ed beams. 'That's the kind of innovative thinking I'm talking about Tarun!'

I look up briefly. *Not exactly innovative,* I want to say. *Vitality did that years ago.*

'So,' Ed continues as I doodle distractedly on my notepad. 'As a department, we've been asked by the board to look specifically at the "P" in Product to imagine the future of life insurance. It's a big project, I know. An important one too. Joe, I need your team to develop at least three innovative ideas and present them to the board in two weeks' time with workable solutions of how we re-establish Prospect's vital role in customers' lives.'

'That's a broad brief,' Joe observes.

'Start by thinking about the three Ps,' Ed offers. 'What do they mean to us now and how do we make them work better in the future? Why not kick off with Tarun's brilliant idea of engaging more with technology to better understand our customers lives. That's the basepoint – *personalisation.*' He writes it on the white board. 'Okay? Anyone have any anything else to offer?'

'What about rethinking what our three Ps actually are?' I say. My voice is unfamiliar, croakily unconfident. I didn't mean to speak and clearly, from the reaction, no one expected me to. I look down at my notepad, at the P words I've doodled. It has felt a bit like playing *Words with Friends* with Joe. And I think it means something.

This Wasn't Meant to Happen

Pi. Pregnancy. Parent. Partner. Pain. Panic. Paralyse. Prepare. Permission. People. Protection. Potential. SuPPort – not strictly a P word, but P-focused. I've circled the word '*people*' and '*potential*' several times.

Ed pulls a painfully sympathetic face. 'Sorry, Sofie,' he says carefully. 'What do you mean?' He looks in my direction, without making eye contact. His manner is kind, benevolent, careful.

'We're a Life insurance company that exists to protect our policy-holders, right?' I sit up in my chair. Try to make myself bigger. Bolder.

'Ye-es,' Ed says slowly, like he's talking to a child.

'And yet in our three Ps manifesto, the word "people" doesn't feature.'

'That's because it's obvious,' Tarun pipes up. 'We sell our policies to *people*, to *protect* them for *profit*.'

Patronising Prick. Two more P's. I'm good at this.

'Is it obvious though, Tarun?' Joe's voice rises confidently from across the room. 'Perhaps Sofie's right. If policy holders are the heart of everything we do, they should be part of our manifesto.' I look at him gratefully.

'I just wonder whether,' I continue, finding my voice, 'rather than focusing on our current value propositions, more innovation might come if we redefine those three Ps themselves? We've talked about personalisation, where the product is geared much more to the lives and experiences of individuals, but only when it comes to their physical health—'

'Fitbits and smartphones, just like I said!' Tarun interrupts. 'Smart*watches* even!' he adds proudly, like he invented them – and the idea of using them to incentivise people's policies.

'Yes, but a version of that exact product which uses technology to gather personalised data has already been rolled out by other insurance companies. We need to innovate here.' My brain has already started working overtime, thinking about the ways in which we could be better serving our customers, based on what I've been through. 'I just wonder if—'

'Sofie!' Ed interrupts without looking at me. 'Honestly, it's *great* that you agree with Tarun as it proves to me that he seems to really understand where I'm coming from.' He looks up from his notes.

'Tarun, why don't you and Joe team up on this "personalisation" angle?'

I am so clearly being sidelined, it makes me furious. I know I have something to offer here.

'Ed,' I say quickly, 'Tarun is so busy with other projects of mine, surely it makes sense for me to take on this new one with Joe? I really think I can bring something to this. I have some quite innovative ideas based on my own experience about how we provide mental-health support and grief supp—'

'Are you sure you're up to it, Sofie?' Tarun cuts in patronisingly. 'I mean, what with everything you're dealing with…' I stare at him, and he has the decency to look uncomfortable. 'You know, because of losing your, losing … it, I wonder if you should be taking it easy, not taking on more work?'

'I lost my baby, not my mind, Tarun,' I snap, my heart pumping with humiliation at how publicly he's belittling me. I pull my notebook up to my chest and stand up. 'And his name was Leo.' *He, not it.* 'I haven't talked about him, because no one has asked, and I don't want to make anyone uncomfortable. I understand it's hard to know how to approach me, but please know that I'm happy to answer any questions anyone might have about him. Now, are we done here, Ed?' I challenge.

'Y-yes, s-sure!' Ed stutters.

'Great. If you don't mind, I'll get started on this project. There's a lot to do.'

I stand up and sweep out of the room, suddenly finding some of that strength, resolve and bravery that Leo has given me.

Chapter Sixty-Three

I don't stop at my desk. I keep walking out of the department, into the lift and then out of the building. On the pavement, I bend over, gasping with choked back emotion.

I stand up and keep walking quickly in case anyone sees me. I don't want to be here. I want to be with Leo. It's not lunchtime yet, but close enough. I know no one will question my absence. I'm pretty sure Ed would rather I didn't come back at all.

'Sofie!' I wince as I hear my name being called and immediately walk faster hoping whoever it is will presume I'm out of earshot.

Joe is panting by the time he catches up to me.

'Hi,' I smile weakly, unable to look at him because I'm so embarrassed.

'Are you okay?' He puts his hand on my shoulder, lightly, and we both stop.

I glance up at him, noticing how soft and kind his expression is, how steady his gaze and demeanour.

'I've been better.'

'Do you want some company? Lunch?'

'It's barely twelve.'

'I told Ed I'm taking an early one. So, where shall we go?'

'The beach?' I reply.

'Perfect. I used to go there on my lunch breaks after Rachel died.'

I look up at him. 'Joe, I need to say something. I'm so sorry I wasn't there for you when Rachel died, not like I should have been. I realise now how hard it must be for you to come to work every day and pretend to be okay. I didn't check in enough because I didn't want to upset you. I didn't feel like the office was the right place…'

'Sofie, I understand,' Joe replies warmly. 'To be honest, I haven't actually *wanted* to talk about her until quite recently; it was all too painful. I wanted to lock my grief up in a box, instead. But I've learned through counselling that not talking about it doesn't make it go away.'

We walk in companiable silence until we reach the promenade of Boscombe beach. I spot a café and suggest that I go in and grab us some coffees.

As soon as I go inside, I'm side-swiped by a memory, a sudden flash of something – longing perhaps – as I think about who Rory and I used to be before Leo died. I feel such an ache when I look around at the couples there, some with babies, that it physically winds me.

Do you know how lucky you are? I want to cry. *Hold on to this version of your life, hold on to it tightly because it could be taken from all of you in a heartbeat.*

I feel my chest constrict with the pain of missing both Leo and Rory. Missing the life I should have had. There is a thin line, I realise, between 'what if' and 'what now'.

As soon as I get our coffees I rush outside. Squinting into the sun, I hand Joe his black Americano. It's odd to see him here – not just outside work, but *outside*. His Scottish skin is almost translucent it's so pale. It tells of a life studying, reading, working and, of course, more recently, grieving. His pristine clothes and immaculately polished shoes look out of place here at the beach. It's kind of like seeing a penguin wandering across the sand. I laugh at this mental image, and he delivers me a quizzical look and a lopsided grin. I notice that *he's* not afraid to make eye contact with me.

He gestures at a bench, and we go and sit down. Joe crosses his left leg neatly and rests his elbow over the back of the bench, his body turned to me in full engagement.

'I know that anything I say will sound pathetically inept in conveying my concern ... but how are you doing?' he says in his soft, Scottish accent. 'And don't be afraid to reply, "fucking awful".'

I think about how it feels to be asked this by someone who understands the complexities of grief, but who isn't directly impacted by the loss of Leo. He's not asking because he wants me back to normal, like Nisha does, or because he wants me to be in the same place in my grief, like Rory does, or because he's worried about me, like Mum is. There's no expectation from my answer. No pressure to be anything other than honest.

'Full Words with Friends?' I ask.

'Yes,' he laughs. He has a strong profile, I note distractedly. Aquiline nose framing kind, intelligent, grey eyes beneath a strong brow. His right knee brushes mine briefly and I try to concentrate, to compose a truthful answer, because with him, I can.

'Bereft, lonely, angry, confused, guilty, broken, ashamed and ... well...' I pause for a moment. 'Just really, really fucking *sad*.'

Joe nods. 'I remember those feelings well, but I've learned the landscape of grief constantly shifts.'

'What do you mean?'

'Well, for example, the sadness stays, but eventually, you might not feel as angry as you once did.'

'I can't imagine you ever being angry,' I say. Joe is the epitome of a gentle giant. I've never seen him come close to losing his temper.

'Oh, believe me, I was fucking furious. But eventually, I realised that emotion didn't honour Rachel, or our relationship. We weren't a couple who fought; we barely ever argued in fact. *She* wasn't an angry person. Stubborn and argumentative, maybe' – he smiles at a private memory – 'but mostly, she was loving, wise, beautiful, messy and unerringly kind. Now the anger has gone, there's more room for the gratitude. I'm just thankful she was and always will be my wife. That's the constant.'

It hits me then, too.

Leo will always be my son. I'll always be Leo's mother.

Joe sees my struggle to hold back my tears.

'I-I'm sorry,' I say, my voice choked.

'Sofie, never apologise for showing how much you love Leo,' he says gently.

Love, not loved. I love that he uses the present tense.

'You've been so strong through everything, Joe... You don't need me blubbing on you now.'

'Why do we perpetuate this myth that strength is silence and courage equals coping? What you did back there was one of the bravest and strongest things I've seen, and I for one am in awe. You stood up for your baby; you protected him like any mother would.'

A snort-like sob escapes and I apologise again as Joe puts his arm around me. 'S-sorry,' I say, trying to articulate the word through my tears.

'Sofie, I'm honoured you trust me enough to show your true feelings.'

'Rory w-won't cry,' I hiccup, pulling away from his embrace slightly. Joe hands me a handkerchief. Of course he has a handkerchief. 'He won't even talk about Leo, not to me anyway.' I regret saying it even as it comes out of my mouth. Like I've been disloyal somehow.

'You know,' Joe says then, 'men really are simple creatures. We like to deal with problems in a binary way, fix them and move on. But grief doesn't work like that. We *can't* make it better which makes us feel useless. So, we put that problem in a box and focus on what we can do: work, pay bills, practical tasks that make us feel like we're coping. But it doesn't mean we're not grieving. The box is there, all the time. We just don't see the benefit of opening it, when there's nothing we can do about it. We'd rather leave it well alone.'

I realise I have no real idea how Rory is feeling. Not only has he locked up his emotions inside a box, but he's also been mostly locked inside his loft office, too.

Joe glances at me as if he can sense what I'm thinking. 'The problem with boxes is they're always there, holding a lot of heavy shit.'

As the lunch break draws to a close, we go and get ice creams and start heading back. Each step feels like I'm walking through wet concrete. I don't want to go.

'Joe,' I say suddenly. 'I'm just thinking about this project to reimagine the life insurance product. When Rachel died, did you feel like it was an effort to do your job? To care about it?'

He contemplates my question for a moment. 'I suppose so. But I also welcomed the distraction.'

'But didn't it frustrate you that as a company and as colleagues, we didn't know how to deal with what you were going through and that your life insurance policy didn't do more for you after she died?'

'I'm not sure,' he considers, 'I guess I just accepted this is how it is. Humans struggle to know how to talk about grief. Life-insurance companies provide financial security through life and pay out in death. What else can we do?'

'A hell of a lot more, I think.' I turn to him, as my thought process starts clearing. 'As a life-insurance company, we don't want to make those big pay-outs, right? We want our policy holders to avoid death for as long as possible. So, to help them we try to educate and influence about living more active, healthy and therefore longer lives. We encourage them to not smoke, to eat a healthy diet, exercise, get regular health MOTs. We constantly motivate them to do so financially through benefits in their policies…'

Joe nods, licks his ice cream thoughtfully. I can see he's wondering where this is going. I look at mine slowly melting in the midday heat, the soft mound sliding down the cone, settling into a sticky, messy pool.

The ice cream? Or my life?

'And yet…' I continue, 'we don't provide the same support during big life moments.'

'No,' he says, 'we don't. Hey, where are you going, Sofie?'

I've thrust my cone at him as an idea occurs to me. 'Joe. Can you tell Ed that I'm taking the afternoon to work from home on our project? I've had an idea. I'll email you once I've thought it through, okay?' Standing on my tip toes, I kiss him on the cheek. 'Thank you, Joe. For everything. You've helped more than you know.'

I walk away, fuelled with passion for my newly forming plan. When I turn back, Joe is still stood there, like a monolith, a marker. Or maybe, a turning point.

Chapter Sixty-Four

I've been sitting in Leo's nursery for the past two hours, reading reports on miscarriage, stillbirth and maternity-bereavement rights, shocked by the experiences of the thousands of women in this country whose babies died before the third trimester, were therefore classified as a 'miscarriage' and aren't entitled to maternity leave *at all*. Just ten days' bereavement leave. Ten working days to mourn a life lost. A family shattered. A future gone.

According to a survey I read by the charity Tommy's, only seven per cent of employees in this country work in a company with a Pregnancy Loss Policy in place. I can't believe that something that affects so many thousands of people each year is so unsupported.

I find myself thinking of Kate and Lena at work. What if one of them has experienced miscarriage themselves? How would I know? Our office culture doesn't give space for that kind of deeply personal conversation and support. It occurs to me that no one at work knowing your baby died must be just as traumatic as everyone knowing.

And what about the men I work with? Perhaps *their* partner has experienced a miscarriage, a termination for medical reasons, an ectopic pregnancy, a late miscarriage, a stillbirth, a neonatal death, and they are having to navigate it while continuing to work. What about couples who want to have a baby but are struggling, who run the gauntlet of their cycle every month, injecting themselves with hormones privately, dealing with the anxiety, trauma, hope, disappointment and all-encompassing fear of infertility? What kind of toll does that take on a person? An employee? A workforce? A society?

I hear the front door open and glance at the time on my laptop. Rory's early. Then I remember he was filming his pre-recorded report about the cat.

'Hi!' I call faux brightly, not getting out of the nursing chair. He opens the nursery door, green eyes as dull as murky seawater as he takes in my presence there. He looks at Leo's urn which is next to me.

'Shouldn't you be at work?'

'I left early. You're back early, too,' I say. 'How did your report go?'

He doesn't reply; he's still staring at Leo's urn.

'Rory?' He blinks, looks at me. 'How was the cat?' I ask.

I see him staring at the picture above my head. L for Leo.

'Hmm … sorry?' he says, still not looking at me.

'Your report? In Southbourne. It was about a cat, wasn't it? How was it?'

'Oh, yes. It was okay. Sorry, Sofie, I need to get on so … if there's nothing else…?'

I look at my once determinedly happy, positive, talkative husband and realise that I barely recognise the person he is now.

'No, there's nothing,' I say quietly. He leaves the room. Goes upstairs. Again.

Through blurred vision, I look back down at my computer, attach the document I've been working on to a new email and write Joe's name. In the subject box I write two words: 'Your help'. Then, I add a kiss and hit send.

Chapter Sixty-Five

It's Monday. I'm in Zoe's office, one printed copy of my report is resting on my lap, another is with her. She turns the pages slowly, mascara-laden lashes lowered, dark, tight curls falling over her cheek as she reads, making it hard for me to see her expression. I emailed her first thing this morning, asking if I could meet with her. She told me to come straight up.

I take this opportunity to look around her office. The room is small but homely, and accessorised with plants and framed photos. One is of a young boy, aged about eight or nine years old, wild hair springing over chocolate-button eyes. He's grinning at the camera, cuddling Zoe and presumably, her husband. A proud mother, father and child. There's another frame on the other side of her computer, but I can't see it from the angle it's pointed at. A homemade, ceramic pot crudely and garishly painted is sat on her desk and filled with pens. My heart aches. I lean forward, to look more closely at the child's photo.

She looks up at me. 'That's Lucas,' she says softly.

'He's gorgeous,' I say, trying not to sound choked.

'Thank you, he's a joy. He's a twin, actually…'

Lucky her. I feel my throat thicken and swell and I force myself to swallow. I don't want emotion to get in the way of this meeting. I need to focus on what I'm here for.

'Sofie,' she says looking at me. 'I know how difficult it's been since you came back—'

'Oh?' I say defensively. 'Who did you hear that from?' I think of Tarun and Ed and wonder if they've questioned my ability to do my job to her. I guess it's only fair. *I've* questioned it.

'I was worried you were coming in here to hand in your resignation.'

I look down. 'I won't pretend coming back hasn't been harder than I expected. I'm just trying to find an authentic way to engage in this work again, to be honest.'

She nods, looks down at my report. 'I completely understand.'

I sit forward in my chair, ready for a difficult pitch. 'I just feel like there is something more we can offer both our policy holders and employees to support them through difficult life events. I don't believe I'm the only one who has experienced baby loss in this company. Statistically speaking, if there are 800 staff here and 250 are women, that means at least fifteen women will be the 1 in 4 that experience miscarriage. Also, given one in 100 women experience multiple miscarriages, two or more of our 250 female staff that could be suffering right now – probably in silence and shame....'

Zoe is still staring down at my report. 'We talk about loss adjustors all the time in this industry, without actually helping people through actual loss adjust*ment*,' she adds with a weak smile. She glances at the photo to the left of her, the one I can't see.

'And that's just the ones whose miscarriages are reported!' I exclaim passionately. 'Who end up in the system and therefore *become* a statistic. So many women, so many *mothers* whose babies die in utero in the first trimester and who don't report it. And then there are those who suffer stillbirths like me, or whose babies die after birth—'

'I know,' she says, glancing again at the photo I can't see, her eyes full of the same life-changing love and loss that I know people see in mine.

Her words echo in my head.

I know.

I understand.

Time and time again she's said those words to me. And then just now. *He's a twin.*

And yet he's alone in the photo. How did I not realise?

'How long ago was it for you, Zoe?' I ask quietly.

She picks up the other photo frame. I don't need to see it to know it's another baby.

'Eight years. Lucas's identical twin died before he was born. They had something called Twin-to-Twin Transfusion Syndrome, which is where the distribution of blood supply is uneven, causing each baby to grow at different rates.'

'Oh, Zoe. I'm so sorry.' I press my hands to my lips, then reach out to her, grasp her hands and we cling to each other for a moment. My heart is both a butterfly and a heavy weight. 'Can I see him?' She nods, passes it over and I see two babies, lying side by side in a neonatal unit.

I blink slowly, trying to stay in this moment of Zoe's, with her babies, and not get thrust back to my birth, my loss. 'What's his name?'

'Nathaniel,' she says, a smile forming on her lips as she says it.

I let those four syllables fill the air for a moment, I can almost see his name gather oxygen and float between us like a love-filled balloon.

'Lucas and Nathaniel,' I say. 'How perfect.'

Tears instantly fill her eyes.

'I'm sorry,' I say quickly.

'No, please, don't apologise,' she smiles, grabbing a tissue from a box on her desk. 'I love hearing their names together. Even after eight years, it makes me feel like he is here again. Their names were always meant to be said together.'

I think of all the messages she's sent to me, the kindness she showed before we even met. 'You've tried to reach out to me so many times, Zoe, I'm so sorry. I-I didn't realise. I've been so wrapped up in my grief I didn't—I couldn't—'

'Sofie,' she interrupts gently, her face full of compassion and understanding. 'I didn't expect you to. We'd barely met, and you were still navigating the impossible early days of your own loss. I wanted to reach out; I hoped I could help somehow. I mean, when you've been through something like this you find you want to do anything you can for those who are suffering through it themselves. It's like being given access to a secret club. You wouldn't choose to be a part of it, but it gives you an instant shared bond with those who are in it too. I can see your pain because I know it so well. And I want to help. And now' – she lifts up my report – 'I think you've shown me a way that I can – that *we* can, together. What you have done here, the ideas you've had, the research-backed insight – it's inspired, Sofie. And I have some ideas, too, about how HR can support this innovation. How long do you have before you need to present this to the board?'

'Two weeks,' I reply.

'Well, if you'll let me, I'd love to be involved. We could meet up after work. Have a drink and talk about it?'

'I'd love that,' I say, then I pause. 'But first,' I say tentatively, 'I'd really love to hear more about Lucas and Nathaniel, if you have time?'

Zoe smiles and her face lights up. 'I always have time for that. And I want to hear all about Leo too. Do you have a photo of him?'

I nod and reach for my bag with tears in my eyes because it's the first time someone other than Nisha, Mum, Sandra or Rory has seen him. And it feels wonderful.

Chapter Sixty-Six

The next morning, I'm in a big, white waiting room alone. Rory thinks I'm at work, but while I was in her office, I asked Zoe if she would sign off a day of my Bereavement leave. Being with her, talking about our journeys with Leo and Nathaniel and Lucas confirmed what I need to do.

Right now, I'm trying to curtail my anxiety as memories of other waiting rooms swirl and engulf me, carrying me back to the scans and appointments I had with Leo. Until the last one where we found out he had died.

I've no idea how long I've been here, but I was the first to arrive when the clinic opened. I'll stay all day if I must. I'm trying not to look at the photographs of babies on the walls; the happy parents; the couples who are waiting here together, hoping for their chance to join them. It's painful, but it's nothing I can't cope with. For the first time in months, today isn't about me or Leo. It is, I realise, a welcome relief.

The door opens and I look up, as I have done each time someone has walked in.

'Sofie?' Nisha says. Her usually impassive face shows shock and disbelief as she sees me sitting on the opposite side of the waiting room. 'What are you doing here?'

Her eyes flicker nervously around the room, at the other people who looked up as soon as she walked in. She's wearing a long, beautifully cut shirt dress and white trainers. Her bobbed, dark hair is centre-parted and pulled back into a sleek, low ponytail. Her almond eyes are perfectly lined with her trademark cat's eye flick. There's not a crease on her; not a hair out of place. On the outside, everything looks perfect; there's no indication of any inner turmoil whatsoever. But I know better.

She sits down next to me, hands clasped on her lap, knees turned inwards, like when she was a gangly teen. She's picked the cuticles around her manicured fingernails. They're red-raw, the only external indication of her inner pain.

I take her hand, stroke it gently with my thumb.

'I'm here for you, Nisha. I know I haven't been for a really long time, and I'm so sorry for that. But I'm here now and I will be for every single step of this journey, until you have your baby. And then you won't be able to get rid of me.' I pause and then add, 'If you still want me, that is.'

'I can't believe you're here. Are you sure this won't be too much for you, Sofie?' she asks tearfully. 'I totally understand if it is, you know.' She swallows. 'I know I said I needed you, but I also realise I've expected too much. And I'm so sorry for that. To ask you to be here … that was huge. I realised that as soon as I left; I just didn't know how to call you. I felt so guilty that I expected you to fast-track to a place you're not ready to be because…' She's gabbling. Nisha never gabbles.

'It's not too much, Nisha,' I say, interrupting her. 'I just needed a bit of time, that's all. You've been in pain, too, and I haven't been there for you, not like you have for me…'

She shakes her head. 'I've been selfish. I've wanted you to feel better so I could have my best friend back. I arrogantly thought that I knew how to fix pain. Typical doctor, eh?' she sob-laughs. 'I should have known that there isn't an operation you can perform or medicine you can give to heal grief. I'm so sorry Sofie…'

'Nisha, no more apologies,' I say firmly, swallowing back any tears that threaten to appear. 'Today is about you.' I go to get up.

She shakes her head, pulls me back, sniffs determinedly as if preparing to share something important. 'I have to tell you something first.' I take her hand and stroke it soothingly with my thumb. 'When I left your house,' she says, 'I went home and did some reading, some scientific research about miscarriage and baby loss,' she says. 'And I came across something that proves that even though they're not here our babies will always be part of us. That Leo literally continues to live on, in you.'

I look up at her longingly, the sound of his name tugging my interest on an invisible string.

'Research has found that from six weeks of pregnancy, a cell exchange begins between a mother and her baby allowing the baby's DNA to become part of the mother's body. This is called a foetal micro-chimerism.' Nisha has gone into doctor mode now. 'It's something that continues throughout the pregnancy, even if the babies we carry doesn't live to be born – and remain for decades after. Possibly forever. Our babies' stem-like cells will have travelled into our bloodstream and some of these circulating cells manage to bypass our immune systems after pregnancy and can even integrate into tissue, physically becoming a part of us, but also protecting us from some illnesses, like certain cancers. They can contribute stem cells, generate neurons in our brain and, according to *New Scientist*, foetal cells contained in the placenta can even *heal* a mother's heart. *Heal it*. You know what that means don't you?' She looks deeply into my eyes. 'They never leave us, Sofie. Our babies never leave us.' She squeezes my hand tightly and for a moment I can't breathe. Her eyes are distant now, but alight. She shakes her head as if trying to process this incredible fact.

I'm speechless. Suddenly, I feel something more than the visceral pain of what I've lost. There's a fluttering that settles somewhere deep inside me. An inner knowledge, now confirmed by science, that tells me he lives there, still. He always will. I'm not alone – and nor is Leo. Or Nisha.

I draw her to me, rest my forehead against hers.

'Thank you, Nisha.' I whisper. I take her hand then, ready to get up. 'Now, let's go and tell them you're here.'

Nisha wipes her eyes, goes to stand up, but sits down again quickly. She looks petrified as she gazes up at me. 'Do you really think I can do this?'

'I have no doubt whatsoever.'

'But what if it doesn't work? Or, what if it does and I can't cope on my own?'

'You won't be on your own, I promise.' I reach out for her hand again. She looks up, tentatively before taking mine, and we walk over to reception together, passing the handful of other hopefuls who are here dreaming of their own families. Intent on both surviving the worst whilst still hoping for the best.

Isn't that all we can ever do?

Chapter Sixty-Seven

It's 6pm. I'm in our lounge, working on my report. I've been here for most of the day, ever since I came back from the hospital.

Nisha has promised to keep me updated on her next steps towards fertility treatment. She's coming to meet me after work next week. It occurred to me that as a doctor, a strategist and a woman, she'd have some insightful ideas about life insurance. I also have another, more personal reason for wanting her to come. But I didn't tell her that.

Rory's not here. I don't know where he is. All I know is that apparently, he didn't go to work today, either, even though he left the house at the usual time this morning. I went to see him at his office in Poole after Nisha's appointment: I suddenly wanted to surprise him, spend time with him outside of our house, away from Leo and everything that is boxed up inside these walls. I thought we could have lunch together. But when I asked at reception, they said he wasn't in.

It's 6:25pm; he's still not home and I've switched on the news for the first time since Leo died because I've just remembered his pre-recorded report is on tonight.

He might not be here, but he's on my screen, smiling bravely into the camera like it's his first day back at school. I feel anxious for him, even though he's done this hundreds of times before.

'I'm here in Southbourne,' he says gravely, his eyes are dark and burnished, prominent shadows evident under his eyes, 'for the unveiling of a plaque in honour of an important and popular resident of my home suburb.' Pause for effect. 'Dave the Cat, known locally as DP or One Stop Cat.'

It's always a cat.

I sit back on the sofa as I watch my husband do the job he's so good at. He looks nervous, though. I notice his hand is gripping the microphone more tightly than usual.

'This furry, free spirit ginger tabby, who died back in 2020,' he continues, 'was a popular pillar of this community. In fact, he was nicknamed "One Stop" due to his regular appearances at the convenience store in Southbourne where he'd often nap on the counter, or he could be found waiting at the pelican crossing where he knew he could cross the road safely. But by far his favourite hang-out was the local community garden and it's for this reason that a plaque has been laid to honour him here.' The camera pans out then and he introduces the woman who raised the funds for it.

I can see he's glazing over as she talks about how much One Stop meant to the community. I sit forward on the sofa, suddenly on high alert. His eyes dart at the camera and then back to his interviewee. In the millisecond that he looks through the lens at me, I can see all of his sadness, loss and trauma, and I can't help but feel angry that his first TV report has been about death. What was his producer thinking?

'Well,' he says at the end of the interview, the tremor in his voice noticeable, 'on behalf of this community, thank you. For this wonderful tribute to a local friend taken too soon... One Stop.' He takes a deep breath and as if being directed, he says robotically: 'Now let's read what it says on the plaque.' He stares at it for a long time before he does so.

'In l-loving memory of our community cat, our DP, sadly gone but never forgotten. We will l-love you for*ev-er*.' His voice breaks slightly on the final words and my heart breaks for him. He takes a breath, almost imperceptibly pulls himself together. 'Th-that's a fitting tribute for a fine cat, I'm sure you'll agree. This is Rory King for Meridien Southwest.' He smiles down the lens, but I can see it cracks just slightly before the camera cuts back to the studio.

I switch off the TV and stare at the blank screen. I know Rory won't expect me to have seen it, because I haven't watched anything other than gameshows for weeks. Do I tell him?

I'm still sitting here ten minutes later when the front door opens, and guiltily, I get up and go out to the hallway where he's taking his shoes off.

'Hi,' I say quietly. He looks up at me; his face is puffy, hair flopped over his face to hide his eyes. 'Good day at work?' I ask.

'What?' He pauses momentarily from untying his shoelaces. His hands are shaking. 'Oh. Yep, it was good,' he says, his voice a monotone. 'How about you?'

'Good!' I reply brightly, mirroring his reply. It's a façade for us both. Rory's still trying to protect me; it's what he's done all along. It's only now that I realise he's cracking under the pressure of trying to hold it together.

He's clutching his phone which is flashing with notifications. He smiles at me brightly, but all I see reflected at me is sadness, shame and secrecy. I see a man so far removed from the one that I know and love, so far from his old happy-go-lucky self that for a moment I wonder how he – no, how *we* – have drifted so far.

'I-I've just been watching TV,' I say. 'I wondered if you wanted to talk … about it?'

'About what?' he says, walking into the kitchen. I follow him, watch as he gets a glass of water. See him lift his phone out of his pocket again so he can look at it as he drinks.

'About your report, Rory,' I say. 'The Southbourne cat one. I-I saw it.'

He puts down his glass. 'Oh,' he says, not looking at me. He washes up his glass methodically. 'I forgot it was on tonight.' He turns to get a tea towel and then dries the glass slowly. Anything to avoid having to look at me. He puts it back in the cupboard.

'It's always a cat, right?' He laughs, but it is hollow.

'Rory,' I say, then. 'You can talk to me.'

'There's nothing to talk about, Sofie. I'm fine.' He looks back at his phone again and starts tapping out a message, sharing his feelings with a stranger instead of me. And it's then that I snap.

'For God's sake, Rory! You're not fine, we're not fine. Nothing's fine and the sooner we both admit it, the better!'

'I don't know what you mean.' Rory looks at me vacantly as I pull my trainers on and grab my keys, one eye still on his phone.

'Where are you going?' he says dully.

'I'm going for a walk…' I say. 'I can't do this anymore. Not until you start talking to me honestly about how you feel.'

And then, I put my rucksack on my shoulder and walk out.

Chapter Sixty-Eight

Before I know it, I've walked for over an hour all the way to Stour Valley Nature Reserve, a two-mile riverside walk flanked by meadows and hedgerows and woodland. Being mid-May, it's still light. Rory keeps calling my phone, but I can't talk to him yet. My old life might be crumbling around me, but out here it feels like something could be growing in its place. My strength, perhaps? Or my resolve that my marriage, my career, the *rules* I used to live so strictly by are no longer working.

In the forest, I can feel the vibrations of the earth beneath my feet. Dappled sunshine moves through the canopy of trees.

I keep walking, feeling the crunch of the sundried, gritty earth and stone pathways, the breeze caressing my tear-stained cheeks, sweat slipping down the back of my T-shirt.

In the forest, I see crops of creamy-coloured fungi huddled together, like groups of tourists in oversized sunhats. I bend down to examine them, testing myself in my identifications by looking carefully for all the dangerous markers that Dad painstakingly taught me all those years ago.

I stop for a moment to look through the branches of the tree, following the proud line of the grand old oak tree's trunk. I feel a sudden urge to feel the bark beneath my fingers, dig into the mossy enclaves and brand my hands with its dark green tint. I lean against the trunk and rest my cheek and ear, then my chest against it. I put my arms around it and close my eyes. Part of me wonders if I will hear it whisper, like in the Enid Blyton books of my childhood.

Wisha wisha wisha.

I know what I would wish for.

I feel the evening sunshine on my face. I stay there for as long as I can, leaning against the tree. Feeling its power, its strength and continual growth, and hoping it will transfer to me. It occurs to me that this tree is Mother Nature. It *is* motherhood.

With my body being held up by it, I'm suddenly acutely aware of being part of something so much bigger. The perpetual circle of life that humans have evolved through since the beginning of time. We're not the first and we will not be the last. There'll always be joy and sadness; hope and despair; war and peace; life and death.

Even though grief constantly tells us that we're alone, life proves otherwise every single day. And nature symbolises all that lives around us. Beyond us. In spite of us. Out here, all human life feels small, a fleeting blessing. If my life adds up to a brief millisecond in Earth's lifespan, then Leo's, who is a part of me, does too.

I close my eyes. Here, in this moment, it feels like his life goes on endlessly. He's this tree that I'm holding. The air. The ground beneath my feet. I close my eyes. Hold *him* close.

Eventually, I begin to walk back along the river. Lost in thought, but also lost in the beauty of this place and this moment. The early evening sunshine is at its most golden now, creating a protective halo of light and warmth around me. The river is perfectly still; there's not a ripple upon it, even from the branches of the weeping willows that caress its surface. I stop for a moment to observe a marbled white butterfly sitting perfectly still on a fuchsia thistle. Just ahead of me, a heron basks in the evening sunshine on the waters' edge. Suddenly it dips its head and emerges victoriously with a fish in its beak and immediately swallows it in one deft gulp. I look to my left and watch for a few minutes in awe as in my peripheral vision, two dragonflies seduce each other as they dance together over the reeds. It occurs to me that nature showcases both birth and death in all its glorious beauty and unexpected tragedy every single day. And yet humans fool ourselves into thinking we can prolong it, escape it, even. But only this middle bit – the living – or rather, our attitude towards it – is in our control.

Just then the butterfly begins beating its wings and I watch it rise effortlessly and majestically in the air. I walk again with more urgency now, suddenly desperate to get home and talk to Rory.

But I'm stopped in my tracks by a blur of red, yellow and gold on a branch above the river. A goldfinch has come to rest on an overhanging branch; it stands motionless for a moment watching me watching him. It's a male, judging by the large, bright burst of red colour on his face and curved beak. When he looks directly at me it feels like time has ground to a halt. A moment later, he launches himself off the branch and I watch him flit over the water towards the fields like a dazzling firework. And then I gasp, because as he does so, a colourful explosion of wings appear alongside him and before I can blink, he's lost amongst the charm fluttering like colourful confetti in the sky.

I feel at once enriched and bereft; lost and found; grief-stricken and grateful – no, *charmed*. And I want to share that feeling with Rory.

Chapter Sixty-Nine

There's no sign of Rory when I get back. He must have gone out for a bike ride, even though I texted him that I was coming home and said that we need to talk; work out how to do this together, this living without our son. I want to give our relationship all the love and effort it deserves. Just as we would have given it all to Leo, if we'd had the chance.

I head upstairs. The nursery door is ajar when I get to the landing. I can just see the side of Leo's urn on the mantlepiece. But for the first time in weeks, I walk past rather than go in. It's my husband I want to be close to right now. And that means seeing the place that he's been hiding away. I continue upstairs to Rory's office. Tentatively, I open the door.

It's dark when I enter. The black-out blinds are pulled down over the Velux windows and the lights are all off. Rory is in here. A blue glow emanates around him, and I stare in shock at the huge, triple monitor that he is sitting in front of. An Xbox sits to one side, large speakers surround the central, enormous split monitor. I knew he'd bought some new gaming stuff, but this is an entire professional set-up that must have cost thousands of pounds. This isn't just a hobby; it's an obsession.

Rory hasn't heard me come in. He's hunched forward in front of the triad of screens, with a headset on. I walk slowly towards him. His back is to me and his hoodie is pulled low over his head. He looks like a teenager. Next to him are two empty bottles of beer, more are scattered around his desk.

'Rory?' I say, then again, louder this time. 'Rory!' He turns, jumps almost in alarm. 'W-What's going on?' He stares blankly at me but doesn't reply. He looks haunted, *hunted*.

'Sofie,' he says. He takes his headphones off, his microphone hanging flaccidly around his neck. 'You're back.'

'What *is* all this?'

'I told you … I bought some new kit,' he mumbles.

'But I thought…' I trail off. I stare at the giant screens, now frozen mid-play and realise what game this really is.

He gazes at the elaborate set-up as if seeing it all for the first time. He looks embarrassed, ashamed.

'I just needed something I could … lose myself in. Does that make sense?'

I nod. The truth is I don't need him to explain. Up here, locked away from view, is a world in which he can fix problems; be a hero. I step towards him, look at the screen. I feel like I need to handle him carefully. 'What are you playing?' It's like I'm talking to a child. The truth is, he's scaring me.

'Right now? *Legend of Zelda: Call of the Wild.*'

'What do you have to do?'

'It's known as an open-world game,' he says, words spilling out of him. 'I play Link who has woken up from a century long sleep and has to try and regain memories whilst stopping the Calamity Ganon from destroying Hyrule.'

'And how do you do that?' I'm struggling not to cry.

'By exploring the world, collecting items, or solving puzzles and side quests. I can paraglide one minute and be swimming or rock climbing the next!'

In the wild, I think. Doing things he used to love.

'I can even cook meals and hunt,' he continues animatedly.

I swim, cook and forage.

We *have* been in the same place, just not together.

'I can make lifesaving elixirs too…' he continues. But he trails off, as if he's just realised the correlation.

I put my hand on his shoulder, then. 'You can win or lose, without winning or losing anything. Or anyone.' This is a world he can completely control.

Without turning round, he bows his head.

He turns on his desk lamp then and the room is completely illuminated. I've been so focused on his elaborate, immersive gaming set-up that I hadn't noticed the rest of it. Now, I can see that is filled with *stuff*. Everything we bought for Leo; everything I thought Rory had sold or put in the garage or got rid of, has been brought up here. In the far corner, I spy the pram, the car seat, a rocker, Leo's highchair, the ocean themed playmat, the baby bath. But in addition to those practical baby items, there's also piles of children's toys, even a trike and balance bike I've never seen.

This is where my husband has been hiding his grief. This is his mess and chaos, all hidden away up here, out of sight. Locked in a box.

This room is Rory's shrine to Leo, just like his nursery has been for me. Like many family lofts, it has become a childhood cemetery of nostalgia for Rory. The difference is, it's for our baby who never came home.

But I can't help but wonder, has Rory bought all this extra stuff to capture the milestones of the child that Leo would have been? Or are they for the child Rory still hopes to have in the future?

'Rory?' I say, finally. 'Why didn't you tell me about all this?'

He looks at me then for the first time in weeks, and suddenly I understand it's his shame that's been stopping him doing so. His pupils dilate with guilt as he begins to sob; silvery tears streak his cheeks. I haven't seen him cry since the day of Leo's service at the crematorium.

'I didn't want you to know. I-I didn't want to upset you. I needed something...' he croaks. 'Somewhere I could remember him, somewhere other than a hospital or cemetery or an urn of ashes. I needed somewhere I could let it out and I didn't want to do that in front of you, so I came up here instead. And then, once I was in here, I found I couldn't leave. I didn't want to leave my boy. I've spent entire nights up here, most nights actually. Gaming helped me forget for a while. Block everything out. But then I felt so guilty that I was trying to forget him, I'd go online and look for things that I think he would have liked. I've been online all night, sometimes. When I haven't been able to sleep, I've come up here. Sometimes instead of going to work, too when I just couldn't face going in.' He sobs, then.

'It's okay, Rory....' He looks up at me pleadingly. 'It's okay,' I say again.

I thread my arms around his neck and draw him close to me. He pulls me onto his lap and buries his head in my chest. I stroke his head gently and we sit there, in front of the computer screen, amongst the toys and pram and baby clothes in this loft that I also realise is a homage to teenage Rory: it's an upgraded replica of the place he grieved for his mum in, after she left.

'It has helped though, you know?' he says once he's gathered himself. 'Being surrounded by all this.' He sniffs and wipes his nose. I can see hope forming in his eyes again, even as the dread settles in my stomach. 'Next time we'll be ready, Sof! We have everything we could possibly need. We'll have much more support from the hospital, too. We can have scans all the time. Look!' he leans down and picks up a box with a bit of tech in it. 'I bought a home doppler! There's so much stuff you can get now, plus tests you can take early on in pregnancy—' The words pour out of him desperately.

'Rory—' I interrupt, then stop. I want to tell him that dopplers should only be used by trained midwives and health professionals, not at home, and this kind of technology is sold with a promise that people can be protected from the worst. But false hope isn't helpful. It's dangerous. And now is not the time.

He looks manic. His eyes are jaundiced with sadness and exhaustion, glazed by hours looking at a screen. He doesn't in any way resemble the man I married.

'I know you thought I just wanted to move on, that I wasn't grieving Leo, too,' he continues. 'But I was, just not in front of you. And I know it will be different, next time. We'll bring our next baby home, I promise.'

I shake my head and get up, step away from him, unable to take anymore. I'm crying as I try to explain, to articulate how I feel.

'Rory, stop. Please. I know how much it means to you to have another baby.' I look around the room again and gasp as it hits me that I have to tell him what I've been so scared to say. 'And if that's really what you want…' He looks up at me hopefully, desperately. I take a deep breath. I need to get these next words out, even though I want to fight against them with everything I have. Looking around me now, I realise it's the only way forward. 'If that's what you really want,' I repeat, 'then you need to find someone else to have a baby with, because that person can't be me.'

Hearing the words that have been in my head for so long makes me want to run to the bathroom and vomit.

'S- Sofie, you don't mean it.' It is a statement, not a question. He is still telling me what I think, how I should feel. He looks at me blankly, eyes opaque with pain. He gets up and stumbles towards me, arms outstretched. He pulls me into an embrace, and I stand there, limply, being held.

I stare at his neck and the little mole that resides there that I have caressed so many times, the skin I've kissed, the strong arms that have carried me through so much and that I thought would always hold me. Now I feel like they're squeezing the life from me, because of Rory's obsession with having another baby.

'You don't mean this,' he repeats.

I pull back so I can look him in the eyes. 'Leo died, Rory.'

'I know, Sofie.' His voice is shaking with the effort of keeping it together. 'And I know Leo dying was the worst thing that could ever happen. But the doctors themselves said it was an anomaly that the cord got wrapped around his neck. We were unlucky and the likelihood is that next time—'

'Please don't say the likelihood is it won't happen again!' I interject despairingly. It occurs to me then that Rory's obsession with considering himself 'lucky' has protected him from a lifetime of grief. It's easier to cope with than the truth. He was dealt a bad hand when his dad walked out, followed by his mum. His gran – whilst wonderfully loving and supportive – could never replace them. He became a lost, lonely kid who turned to an online world for comfort. The truth is, he isn't luckier than most – because both life and luck are entirely random. Everyone is thrown both good and bad.

'We have to have hope, Sof. What else is there?'

I stare at my desperately deluded husband with strengthened

resolve. 'Rory, you've got to stop reframing denial as hope. I know it's your coping mechanism, but it means you don't deal with reality. You haven't for years, ever since your mum left.'

'Hope isn't denial!' he exclaims. 'It's a decision. It's choosing to find possibility even in the darkest times. I choose hope, because life doesn't feel bearable without it. I don't want to give up on having children. And,' he adds, 'I don't want to give up on us, either.'

I reach out and touch his cheek, and it feels as though I could be doing so for the last time. I rest my forehead against his, then. 'But, don't you see, Rory,' I whisper hoarsely as tears flow unstoppably down my face, 'you're still fighting for the baby first, not me.'

A silence falls between us. Nothing I say now can change his mind: he'll only ever believe in luck; he'll always hinge his life on hope and want to play the same hand again and again. Always hoping for a different result.

'I've changed, Rory,' I say eventually. 'I want life to be different because we *had* Leo, not because he died. I can't be who I was before we lost him … and I don't want to be.'

I sob, and snot seeps out of my nose. I wipe it carelessly with the back of my hand. It feels like in losing Leo I also lost the plug that used to contain everything about me so neatly. Before him, I hid messy emotions away behind order, neatness, togetherness. This body that has shed blood, mucus, tears and grief for months is unable to hide anything anymore. It's all coming out. I'm wild. Free.

'I love you, Sofie.' Rory puts his hand to my face and our lips meet with our tears in one messy, beautiful, desperate kiss.

'I know,' I reply. I feel like I'm being held by my husband for the first time in months, rather than just held up by him, but it's not enough. It's like we've come together again, but only to come apart.

'Sofie…' His puppy-dog eyes are pleading, his brow concertinaed in despair. He doesn't finish his sentence. I glance at his monitors, at the game still frozen mid-play. We've both learned that so much of life, in the end, isn't about choice. We are not in control. We can't be. Not when there are other players and an entire world of elements to navigate our way through, too.

He drops his forehead, so it rests against mine.

'I need some time, some space. We both do, I think. I'm going to pack a bag and go home for a while. To Mum … and Midge. I'll let you know when I get there, okay?'

And then, with one lingering kiss on Rory's lips I head towards the door, stepping over all the boxes of baby stuff, like they're little landmines.

Part IV

1. A 'unit' is that by virtue of which each of the things that exist is called one.
2. A 'number' is a multiple composed of units.

Euclid – *Euclid's Elements*

Chapter Seventy

'Sofie!' Mum looks down at my suitcase. 'Is everything okay?' She glances behind me into the night expecting to see Rory exiting the car. I'm trying desperately not to cry. I'm worried that if I do, I won't stop.

She places her hand on my face and gazes at me. 'I take it this isn't a brief visit?'

'Honestly Mum? I don't know...' Then I break down because I've no idea what happens next. I've emailed Ed and Zoe and told them I won't be back in until Monday. I just need some time away, to work out what I'm doing.

'Oh, my love,' she embraces me. She takes my suitcase and leads me gently inside. I stand for a moment, looking around. Feeling utterly lost.

'Pop your case in the spare room and I'll put the kettle on.' She scurries off to the kitchen, but not without giving me a last, fretful look of concern.

As I walk through Mum and Midge's sweet, comfortable house, I realise it's devoid of memories, or at least, my memories. But when I walk into the spare room, my past hits me, as it always does. My old wildflower bedspread from when I was a teen covers the single bed. Even though I haven't ever lived here, there are photos of me everywhere. On the vanity unit, on the walls. There's me as a baby, with

Mum, with Dad. There I am as knock-kneed toddler in a pair of grubby shorts and a once-white T-shirt, grinning wildly in the middle of a field with a bunch of primroses in one hand and a basket of fruit in the other. Dad's crouched next to me, arm around my shoulder and gazing solemnly into the distance.

There's one of Mum and Dad on their wedding day in Denmark, too. Mum's barefoot, wearing a bohemian balloon-sleeved, empire waist dress covered in tiny lace flowers and a beatific smile. Dad stands proudly next to her, beaming beneath his thick beard, wearing a wide-collared linen shirt open almost to his waist and tucked into shorts. Mum's leaning into him, head almost in the nook of his armpit. He holds her possessively around her waist, his hand so big that it seems to encompass her entire stomach. They look so young. So happy.

Further down, there's a photo of me aged around six, in full fishing regalia. I'm on a boat with Dad. We're holding a gigantic trout between us and smiling into the lens. In another, we're in the garden at our makeshift outdoor kitchen, making elderflower cordial. A joyous photo of the three of us outside Per's Place on the day it opened is next to the last family photo we ever took. A timer shot, taken on a tripod, the three of us with me in the middle proudly holding my GCSE results up. Dad's holding a beer aloft, grinning like he's the one who aced them, not me.

Eight months later, Dad moved out. By the following summer, he was dead.

I unpack the memories at the same time as my suitcase. I take out Leo's memory box and his little urn that was resting on top of my hastily thrown in clothes, and pull it into my chest. For a moment, as I look across the undulating Purbeck fields beyond the garden, I realise *this* is my mum's version of both Leo's nursery and Rory's loft. Here is where she keeps the special pieces of a lost childhood. To mourn *and* cherish.

Gazing out of the window, past the stone garden wall and the fields beyond, I take in the purple haze of the sunset and the glorious sense of being in the right place. The heavy solidity of the urn in my arms makes me aware, with visceral certainty, that I didn't scatter Leo's ashes in our garden like Rory wanted me to, because deep down I knew that the house Rory and I live in wasn't going to be ours forever.

I think of Rory there, alone, and suddenly, it feels like all my breath has been squeezed out of my body. I miss him so much already. But I also know I've done the right thing. I rang Sandra as I left, asked her to go and be with him. I know she will look after Rory, as she always has done.

I walk over to the boxes in the corner of the light-filled room to distract myself. Dust motes dance and twirl before my eyes as I bend down and look at the writing on top of them. *Per's stuff*. *Sofie's schoolbooks*. Others are labelled *Old toys* and *Baby clothes*.

One box is open. I sit back on my haunches and rifle through it, pulling a handful of paperwork out. Dad's death certificate is lying loosely on the top.

I put the certificate to one side next to me, not really wanting to look at it, and go through the other paperwork, smiling through tears as I find a stack of homemade cards I sent to dad as a child: birthday, Christmas and Father's Day ones covered with ever-improving childish scrawls and paintings; some with pressed wildflowers – delicate ink nature drawings of birds when I was older. One that I pull out is quite impressive, given my limited art skills. It's a watercolour of a male goldfinch with its young. I must have been about eleven when I drew it. Inside I'd written, 'Dad, you're my lucky charm'. I think of the goldfinch I saw earlier at Stour Valley Pasture, pull the card close to my chest and weep.

Chapter Seventy-One

'There's a cup of tea here, whenever you're ready,' Mum calls.
'Okay,' I call back shakily. Wiping my eyes, I put on an old hoodie for both warmth and comfort then walk into the small, cosy farmhouse-style kitchen. Mum is at the square pine table, Midge next to her. It's past 11pm and they're both in their pajamas.

'Hi, Midge,' I say kissing her affectionately on the cheek. 'Sorry to burst in like this. I'd have called ahead, but I—'

'Sofie, please', she interrupts softly, eyes creasing into half-moon crescents. 'You're welcome here anytime.'

'I wish it was in happier circumstances.' I smile weakly.

'What's happened, love?' Mum asks, her face wracked with worry. She pushes a mug of tea in front of me and I stare into it and take a deep breath.

'Rory and I are having some time apart. We need some space to work stuff out.'

I cling on to my mug like it's a support rope, feeling the heat burn against my skin.

I see Midge touch Mum's hand lightly; they glance at each other. There is, I realise, a constant conversation of love and support between them.

'I'll leave you two to it,' Midge says and stands up. Again, once upon a time I'd have welcomed her departure, but this time I reach out for her hand. 'Please stay, Midge,' I say. 'You're my family, too.' Midge's face caves a little with emotion, but she centres herself quickly. She sits back down at her place at the table, in between Mum and me. It is, I realise, exactly where she's meant to be. A place where she can give support to us both.

Chapter Seventy-Two

It's just gone 4am, but I can't sleep. I've been lying awake thinking about how little we know about other people's lives – past and present. Mum, Midge and I spent hours talking about everything, my relationship, theirs, Dad. Our lives. His death. A death that has never quite added up.

Even though it's barely dawn, the birds have begun their alarm call, their collective voices sounding like any family around a breakfast table: chattering, musing, deliberating, demanding, arguing, celebrating a new day with each other.

Leo's urn is on the windowsill. I like to think of him looking out over the fields of my home. That's what this place is I realise: home. Not this cottage – this will always be Mum and Midge's – but this landscape. This isle. A place that I tried to sail from but that's always been trying to pull me back. Now I'm here, I'm not about to leave in a hurry.

I pull on a dressing gown. Even at this hour, there's a warmth in the air that tells of sun-filled days to come. I pad across the room to the pile of boxes in the corner I started looking through last night. All things Mum just hasn't been able to bring herself to get rid of.

After last night's chat, I need to find what I've always feared. Solve the equation.

It doesn't take long. It's there, near the bottom of the first box, a

This Wasn't Meant to Happen

folded-up piece of lined A4 paper slipped into an old wildflower book on the page about Myostosis scorpioides, otherwise known as True Forget-Me-Not.

Crumpled and slightly yellowed with age, softened from what feels like many times of being opened and folded back again, I unfold it myself for the first time and begin to read. As I do, I feel the ground beneath me tip. But I find the strength to steady myself. Carry on.

I'm still clutching the piece of paper in my hand when I walk into the kitchen. It's barely 5am; Mum's sat at the table as if she's been there all night, waiting for me. There's a cup of tea in front of her. Another one is opposite her, steam rising like a ghostly spirit. It feels like she's been waiting for this moment. This conversation. Her face is pale, drawn, bloated and blotchy with tears. Her eyes dart from my face to the piece of paper and back to my face again. Shakily, she puts her mug down. She looks like she hasn't slept a wink either.

I walk over to the chair opposite hers and I place Dad's suicide note in between us. I stare at it and my tears blur his words as I read them over again. I've always wanted to believe that the man I knew would never have taken his own life. And yet, I've also never really believed that he'd fallen. I look down at the words that will now be imprinted in my memory forever.

To my girls,

It is my will, not my wish.
It is an ill, not an itch.
I have tried, I have failed.
I've loved and now, I have bailed.
I leave you, for more.
You both, I adore.
My love will continue.
Your love, my window.
I'll be there looking through.
Forever, looking after you.
This isle, the hills and the sea

Hold my love for you eternally.

Per x

I reach over for Mum's hands, and we sit there, together staring at the note between us. Her blue eyes have darkened to midnight.

'Why didn't you tell me, Mum?'

She looks out of the window to the misty covered hills beyond.

'I wanted to protect you – and him, too.'

'I always suspected, you know,' I say quietly. He knew those paths so well he'd never have fallen. And there was no real outcome from the police enquiry. Nothing added up. 'People talked, too…' I continue. 'They said he was depressed, in trouble financially. Drinking, gambling … people often saw him going into the bookies in Poole.'

'It's not easy to keep secrets around here,' she murmurs. 'I didn't want you to think badly of your father or for him to be defined by how his life ended, when how he lived – for the most part – was so beautiful. He saw the world differently from most people; felt everything more fiercely, from the earth's vibrations to the ones in his heart. He was complex, Sofie, but the most important thing about him was that he loved you – and he loved us – right to the very end.'

'I feel like I didn't know him at all.' I exhale, trying to hold back the tears now that the suspicion I've held for years is now fact. My strong, stoic dad committed suicide. I didn't want to believe it of him. I think it's why I've never properly asked.

'Of *course* you did,' Mum says emphatically. 'You know he was loving, fun, deep-thinking and enormously passionate about nature. You also know that he was a natural loner and prone to deep bouts of depression. He'd disappear for days on fishing trips, leaving me to deal with everything – especially after we opened the café. You know that he sought solitude; was an extroverted introvert that loved nature more than people – including us, sometimes. Do you remember as you grew up, begging him to take you foraging with him? The hours you spent waiting at the window for him to come home?'

I stare down at the note on the table, these memories twisting and reforming to create a more honest picture of Dad than the childlike one I've painted since his death. I remember spending hours in the garden waiting for him to return from one of his lone trips. How, when I'd ask if I could go with him, he'd often tell me that he was going to more difficult places than I could get to.

It seems, in the end, that was closer to the truth than I'd realised.

I'd sit and watch from the swing seat as he walked to the bottom of the garden, opened the gate and walked across the fields and into the distance until he was just a dandelion helicopter seed on the horizon. I'd try and wait for him, but he'd be gone for hours and inevitably Mum would call me in for tea, or I'd find myself being woken up by her and carried to bed, having fallen asleep right there on the swing seat.

Then I think of how much he changed once the café was open. How much pressure he seemed to be under and how eventually, he detached from it – and us.

As ever, Mum reads my mind.

'The café was his dream, but he couldn't cope with it. The pressure of running a business completely overwhelmed him. He did his best to manage; he even hid how hard he was finding it from me. He started drinking, much more than he'd ever drunk before. I knew all those evening "walks" he went on were to various pubs. And yes, when we were in financial difficulties, out of desperation he gambled our savings to try and save the business. Then we had to remortgage the house. I'd no idea how deeply in debt we were until after his death and I had to deal with the creditors. Finance was his real downfall in the end, Sofie, not our marriage, and not you. In fact, you were the reason he kept going for so long. We'd waited such a long time for you after all...' She stops, her words hanging in the air over my head like a baby's mobile. 'He saw you and the café as his legacy.'

'Is that why you worked so hard to save it?' I ask. She nods.

'Not out of guilt?'

Mum tilts her head, shakes it. 'I only grew closer to Midge after your Dad had died. She became a friend from the moment she moved in to the flat and then the house, but that was all. And I was too wrapped up in my grief for Per to even think about another relationship for months after. Not least because I'd never been in one with a woman before. Falling in love with her surprised me as much as it surprised you.'

I nod tearfully. I didn't know it was so important to me that she loved dad until the end. And, I realise now, her enduring act of love has been to dedicate the rest of her life to the memory of a man's dream. A man she loved but couldn't save.

'You've done a good job with the café,' I say, my voice choked with emotion. 'Dad would be proud. And I also think he would be so happy that you're happy.'

'Do you think so?' Mum's face folds in on itself, then and I see the strain of the last eighteen years in the fault lines of guilt and worry indented deeply into her skin. I realise she's carried her suitcase of grief alone for years. 'I always feel like I'm just grasping on with my fingertips, and maybe I should just let go. But it's all of him I have left…'

I get up and we hug. She pulls away first and looks at me, wiping my eyes gently with her fingers and brushing back loose tendrils of hair from my face. She might feel small to me now but I also realise how strong she is. How strong she's always been, not just for me, but for Dad, too.

'I understand why you told him to leave, Mum. I know how hard you tried. For years, I thought you'd pushed him away, but I realise you were always trying to save him.'

'My biggest regret is not confronting him about his depression or his drinking, I realise I was enabling him by not doing so. I thought I could shock him into changing his life by telling him to leave. I wanted him to see what he stood to lose if he carried on like he was. I never thought—' She stops and presses her hand to her lips again, unable to finish that sentence.

'It wasn't your job to save him, Mum,' I say, taking her hand. 'He had to want it for himself.'

I sob as I think of how Rory has worked so hard to keep me happy over the years: enabling my fears, fuelling my coping mechanisms while asserting his own. In the end, it hasn't helped either of us.

'You do know you're very different from your dad, don't you, Sofie?'

'How can you be so sure?' I ask tearfully.

'Because when you were barely an adult yourself you got through the worst that life had to throw at you and found better, braver answers than he did. You found it in friendship with Nisha, in your studies, your work and then, in love. Your dad would have approved of Rory, you know. And he'd be so proud of you. *You* were his real dream, Sofie.' She pauses as this notion settles around me in a beautiful haze.

He would be proud of me.

'You're much stronger than me, too,' she says then. 'You have chosen to confront your grief for Leo; not pretend it didn't happen, like I did. And like Rory has.'

I look up.

I stroke her hand, urging her on. I want her to find her voice. Her truth.

It seems like a lifetime before she speaks again.

'I lost babies, too, Sofie. Before I had you. Many times.'

Beyond us, below us, I hear the waves crash against the cliff face, over and over again.

Chapter Seventy-Three

Mum and I stand together staring out to sea. It's barely 6am and there's not a soul to be seen. We got straight into the car after her revelation. I knew she'd need air, space and the freedom to talk side by side. Mother to mother. I drove us to South Beach and then we walked the Southwest Coast Path to where Old Harry Rocks proudly stands. This feels like a conversation Dad should be here for.

It's a place where the sea meets the land, the past meets the present and gives a clear view of the future, words can be carried on the wind and tensions tossed into the tide. The rocks may be eroding, beaten by wind and waves, but still they stand.

We hold hands, looking out at the expanse of ocean. The unexpectedly warm morning swishes her skirts around us, summer-scented breath tickling our faces as if encouraging us to talk.

'Tell me, Mum,' I say gently.

She stares into the distance, as if looking for something she's never been able to find. She doesn't move, she barely blinks as she stands next to me like a statue. No, like a rock.

My rock.

I lead her over to a bench and we sit down, arms brushing against each other, close in a way that we haven't been for a long time.

'It's okay to tell me, Mum. I don't need you to protect me anymore. I want to know about your babies, the ones that came before or after me and shaped the person you are. The mother you are to me.'

Then, as she looks out to the still ocean, she tells me about the pregnancies she lost at twelve weeks – just after their wedding day – thirteen weeks, nine weeks, and then finally, twins at eighteen weeks. All before me. She never had the chance to hold them. No photo, footprint, no memento of them. No proof that they were ever here; that they existed.

I think of the wedding photo of Mum and Dad that used to hang on the stairs in our house, which hangs in the cottage's spare room now. It has never occurred to me to look at it and see anything more other than a happy couple on their wedding day. Now, the billowing vintage 1970s dress – decades out of date when they married in the '90s - and the pregnancy-friendly empire-line – makes sense. And Dad's hand stretched across her waist and what I realise now was her slightly rounded tummy. It all makes sense.

'You weren't given any help? Offered counselling?'

Mum shakes her head. 'Miscarriages and late pregnancy loss just weren't talked about in the way they are now, Sofie. The whole experience was intensely private. We didn't talk about giving birth, having sex, or postnatal depression back then, either. You just were pregnant and had a baby and got on with it, or you didn't, or couldn't, or you tried and failed. It didn't occur to me to talk about my struggles with anyone other than Per and the medical staff we were dealing with. Even before I met Per, I'd never been close to my own parents. They were old-fashioned. They wanted me to marry a local boy, have lots of children and that would be my life. They were horrified when I met Per and told them I was moving to Denmark with him. They made it clear that my chosen path was not one they wanted to be part of. After we got married, I knew I could never tell them that I'd also been pregnant and lost the baby. They would never have spoken to me again.'

'It must have been so hard for you, Mum.' I can't imagine going through what I have with no family support.

I'm lucky.

The words whisper through my mind, like a gentle breeze.

I think of her at Leo's bedside, how hard she found it to hold him and how when she did it felt to me like he was hers, somehow, too.

Now the enormity of that moment as experienced by her hits me. I think of how holding Leo must have taken her back to the loss of her own babies. But she put aside her pain to try and support me.

'What were their names?'

She blinks, processing the question I can tell she's never been asked. Her eyes cloud, then clear. 'I didn't name them … not officially. But I've always thought of the twins as Eilish and Elijah.'

I think of the babies I met in the town hall when I was registering Leo's death – one was also called Elijah. At least I know my Leo has an Elijah to play with now.

When Leo died, I felt like I was standing on a fault line alone; yet my mum was always there too. Along the way, I've also learned Nisha was too, and Zoe from work, and Jen, who I met in the café. And that's just a handful of the thousands upon thousands of women – the millions, billions – who have been through the trauma of baby loss, at different times, in different ways and circumstances, since the beginning of humanity.

I'm not alone.

I hear the distant cries of the peregrine falcons that often circle these rocks.

'I wish I'd told you all this sooner, Sofie,' Mum says quietly. 'I was just so afraid of causing you stress during your own pregnancy.'

'I can't imagine what it must be like,' I say at last. 'To not have anything to remember your babies by. To not have been able to talk about them to anyone…'

I think of how desperate I've been to talk about Leo. And how strange and isolating grief is, that you can be surrounded by so much love and support and yet still conclude that you're alone. I grasp her hands.

'I know I don't say this enough, Mum, but I'm so lucky to have you. And to have had Leo – if only briefly. I'm so glad I got to hold him. And thankful that you did, too. I know now how hard that must have been for you.'

She looks at me with such love and such sorrow then that it feels like she's not just looking me, but all her babies.

'Sofie, I need you to know that having you has been the greatest gift of my life.'

I put my head on her shoulder, and we sit like that for a while, just holding on to each other as the waves crash below us and the sun continues to ride up in the sky, sending bright streamers of colour dancing through the air.

It's a while before I speak again.

'Do you still think about your babies?'

'Of course.' There's a brief pause and then she turns to look at me, touches my face. 'But not as much as I think of you. From the moment I held you in my arms, I chose to focus on you and the future instead. You ended my journey with joy and hope, until…'

'Until Leo?' I say lifting my head from her shoulder. 'Is that why you didn't have more children after me?' I'm determined for this to be about her, not me. She's waited so long to have her story heard.

She nods and turns to face the sea again. 'You were our miracle and we wanted to focus on that. We were so happy, so grateful and excited for our life together. And it really was idyllic. It was why we called ourselves The Tremendous Three … do you remember?'

I nod, feeling choked. That family nickname was a nod to my Enid Blyton childhood on Purbeck, where she set her Famous Five books. It'll always have a deeper meaning now, knowing what they went through to have me.

'Per always said *you* were the missing piece that completed our picture. We chose not to tell you about the older brothers and sisters that might have been because … well, why tell you about a gift you could never have?'

'Didn't I ever ask, though?' I interject. 'About having siblings?'

Mum nods. 'A couple of times, when you were about four or five. But you seemed content when Per told you that we'd used all our love and luck having you and that you were more than enough. You never asked again. You were a solitary child, anyway, unsurprising given you were so much like your dad.' She smiles nostalgically. 'You just didn't seem to want siblings in the way that other kids did. It wasn't until you met Nisha that you found a real kinship – and then she became as much of a sister as a friend, anyway. I told myself that I'd tell you one day, when you were old enough but then…' she trails off.

'Dad died,' I finish the sentence for her. We begin to walk slowly along Ballard Down, arms linked.

'His death impacted you so hugely,' she says. 'Your entire view of the world changed; you became cautious and afraid, wary of life and of love. And then when you met Rory, I watched your essence come back. You glowed again from the inside out. It was so beautiful to see. Once you were married, I wondered if I should talk to you about my pregnancies, but you were so sure you didn't want to have children, I didn't think I'd ever have to.'

'Your reaction makes sense now.' I think of how shocked Mum was, how she could barely speak.

'You don't experience loss and grief like that without carrying the trauma of it forever. I was so scared for you when I found out you were pregnant as it brought back my own experiences. And when Leo died, I felt I was to blame. Maybe if I had told you....'

'Mum, don't.'

She looks at me, her eyes full of anguish. 'I've blamed myself every day since then, wondering if you'd known my history, if the doctors had known, then perhaps...' She puts her hand up to her mouth and I immediately wrap my arms around her.

'Mum, stop. It wouldn't have made any difference,' I tell her firmly. 'It was a complication with the cord, you know that. I carried him to full term. My experience was different from yours; it wasn't your fault.' I pause. 'It wasn't *anyone's* fault.'

I realise as the words leave my lips, that I'm not just saying these words to her, but to me, too. I pull away and look her directly in the eyes. I can see myself reflected back in them then, not just as her daughter, but as a mother, too.

'You *did* protect me, Mum. You gave me nine months of happy memories. If I had known about the babies before me, I don't think I'd ever have been able to relax or enjoy my pregnancy at all. And I did, Mum, I did. I had so much hope...'

We arrive in front of a stone bench engraved with the words 'Rest and be thankful'.

We sit and take in the wildly beautiful panorama. In that moment, I feel the weight of history all around us. This coast reminds me that life and death, the sea, this very landscape – even Old Harry

Rocks – were once part of something much bigger until they were separated by forces beyond their control.

I look down at Mum's arm, which I'm holding. I think of the life-long impression our babies have made on us. The babies who are here and yet are not. Who are born but don't stay; whose footprints didn't get to grace the earth, but nevertheless walk alongside us forever.

I cling to what I know, which is how longed for, how *loved* Leo was; how much he has changed my life; how I'll never be without him, even though I have to live the rest of my life that way. And that is thanks to Mum. And Rory, of course.

Rory.

I begin to cry. Mum draws me close to her again with one hand and I put my head on her shoulder.

'Do you think you and Rory could try again?' Mum asks.

'I don't think I have the strength. I'm too scared of what I stand to lose.'

'Scared and scarred,' she says, kissing my head. 'I understand, Sofie, believe me I do. The courage it took for me to get to a place where I was ready to try again after each miscarriage felt immense. Too big, at times if I'm honest. It was your dad who had to convince me…'

I turn, head tilted, ready to listen to this new piece of information about Dad. Seagulls circle overheard as if waiting for new scraps, too.

'He was always quick to rationalise our babies' deaths in a way that I never could, but I think that was only external, his way of appearing like he'd dealt with it. I think it had a bigger impact on his mental health because he didn't talk about it. He'd just say, "Life is not holding a good hand, it's playing a bad hand well." I found his proverbs so romantic when we first met, but over the years, it began to frustrate me when he quoted things like that, because he wasn't really expressing his own emotions.' She smiles, sadly. I think of Rory's catchphrases and completely understand. 'Also,' she adds, 'I realised that most of them made no sense whatsoever. Do you remember this one?' She clears her throat and puts her hands out in front of her as if presenting it on a plaque. 'Everything has an end…' she trails off and looks at me, waiting for me to finish it.

'Except a sausage, which has two,' we say in unison. Then, we start laughing until we're crying again. As I look across at Old Harry Rocks it feels that now, more than ever, Dad is with us, watching as this difficult conversation plays out. A conversation which has brought Mum and me closer than ever before.

'What's next, then?' Mum asks as we start to make our way back to the car.

I shrug. 'I go back to work I suppose.'

She looks at me with raised eyebrows. 'Is that what you want? Because there is another option you know…' She glances down, looks at our entwined hands. 'You could come and work at the café. Become a proper partner in the family business. Midge and I would love to have more time with you, and I saw how much you loved it when you worked there recently. To be honest, I can't do this forever…'

I think of the café, of the legacy Dad left behind. Mum's right. I did love the two weeks I spent there and the Saturdays since. My morning walks, the time spent creating new recipes in the kitchen, the connection with nature again. I have so many ideas I could implement there, too, not just to help me and the business but other people too. I have a vision of running grief workshops there, foraging walks … so many ideas, but they're just dreams. And dreams aren't made of anything solid. Dreams don't pay the mortgage. Plus, I've finally worked out how to make a difference at Prospect and I'm determined to see it through.

'I'm not going to pretend I didn't think about it, when I was there. But being an actuary, Mum … it's what I know; it's who I am.' Just saying those words makes me feel empty.

She tilts her head, looks at me intently with her pale blue eyes. 'Is it, love? Or is it just who you were just determined to become, to protect yourself?'

'My career gives me financial security,' I say automatically. 'Of *course* I've prioritised that because of what happened to Dad.'

'And yet you want to stay there, but walk away from a marriage that gives you love, happiness and support?'

A lone tear falls from my cheek.

'It's more complicated than that, Mum.'

Mum clasps my hand. 'Sofie, my darling, I understand that Dad's death made you determined to make choices to protect yourself. But his death wasn't just caused by his financial decisions, there were so many other factors involved. I know that losing Leo has made you question your life. And I know it's frightening to let go of the things that you believe protect you the most. But ask yourself this, if you were to put love, happiness, fulfilment and financial security in order, which would you sacrifice first?'

I exhale, throw my head back and look up at the sky.

'Rory and I want different things, Mum. I don't know if we can resolve that.'

'You could be brave,' she offers. 'Take a chance like you did with Leo…'

'I honestly don't think I have it in me. Perhaps I'm just not as brave as you…'

She grips my hands and leans her face down to look in my eyes.

'Sofie, you've already shown more courage than surely even you could have believed possible. You've survived the worst and you're still standing. Different, reformed, maybe,' she nods in the direction of Old Harry Rocks, 'but also still *here*. And if you can survive that, you can survive *anything*. There's nothing left to fear.'

I close my eyes, focus on the feeling of peace it brings to have my experience positioned this way. I *have* been strong. Leo has made me not just a mother, but a fighter, too – and fighters get back up again after they've been knocked down, don't they? I'm getting back up again, just maybe not in the way anyone wants me to – or expects.

It's about what *I* want now.

Chapter Seventy-Four

The boardroom is a large, plush room on the top floor of Prospect House. It feels like an entirely different building from the basement we actuaries work in, it's so light, fresh and modern.

Gigantic plants stand proudly in expensive looking over-sized pots. One side of the room is lined with tables where the catering team have set out urns of tea and coffee and plates of pastries. The room is filled with board members and senior management; there's a low hum of murmurs, occasional coughs, the clink of cups and saucers.

The presentation title is up on the screen behind us: *Ensuring the future of Prospect Life – and our workforce.*

I'm standing next to Zoe, clutching my notes. Nisha is behind us, next to Joe. She's been working closely with Joe all this week using her contacts and professional insight. I've enjoyed watching them, heads bent together, chatting intently like they've known each other for years. I can't believe I didn't think of introducing them properly before.

It's been a week since I left my home and my marriage and moved back in with my mum. I have spent the last few hot summer evenings here with Zoe, Joe and Nisha, working on this presentation, compiling our research for a pioneering new vision and product. Each night, I've driven home to Mum and Midge's house, exhausted but happy. Even though her new house in Brocklehurst isn't that far, Nisha has slept over with me too, just like the old days. We've talked about everything – Rory, Andy, our careers, our fears about having, or never having, children. Nisha even confessed a tentative interest in Joe, which I was obviously thrilled by. But I'm also determined to not push anything or interfere. I've learned there is no formula for love; you just have to believe in something – or someone – enough to take a risk. But I do have a good feeling. Someone I know would probably call it hope.

My hands are trembling, mouth dry. I take a sip from my bottle of water. Take a deep breath.

I can see Ed a few rows back; Tarun is sat next to him, one leg crossed over his knee, arms folded, like he's waiting for us to fail. There must be thirty-plus senior members of the company here.

Alan, the CEO, stands up and impresses on us the importance of the day's event. Then Jim, the CFO, talks about plunging profits, accountability and expenditures before he introduces us.

I look at Zoe who gives me a nod, then I look over my shoulder; Joe gives me a thumbs-up; Nisha smiles and Zoe and I step forward. We're ready.

'Good morning, everyone,' I say. My voice cracks a little and I cough to clear it. 'My name is Sofie King. I'm Pricing & Valuation Actuarial Manager at Prospect and also…' – I pause, take a deep inhale – 'a newly bereaved mother to my son, Leo.'

I pause to give his name the space it deserves in the room. People shuffle awkwardly in their seats. Chair legs scrape along the floor as they're adjusted. Heads are lowered. Some nervous coughs. Only once there's silence again do I continue.

'Leo was stillborn on February 16th this year, thirty-nine weeks into my pregnancy. I miss him every day…' My mouth dries; my chest constricts. I stop, swallow, uncertain if I can do this. I stare at everyone blankly. I can't. I can't do this. Zoe squeezes my hand and I look at her desperately.

Still holding my hand, she takes over.

'I'm Zoe Ansell, HR manager and mum to my boys, Lucas, who is 8, and his twin, Nathaniel, who died after complications at birth. Today,' she says, 'we're here to talk to you about risk and loss.'

She looks at me to check I'm okay to continue, and I nod. I'm doing this for Leo. For Me. For Rory. My Mum, Nisha. Zoe, Jen. Anyone who has ever been through this trauma.

'A year ago, I became unexpectedly pregnant,' I say. 'As an actuary who avoided risk, it was a big leap of faith. Those nine months were so magical, every moment I spent being pregnant helped me to let go of fear and believe in the best possible outcome. Until, at thirty-nine weeks, my baby stopped moving and we discovered Leo had died in utero. In that moment my whole world collapsed.' I pause, take a deep breath to compose myself.

'I spent weeks unable to get out of bed, paralysed with grief, unable to face the world, let alone work. Since then, I've spent hours in my head feeling isolated, ashamed, alone. Not knowing how to share my grief with anyone, not even my husband. He has hidden his grief, too, to try and protect me, convinced by society that he must be the strong one.' I look around the room and see the audience of mostly men, listening intently. 'Which led to a breakdown of his own. He's currently on compassionate leave from his workplace.'

Rory and I have kept in contact this past week, by text. He told me the TV station had offered him a further month's paid bereavement leave which he's decided to take. I'm glad. He couldn't continue as he was, boxing up his grief. Pretending he's okay when he is so far from it.

I take a deep breath. 'Contrary to how I might seem standing before you today, I'm not the person I was before Leo died. I'm not the employee I was, either. I'm less able to cope with office life. I can't deal with the deadlines, or the politics. I lose focus often, because my thoughts are full of Leo. I'm desperate to talk about him but I know it'll make people uncomfortable, so I stay silent.' I stop then, my emotions suddenly threatening to derail me.

I feel Zoe inch closer; she puts her arm around me for support.

I give her a smile of thanks. 'But I also know I can still add value, just not in the way I did before. Since Leo died, I've questioned everything about myself, the world and my place in it. What's my purpose? How can my experience help someone else? How can I make Leo's life – and mine – mean something? Because no matter how painful his loss is, having him is something I'll never forget – or regret.' I look around the room. 'I'm sure you're wondering what this has to do with insurance. Well, Zoe and I have experienced real-life risk and loss. These are two words we use every day here, but do we as a company ever stop and think about what they mean?'

I pick up the dictionary we brought with us and begin to read.

'Risk is a situation involving exposure to danger; sometimes hidden, sometimes not. In life insurance, risk is the possibility of harm or damage against which something is insured.'

'Loss,' Zoe picks up, brushing her curly dark hair back from her face before taking the dictionary from me, *'is the fact or process of losing something or someone.'* She looks at me. 'We both have extensive experience of that.' She reads on. *'It can also be an amount of money lost by a business or organisation.'*

'Hopefully not so much experience of *that*, thanks to my department,' I add and there's a ripple of laughter. 'It's true that in recent years,' I continue, 'we as a company have experienced more losses than we'd like But what about the *personal* losses in the company? Do we ever monitor those?'

'Loss,' Zoe reads another definition, *'is a person or thing that is badly missed when lost. Not just death, but for example, when a relationship breaks down.'*

I immediately think of Rory and my breath disappears.

'Can I ask now many people here have experienced loss of a loved one in the last year?' she adds. 'Whether that's a parent, child, sibling, grandparent, partner…?'

There is an immediate flurry of hands. At least a dozen hands in the room are raised.

'Did you know,' she asks, 'that ten per cent of employees are likely to be affected by bereavement at any anyone time? That's ten per cent of the workforce suffering, often in silence.'

She looks around the room. 'We *know* that good mental-health support is vital in the workplace, and I know there's more that can be done at Prospect. Sofie and I believe that by knowing our employees' personal stories as well as our policy holders', we can create new compassionate ways to work through grief, whilst at work.'

Joe steps forwards, then.

'Three years ago, my wife Rachel died. A year after we married, she was diagnosed with a particularly aggressive form of bowel cancer. She was thirty-six when she passed away and I still miss her every day. But I also know that she wouldn't want to me to mope; she wouldn't want me to feel isolated, or alone.' He quickly glances at Nisha then back out at the room. 'She'd want me to love again, make as many friends as possible, follow my dreams and do something positive with my life. Something with purpose.' He sits down.

'We're all connected by loss,' I say, taking over. 'Death is our most common denominator and yet it is the one thing we refuse to discuss; nor do we know how to help each other when it happens. What if at Prospect we talked less to our policy holders about how we measure risk and focused instead on how important risk-taking is when experiencing both the joys *and* losses of life? That way we could market Prospect Life as being a champion, not of how cautiously we live life in order to preserve it, but of how purposefully we take risks, so we can make the most of every day?'

I press play then on a short film we've made about risk and loss. It shows groups of people in different, happy situations: going to uni, getting married, in hospital, at work, pregnant, giving birth. It then shows Rachel in the hospice, Nisha talking to parents of young patients, whose lives have been impacted by illness and grief. The video finishes with the picture of Rory and me cradling Leo, the day I delivered him.

The film finishes with a tag line.

At Prospect we believe that we may only have one life, but we have many opportunities to find love, be happy, make a difference. We want you to risk it all for what you love, knowing that whatever happens, through happiness and heartbreak, we will be there to protect and support you every step of the way. This is our purpose.

One life. One Purpose. One Prospect Life.

Dissonant claps turn into a roomful of applause. Once it dies down, I click and a new slide appears that simply says THE FUTURE *PROSPECT* OF LIFE INSURANCE.

'Shockingly, nowhere in our research about how to live well, have we found an insurance policy that actively rewards looking after your *mental* health in the same way that we do physical health. No one in this industry currently actively engages with their customers during difficult times to ensure they're getting the necessary medical or talking therapy they need. The insurance industry simply hasn't made a definitive correlation between the impact that bereavement, depression, anxiety and PTSD can have on a person's life – and the longevity of it.'

'But what if Prospect could be one of the first of these pioneering companies to fast-track change by introducing a mental health focus in our policies?' I click again. 'What if we created partnerships with charities or counselling groups that deal with grief, or loss, or addiction – something Vitality does with gyms and nutrition companies? The mental-health movement has been growing so quickly over the past decade, it seems obvious that it should be reflected in life-insurance policies.'

I sit down and Nisha stands up and talks about her experiences dealing with bereaved parents. She passionately and articulately outlines the real difference that proper financial cover and emotional support would make to these families.

Joe takes over, then, presenting our vision of a new kind of policy. With Nisha's help, he's been able to speak to hospital bereavement services, registered counselling groups and mental-health charities who are eager to partner up. He's pulled together a comprehensive set of stats, predictive models, and guidelines.

When he's finished, he steps aside, allowing me to stand up one last time.

'We believe that *Prospect's 3 P's* should be *Personal Partnerships with Purpose*. Policies that focus not just on how long people live, but how *well* they live – how well we *all* live. *That* is our vision for the future of life insurance.'

I sit down and a second later, applause erupts around the room once more.

Chapter Seventy-Five

'Pub?' Joe says to me, but looking in Nisha's direction as we emerge from Prospect House at the end of the day. Zoe had to rush off to pick up Lucas from school. When she had mentioned it, I was hit by such a visceral longing for a future in which I could do the same for Leo that I felt dizzy. I closed my eyes as I leaned into her and we'd hugged, squeezing each other tightly, before she left.

Nisha escaped straight after our presentation. She didn't have to stay for the rest of the arduously long day listening to the talks given by other teams, but we agreed to meet here after work so we could go for a drink together. Joe smiles and waves at her and as she waves back at us; I can see the hint of a blush creeping up her neck.

'You know, I'm afraid I can't, Joe,' I say faux apologetically. 'Things to do. People to see…' This is true.

'Ri-ight,' he says glancing at me before his eyes and attention avert to Nisha. 'Important, is it?' he adds distractedly.

'Tell Nisha I'll call her, okay? And, Joe? She's a constant by the way, not a variable.' I touch his arm, smile knowingly and start to walk away.

When I said I wasn't going to interfere, I didn't mean I wouldn't give them a nudge in the right direction.

'Sofie!' Nisha calls, then, and I pick up my pace a little. I hear her call again and only once I know I'm a safe distance, I turn round and still walking backwards I wave at her and smiling, I shout, 'You're welcome!' I know she'll understand what I mean.

Then, I take one last look at Prospect House, knowing I won't be back for a while.

Sometimes the hardest decisions just seem fall into place when they have to. After the presentation, I spoke to Zoe and told her that it had been a mistake for me to come back so soon. That I'd changed my mind and would like to take my full year of maternity leave – the leave I would have had if Leo had lived – and use it to work out the next stage of my life.

I feel sad to not see it through but I also know that working full-time just isn't tenable. I can't manage my grief and the workload that would be expected of me.

'I understand, Sofie,' Zoe said. 'Selfishly, I'm sad to lose you when I've just got to know you, but I'm so happy you're choosing to do the right thing for you.'

I get on the bus, heading back to Purbeck and the place that feels like home again. I'm proud that I took a risk, and it paid off and that maybe what we've done today will make a difference. But I'm equally proud that I've walked away, because it will make a difference to me.

Once in my seat, I send a quick text to Rory to say what time I'll be at the pier. I messaged him earlier to see if he'd be happy to meet up. Of course, he agreed.

I watch out the window as the sun breaks through a cloud.

It's then that I'm filled with something that seems to inflate from within. It isn't happiness, I'm not quite there yet. It's something else. Something like … hope.

I observe it from the outside at the same time as I feel it within, like I'm reacquainting myself with an old friend.

But this hope doesn't feel forced, or ephemeral as it has in the past. It isn't an idea; it's a state of being. It's there *because* of me. And Leo. It is hope inspired by action, backed up with hard work, support and an understanding and appreciation of my own grief. An understanding of my journey. My*self*. It's an acceptance that whilst we can do everything we can to learn from the past and find ways to heal and help others in the future, hope can never be guaranteed. But I've realised that the process of committing yourself to it is enough.

And as I think of Zoe, Joe, Nisha, Mum, Midge and of course, Rory, I've learned that you can't do that alone.

Chapter Seventy-Six

We meet at Swanage Pier a little after 6pm. He's standing at the end, his back to me staring out to sea. A light summer rain has begun to fall which I'm woefully unprepared for. Rory's wearing a light waterproof over the top of his hoodie. The wind whips up and tugs his hood down and he turns, as if sensing my presence.

I start to walk towards him and then, slowly, he does the same. We eventually meet at the spot – our spot – the place where he proposed. The place where we laid a plaque announcing Leo's due date.

It's been a week since I left our house to go to Mum and Midge's. It's the longest we've been apart since we met, seven years ago this September. I think of the people we were back then, the person I was – and how much I've changed. I'll always miss that version of me, but I'm also starting to accept, embrace, even *like* the person I've become.

'Hi,' I say. I'm looking down at the plaque because I can't bring myself to look up at him. The space between us still feels enormous, even though we're only inches apart.

'Hi,' he replies quietly. We turn and walk together slowly, in parallel, hands pushed into pockets to protect from both the cold and the bitterly harsh reality of where we find ourselves right now. We head to the end of the pier and find a bench, a place to sit together and talk.

'I'm so glad you called,' Rory starts, his words spilling out quickly. 'I really wanted to call you, but I-I knew you needed space…'

'I did,' I say. 'I do. But I know we have so many things left to say, too.'

'Can I go first? Please?' Rory gazes at me, his expression so full of puppy-like desperation it physically pains me. I nod.

'I don't know where to begin.' Rory's voice cracks. He turns to me, green eyes sick with worry. 'I- I was scared this wouldn't happen. That I wouldn't get the chance—' He stops, takes a deep breath to compose himself.

I don't speak. This is his time now.

'I want to say I'm sorry, Sofie, for everything. I know I tried to accelerate you through your grief because I couldn't handle it. Losing Leo, well, it felt too big, too overwhelming to deal with. I wasn't brave enough to sit with it like you have. I just wanted to either put it away or put it on show in public, in a way that made it look like I was coping, whilst also hiding away from it in real life. I've found a counsellor, since you left, and I've been to my first session. It was helpful, but hard. Really fucking hard.' He laughs hollowly.

I nod, but don't interrupt his flow.

'Therapy was long overdue. Not just since Leo died, but since Mum left, too. I think I lost myself a long time ago; became the person I am based on an image I believed that people would like. I felt I always had to be positive, happy, buoyant because if I was less than that, the people I cared about would leave me. When I met you, I forced you do the same because I wanted to control every outcome and make it good. I haven't ever been able to deal with problems in an adult way; I couldn't handle things not working out. Losing Leo … well, it was impossible for me to be positive anymore and that scared me. So I hid in a false world where I could be a hero and also in an imaginary future where everything would be okay, trying to convince myself that having another baby would make it better. I know this made you feel like I was forgetting Leo. I also know you felt like I'd left you long before you left me.' He bows his head then.

A part of me longs to reach out and take his hand, but I don't. He looks up.

'I know now that I can't fix the fact the Leo died. Nothing will ever fix that; my focus is on fixing me. And hopefully, us.' He turns his head and looks at me, then: his eyes are filled with tears. 'I'm so sorry, Sofie. For not sharing how I was feeling with you. For boxing it all up. I've already sold all the gaming gear,' he continues, swiping his hand across his eyes. 'I need to find a more positive way to deal with my grief. Something that fires me up and makes me feel like I can conquer things, but for a cause this time, not an online score, or for likes and comments. I've started climbing again,' he says cautiously. I understand why: the old me would have been horrified, but the new me is happy for him. 'I've been meeting up with my old bouldering mates; I want to challenge myself in a positive way. I'm thinking I'd like to do something to raise some money in Leo's name. I need to work out who I am again as a father to a baby who isn't here, but also, hopefully, as a husband to a wife who *is* here.' He exhales in relief, letting go of something heavy he's been carrying for a long time.

I don't say anything. No more false hope.

We sit in silence for a while, listening to the sound of the circling seagulls' plaintive caws. For me, there is no clear way forward right now and no safe path back. We are both a couple of weak, vulnerable pawns on the same side of the board, trying to navigate how to get to the other side safely. How many other relationships have faced a different future from the one they imagined after a devastating loss? Ended up facing checkmate.

'Rory,' I say, eventually. 'I'm so glad you've been brave enough to tell me what you need, but I need you to know that I've made some decisions, too.' He stares at me and I can see that he still has hope. Even after it all.

I take a deep breath and stare straight ahead. 'The first decision I've made is to leave my job.' He looks at me, clearly shocked. 'It's a risk but I also know it's the right choice. I had to let go of it as a safety net, which is what I've realised it has always been for me.'

'That's a big decision,' Rory says, a little of his old self – his old confidence – returning, now that the subject is me. 'In the past, we'd have talked over something as big as this together.'

I turn to him, then. 'But things are different now, Rory,' I say firmly. 'I know what I want, and it's not what I've thought all these years.'

He frowns, a shadow passing over his face. 'What does that mean...?'

'You were right. I do have to take risks and you have been my safety net too, my anchor, actually. You can't be that anymore; nor can you be the person that fixes everything for me. It's up to *me* to work out how I want to live my life. I have to make my own decisions – about everything. My work, where I live, what I do with my body...' I trail off.

'Sofie, that's not fair...'

'Isn't it?' I push back, gently. 'I so appreciate you telling me where you're at, Rory, and for apologising for trying to control how I grieve, but the one thing you've never ever taken responsibility for is constantly pushing for us to have a baby, no matter how many times I protested, or said I wasn't ready.'

'You blame me,' Rory says dully. 'I knew it.'

'No,' I reach out then and put my hand on his. 'That's not what I'm saying. I don't blame you and I don't regret having him, not at all, but I also can't go back to a version of my life where you get to be in the driving seat. I changed when Leo died.' I take a deep breath. 'And now I think I need to change my life, too...'

He bows his head, as if doing so will stop me from continuing.

'I want to sell the house, Rory.'

He looks up at me then, eyes full of distress.

'Mum has offered me the flat over the café...'

Rory opens his mouth to speak.

'Hang on, please, let me finish. I want to invest my money from the sale of our house in the café, maybe even in time in a plot of land too. I can see myself working towards taking over the business from Mum and Midge eventually and I like the idea of building a home. A place I can imagine staying in forever. Somewhere, if you agree, we can spread Leo's ashes.'

'Can I be involved in that plan, too?' Rory pleads. 'That new life?'

'I don't know.' I gasp, trying to take a breath because I'm not sure I can see it, no matter how much I wish I could. And that's when I break down.

'Having and losing Leo changed me, Rory,' I say, eventually, when I've composed myself. 'I don't want to be stuck in the office and in the house anymore, avoiding risk at all costs. I want to walk every day, swim in the sea, kayak and do all the things I used to love as kid without fear. Leo made me strong and he made me brave and he made me realise that this life we have, it's precious. And I want all that, I want it for us both.'

'Together, or apart?' Rory says, his face wrought with pain and confusion.

'I don't know,' I say, honestly. 'Right now, I just want us both to feel that the life we have from now on fits the people we have become. And we need some time apart to figure that out for ourselves. But no matter what happens from here, regardless of our family's shape or size in the future, whether we go our separate ways or not, we will always be Leo's parents. I touch the necklace Rory gave me, feel the inscription beneath my fingers. 'To infinity.'

Rory nods weakly, his eyes as grey and fathomless as the sea.

Chapter Seventy-Seven

It's a characteristically dark Friday morning in early December. The wind is whipping across the sea; tumultuous waves rise and crash just beyond the rocks of Peveril Point. The sky is gun-metal grey, heavy with intent. Half of Purbeck seems to have chosen to seek shelter, warmth, comfort and nourishment in the café. And who could blame them? The Scandi-themed Christmas decorations are up; the café is covered with fairy lights and greenery; we have Nordic Christmas trees in pots around the edge of the café space and evergreen wreaths in the big front windows. For the past six months, I have loved looking out to the sea each day, that stretches for miles beyond the cafe; it's like a piece of living art. And if I glance out the corner of my eye, I can always see Old Harry Rocks standing stoic, sentinel, watching over us all.

This is the first Christmas since Leo died. I can't believe it's been almost ten months; he's now been gone as long I carried him. But whilst the grief is still raw, I also know that I'm exactly where I need to be and Leo is instrumental to that. I also feel that Dad helped bring me back here, too.

The one-bedroom flat above the café has provided the best temporary-but-stable home for me these past few months. It's not perfect by any means, but it's all mine. I miss Rory, of course I do. This hasn't been easy: there is a huge hole in my life where he once was. But I know I must find my own way of living without Leo now, before I can even think about a future with him – or anyone else.

One thing that has been easy was selling our house. And I've also had an offer accepted on a plot of land in Wareham, a beautiful expanse of a few acres with a view of the sea. We've found the perfect spot there to scatter Leo's ashes. One day, I hope to build a house here, but for now at least I know I'll be able to visit him every day.

My life has changed immeasurably because of Leo – and I'm so grateful to him for that. I still have my routines – I'll always be a creature of habit – but these days, my routines are led by my heart, rather than fear and anxiety. Every morning, I get up at the crack of dawn and go for a walk around the coast and the hills of my childhood, wearing my old walking boots, carrying my foraging basket in my hand and my rucksack – full of Dad's old tools – on my back. I've completed some local foraging courses, no longer solely looking at numbers and reports but being out in the fresh air doing what I love.

With every walk I take, I feel Leo and Dad with me. In a charm of goldfinches gilding the sky above the common pink heather and burgeoning hedgerows that line Hartland Moor down to Corfe Castle. Or when the swallows and geese arc over the skyline in an 'L' shape. Sometimes, Mum comes with me to watch the early morning mist spilling dramatically over Purbeck ridge and settle over the fields of gold. I play the song often as it makes me think of Leo. But I can never listen to it without thinking of Rory, too. Occasionally, over the past few months, we have met up. We're not out of the landscape of each other's lives completely.

Nisha has been my rock throughout it all. Even during these cold winter months we're in now, we meet up to go wild sea swimming on Middle Beach like we used to do as kids, taking flasks of hot tea and leftover pastries from the café to have afterwards. It feels liberating and healing and gives us a chance to connect – not just as the women we've become, but the friends we've always been. She and Joe have officially been a couple for six months – they count their first date as their trip to the pub after the presentation – and they are both so happy. Nisha has put her search for a sperm donor 'on ice', as she puts it. Joe is moving in with her next month. 'Why wait?' she said to me, 'when it feels so right.'

Twice a month, I go into Prospect to run Lunchtime Foraging Walks for the staff. Everyone is welcome, but I've found that it's those employees who are going through a difficult time who tend to come: walking together inspires conversation, insight, understanding, connection. I need it as much as they seem to.

Somewhere amongst all this, my grief has become rooted in a place where beauty and hope can grow around the pain.

I peer out into the café. I've officially become a partner in the business with Mum and Midge, too. It's changed a lot these past few months: the back bar and service area has been tiled with beautiful, scalloped tiles in aquamarine, like a mermaid's tail; the old counter has been replaced with sleek marble. Fishing nets and local art line the walls, but we still have the big shrine to Dad; the photo of him and me on the boat still sits proudly beside the till area. On the back wall against the tiles are a series of twine-bound twigs wrapped with fairy-lights, which Mum and I have hung to form the shape of the 'Leo' constellation. We wanted him to be part of the café, too.

When I'm in the kitchen and the printer is going ten to the dozen and I'm rushed off my feet, I feel alive. I love seeing the place packed with people; hearing the hum of happy chatter that reverberates inside.

'Have you got those two cured Salmon Gravlax *Smorrebrod* and Pickled Herring for table eight? I also need two of the *Gronkaal* soup please!' Mum calls into the kitchen, making me jump.

I pull myself together. It's 2pm and I'm meant to be finishing off the final late lunch orders in the café, whilst also prepping for this afternoon's event. As well as bringing back some of the Danish food that dad was so passionate about, using his foraging knowledge, I decided to put my stamp on things. I wanted this café to be a place where groups of like-minded people can come and share their stories, connect.

So, as well as having a full refurb inside, I convinced Mum and Midge that we should invest in a side extension with a private room to host events. It was finished last month.

'Coming right up!' I wipe my hands on my messy apron and put the finishing touches on the lunch plates. I ladle the Danish-recipe green kale soup into two bowls, add a chunk of rye bread to each of the side plates and ping the bell to alert Midge that they're at the serving hatch.

Midge comes in and grabs the plates, panting a little with her hand on her hip.

'Ready for this afternoon's session?' she asks with a smile.

'As I'll ever be!' I think about the monthly meetings we've called 'Per's Pals', which we'll run in the private room from now on because, in the few months we've been going, they've grown beyond expectation.

These meetings for bereaved mothers are my way of giving back: creating a community and a safe space to meet up with others who understand what they're going through.

When I introduced Nisha and Jen a while back, they got on so well, we decided to meet up again the following week. Then I invited Zoe, who also invited a friend of hers from uni called Annette, who had been through several IVF cycles. She and her partner Simone have just started their adoption journey. Jen also brought a colleague of hers called Serena, who has experienced three losses between twelve and twenty-two weeks.

Last month, simply through word of mouth, the number around the table had reached twenty-five. The extension was nearly finished, and I realised we had the space and the need and so we put up a poster in the café and waited to see what happened.

To our amazement, over sixty bereaved mums of all ages and stages of grief came along. We had to close the café to host it in the end, and I divided everyone into groups to make it less overwhelming for people to talk. I started by asking everyone to introduce themselves in their group and share their baby's name and their birth experience – just like we would have done at an NCT morning. After that, the conversation and the tears flowed easily. It was the most emotionally gruelling, uplifting and inclusive hour of my life. I encouraged the groups to mix and then created the WhatsApp group, Per's Pals, so we could continue to talk after the session was over. The following week, I asked everyone to meet again but this time on the beach.

'Now we're able to talk about our babies to each other, I want us to walk with them,' I said. 'We're going to get outside, connect to nature and find space for our grief. All you need to do is wear suitable shoes and waterproofs, and I'll bring the rest.'

We've been a few times now, in small groups, and I'm teaching them all about plants, fungi and flowers, getting them to notice and identify different species. We forage and learn, but mostly, we connect with our babies and our shared grief.

We want to turn Per's Pals into a registered charity and we're planning several events for next year. Eventually, there will be Per's Pals meetings for all kinds of loss: I've contacted registered Bereavement counsellors to run these groups. And of course, we will also run one specifically for those who have lost a loved one to suicide. I think Dad would be happy to know that his café is helping so many people.

We're also planning to offer our private room for hire to local businesses around the Southwest. Businesses like Prospect – who, of course, are already on board – to send employees struggling with grief to their own Per's Pals sessions.

Today, our private room is playing host to some bereaved dads.

Rory met Marcus at a group counselling session. Marcus had experienced severe depression after the loss of his baby. His relationship had not survived – and neither, nearly, had he. Rory is determined to create a community of bereaved fathers who can help support each other positively. He already has plans for a charity triathlon next year.

I smile at him, marvelling at how different he looks. His trademark easy, laid-back gait is still there, but the newsreader quiff has long since grown out and he's sporting a beard out of choice – not grief. His wardrobe of smart coats has been replaced by a RAB waterproof; his camera-friendly smart trousers are gone in favour of all-weather shorts and hiking boots. Much like my dad used to wear, I realise. He looks tanned, fit, healthy. Happy.

We're not back together, but as I said to Rory the other day after our couples' grief counselling session – something we agreed to have before making any sort of rash decisions about divorce – it might have been luck that brought us together, but it takes hard work, patience and perseverance to make a marriage last. After Leo died, it felt like the safety plug had been pulled on our relationship. We'd faced the worst, and seen each other at our worst, too. But now we know there is beauty and strength in that. We're no longer under the illusion that we are blessed by Rory's so-called 'Kingsmet'. We know we're not perfect; we know that good things won't always happen to us. But if we do choose to be together, it's because we'll believe that what we have is worth fighting for.

Right now any relationship other than with myself feels like a distant rainbow stretching over the horizon; I'm focusing on finding joy in what I *can* see in front of me. And purpose in the new power that I *know* is within me.

Thanks to Leo, I'm not alone; I'm not scared. I'm brave. Resilient. I am enough.

Epilogue

It's a bright, beautiful February day – exactly a year to the day that Leo died.

I walk across the meadow – officially now *our* meadow – next to Rory who is holding tightly on to Leo's urn. In turn, I am holding tightly on to Rory. We're flanked by Mum and Midge, but also Sandra, Zoe, Jen, Nisha and Joe, all of whom are clutching yellow daffodils. The sky is abnormally blue for the time of year. Bright, warm sunshine is flooding the land, burnishing the fields gold.

We walk towards the old white willow tree that I spotted on my first visit to this land. I knew immediately this was Leo's forever place, wrapped as it is by ancient earth and the endless sea. I become breathless suddenly, the familiar heavy boot pressing down on my chest.

I think of what Nisha told me all those months ago, that it has been scientifically proven that from the start of pregnancy our babies' cells cross into our bodies and become part of our tissue. Physically part of us, forever, whether they're born or not, whether they live beyond our wombs or not. They change us; they can even heal us. Nisha and I, and the women I've met along the way who are walking the same path, have realised that through our experiences with our babies, we can heal each other, too.

I think of what Nisha told me just yesterday and find myself smiling through my tears.

'*Joe and I are having a baby, Sofie,*' she'd said.

'*I'm so happy for you,*' I'd replied, hugging her tightly and I meant it with every fibre, every cell of my being.

Those of us who walk the earth without our babies will never get over their loss, but that doesn't mean we can't, in time, share the joy of new life once more – for others and maybe, even ourselves.

Rory and I know that Leo's footprints will flank us forever. He'll be with us on every walk across the hills and beaches of this glorious green isle, in the fossils we may find on the beach, amongst the wildflowers I forage, the sea that surrounds me on a morning swim, the leaves beneath our feet, the flowers that unfurl each spring, the earth between our fingertips, the trees that arc above us.

He is our world. He's part of what Rory and I add up to and he always will be. He is the sum of our hearts.

As we stand gathered with our friends and family and all the other people who know and love Leo, Rory puts his hand lightly on my shoulder and presses play on the song we've chosen. Sting's 'Fields of Gold'. Clutching the urn tightly, I look up at Rory – my husband and father of my child. In that moment, he leans down and drops the lightest, softest of kisses on my mouth that is so full of love it takes my breath away.

I'm so thankful that Leo has gifted us both this new beginning. Whether there are children in our future or not, our time apart has taught us that we can live together both with and without him.

Then, we take it in turns to put our hands in the urn and as we open up our fingers we watch Leo settle finally into the land; the place where both he and Per and Rory and I and our families' roots will always be.

To infinity.

Author's Note

I'm a mother of four children. My first two – aged fifteen and thirteen at the time of writing this note – were straightforward pregnancies and births. It was a huge shock when my third child, Poppy, wasn't. Like my other children, having her has also become my most cherished and life-changing experience. Unlike them, I've had to learn to live without her.

I carried Poppy for just under twenty-four weeks until the day I delivered her, knowing she had already died. I was petrified of the experience. I knew I had to be brave for her; I wanted to be the best mum I could be in the moments I was able to do that for her. But in the end, it was Poppy who carried me through the fear and pain of that life-changing experience, to a place of peace.

In the moment when her little body left mine, I knew we were bonded forever. Each other's beginning and end. As I lay back on the bed, comforted by my husband, I remember feeling like the painful contractions of the birth had been replaced by the unbearable contradiction of our situation. Hearts full of love, but desolately empty. A baby with a name but no birth certificate. Parents to a baby we'd never take home. I didn't know how I would go on without her, but I also knew I had to. And I knew that my life would never be the same again.

Author's Note

Life carried on, but I battled with the paradox of my situation. My body which had carried her was now a constant reminder of what I'd lost. I felt disconnected from myself and the person I used to be, but I also knew I had to find a version of myself that Poppy would be proud of. I was deeply grieving for the baby I'd lost, whilst also incredibly grateful for the two beautiful children I had. I was entirely changed, yet I didn't want to be treated differently by anyone. I couldn't bear the idea of telling people what had happened to my baby, but I also wanted to shout about her from the rooftops. I wanted to work, but didn't want to do the job I loved because it would take me away from my pain, which meant it would take me away from her. I knew writing could be healing, but I felt strongly that I needed to lean into the loss, to feel it all in real time – not romanticise it for the sake of others or be tempted to lose myself in a fictional world that might temporarily block out the pain but cause deeper problems in the long term.

I received counselling and was encouraged to write down how I felt. But I refused. I knew if I put pen to paper, what would come out would be a neatly packaged version of grief for public consumption. Something I could wrap in a bow and present in a palatable way to the reader. As an ex-journalist and author, I didn't know how to write *without* it being published. As such, I knew I wouldn't be authentic about the true trauma and devastation I felt. I would be accelerating my grief to an acceptable place for the sake of how it would look to others.

I spent months doing anything *other* than write. I became obsessed with colouring-in books, a pleasingly controllable activity that allowed me to acceptably stay within the lines of expectation – something my pregnancy had not allowed me to do. I baked extensively; I took my preschool daughter out of nursery to spend more time with her; after they'd gone to bed, I watched old musicals whilst sorting my son's Lego into colour-coded boxes. I tidied rooms, organised cupboards. In short, I found peace in doing things that created order and sequence, when my mind was such a mess. Eventually, I started running – further and faster than I'd ever done before. It was something which gave me space to grieve, whilst also allowing me time to grow. It was only then, out in the open air on my own that I slowly

Author's Note

began to piece myself back together. To notice the beauty of the world around me, feel Poppy next to me in the fields I passed, the wildflowers I saw, the sun that seemed to follow me everywhere. I ran with a friend who was grieving too, for her mother who had died of cancer. It was here I found real connection, the 'good grief' that also inspired Sofie's rewilding as she steps back from her career as an actuary and finds comfort in her childhood love of foraging. Being in nature gifts her an everlasting connection with her baby boy and breathes life into her. A new life. One that has the space for him to exist next to her, too.

One of the many contradictions of late baby loss is that amongst the darkness, sorrow and grief there is beauty to be found both in the birth and the loss. There's the pride for the baby you briefly hold in your arms – and for yourself, that you somehow survived the most traumatic of experiences. Late baby-loss mothers hold memories of their babies' births close because we know they will be all we have. We also know that people are frightened of it. No one asks a baby-loss mother what the birth was like, what her baby weighed, who he or she looked like, or sometimes, even their names. And in that fear, that silence, our sweet, special memories of our babies become shameful.

I always knew that I wanted the reader to experience with Sofie the moment she gives birth to her stillborn son. I wanted it to read as an awfully beautiful, awe-inspiring birth: full of exertion, trauma and pain but also full of pride, beauty, love and even, at times, the dark kind of humour that grief and trauma incites. More than anything, I hope that it gives a voice for the women who may have felt unable to share their own birth stories for their babies who exist in their hearts, but not their arms.

I felt strongly from the moment that I started writing this story that I didn't want Sofie's son's death to be reduced to a plot twist. I have always wanted everyone to know what they are reading from the moment they pick up this book. Yes, it's about grief and loss, but it is also overwhelmingly about love. Motherly love, of course, but also self-love, supportive love from friends, colleagues, the community and also marital love. Love for better or worse. Truly, there is nothing worse for a couple to face than losing a child.

Because after that loss the problems just keep coming; the differ-

Author's Note

ences in how men and women grieve, the pressure to be okay, to move on from family and friends, the added trauma of trying to work out if you want to try again. This is something Sofie and her husband Rory go through as I wanted to depict the desperate pull in different directions: fear versus hope. Future versus past. A beginning versus an end.

I remember all these feelings vividly. But unlike Sofie, I knew even as I was grieving the baby I lost, that I desperately wanted another baby one day. It took longer than I expected – three years, in fact. Just as I was ready to give up – and a month after running a half marathon in Poppy's memory and for the baby loss counselling charity *Petals* – I fell pregnant at age forty-one. My younger son, Rex – now seven – was the rainbow I never gave up on.

I tentatively started to write this book five years ago, just after Rex had turned one, because I finally felt ready to write truthfully about my experience in the only way I know how – through fiction. I wanted to write this book, not as a memoir, or a self-help or survival guide but as a story that would reach the hands nd hearts beyond those who have suffered the loss of a child and who know it intimately. This book is for them, yes, but it is also for the partners, friends, sisters, mothers, fathers, grandparents, aunts, uncles, cousins and colleagues who might need to find a way to support someone through this experience in the future.

Because the statistics show that it *will* touch us all in some way: one in four women experience pregnancy loss. One in four. It's a huge number, isn't it? Hard to take in, when you stop to think about it. Because if one quarter of pregnancies end in loss during pregnancy or birth, if one *quarter* of all the pregnant women in the world have their hearts broken, future obliterated by the unimaginable – the unfathomable – then *all* of us at some point in our lives will know someone who will experience this life-changing trauma.

I know I was changed forever when Poppy died ten years ago, but I have always believed that she changed me for the better. It took me a long time to learn how to talk about it, but once I did, I couldn't stop and that's why I have taken it to the page. Poppy was the reason I temporarily gave up my writing career, but she is also the reason that I have started again. And I'm doing it with renewed love, understanding, passion and compassion too. This book simply wouldn't exist without her. Thank you, my sweet girl.

And thank you, for reading it.

Baby Loss Bibliography

Over the past decade, I've read each one of these books on the list and they've all brought me deep comfort and insight in different ways. I would recommend them all to anyone who has experienced the loss of a baby or child, in pregnancy or after.

The Baby Loss Guide by Zoë Clark-Coates
Beyond Goodbye by Zoë Clark-Coates
Pregnancy After Loss by Zoë Clark-Coates
Ask Me His Name by Elle Wright
A Bump in the Road by Elle Wright
You Are Not Alone by Cariad Lloyd
The Worst Girl Gang Ever by Bex Gunn and Laura Buckingham
Beyond Grief by Pippa Vosper
Life, Almost by Jennie Agg
Grief Works by Julia Samuel
Tiny Beautiful Things by Cheryl Strayed
Wintering by Katherine May
A Heart That Works by Rob Delaney

Baby Loss Charities

Tommy's
Sands
Petals
Saying Goodbye
Aching Arms
The Lullaby Trust

Acknowledgments

My pregnancy with Poppy was not as I expected, nor has this book had a straightforward journey into the world. Throughout it all, I've been lucky enough to be supported by the best people in both publishing and my personal life.

I wouldn't be writing this page without my agent, Lizzy Kremer, who accepted my deeply messy story of grief, pain, survival and hope without question and then guided me gently through all the inevitable rewrites it required. Lizzy, you have exhibited continued care, compassion, consideration and patience beyond expectation. Thank you for believing this book had a purpose and place in the fiction market and for fighting tooth and nail to get us here. I'm so grateful to you.

To Orli Vogt-Vincent, your reassuring emails and forensic collation of baby loss statistics to support the book's submission kept me going when the rejections began to trickle (and then flood) in. Thank you for being such a passionate and insightful contributor, not to mention such an articulate advocate of this novel and its sensitive subject matter.

During that difficult, deeply disappointing submission process, all I could do was hope that someone would eventually see what I knew. Women outside the baby loss community *need* to read stories like this in all their impossibly hard, heartbreaking and hopeful glory, and where better than in fiction? Here, the true depth of our bravery, strength, love and gratitude can be revealed and reflected to us safely, in place of the silence, shame and stigma created by our society that dictates these difficult experiences should be hidden away.

Thankfully, Charlotte Ledger, my editor and publisher of One More Chapter was that one special person. Charlotte, I'm forever grateful for your emotional foresight and fortitude, profound understanding of grief and willingness to take a risk on this book. I love our conversations and hugely appreciate how carefully you listen, how much our beliefs for this book align and how mindful you've been at every single stage of this journey of both the fragile material (and author) you're handling!

That you have surrounded yourself with an equally wonderful and sensitive editorial team is no surprise. Thanks to Arsalan Isa, whose organisational skills are beyond measure and to Kara Daniel for keeping my proofreads on track. I'm in awe of my line editor/word wizard Caroline Jane Hogg who managed to sensitively find a quite brilliant way to cut a huge chunk of the book without impacting Sofie, Rory and Leo's story. And to copy editor Federica Leonardis for ironing out all the fluff and flaws. You've each left your imprint on this book with the lightest, most expert touches. To Emma Petfield and your excellent marketing team, thank you for making it clear from the get-go that you believe everyone should read this book, and that you'll do everything in your power to make it so.

To Adele Groyer and Hannah Beckett, I'm sure you'll have forgotten patiently talking me through what an actuary does as it was so long ago. Hopefully, you'll have forgotten my embarrassingly basic questions! Suffice it to say, Sofie's career wouldn't play the part it does in this book without your excellent industry insights and explanations.

Cesca Major – my official first reader – only you could make this hermitic writer say 'yes' to a 5-day writing retreat. That you then offered to read my grief-riddled ramblings and impart such helpful feedback gave me the confidence to submit my MS to Lizzy. You're an inspiration and I'm so grateful for the friendship, support and encouragement you've provided from afar.

Nick Smithers, my high-kicking college partner/faithful writing friend of thirty years. Our hours (and hours) of phone calls always feed my soul and your notes on the early drafts of this book were as invaluable as ever. Rory would not be the man he is without you. And I would not be the writer I am, either.

Hannah Morrison, you'll hate me thanking you here so I'll keep it short and just say you can red-pen my pages any day. And Abby Boden, our mutual friend and third spoke in our friendship wheel. I hope we all continue to walk/yoga/paddleboard/wild swim/drink wine together into old age. (Ok, mostly the walk, yoga and wine-drinking for me!)

To Emma Evans and Louisa Gordon whose friendship (not forgetting our fabulous Theatre Club) has brought so much light and laughter to my life over the past decade.

Paige and Greg Toon, fellow Cambridge-dwellers, writing/publishing industry experts and wonderful friends. Thank you for the (almost) fifteen years (how?!) of laughter, wisdom, support and understanding. Your belief in both me and this book sustained me (as did the prosecco and porn star martinis…).

To Emma Wood, the most loving and fiercely proud mama I know. Your angel twins Harriet and Matthew are so lucky to have you, as are your four boys.

Nadine Johnston and Clare Sutcliffe, you approached me with such care, thoughtfulness and kindness in the dark days after Poppy died. Thank you for reaching out when I felt so alone. This book is for both your babies, too.

To the entire baby loss community who have made me feel part of something beautiful, not broken. Deep thanks and gratitude to the many incredible advocates who continue to give a voice to our community and make us feel seen. In particular: Zoë Clark-Coates from the charity *Saying Goodbye*; the wise, wonderful Elle Wright (thank you, Giovanna Fletcher, whose book launch I stalked Elle at); Jennie Agg; Dr Michelle Tolfrey; Pippa Vosper – I'm in awe of the incredible work you all do that is powered not by loss but pure love.

To my mum. Thank you for loving Poppy so much and for keeping her alive in your heart. I'm forever grateful that you are the same sweet, kind, loving nanna to her as you are to all four of your grandchildren.

Rachel Cavanagh, *good grief* I can't describe the gratitude I feel that our losses led us to each other. To walk (and run) this difficult path in the sunshine alongside you has been a blessing and an honour. I truly consider our decade-long friendship as one of the greatest gifts that Poppy has given me. Thank you for being the person I get to share her with and for sharing your beautiful mum, Marlene, with us both. I know she's looking after her for me.

To the love of my life, Ben. Whilst I sometimes doubted that I would survive the experience of losing Poppy, I never for once doubted that we would. Like Rory and Sofie (but also very much *un*like them) our grief paths have often been very different, but you've never swayed from being by my side. I'm so proud of us. And I'm so grateful for our family that, whilst forever missing a little piece, also manages to feel whole.

Barnaby and Cece, you two helped me navigate the darkest days and still find joy and laughter in them. You taught me what strength and resilience were when you were too little to know you were doing so. You've encouraged me to keep writing this book and even though it took years (you were tiny when I first started, now you both tower over me!) you never stopped believing I could. I'm so proud of the young adults you've become, and I love you both more than I can say.

Rexy Scrumptious, truly, my real-life rainbow. You're the bundle of unexpected mayhem and mischief that came along just as I'd given up hope and whose presence healed my heart enough to write this book. One day you'll know you have another big sister (who you would have undoubtedly also wrapped around your little finger). She knew our lives would be better with you in them and she was so right. We all love you so much.

Finally, to my beautiful baby girl, Poppy. Keep shining your light brightly knowing that this book is because of you, for you, forever and for good. I love you little one. I would do it all again for you.

The author and One More Chapter would like to thank everyone who contributed to the publication of this story...

Analytics
Abigail Fryer

Audio
Fionnuala Barrett
Ciara Briggs

Contracts
Laura Amos
Inigo Vyvyan

Design
Lucy Bennett
Fiona Greenway
Liane Payne
Dean Russell

Digital Sales
Laura Daley
Lydia Grainge
Hannah Lismore

eCommerce
Laura Carpenter
Madeline ODonovan
Charlotte Stevens
Christina Storey
Jo Surman
Rachel Ward

Editorial
Kara Daniel
Caroline Jane Hogg
Charlotte Ledger
Federica Leonardis
Jennie Rothwell
Sofia Salazar Studer
Emily Thomas
Helen Williams

Harper360
Emily Gerbner
Ariana Juarez
Jean Marie Kelly
emma sullivan
Sophia Wilhelm

International Sales
Peter Borcsok
Ruth Burrow
Colleen Simpson
Ben Wright

Inventory
Sarah Callaghan
Kirsty Norman

Marketing & Publicity
Chloe Cummings
Grace Edwards

Operations
Melissa Okusanya
Hannah Stamp

Production
Denis Manson
Simon Moore
Francesca Tuzzeo

Rights
Ashton Mucha
Alisah Saghir
Zoe Shine
Aisling Smyth
Lucy Vanderbilt

Trade Marketing
Ben Hurd
Eleanor Slater

The HarperCollins Distribution Team

The HarperCollins Finance & Royalties Team

The HarperCollins Legal Team

The HarperCollins Technology Team

UK Sales
Isabel Coburn
Jay Cochrane
Sabina Lewis
Holly Martin
Harriet Williams
Leah Woods

And every other essential link in the chain from delivery drivers to booksellers to librarians and beyond!

One More Chapter is an
award-winning global
division of HarperCollins.

Subscribe to our newsletter to get our
latest eBook deals and stay up to date
with all our new releases!

signup.harpercollins.co.uk/
join/signup-omc

Meet the team at
www.onemorechapter.com

Follow us!

@onemorechapterhc

Do you write unputdownable fiction?
We love to hear from new voices.
Find out how to submit your novel at
www.onemorechapter.com/submissions